COMMUNITY ENTERPRISE AND COOPERATIVE DEVELOPMENT

COMMUNITY ENTERPRISE AND COOPERATIVE DEVELOPMENT

Editor
Johann Angermann

DPH
DISCOVERY
PUBLISHING HOUSE

Published by:

DISCOVERY PUBLISHING HOUSE
4383/4B, Ansari Road, Darya Ganj
New Delhi-110 002 (India)
Phone : +91-11-23279245; 23253475; 43596065
Mobile : +91 9811179893 / +91 9871656464
E-mail : discoverybooksindia@gmail.com
orderdphbooks@gmail.com
namitwasan9@gmail.com
web : www.discoverypublishinggroup.com

Community Enterprise and Cooperative Development
Edited by: **Johann Angermann**

International Standard Book Number: **978-93-6224-013-2** (Hardback)

Printed at:
Infinity Imaging Systems
Delhi (INDIA)

PREFACE

Community-based entrepreneurship emerges as a pivotal mechanism for unlocking the latent potential within marginalized and underprivileged communities that stand disconnected from the broader economic mainstream, playing a crucial role in fostering social betterment and upliftment. This form of entrepreneurship is deeply rooted in cultural norms and values, leveraging shared resources, establishing linkages, and building upon mutual trust among community members. These elements are cultivated through intimate personal relationships, which are essential for the smooth operation of economic activities within the community. Entrepreneurial endeavors that focus on generating local public goods for the community are viewed as having a distinct advantage when compared to purely market-driven activities. This is because such community-focused initiatives are more attuned to the specific needs and aspirations of the community, thereby contributing more effectively to local development and well-being.

Cooperatives stand out as enterprises that are inherently aligned with values and principles, making sustainable development an integral part of their operational ethos. These enterprises are guided by a set of core values and principles including equity, solidarity, democratic management, and a strong commitment to environmental stewardship. These guiding principles prioritize the welfare of human beings over the accumulation of capital, thereby embodying a value system that places significant emphasis on social equity and environmental sustainability. This approach is in harmony with the Sustainable Development Goals (SDGs) outlined in the United Nations 2030 Agenda, which seeks to address a broad spectrum of environmental, political, and economic challenges confronting our society. Among these goals, SDG 8 focuses on promoting sustained, inclusive, and sustainable economic growth, alongside ensuring full and productive employment and decent work for all. Meanwhile, SDG 10 aims at reducing inequalities within and among countries. The vital contribution of cooperatives in advancing the SDGs has been acknowledged both within institutional frameworks, by entities such as the United Nations Task Force on Social and Solidarity Economy and the International Co-operative Alliance's Cooperatives Europe, and through academic research, underscoring the alignment of cooperatives with the SDGs.

Cooperative firms are increasingly recognized as an optimal business model for addressing these challenges, offering a management structure that benefits all stakeholders involved. Recent scholarly work has underscored the significant role these companies play in enhancing the business landscape of local communities, thereby spurring economic development in these regions. The intrinsic nature of cooperative firms, which inherently encourages socially responsible behavior, positions them as a key vehicle for promoting economic prosperity and social well-being in local areas. This emphasizes the importance of cooperative enterprises not only as economic entities but also as catalysts for social change and development, reflecting their commitment to creating a more equitable and sustainable future.

The book "*Community Enterprise and Cooperative Development*" serves as a comprehensive guide for individuals and organizations interested in the foundational principles, operational strategies, and sustainable practices of establishing and managing community enterprises and cooperatives. This book is designed to elucidate the concepts of collective business models that prioritize social objectives, community welfare, and economic sustainability over individual profit maximization. It offers readers insights into the mechanisms of successful cooperative development, including governance structures, financial management, member engagement, and the social impact of community-based enterprises.

Intended for a diverse audience, this book targets community leaders, social entrepreneurs, economic development practitioners, students of social and economic sciences, and anyone with an interest in cooperative models and community-driven economic development. It aims to inspire and equip these readers with the knowledge and tools necessary to initiate, expand, and sustain community enterprises that can contribute to local development, economic resilience, and social cohesion. Including case studies, theoretical frameworks, and practical strategies, the book seeks to foster a deeper understanding of how cooperative and community enterprises can be pivotal in addressing contemporary economic challenges, promoting inclusivity, and enhancing the quality of life within communities.

I would like to express my sincere gratitude to the numerous individuals and organizations whose contributions have enriched the content of this book. This work would not have been possible without the valuable information sourced from widely regarded references.

I extend my heartfelt thanks to the editors, researchers, and experts whose pioneering work has laid the foundation for the topics covered in this book. Their dedication to advancing knowledge in their respective fields has been instrumental in shaping the content presented here.

Editor

CONTENTS

1 INTRODUCTION TO COMMUNITY ENTERPRISE AND COOPERATIVES

INTRODUCTION

Community enterprise and cooperatives are innovative models of economic organization that prioritize community well-being and collective ownership. Unlike traditional businesses driven solely by profit, these entities are founded on principles of democratic decision-making, social responsibility, and equitable distribution of benefits.

Community enterprises are businesses owned and operated by the local community, aiming to address specific social, economic, or environmental needs. They often emerge in areas where traditional market mechanisms fail to meet the diverse needs of residents. By harnessing local resources and expertise, community enterprises foster self-reliance, empower marginalized groups, and build resilient communities.

Cooperatives, on the other hand, are member-owned organizations where individuals join forces to meet common needs, such as affordable housing, access to healthcare, or fair labor practices. Members democratically control the cooperative's operations and share in its profits or benefits, ensuring that decision-making reflects the collective interests of the community.

Both community enterprises and cooperatives embody principles of solidarity, inclusivity, and sustainability. By prioritizing social impact over individual gain, they contribute to more equitable and resilient economies, fostering a sense of belonging and shared prosperity among community members.

THE NATURE OF ENTERPRISE

"Enterprise" gives a mixed message. On one hand, linked to entrepreneur, it can be seen as the activity of someone prepared to take risks with the resources with which he or she is entrusted, in order to gain a personal profit. In the age of "Greed is Good" increasing numbers of entrepreneurs, when caught in their activities, are finishing up as "white collar" criminals. On the other hand, "enterprise" comes from the French, "entre" meaning "between" and "preneur" meaning "taker". In this second meaning an "enterprise" is a form of organisation that takes people from where they are to where they would like to be. In this context the "entrepreneur" is someone who develops an innovative way of meeting an emergent need in the community, a creative individual who inspires others with his or her leadership, to achieve a goal not possible otherwise. But this too is a mystification of another possibility. Neo-classical economics argues that the most economically efficient organisations are privately owned enterprises, competing in a "free market". They are characterised it is said by "perfect competition", and in a situation where consumers, making rational choices about costs and benefits have "perfect information" about the consequences of their choices forever into the future. It is further suggested, that government operated enterprises are by nature bureaucratic, inflexible and inefficient, by comparison to those that operate in the market-place.

But the reality few of these conditions exist in the real world. The conditions of "perfect entry" – where individuals can freely enter any industry to establish themselves as competitors to an existing enterprise - have not existed since the early 19th century. Despite massive market growth has seen the number of automobile manufacturers in the USA, for instance, fall from 5,000 in 1895 to 4 in 1995. Today of the world's 100 largest economies, 51 are now corporations, only 49 are nation states. The economic impact of these trans-national corporations has been continuously growing throughout the 20th century, despite the fact that since the 1970s, their number of employees has been falling rapidly. Clearly, in these circumstances the costs of "perfect" competition are so high, and so damaging to the sense of community, that "free markets" do not really operate.

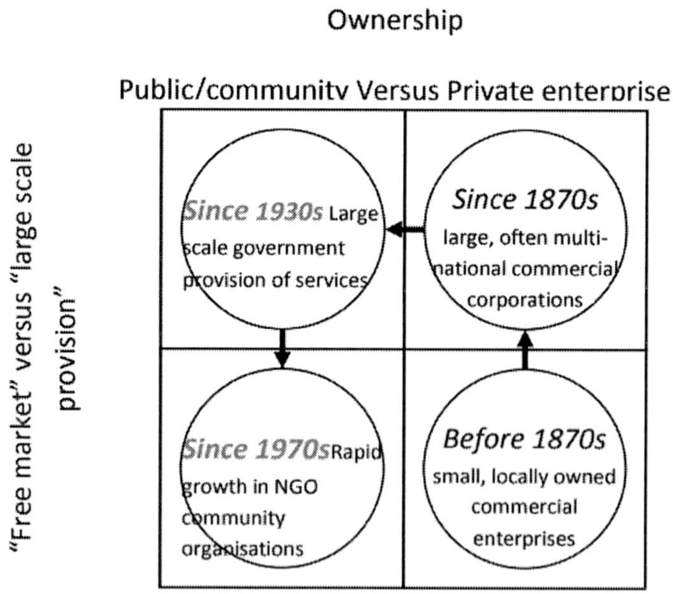

Figure 1. Mixed economy at community level.

Source: https://dragondreaming.org/wp-content/uploads/2020/01/Fact-Sheet-Number-19-Community-Enterprise.pdf

From the 1930s depression government provision proved to be the best way of maintaining both aggregate demand as well as providing a form of enterprise to meet many community needs that could not be delivered by markets. Public education, public health, welfare provision and many infrastructure developments are only possible through funding from the public purse. This is especially true in those areas where a "fee for service" would result in worsening conditions of social equity, and a rising gap between rich and poor. But in recent years, whilst community social and environmental needs continue to grow, the growth of government tax revenues have threatened overall corporate and community prosperity. In these cases not-for-profit community organisations have shown an importance that was previously not recognised.

Thus rather than a single form of enterprise we find in fact there are four types, creating historically a highly "mixed economy", as follows

In the so-called "developed" world there has generally been a "mixed economy" of four kinds of organisations working at community level – determined principally by the specific economic, social, political, cultural or environmental nature of the local community involved.

COMMUNITY ENTERPRISE

A community enterprise is one that is located in a community and members of the community are the owners, managers and employees. In addition to the economic benefit, community enterprises often have the added dimension of trying to improve the communities in which they are based by bringing additional social benefits (for example improving livelihoods of members of the community, building community cohesion, drawing on the strengths of the community, promoting the community, promoting gender equity and youth empowerment) and operating in an environmentally sustainable way (for example practicing sustainable use of resources, minimising negative environmental impacts due to pollution, promoting conservation of biodiversity).

Community enterprises in the Caribbean depend heavily on natural resources; this is especially so for those located in rural communities. They range from community ecotourism initiatives, to development of craft products, to greenhouses and production of organic cocoa, coffee and honey.

Community is a much misused word. It comes from three separate components

- Com = means "with" or "together" (in Latin)
- Munis = means "the changes or exchanges that link" (in Proto-Indo-European)
- Ity = comes from "Itatus" (in Latin) which means "local", "small" or "intimate"

Thus "Community" means "the local links or exchanges that tie us together". An authentic "community" is one that is inclusive of difference, is cohesive without being a clique, and is directed outwards towards the wider world, whilst being focussed on achieving the needs of its members. An authentic community is thus characterised by the quality of communication amongst its members. We don't have many truly authentic communities.

Most of what we call communities are just accidental groups of people who have something in common –

- Geographical Communities – are people who live in proximity
- Organisational Communities – are people linked by need or organisation
- Cultural Communities – are people linked by a shared culture

Enterprise is also a much misunderstood word. It comes from two words in French –

- Entre = between
- Prise = to take

Thus an enterprise is something that "takes you from where you are now to where you would like to be in the future".

Taken together a Community Enterprise refers to the development of an innovative community based institutions that enable a higher degree of collaboration between the four sectors operating in a local area.

A community enterprise exists when the four kinds of enterprise present in a local community, namely –

- Small to Medium Locally Owned Businesses
- Large, Externally Owned and Managed Corporations
- Government Agencies and Instrumentalities, and
- The Non Government, not-for-profit Sector

Work together to achieve beneficial outcomes that none of them could achieve by working alone. It can be described best in the following diagram.

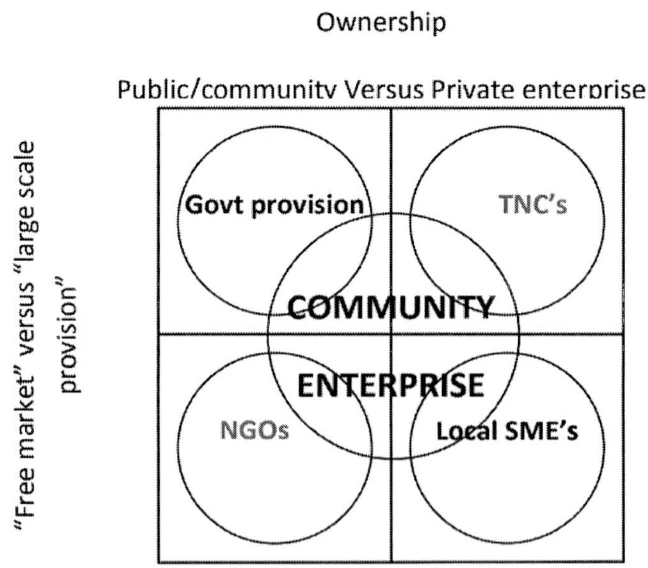

Figure 2. Community enterprise.

Source: https://dragondreaming.org/wp-content/uploads/2020/01/Fact-Sheet-Number-19-Community-Enterprise.pdf

Any community group that has decided to organise and run its own project has made an important decision – its members have become active Community Enterprise participants in local their Community Economic Development. The members have common aims and alone they are unable to achieve these aims, but by banding together and working in partnership with other organisations in their community it becomes possible to work towards these aims and (hopefully) achieve them. Development for the local community by the local community ensures that their dependence upon government bodies, large external companies and other agencies over which local people may have little control, in fact best meet community needs.

Peter Kuenstler writing about Community Enterprises in Western Europe states "One of the characteristics of local initiatives is that they are frequently 'mixed' undertakings, that is to say not only a commercial or trading objective, i.e. to supply a product or service in return for payment, but also a social purpose, to provide a service for which users may not have to pay, but which is provided either through the commercial activities of the project or through a grant from an outside body".

George Burt, of Community Business Scotland, considers a Community Enterprise has the following criteria. Thus a community enterprise provides some or all of the following;

- is a trading organisation
- is owned and controlled on behalf of a local community
- creates jobs for local people in new enterprises
- stimulates all aspects of community economic development
- provides services for a community
- helps or finances projects of community benefit
- provides facilities and training to help others create employment
- does not distribute its profits to its members
- re-invests its profits for community benefit

There are ten major ingredients of successful Community Enterprises.

1. ***An Integrated Approach:*** the goals of community enterprise are never solely economic; nor are the goals solely social, or cultural, or environmental. Community enterprise developments must be integrated if they are to be effective. They are organised to meet important interests of the whole community. Accordingly their goals and strategies relate to the whole community – to its social, economic, environmental and cultural elements. These are precisely the requirements for Local Agenda 21, needed to develop Ecologically Sustainable Development, agreed to by the Australian Federal Government at the Rio Earth Summit in 1992. It has also been supported by the Australian Local Government Association (ALGA) in its push for Integrated Local Area Planning (ILAP).

2. ***Not for Private Profit:*** Many community enterprise projects get confused by this point. Community enterprises need to make a financial profit in order to survive. However, in a community enterprise, "profits" are a means to some other community "end" rather than an "end in themselves". The goal of a community enterprise is not to accumulate money, or pay dividends to members, but rather to ensure that any profits made are used for the benefit of the whole community. Community enterprises thus are very concerned with what is being called the "triple bottom line". Not only are they concerned with financial viability and profitability (the "bottom

line" of a conventional private enterprise), but they are also concerned what is happening to the "social capital" and the "ecological capital" of their communities too. Profits made from trading enterprises are usually reinvested to grow the "social", "cultural" or "ecological" capital of the community.

3. ***Not for Personal Gain***: Community Enterprise projects, unlike most traditional small businesses, private companies or cooperatives, are not organised to provide personal financial gain for their members. Members' benefits may come, however, indirectly, through the improved access to important goods or services arising for the project. For instance, a rental housing cooperative would be an example of a Community Enterprise, as members are able to provide in an important way for their housing needs. A non-rental, equity housing cooperative, however, would not be a community enterprise, as on the sale of their equity, private individuals stand to make a financial gain.
4. ***Local Control:*** Community resilience and self reliance can only be attained through a process of development which is largely locally initiated and locally controlled. Again this can lead to confusion. No community in the globalising world market can now ever be totally self-reliant. Through their taxes, local communities provide for government to provide programs on their behalf. They demand and are right to expect that government spending occur in their locality. The profits made by large companies, or the repayments on bank loans are generated by local communities, and there are many excellent examples of community enterprise created by working in partnership with such agencies, Nevertheless, it is important that members of a community enterprise realise that while, training, education, information, support and assistance, and even some funds may come from outside the community, it is by making decisions locally that the success of a community enterprise can be assured.
5. ***Belief in Managing Their Own Affairs:*** Community Enterprises therefore must believe in themselves and their abilities to manage their own affairs. They must have faith in the potential of the people of their community, and trust that people are capable of coming together for the good of the whole community, rather than just be motivated by narrow self interest. Acting out of such a belief, and motivating others to do the same, builds the social capital of a community, reduces any distrust and increases the economic returns to all enterprises – small private enterprises, large corporate enterprises and government service provision.
6. ***Democratic Consensus in Decision Making:*** Conventional management and organisation structures tend to draw the power of decision making away from the members as a whole, who may meet only once or twice a year, towards a small group of people involved in the executive or management committee which may meet monthly, or even fortnightly. This anti-democratic tendency can lead to conflict between members and management, which can reduce the effectiveness of community enterprise, unless managed properly. Seeking every opportunity for

consultation and involvement of all stakeholders in the community, can help the committee ensure that executive members do not get trapped into a cycle of "overload – overwhelmed – burned-out – resign – seek new members". It can also continually mobilise the energies and the interest of a far larger group than conventional "committee meetings" can generate. Participatory democracy, involving various methods of consensus decision making, can be very helpful here. At the same time, it is important that for those urgent unimportant decisions (eg which post office should be used to buy stamps), should be left to the individuals who are engaged in those activities, without needing to be answerable to a committee for their actions. Seeking order, decision by committee frequently provokes paralysis. Dee Hock has shown "Chaordic Organisations", those that exist on the edge of Chaos, are more successful in promoting and empowering their participants to be innovative and creative, adjusting rapidly to changing circumstances.

7. ***Small is Frequently Beautiful:*** Our culture tends to be obsessed by "bigness". People who get involved in community enterprise can also become addicted to this as a criterion of success. But big projects do not start in a vacuum. They are the result of the success and growth of previous small projects. If you hear someone describing your project as a "small local effort" this should be regarded as praise, not as condemnation. Such efforts are owned and managed locally; it is located and controlled by the host community; it provides work for local people; makes use of locally available resources, both human and material; serves local needs through providing improved access to products and services; enhances local capacity and community adaptability; builds social vitality and rarely does much (if any) damage to a local environment. As Tony Judge, of the International Association for Associations has said, building strategic partnerships between very different kinds of organisations achieves far more than any single organisation trying to got it alone. Community enterprise, thus organises a local ecology of organisation structures by enhancing communication between non-government community organisations, government agencies, large corporations and small, locally owned businesses. This work may be small, and almost invisible, but it is crucial to the success of community economic development.
8. ***Community Economic Development:*** Traditional community development initiatives in developed countries have tended to focus upon social, recreational, cultural, health and education initiatives. Economic development in the past has been left to major business corporations and State and Federal Governmental planners. Not only has this tended to favour "big projects" in "large communities" at the expense of "little projects" in small communities, which have suffered as a result, it has also tended to reduce local control, and local resilience to the buffetings of changes in commodity prices or government policies. Community Enterprise is they key strategy that puts economics back into the heart of Community Economic Development. At the same time it does not reduce the importance of the social, cultural or

environmental. Rather it augments their success by giving them access to funding that they would otherwise lack, reducing their dependence upon government handouts or corporate sponsorship.

9. ***Involvement of Training and Education:*** The most successful community enterprises are what Peter Senge calls "learning organisations". Learning organisations work because they are "value driven" and mobilise voluntary input far in excess of the work generated from any contract, wage or salary. They also tend to promote change from the inside out, rather than have change forced upon them from the outside in. By having their "eyes wide open", learning organisations are constantly receiving signals of many kinds that reflect upon their performance, and are able to discriminate between a "meaningful signal" and meaningless background "noise". Through review and evaluation, the "learning loop" is closed. Thus recurrent, lifelong learning for all involved is fundamental to the success of any community enterprise. Community enterprises need a hunger for information and awareness about how things could be done better, that should be shared by all people involved. If there is a better book keeping system, for instance, get someone trained to implement it. If you hear of a community that has been successful in fostering community involvement, check them out and learn from their experience. It may prevent you from having to reinvent the wheel. Education in this way is not something that is contained in schools or academies, set apart from life. Education in a successful community enterprise becomes a part of life, as inseparable as breathing.

10. ***It Takes Time:*** Community Enterprise projects are developmental, and development cannot be hurried. One cannot prise open the petals on a rose bud, it proceeds at its own pace. Community enterprise projects are there for the long haul. Whilst they may be able to take rapid strides, or capture a temporary opportunity, their impact usually will only really be felt over many years. This does not mean that people need to commit themselves for an organisation forever. It rather means that the community enterprise structure is one that should facilitate new, less experienced but more enthusiastic people to join easily, and "older" more experienced people, who may have little more to contribute, to leave gracefully, without forsaking or losing valuable lessons that may have bean learned the hard way. This prevents a small group of declining numbers being left "carrying the can". Ensuring that each person who leaves gets replaced, in advanced, by someone who would be better at doing the job than they were, would go a long way to securing the stability of community enterprise structures. Finding ways of giving everyone the chance to participate in making the really important decisions, is a great way of sharing any burdens and keeping enthusiasm high.

ORGANISING FOR COMMUNITY ENTERPRISE

A Community Enterprise is thus highly malleable, involving an adaptable structure to take account of the needs and situation of the circumstances found in a particular locality. Community Enterprises have taken the following forms

- A Not-for-Profit Incorporated Community Association (under the WA Incorporated Associations Act 1987) that runs a local business
- An enterprise arm of a local organisation, Service Club, Progress Association or local Chamber of Commerce (Rotary run Swap-Meets, or Market Days are an example)
- A particular project auspiced or sponsored by a Local Government Authority (The Narembeen Community Telecentre is a WA example)
- A non-distributing Cooperative Company (under the WA Cooperative Companies Act 1947-93. The Mt Barker Cooperative operates in such a fashion)
- A Community Foundation, or charitable body, having tax deductable status (The Mid West Community Foundation established in Moora sought such a structure)
- A Community Trust, in which the beneficiaries of a trust business are named as a particular community. The recently formed WA Community Foundation operates in this way.
- A community based Credit Union in Maleny, Queensland, is at the hub of a variety of Community Enterprises, including a LETSystem, Food Cooperative, and others.
- A corporate out-sourced local government function – such as the award winning Emergency Services Program in Margaret River.
- A Business Partnership – in which a number of these agencies work together in a structured form, as with the proposed community owned windfarms in Geraldton and Denmark.

As the following above diagrams show, a Community Enterprise can incorporate a wide range of players for a wide variety of functions. In Western Australia Community Enterprises have undertaken a range of functions including

- ***Establishing Profitable Enterprises:*** that are essentially small business, to either employ local people, or create a capital base that can be used for other community benefit (eg. The Cunderdin Hotel was managed by a Community Enterprise that used to profits to build and run a community based swimming pool, long before they became common in Country Towns). The proposed Turner Rd Caravan Park, to be run by the Augusta Community Development Association, or the Margaret River Design Centre, being proposed by the Alternative Technology Centre are classic examples of such Community Enterprises.
- ***Running Marginal Enterprises:*** There are many enterprises that the private sector would not consider undertaking, but which a community enterprise, by mobilising volunteer assistance and drawing upon social capital, can run effectively. This may involve a community taking over an existing enterprise which would otherwise by lost to a community. Except that the people investing stand to make a personal profit, the growth of the Community Banking movement, sponsored by the Bendigo Bank is otherwise a classic example of such marginal business enterprises, mobilising community based social capital to run enterprises which have been judged to be marginal by conventional banks.
- ***Seizing Opportunities:*** Once a Community Enterprise structure is

established, it may facilitate a rapid response to a temporary business opportunity which would otherwise disappear, or not be taken up by a locality. The Community Enterprises in the town of Hyden in WA have repeatedly demonstrated the effectiveness of this approach. Equally the "debranching" of the major banks have provided opportunities for community enterprise banking, in which local communities have worked in partnership with Bendigo Bank to achieve outcomes impossible for the parties if they had been forced to work alone.

- ***Promotion of Community Entrepreneurship:*** Community Entrepreneurship is a special kind of local leadership which can effectively assist a community build a vision for itself, and then helps the community build a bridge between where they are now and where they want to be. Business Incubators exist in Tambellup, Balingup and elsewhere to foster such an enterprise spirit. In Western Australia, the Community Builders Program and the Community Opportunities Workshops of the Office of the Minister for Primary Industry, and the Small Town Economic Planning Program of the Department of Commerce and Trade have in the past assisted with the building of such Community Entrepreneurship.
- ***Providing Community Services:*** A community enterprise may also undertake any activity that benefits a local community. For instance many Telecentres in Western Australia (which are very successful Community Enterprises) publish local newspapers, and share resources with local libraries and other community services which may otherwise be only available on a much more limited basis than at present. Community Enterprises may also provide for such services to senior citizens, youth, or mothers of young children.
- ***Sponsoring Community Activities and Events:*** A community enterprise may organise major community events that can be of major cultural, social, and economic benefit to a local community. The Dowerin Field Day, brings an estimated 80,000 people to a town that otherwise has a resident population of only some 800 people. Many examples of such events exist in Western Australia, for instance the Nannup Folk Festival, the Bridgetown Blues Festival, the Balingup Small Farm Field Day and its Medieval Fair are just a few such examples.

INTRODUCTION TO COOPERATIVES

Cooperatives are businesses organisations that are owned and run by a group of individuals for their mutual benefit. Within a legal context they are an association or corporation established for the purpose of providing services on a non-profit basis to its shareholders or members who own and control it. Cooperatives exist for all types of reason, to provide housing, food, and energy to running businesses such as bookshops to artist cooperatives and beyond. Cooperatives have existed in some form or another ever since human beings began to organise themselves for their own mutual benefit, many tribes organised themselves along cooperative lines as a means of securing resources and allocating work within their particular group or community. These cooperative structures were then used when trading with other tribes and communities within the locale as a means of ensuring fairness.

Cooperatives within a Historical Context

The idea that people that should form into groups for their own mutual benefit was further developed by the Welsh Social reformer Robert Owen, who in 1810 got together with his partners and purchased a Mill from his Father-in Law David Dale.

From this point onward Robert Owen and his partners introduced better work conditions for their workers and offered them discounted goods via their retails shops, as well as sharing the profits from sales amongst the employees. Owen continued to develop these cooperative ideas through writing books and travelling round the UK doing lectures to promote these new ideas.

Further to this, in 1844 the first cooperative enterprise was developed when The Rochdale Society of Equitable Pioneers was founded. Historically this enterprise was taken as the model to develop further Cooperatives and is the basis of the modern Cooperative Movement that we have today.

A Working Cooperative in Action

There are dozens of cooperative up and down the country that offer a variety of goods and services. An obvious example of a fully working contemporary cooperative that is very prominent within the wider Market framework is the Cooperative, known by many simply as the Co-op. The Co-op boasts over 6 million members and provides employment for over 110,000 people across the UK.

At the other end of the spectrum there are smaller grass roots community run cooperatives both here in the UK and all over the world, and this seems to be something that is gathering momentum due to the workers valued involvement and input, the social investment, and the general resilience of cooperatives compared to Market place models of trading and producing goods.

What is encouraging within a UK context is that there are many medium sized and smaller cooperatives that focus on food and the distribution of food, such as the Suma Whole food Coop, Organiclea in London, and Manchester Unicorn Cooperative grocery, to name but a few. These cooperatives provide healthy organic and ethically sourced produce for people all over the UK with Suma, and across Manchester and London, and are thriving; they are thriving because they have developed links with the local community whilst at the same time ensuring that suppliers are paid a fair price for their produce.

Cooperatives Help to Develop a Permanent Culture

Cooperatives are an important organisational structure as we move towards the development of a Permanent Culture and away from the temporary exploitative short term 'quick buck' approach of free Market economics and Neoliberalism.

Their importance lies in the fact that they are run collectively and mutually, and because of this Cooperatives are much more resilient and people centred than a top down structure where those at the top make decisions based on their personal interest as opposed to the interests of all of those involved in the business or organisation. If we examine the underpinning principles below that govern and guide the modern cooperative we can see that these principles embody a great many of the things that we need to bring about a Permanent Culture, such as inclusivity, equality, fairness, access and participation to democratic processes.

Cooperative Values

The cooperative values serve as guidelines for all co-op organizations and their members. There are six main cooperative values:

- ***Self-help:*** Co-ops are geared towards creating a community where every member benefits equitably. To accomplish this ideal, members need to help themselves while also helping each other.
- ***Self-responsibility:*** Much of the cooperative ideology is based on the idea that each individual member is individually responsible within the group. They should be responsible and play their part on their own, without the need for external motivation or incentive.
- ***Democracy:*** Democratic structure is crucial to running a successful cooperative. The organization exists so that all members have control, and no one individual holds more power than the others. Members choose representatives by way of voting, and each individual has one vote per election.
- ***Equality:*** Each member of a cooperative should benefit from the same rights, based on their level of contribution.
- ***Equity:*** Cooperative organizations should treat all members fairly, without any form of discrimination. Equity is essential to creating a harmonious relationship among all members.
- ***Solidarity:*** The members within a cooperative form a unified organization where all the individuals support one another. Each organization also supports other cooperatives to form a united network.

In addition to the main cooperative values, there is also a set of ethical values. They are traditional ethics established by the founders of the cooperative organization. All co-ops function under the ideals of honesty, openness, social responsibility and caring for others. These values act as the foundation for cooperative principles. The principles are essentially guidelines for how members can successfully integrate and practice the core co-op values in every area of their organization. Both the values and principles are crucial in all areas, from everyday operations to elections and policies.

COOPERATIVE PRINCIPLES

One of the ways cooperatives differ from other business structures is their adherence to cooperative principles and values that reflect social, political, and business concerns. Cooperatives trace the roots of these principles to the Rochdale pioneers, who established the first modern cooperative in Rochdale, England in 1844. These principles have been refined, adapted, and reinterpreted over time. The seven principles used by the International Cooperative Alliance today are generally accepted by cooperatives worldwide. Cooperatives are also based on the values of self-help, self-responsibility, democracy, equality, equity, and solidarity. Cooperative members believe in the ethical values of honesty, openness, social responsibility, and caring for others.

The cooperative principles are:

Voluntary and Open Membership

The members are the most important part of a cooperative. Without dedicated and participating members, no co-op can succeed. To gain such a group of individuals, all co-ops need to remain voluntary organizations with membership opportunities for all. They should be open to any persons who are able and willing to join, accept responsibility as a part of the organization and can use the organization's services. It also protects members and interested individuals from any form of discrimination. Cooperatives accept members voluntarily, meaning they cannot discriminate based on gender, sexuality, social status, race, political affiliation, religion or any other personal details. As long as individuals are willing to follow the core principles and values of the co-op, they can become members.

This principle protects the fundamental human rights of interested individuals and members. It establishes that no person or organization can turn an individual into a willing co-operator and that their involvement has to come from a place of genuine interest. The voluntary membership also provides individuals with freedom of association. They can exercise their free will and decide if and when they wish to join and leave the organization.

Democratic Member Control

Cooperatives are founded on the ideals of democracy. Every member plays an integral role in making decisions that affect the organization as a whole. The cooperative makes crucial choices, adds or reforms policies and elects new representatives as a group. All of the members have equal voting rights, with one ballot per individual, and elected officials hear every person's voice.

Since all members are affected by the co-op's choices, as they all hold the same status, it's natural that they should have the power of decision. It's a vital part of all operations, from the day-to-day schedules to broader issues that will affect the future of the co-op. Providing a democratic structure ensures all members have a fair stake in the organization and that their opinions and observations are considered. Healthy debate is also essential for a working democracy.

Beyond creating a fair method of decision-making, it engages all members and serves as an incentive to participate. If members know their votes count and are valuable to the good of their organization, they will be more willing to participate in democratic practices as well as daily operations. Democracy also ensures those in elected positions are held accountable for their actions. If members decide an official is abusing their power or not considering the good of all members, they can take steps to solve the issue as a group.

Members' Economic Participation

To maintain fairness in all areas of the cooperative, members need to contribute equitably to its economy. They should also maintain democratic control over the collected capital. A portion of the capital is considered the property of the group.

Should there be any surplus capital, the members decide where to distribute the money. Surpluses typically go towards:

- Developing the cooperative or creating reserves
- Benefitting members equitably based on their transactions
- Supporting membership-approved activities

Creating an equitable and democratic economy is essential for several reasons. For one, it establishes that capital supports business pursuits but doesn't rule how the cooperative operates. Money should always be considered a servant of the members. It is a means by which the co-op can develop and grow. Additionally, creating a democratic process for allocating capital ensures the co-op spends it with its people in mind and prevents any major excess.

Autonomy and Independence

While each member has their own freedoms within the cooperative, the organization itself is also an autonomous and independent entity. The members of the co-op determine everything it does, which allows the co-op to function independently. The organization needs to be self-sustaining for each member to be able to exercise his or her freedoms within the structure.

The autonomy of the cooperative is also essential to outside collaboration. Co-ops can decide to enter business relationships with other organizations or raise additional capital from outside investors or sources. This principle ensures they keep their democratic and independent structure regardless of who they enter into agreements with. It even extends to arrangements between co-ops and external governments. The terms and conditions should always include group autonomy.

Maintaining an autonomous and democratically run organization is essential to cooperation. Without these two factors, co-ops would have no self-identity and would have no unique connections to share. They also ensure the members can continue to run the co-op by self-governing, regardless of their relationships and agreements with commercial entities and national governments. Securing democratic practices is especially important when it comes to working with sources of capital.

Education, Training and Information

To run a co-op successfully, promoting and spreading education is a necessity. Every individual involved with a cooperative needs to be well informed about the way they operate, their purposes and the responsibilities of each person. Members, employees, managers and elected officials all need continual training as the cooperative evolves and changes over time. If they are well versed in the co-op's policies, regulations, values and principles, they'll all be able to contribute more effectively to its development.

But education shouldn't stop at the cooperative's internal members. It should also extend to the surrounding community and the general public. Members can teach others about the beneficial nature of cooperative businesses and encourage interest in their organization. Informing younger generations and community leaders not only creates outside approval and awareness, but it may also encourage interested individuals to join the organization.

Internal and external education are both necessary parts of cooperative practices. Continual member training helps cooperatives develop, advance and adapt to new technologies, helping them become better business entities. It also supports co-ops in adjusting to other changes, such as changes in laws, social trends or the economy.

Beyond the cooperative itself, education encourages the spread of information. It helps create relationships with universities and supports research regarding the cooperative movement. With formal research, co-ops can help spread the educational material to governments and officials and inform future policies. Teaching the wider public about the history, principles and day-to-day operations of a co-op can create a stronger, more supportive local community.

Overall, continual education is crucial for a cooperative to function. Regardless of how far a co-op's outreach goes, there's always a core purpose in mind — to nurture a more complete understanding of the nature of cooperation as well as to emphasize its benefits.

Cooperation among Cooperatives

While co-ops are independent of one another and run by autonomous individuals, they also need to work together harmoniously. Creating a larger network of cooperatives — locally, regionally, nationally or even internationally — allows independent organizations to better serve their members. Each co-op brings its unique abilities and contributions to the table, and they function with more strength as a unit. Not only do individual members benefit from the connectivity, but it also helps the cooperative as a whole. Developing larger structures that span multiple cooperatives strengthens the movement through combined efforts and support. The networks can then work together across organizations to better serve their members. They can also choose to work with other structures that will serve the common good of the members and the movement as a whole. Creating a stable structure establishes independent co-ops as both social and economic entities in relation to other groups and organizations. Forming these networks allows co-ops and their collaborators to gain a mutual benefit from one another, rather than to compete against one another for profit, like non-cooperative businesses. Working together emphasizes the value of solidarity.

Concern for Community

All cooperatives focus on their internal communities, but they are also concerned with their local communities outside of the organization. Co-ops source materials from and invest in local suppliers to contribute to the community's sustainability. While the group works as a unit, each member should also take it upon themselves to contribute to the community in some way. The cooperative and surrounding network should encourage them to serve with pride.

But sustainability doesn't stop at the local level. Community goes as far as a worldwide reach, and cooperatives should think and act on both a local and global level. Members can work towards approving policies that consider the community at large. Maintaining local and global concern is important for several reasons. As other principles dictate, cooperatives are independent organizations that work best in a collaborative effort. So, each co-op should have their own way of contributing to sustainable development, but they should also work within their networks. This enables cooperatives to take action on a level that can affect the world. Not only are co-ops directly affected by community development, but they can also have a great impact if they work together.

TYPES OF COOPERATIVES

Cooperatives vary depending on the service offered and the way that the members are organized. They also differ depending on the economic activity, how members use the Cooperative and kind of management.

There are six types of classification: Agricultural Co-op (known in Manitoba "New Generation Co-op"), Consumer Co-op, Credit Union, Housing Co, and insurance Co-op and Worker co-ops. Those types of cooperatives include producer/marketing, retail supply, utilities, cable television, agricultural services, fish marketing, child care, farmers' markets and community service.

- Producer / Marketing Cooperatives
- Consumer Cooperatives
- Worker Cooperatives
- Housing Cooperatives
- Financial Cooperatives
- New Generation Cooperatives
- Multi-Stakeholder Cooperatives
- Non-profit Community Service Cooperatives

Producer / Marketing Cooperatives

The Producer Co-ops were one of the first kinds of Cooperatives developed to explore and provide solutions to the farmers' production in the early 1880s. Producers Co-ops are also known as marketing co-op where the members provide the co-op with the same production that the co-op markets in a processed or value-added form.

The Co-ops' mandate is to commercialize the members input by seeking the best price possible on the market. In Manitoba many groups of suppliers are organized into marketing co-ops to meet the marketing requirement and to explore and access the market for their product.

These Producer Co-ops include farmers, artists, harvesters and fishers seeking out and selling to end users to earn and retain the benefit of their owners/producers.

Consumer Cooperatives

This is one of the best known forms of cooperatives. They are owned and controlled by the people that buy the products and services sold, managed or distributed by the co-ops.

Their mandate is to acquire the products and services required by their members at the lowest possible cost with the highest possible quality. These co-ops can operate in three different ways; as buying clubs where products and services are obtained by the co-op only when the members place an order; as retail stores where the members come in to shop; and as service providers where members order the service, such as cable television, internet access, insurance, water or natural gas.

In Manitoba there are general stores, gas bars, farm supplies, furniture stores, funeral services, natural gas utilities, water utilities, internet access and cable television co-ops serving the needs of their members.

Worker Cooperatives

Worker co-ops are identified as the third type of Cooperative owned and controlled by their employees. The purpose of the worker co-op is to create jobs for their members and allow them control of their workplace. Members provide the capital to finance the business, each sharing the costs and risks of ownership. The management of a worker co-op is concentrated in the business part and classified as a third type of co-op where the members are employees. Usually the worker co-ops are services co-op offering services to other business and they are generally printing, nursery schools, cleaning, consulting, delivery, manufacturing and food services.

Major benefits to the employee-members include involvement in the policy-making process, through the election of a Board of Directors, profit sharing through patronage allocations, and a quality of work life that is established by the membership.

Housing Cooperatives

Housing co-ops are developed to resolve the living need by offering an affordable and secure housing in a viable community. The members are tenants/ owners having the ability to manage and control the co-op.

There are two types of housing co-ops under Manitoba legislation, "Not-for profit" (a defined term) and all others.

Not-for-profit housing co-ops are those where Articles of Incorporation specify that they are not-for-profit, that file income tax returns as a not-for-profit corporation or that have received from the Government of Canada or the Government of Manitoba or an agency of either one of them, a subsidy or assistance of a type that assisted with or reduced housing costs.

The Not-for-profit housing co-ops are subject to the following restrictions:

- They cannot issue investment shares
- They must conduct at least 90% of their business with their members
- They shall carry on their business without the purpose of gain for their members
- They may not be continued under any other legislation
- They may not amend their articles to change to any other type of co-op
- On dissolution their remaining assets must be given to:
    - another not-for-profit housing co-op
    - Manitoba co-op with similar objectives and limitations
    - charitable organizations with similar purposes

Most housing co-ops in Manitoba are not-for-profit and were built with assistance from both the Government of Canada and the Government of Manitoba to provide affordable housing for low and moderate income families.

Resident members purchase membership shares of the co-op in relatively small amounts (less than three months housing charges) and pay housing charges to cover mortgage interest, utilities, repairs, taxes, depreciation, management, administrative and other operating costs.

When members leave the co-op they are entitled to have their shares redeemed by the co-op for the same price paid by the members unless the co-op has a deficit and is prevented by legislation from redeeming the shares.

The other category of housing co-ops does not have the above restrictions and set their own rules for the amount of equity required to become a resident member and how members deal with their occupancy rights and shares when leaving.

In most instances the exiting member gives the prescribed notice and on the exit date is no longer responsible for the housing charges and receives the acquisition price for the membership shares upon redemption less any pro rata portion of any capital impairment. In some of these co-ops the share capital is modest and similar to the not-for-profit housing co-ops and the co-op and the members' cash flows are not significant. Other equity requirements are higher and members can reduce the monthly housing charges by increasing the share capital investment.

However, upon leaving, the housing co-op may have to increase its mortgage, as the incoming member may not be able to invest as much in share capital as the exiting member. In these cases the exiting member may have to wait some time before being paid for all the shares redeemed. This can also put stress on the co-op if the mortgage holder does not feel the cash flow of the co-op is sufficient to warrant additional financing. Others are set up so that the exiting member is responsible for the housing charges until a replacement resident member is found.

The new member pays the exiting member market value for the right to occupy the housing unit and the housing co-op records the transfer of equity and charges the new member an initiation fee. The housing co-op, although it still must approve the new member, receives the transfer fee but does not have to concern itself with the redemption of shares.

Financial Cooperatives

The financial co-ops were initially based on consumer co-ops offering financial services to their members. Financial co-ops were started in rural communities providing farmers with micro credit during the early 1900s and they were known as the people's bank or credit unions, and saving and credit cooperatives.

These special types of co-ops often come under legislation developed for the uniqueness of the financial services being provided to their members, deposit taking, loans, trust services, and insurance. Credit Unions (in English Canada) / Caisses Populaire (French Canada) are the most recognizable or best known of the financial co-ops. Like other co-ops democratic control is in the hands of their members/owners.

These co-ops have the mandate to provide their members with financial services at the lowest possible cost and the highest possible return. These services include a variety of deposit vehicles, mortgages, loans, lines of credit, safety deposit boxes, financial planning, estate administration and insurance.

New Generation Cooperatives

New Generation cooperative or New Formula to view and operate a Co-op and they are the latest buzzwords in the co-op community describing a variation on the traditional co-op, yet, retaining the critical co-op principles. New Generation Cooperatives (NGCs) represent an emerging trend in agriculture, forestry, fishing and other industries that are supplied by producers. These are distinct types of cooperatives formed to enable members to process raw commodities. As a result, members not only receive market prices for their produce, they also gain the opportunity to profit from processing and marketing these value-added products.

It is primarily the financial structure and membership requirements that distinguish NGCs from the more traditional cooperatives. Typically, higher equity investments are required by members in order to establish a processing plant. Furthermore, the number of members is limited to those who purchase delivery rights, as well as by the processing capacity of the plant. Because of the unique structure of NGCs, members feel a greater degree of personal ownership and a stronger commitment to the cooperative.

These Cooperatives are referred to as new generation because of four distinct variances from traditional co-ops:

- The focus is on the value-added processing or manufacturing of raw commodities delivered to the co-op by its members and the marketing of the resulting products.
- A significant equity investment is required by each member, with the total initial equity contribution being a major portion of the gross project costs.
- A two-way contract between the member and the co-op requires each member to deliver, and the co-op to accept, an agreed-upon amount of the raw commodity for each delivery right (special investment share under Manitoba legislation) owned by the member.
- Membership is limited to the number of special investment shares (delivery rights) required to be sold by the co-op to its members in order to meet its processing capacity.

THEORETICAL FRAMEWORKS: ROCHDALE PRINCIPLES, SOLIDARITY ECONOMY, SOCIAL CAPITAL THEORY

Rochdale Principles

The Rochdale Principles are a set of ideals for the operation of cooperatives. They were first set out by the Rochdale Society of Equitable Pioneers in Rochdale, England, in 1844, and have formed the basis for the principles on which co-operatives around the world operate to this day. The implications of the Rochdale Principles are a focus of study in co-operative economics. The original Rochdale Principles were officially adopted by the International Co-operative Alliance (ICA) in 1937 as the Rochdale Principles of Co-operation. Updated versions of the principles were adopted by the ICA in 1966 as the Co-operative Principles and in 1995 as part of the Statement on the Co-operative Identity.

1. Democratic Control

One member one vote irrespective of member's shareholding or the amount of purchases made in the store. Democracy was at the very root of the agitation for the Charter and an essential foundation for the co-operative.

(NOTE: The members of the Co-operative Wholesale Society (CWS) were not individuals but Societies of widely varying scale. In this case, the members voting rights depended on the amount of purchases made from the CWS. This is still the way that the CWS successor 'The Co-operative Group' organises voting rights for their corporate members).

The Pioneers left very little to chance. They were cautious, practical and experienced people. They set out their rules in detail in 1844, then amended them in 1845 and 1854. They expressed eight fundamental principles. The first was democracy, the principle of one member one vote. There is nothing remarkable in this, since it is what Chartism was all about, and in their chapels and friendly societies and trade unions, the Pioneers would be familiar with it. What was remarkable was that they were applying it to business; they could have given votes in proportion to share capital, as in capitalist firms, or in proportion to purchases, but here power was shared out to persons not to property. Persons also meant women; though they do not seem to have taken an active role in the Society at this stage. Beatrice Potter pointed out that forty years before married women were allowed to keep their own property, women members got some control through having their own share account; the cashiers insisted that husbands who wanted access to it go through the courts first.

2. Open Membership

This goes closely with equal voting rights. Anyone can buy a £1 share and become a member on equal terms with the existing members. It prevents members selling their shares at a profit. The £1 share can never rise above the value of £1.

The second principle was open membership. At first they limited the number of members to 250, probably because they had not yet realised that they could grow by opening branches, and because they did not have much legal protection; the 1852 Industrial & Provident Societies Act, which some influential supporters sponsored for their benefit, gave them proper legal status, (though full limited liability was not granted until 1862) and so after this, membership was allowed to grow and grow. The Act allowed them to sell to non members, but this remained the exception, the rule being that the members and the users of the co-op's services were one and the same. The important point about this principle is that it was a generous one. It allowed new people to come in on a down payment of only a shilling, making the social wealth built up by past generations instantly available to newcomers. There would be none of the hoarding of profits by the original shareholders that we find in capitalist companies. The application of this principle can be judged a success; having aimed at a membership of 250, by 1880 the co-op had over 10,000 members, a large proportion of the local population.

3. A fixed or limited capital on interest on capital subscribed to the Society

This goes back to the time of Robert Owen's advocacy of "villages of co-operation" and was already well established in the Movement. Sometimes local co-operative societies which had sprung up in the 1820's and 1830's has not applied this principle. Some of them had received capital as gifts and others had divided their profits, if any, according to the sums they had subscribed to the venture. This principle set a standard for the building of the Co-operative Movement.

The third principle was fixed and limited interest on capital. 'Fixed means that interest does not rise or fall with profits as it does in a capitalist company, and 'limited' means that the Society will only pay out for capital what it absolutely has to in order to finance its own development. It was one of Robert Owen's principles, that while capital has to be paid for, it should not enable the lender to cream off the surplus made from the labour of others. In this case the rate was fixed in 1844 at 3.5 per cent, then set at varying rates by members meetings, until in 1854 a maximum of 5 percent was written into the statutes. Holyoake points out that many co-op's had failed because they refused to pay interest on capital at all, but the Pioneers were pragmatists; they recognised that in order to attract capital they had to pay for it and that owners were entitled to some payment for the risk attached to lending it.

4. The distribution of the surplus, after the payment of interest and collective charges in dividend to the members in proportion to their purchases

The fourth principle; distribution of the surplus as dividend on purchases, the famous 'Co-op divi'. This was the decisive step in breaking with the old Cooperative Movement which had assumed that surpluses would be built up until a co-operative community could be formed. There are in fact three kinds of people who can benefit from surpluses: those who lend capital, those who work in the business and those who are consumers. The distribution on the basis of purchases marked the Society off from both capitalist and worker owned enterprises and turned the Pioneers (though they may not yet have realised it) into a consumer co-operative. There was nothing remarkable in this. Though one of the Pioneers, Charles Howarth, had to reinvent the idea (perhaps because it had been frowned upon by strict Owenites. Alexander Campbell, the 'father of Scottish co-operation' had been recommending it ever since 1822, and there were in fact several co-op's which had been using the dividend principle since the mid 1820's, including Lennoxtown in Scotland and Meltham Mills in Yorkshire. A meeting of the First Western Union Co-operative Society in 1832 had reported that dividend on purchases "would confer immediate benefit upon all those who dealt extensively at the store and remove the discouragements which the most zealous and persevering co-operators had hitherto experienced".

In practice it did just that. Holyoake tells some remarkable stories of poor people who, having been in debt to shopkeepers for thirty or forty years, suddenly found themselves with money in their pockets and £20 in their share account. Though the dividend was low at first, three pence in the pound, it rose steadily until the Society was paying two shillings and sixpence in the pound (twelve and a half p). One old man claimed that in 11 years he had accumulated £77 in dividend, which had kept him out of the poor house in his old age.

5. Cash Trading

The fifth principle was cash trading. This may seem unimportant today, and is no longer regarded as an essential principle, but to the Pioneers it was most important; though they knew it would restrict their membership, they felt so strongly that they wrote into their rules that any officer giving or taking credit was to be disqualified from office and fined ten shillings. There was a universal dislike of being in debt to shopkeepers, but more than that, there was a realisation that previous societies had foundered on credit. As Holyoake said:

"So many co-operative experiments had been stranded by credit, that an almost universal opinion was prevalent, not only in Rochdale, but throughout the country and in Parliament, that co-operation was an exploded fallacy".

Again, the principle seems to have paid off because, though its strict application in the early years undoubtedly limited its growth, the Society grew anyway.

6. Selling only pure and unadulterated goods

The sixth principle was selling only pure and unadulterated goods. This was not a written rule, but appeared in an important statement of first principles in the Almanac of 1860. We might think that providing wholesome, and untainted food and giving full weight and measure to the customer ought to be taken for granted in a consumer owned and controlled business. Yet there were considerable trading risks involved. Take the case of the flour which, though produced in their own mill, was rejected by members because it was browner than usual. Holyoake tells us that the directors could have bowed to pressure to add chemicals to whiten it, but that this was so much against their principles that they preferred to take the risk and after much discussion with the customers the pure flour eventually gained acceptance. Looking back on the story many years later Holyoake added this comment; "The members had become more intelligent; they had learned the nature of good flour when they had it; their tastes were better educated than that of many gentlemen of the middle class, and the Directors were able to tell the purchasers, in a reckless manner 'if they wanted to adulterate the flour they could do it themselves' ".

More generally, the effect of such commercial honesty was that buyer and seller were able, for the first time, to meet as friends, without suspicion on either side. Their surroundings may have been humble, the warehouse at Toad Lane unfashionable, but the relationships between the people were of the highest quality. Members were able to send their children on errands to the store, knowing that they would not be taken advantage of, and that all would be treated alike and given the right quantity and quality of provisions. Adulteration remained a feature of commercial life well into the 20th century, but as Holyoake describes it, the members of this humble co-op had gained access to goods which even the well off could not be sure of obtaining.

7. Promotion of Education

The seventh principle was Education. The famous rule appears in the 1854 statutes, that a separate and distinct fund be set up for the 'intellectual improvement of the members' and their families. It was to be funded out of a 2.5 per cent levy on surpluses, and to have its own committee of 11 members, appointed at the annual meeting. The rule was a way of making systematic what the Pioneers had always done: as Owenites, they believed that only through basic education could people's characters be changed, and as followers of Dr. King that only through acquiring commercial skills could they trade successfully. In 1846 they were already holding regular Saturday afternoon discussions at the store, and in 1848 they were able to set up a newsroom and book department, buying up the library of a failed people's Institute. By 1850 they were running their own school and adult education classes, and by 1860 had established the principle that each branch should have its own newsroom and library above the store.

So keen were they on education that they had originally proposed a levy of 10 per cent on surpluses, but because education had (through an oversight) not been included in the 1852 Act, the Registrar of Friendly Societies would not let them register it. The contest with the registrar lasted several months, but eventually the 2.5 percent seems to have been agreed as a compromise: it is a compromise that many co-op's since then have found hard to live up to, but which is always cited as the measure of how committed they are to education. It caused disappointment at the time: Holyoake comments bitterly that the law seemed to prohibit workers from educating themselves, but the government refused them the vote on the grounds that they were not educated.

8. Political and religious neutrality

The eighth principle was political and religious neutrality. Political neutrality was assumed from the start, at least between different types of working class radicals: Chartists, Owenite Socialists, Corn Law Leaguers and so on. Religious neutrality was also assumed from the start, because among the Pioneers were Owenite secularists and members of a Unitarian congregation; at least one of them, John Garside was a local preacher. So they were reared in what Holyoake (himself a militant atheist) called 'a school of practical toleration'.

Without this principle of religious neutrality, they might have been regarded by their contemporaries as adherents of Owen's 'Rational Religion' or Holyoake's Secularism. But in their early days, it is unlikely that they expected to attract anyone from the more securely established religious sects. Of the Pioneers themselves, there was a "Cookite" (a brand of Methodist Unitarian indigenous to Rochdale), Swedenborgiens (also associated with Unitarians) and a local preacher, but the others had no religious affiliations.

Finally, in the 1854 statutes, the Pioneers added one more principle, that of disposal of net assets without profit to members; in the unlikely event that the Society might be wound up, the trustees would have to pay everyone what they had in their share accounts, and then distribute the rest of the assets to other co-operatives or to a charity.

This means that no one would be tempted to break up a co-op just to get at the assets. It is a rule which, with open membership and continued growth, they did not really need, but which has become crucial to the success of worker co-op's; in France, for instance, the state insists on it, and so the worker co-op movement has had a firm basis upon which to build. This is now enshrined in British law.

The Rochdale Equitable Pioneers Society built the foundations of the Cooperative Movement which has grown to its present day strength. Many of the issues which the Pioneers had to deal with are the same as the present day Cooperative Movement has to face. An understanding of the road which previous generations of co-operators took will help us in the modern day Co-operative Movement.

The Solidarity Economy: A Plural Theoretical Framework

The distinction between infrastructure and superstructure that underlies the project of securing the economy's independence is deeply questionable today. The fact that economic development now depends on harnessing cultural production through information and communication technologies has blurred the boundary between materiality and social interaction, thereby promoting their permeability. Given the unprecedented risks entailed in the contemporary expansion of the capitalist system, the search for an 'alternative economy' has resulted in strong initiatives of which the new social movements are but one expression. But perhaps we should first take stock of how some of the social changes they propose reflect the theoretical assumptions of the orthodox economics they oppose.

There is a great temptation, in the name of radicalism and following the example of neo-classical theory, to disclaim or remove the political dimensions from economy. For sure, as we know from bad experience with community projects, to conceive of social transformation solely in terms of economic practice makes political mediation impossible and encourages faith tinged with religious or moral fervour to fill the gap. The lessons of the past allow us to recognize the dangers with ease: the dominance of avant-gardes and lone prophets with a mission to liberate the truth from present realities and to illuminate the future; a proneness to squash initiatives on the grounds that by themselves they will not overthrow the logic of the system.

Such a vision of another economy, of another world can hardly contemplate the democratic conditions of its own realisation. Here, we want to show that the debate over different meanings of the economy should be reopened in this light. Without it, any discussion of the levers of change or of the conditions of transition would be impoverished. Our task is to understand and explain those dimensions of economic life that have been obscured by the naturalisation of the economy's current dominant form, if we are to harness our efforts at making them intelligible to an idea of socio-political transformation sustainable in public debate. To follow in the footsteps of Mauss and Polanyi, taking their contributions separately and together, opens the way to an emancipatory project that is explicitly mindful of a politics that, paradoxically, revolutionary rhetoric banishes in the name of effectivenesss.

The Plural Reality of the Economy: An The plural reality of the economy: An Analytical Framework

The striking convergence between Polanyi and Mauss comes from the fact that both based their economic analysis on a critique of the reductionist assumption that explains economic action solely as the expression of material self-interest. Both held that economic behaviour could be an expression of a sense of belonging or of interest and disinterest combined, such interest being wider in scope than the merely material. They both inferred that economic reality is inevitably plural and that this is masked by utilitarian analsysis.

Polanyi, in particular, underlined the heuristic value of returning reflexively to the definition of economy. The meaning of the word 'economy', as we currently use it to designate a certain kind of human activity, swings between two poles. The first, 'formal' sense stems from the logical character of means-end relations: the definition of economy in terms of scarcity comes from this. The second, 'substantive' sense emphasises the relations of interdependence between people and the natural surroundings from which they derive their material being. In this definition, such substantive conditions are basic to the economy. This distinction between an economy of scarcity and one linking people to their environment was revived from the posthumous publication of Menger's Principles, a foundational work of neo-classical economics.

There Menger suggested two complementary directions that economics might take: one based on the necessity of economizing in response to insufficient means; the other, which he called 'technoeconomic', flowing from the exigencies of physical production without reference to the abundance or inadequacy of the means available.

These two approaches to the possible development of the human economy proceed from "essentially different assumptions.... (but) both are primary and fundamental". This argument was forgotten by his successors in neo-classical economics who chose to privilege Menger's price theory and reduce his approach to a formal one alone, protected by the absence of an English translation of the posthumous edition of his work. Polanyi held that this reduction of the field of economic thought led to a complete rupture between the economy and life, a comment expanded upon by those economists who have taken the trouble to reflect on the epistemology of their science

Polanyi draws on this distinction to underline the two characteristic features of the modern economy.

First, the growing independence of an economic sphere that becomes identified with the market

Passet has traced the stages, from the Physiocrats to neo-classical theory, of a long process of withdrawal in which sidelining the substantive meaning of economy led to confusion between the economy and the market. The Physiocrats worked out the concept of economy by referring to the market as a mechanism linking supply and demand through prices; but, for Quesnay as much as for the founder of the classical school, Smith, if the economy was granted the characteristics of a market, the economic sphere was not separated from the rest of society.

Thus for Smith the value of a good is based on the costs of its production; Ricardo extended this idea to a labour theory of value that Marx used for an unprecedented attack on the the liberalism advocated by the classical school when he defined capitalism as a system of labour exploitation. In reaction to this radical challenge, the neo-classical school threw out these assumptions and based value instead on the principle of utility/scarcity.

Now a pure economics could be defined as a "theory of price determination under hypothetical condition of absolutely free competition" from which all phenomena outside the market were excluded, except when neo-institutional economics tries to explain market failure or when the economics of organizations only recognizes other solutions after treating the market as the principle of first resort.

Second, identification of the market with the selfregulating market

Rationalist and atomistic assumptions of human behaviour allow economists to aggregate individual behviours by means of a deductive market model without taking into account the institutional framework of its form.

To conceive of the market as self-regulating, that is, as a mechanism linking supply and demand through prices, overlooks the institutional changes necessary for it to happen at all and indeed the structures without which it could not function. Rosanvallon has described this economic ideology as "the reduction of trade to the market conceived of as the only natural form of economic relations...Exchange, which must be equal, is taken as the archetype of all other social relations...A natural harmony of interests is enough to sort out the world market; political mediation between people is considered to be useless or even harmful". With the arrival of the neo-classical paradigm, economics was able to study rational interested bevaviour with formal mathematical rigour. The market could be understood solely in terms of the pursuit of maximum profit.

Consequently, to these two points of Polanyi's we may add a third much emphasised by many authors including Marx: identification of modern enterprise with its capitalist form

In a capitalist economy based on private property in the means of production, the creation of goods is tied up with the possible profit for holders of capital. The firm is a "profit-making unit whose organization is geared to the hazards of market transactions, always with the aim of taking advantage of the exchange", according to Weber who adds that "capital accounting thus underpins the rational form of an economy of gain" since it allows calculation of the surplus produced" in relation to the money value of the means employed by the firm". The establishment of the joint-stock company in law provides the means for an unparalleled concentration of capital, since property rights may be exchanged without their owners having to be aware of it, with the stock exchange offering a parallel guarantee of converting their assets into cash at any time. "To the extent that capital accounting has become universal and with it the opportunities for market transactions, from now on it shapes perspectives on commodity exchange as much as those on production".

If Polanyi revealed a plurality of economic principles, Mauss acknowledged a plurality of property forms and insisted that economic organization is always a complex combination of economic types that are often opposed and that these are shaped by evolving social insitutions. "Property, law, the organization of work – these are all social facts, real things corresponding to the real structure of society. But they are not material objects; they do not exist outside individuals or the societies that make them and keep them alive. They only exist in the minds of men brought together in a society. They are psychic facts.

Economic facts, such as property rights for example, are themselves social (value, money etc...) and therefore constitute psychic facts like all the other social facts to which they are connected, conditioning and being conditioned by them". If individual property cannot be called into question without restricting freedom, we could still add "national and collective property and other economic forms above, alongside and below that level"

There is not just one mode of economic organization expressive of a natural order, but rather a set of forms of production and distribution exist together. "There is no such thing as an exclusively capitalist society...There are only societies with a dominant regime or rather, to complicate matters further, with instititutional systems more or less arbitrarily defined by the dominance of one or other of their elements". For Mauss, social action and practice are the result of individual representations made standard by political institutions; these define a framework within which practices unfold, influencing their representation in turn. Institutions change because they are social conventions which at once express and limit the field of possibilities. Studying them allows us to gain "sharp awareness of the facts and a grasp, if not certain knowledge of their laws" and helps us also to emancipate ourselves from the 'metaphysics' in which 'ism words' like capitalism are soaked. To assert the existence of a capitalist society implies perfect coordination of individual representations, the idea that capitalist dominance exists in reality, whereas "an economic system is made up of contradictory institutional mechanisms which cannot be reduced one to the other".

So the contribution of Polanyi and Mauss may be understood as an analytical lens that allows us to grasp the plural character of economic reality by demonstrating the existence of a number of principles of distribution and production, while drawing our attention to the institutional forms in which the market is embedded. The idea of a plural economy does not presuppose any consensus; it offers an analytical lens through which we can marshal the facts and throw light on the complementarities as well as the tensions and conflicts between economic opposites.

Democratic solidarity: a central : a central concept in resistance to market society concept in resistance to market society

With this framework in mind, we can now decipher the mechanisms through which resistance to market society has been manifested. From this point of view, there is a relationship between reciprocity and redistribution that is particularly modern, as Mauss showed us in the conclusions to The Gift.

Even so, we should not idealise solidarity. The inclination to help others, developed as a constitutive element of responsible citizenship, carries the threat of a "gift without reciprocity", allowing limitless gratitude as the only return and creating a debt that can never be redeemed by beneficiaries. The relations of personal dependence promoted in this way risk trapping the recipients in a permanent position of inferiority. In other words, this philanthropic solidarity brings with it a mechanism of social hierarchy and support for the inequality that is built into the social fabric of the community.

In contrast to this 'benevolent' version of solidarity, however, there is another that would stress the democratization of society through collective action. This second version assumes the legal equality of the people involved. We find it in different continents over the two last centuries; it does shape social reality to some extent in South America and in Continental Europe.

If we trace its origins, the depth of the democratic solidarity emphasized by advocates of the 'solidarity economy' is as much historical as theoretical. The concept of solidarity has been mobilised to limit the disruptive consequences of the market economy, of what might be called 'utopian capitalism'. Besides, democratic solidarity has two faces – one of reciprocity designating voluntary social relations between free and equal citizens, the other redistribution, designating the standards of service drawn up by the state to reinforce social cohesion and to redress inequality. History shows that, from the eighteenth century, people generated proliferating means of public association which in the first half of the nineteenth century focused on the demand for new forns of work organization. In this case, democratic solidarity took the form of voluntary reciprocity bringing together citizens who were free and equal under the law, unlike the charity and philanthropology that thrived on unequal conditions. When the liberal prophecy failed and the removal of obstacles to the market did not lead to a balance between the supply and demand for labour, a large number of responses emerged to solve the social problems involved through the self-organization of the people themselves. Worker and peasant associations worked together, provided mutual aid and made collective demands. They initiated an economic project based on brotherhood and solidarity that refuted entirely the attempt to draw a line between the economy and public life. Eventually, however, with advances in the efficiency of capitalist production and some repression, this outburst of reciprocity ran out of steam. Then solidarity increasingly took on another meaning, that of a social debt between classes and generations whose management through the organization of redistributive flows was the state's primary responsibility. At the same time, the movement to form public associations became established through spawning new insitutional forms, such as unions, mutual insurance companies, cooperatives and non-profit organizations. So, it gave way to forms of socio-economic organizations but they have not escaped the consequences of becoming commonplace. The union movement distanced itself from this tendency in pressing for a redistributive welfare state and for recognition of workers' rights in businesses. The state developed a specific form of social organization which facilitated the extension of the market economy while reconciling the workers to the citizen body at large. One cost of the ensuing security, however, was that political examination of the economy was dropped. The project of a plural economy faded away.

Nevertheless, the relative democratization of the economy, achieved with much struggle, was won in the name of solidarity. This concept was linked to the emergence of sociology in that it made a break with the contractarian vision of liberal individualism and, having been at first organized with an economic mission defined by reciprocity, it was then expanded into a system of public redistribution that included the voluntary associations under its supervision. Moreover, the way that associational activity and the public sphere co-evolved is one of the great lessons to be learned from such a historical retrospective. It is not a question of replacing the state with civil society but rather one of combining redistributive solidarity with a more reciprocal version in order to rebuild society's capacity for self-organization.

Democratic solidarity introduced egalitarian reciprocity between citizens into the public sphere at the same time as establishing the principle of redistribution through the state.

What is peculiar to modernity, therefore, is first reciprocity based on equality in the public sphere. Despite the constant risk of falling into a strategic or functional mode of expression made all the more violent by being masked in a discourse of free speech, reciprocity between equals is essential if we are to bring questions arising from everyday life to independent arenas for public debate with the potential to express society's need for self-determination. In order for the gift not to become frozen in asymmetrical dependency, is must be circumscribed by a system of relations which, by submitting it to collective rules designed to stabilize the conditions of its circulation, makes reciprocity between equals possible and allows for donor and recipient to switch places.

The second distinctive feature of modernity is a system of public redistribution whose rules are fixed within a framework of representative democracy. The transition to a democratic solidarity based on redistribution by all means may lead to the opposite of freedom if its source is a public authority whose aim is to subject everyday life to control by bureaucracy. But the risk of such an eventuality does not undermine the interdependence of reciprocity and redistribution. The difference between them should not make us forget their common birth, as their shared reference to solidarity confirms. Solidarity related to public redistribution unites freedom and responsibility, since mutual obligation underlies the freedom that comes from having the confidence to pool resources. It is an extension of the spirit of the gift as put forward by Mauss. For Jaurès social insurance is a right which "comprises the interplay of reciprocal duties and sacrifices, a sphere of mutual giving", what Castel called 'social property'; with the proviso, Jaurès added, that it should not be a "wheel of state" but "a living product through which the workers will exercise their strength today and the apprentices their control of tomorrow". In the hands of Mauss and Jaurès, therefore, the concept of democratic solidarity points to close relations between the gift, reciprocity and redistribution, rather than emphasizing their differences.

From the 'double movement' to a From the 'double movement' to a plan for transformation

The economy under conditions of modern democracy therefore is caught in a double movement: the first expresses a tendency towards becoming disembedded, the second is the opposite democratic tendency to re-embed the economy.

The first movement expresses the dominance of the formal definition of economy. Economy is conceived as a combination of the self-regulating market and capitalist society: the project is to make society indistinguishable from its own economic mechanism. A market economy without limits leads to a situation where the market is allembracing and sufficient by itself to organize society; the public good is realised by the pursuit of private interest without any room for political debate. This invasive utopia of the self-regulating market differentiates modern democracy from those other human societies where aspects of the market might be found, but without the aim of putting them together into an autonomous system.

It proves impossible, however, for the market society to attain its goal, since society itself balks at the prospect, by having recourse to the idea of solidarity, in particular. The institutions that may be enrolled into controlling the market are many, embodying might call a centring/outflanking of the market. This is the core of a second movement reintroducing a substantive approach to the economy through three main developments.

The principle of redistribution is mobilised against the reduction of the economy to the market

There is another pole intrinsic to modern democracy, the non-market economy in which goods and services are allocated by means of redistribution. The market economy could not fulfill the promise of social harmony it once made. On the contrary, as social problems mount, it becomes necessary to put forward institutions that are sensitive to its destructive consequences and able to counteract them. If the idea of basing the economy on reciprocity has become rasther blurred, redistribution as an alternative economic principle to that of the market has emerged as the result of public action. The state confers on citizens individual rights allowing them to benefit from social insurance against risk and in the last resort public assistance for the underprivileged. Public administration is thus defined by payment of goods and services with a redistributive dimension (from the rich to the poor, the employed to the unemployed...) according to rules issued by a public authority that is subject to democratic control.

In response to the notion that the market must be selfregulating, it is confined by a process of institutional embedding

If disembedding of the market is a feature of modernity, this has been frustrated by society's repeated reactions aiming at « socialising » the market, that is subjecting it to a body of rules derived from a process of political deliberation. In other words, the modern market economy is defined by a tension between disembedding and embedding processes. In twentieth century history, the drive to establish a self-regulating market in the place of various regulated markets itself gave rise to the development of regulatory frameworks. "The majority of markets today consist above all of rules, institutions and networks that frame and control the conditions under which supply and demand meet". But these are opposed in their turn by spates of deregulation calling for "various markets to be brought into line with the impersonal idea of perfect market competition, that is for the desocialisation of markets".

To which we should add attempts to found and get established non-capitalist enteprises

The basic model of the firm in neo-classical theory is one where property rights are held by investors. In this context, the aim of the firm comes down to profit maximisation, to the accumulation of finance capital. Labour is subordinated to this accumulative logic. In contrast to this dominant model of economic theory, some analysts have demonstrated a variety of property forms, that is, different kinds of persons holding property rights and thus able to shape the aims of a firm. The purposes of a firm depend on the configuration of property rights and on those who hold them. Unlike capitalist firms, some enterprises are not owned by the investors, but by other types of participant whose aim is not to accumulate capital. There are potentially as many property forms as types of participants, including workers, consumers etc. There have been many studies of organizations whose owners are not the investors. The literature on workers control (autogestion) naturally leans to firms organized by workers. Analysis of the world of cooperatives equally focuses on enterprises controlled by consumers and suppliers. There is today a wave of so-called social enterprises whose 'social' character does not necessarily depend on their being collectively-owned. When judging an economic activity, other criteria come into play than financial profit: access to supplies, the quality of performance of a service etc. Economic action in these terms thus reflects a kind of reciprocity where "true worth lies in the tie" more than maximization of individual interest.

So we have a variety of responses to the utopian experiment of market society: the mobilization of different economic principles, the development of institutions restricting the market sphere and issuing rules for it, the adoption of non-capitalist property forms.

Neo-liberalism brought back the utopian idea of a market society. The content of the democratic reply then proves to be crucial. At worst, the desire for liberation risks turning into its opposite – the sort of identity tensions that can produce confrontation between 'Mac World' and 'Djihad'. The globalization of the market and its extension into areas never touched previously finds its corollary in the rise of religious fundamentalism. If the risk of such confrontation is real and confirmed by events, it has already shown its incompatibility with democracy in the course of the twentieth century. History tells us that, when an economic worldview becomes an end in itself, there is no room for an alternative human project to be decided through democratic process. Market extension "meets a countermovement checking this expansion in whatever ways are necessary for society's protection". This is the route, according to him, to a "great transformation" to liberate society from the threats that economic liberalism brought on its head.

The fascist and communist regimes tried to go in this direction; it led to the destruction of freedom and the reign of oppression. Unfortunately no great transformation yet has been able to reconcile freedom and equality. Of course, there was a compromise between market and state during the period of expansion after the Second World War. Fordist and welfarist industrial societies imposed social rules on market economy through legislation and collective bargaining along with a vast apparatus of non-market redistributive economic forms. But this compromise had a reversible character, as proved by the neo-liberal offensive exempting the market from certain social rules that were conceived of as rigidities and by delegitimizing a non-market economy weakened by bureaucratization and the subjugation of users. That reversibility is all too obvious today. The fact that social progress is conditional on deductions being levied on the market economy opens up a contradiction: on the one hand, it would be desirable to restrict the market so that it does not extend into every sphere of human life and solidary relations might be preserved; on the other, it is just as desirable for economic growth to be as high as possible in order to yield the maximum returns to finance redistributive systems which testify to the solidarity betwen social groups.

In order to escape from this apparent impasse, it becomes necessary to take into account all the steps that concretely reject the ceaseless commoditization of social life. This is the full significance of initatives undertaken in the solidarity economy. In their many-sided ways, these help to challenge developments that neo-liberal ideology represents as inevitable. If such initiatives were in a position to extend enrolments beyond their immediate constituencies, to increase their commitment to and involvement in matters of public regulation and to ally themsleves with social movements who share their goals, they could contribute more effectviely to the democratization of economy and society.

Social Capital Theory

As social capital, dubbed "the missing link" in economic development, is further explored, the focus is on its recognition as one form of the nonmaterial capital regarded as an important production factor especially within communities. The analyses of the intellectual evolution of social capital by Bourdieu, Coleman and Putman also attempt to construct a consistent and general theoretical framework to avoid reductionist economics. Lastly, an overview of the criticisms levelled against the concept of social capital is portrayed in line with its recent tremendous extension in scope and depth.

Social capital as relationships, attitudes, norms, values and institutions that govern how people interact and contribute to mutual socioeconomic benefit. It simply means that the links that people hold and share enable them to trust each other enough to work together and so to benefit collectively. The essential characteristics of social capital extracted from viewpoints include intangible substances such as goodwill, fellowship, sympathy, trust, love etc.. Its structural dimension that involves networks, ties and connections between people represents features of social organisation that can improve the efficiency of society by facilitating coordinated actions. However, due to its contested wide usage and the looseness of its application, vigorous debates continue between sociologists, political scientists and economists whether social capital is really, "capital", or whether it is constructed, produced or an endowment.

The rationale behind the conceptualisation of social capital was to complement the economic analysis in development and to highlight the importance of social relations as an accessory in the development process. While differences in the conceptualisation of social capital remain, there is an agreement between sociologists, political scientists and economists that social capital is unique because it is relational. This means that a person must be related to others because it is in the relationships with others and not with the self where the actual source of the social capital related advantage is. Social capital cannot be a private property of any person; it exists only when it is shared. An example illustrates further that, "whereas economic capital is in people's bank accounts, human capital inside their heads, social capital inheres in the structure of their relationships" and has public good characteristics.

The nature of the structure of these relationships tends to be horizontal or vertical, with the former being closed and homogenous as seen with families, friendship circles, community networks and institutions. The latter is found in socially heterogeneous groups like formal institutions and cross-culturally. It is the social capital inherent in these structural relationships or associations that produce private or public goods to individuals or collectives. Adages like "it's not what you know, it's who you know what matters" and "my connections can help me ... I know people in high places" illustrate the resourcefulness of social capital, qualifying it as an "asset" to be called upon when needed for help, enjoyment or profitability. What remains central to the definitions of social capital offered, remains important, namely the "resourcefulness of relationships of mutual acquaintance brought about by social organisation and connections of people sharing instantiated informal norms that promote cooperation between two or more individuals"

For the purposes of this study, define social capital as the obligatory norms of reciprocity, respect and trust, and social relations embedded in the social structures of society, that enable people to coordinate and cooperate for the good of collective outcomes.

Theories of Social Capital

The notion behind the concept of social capital that social relations as well as social structures have the potential to generate benefits for individuals and collectives, can be traced back to the works of classical authors from a variety of fields For example, Hanifan, a state supervisor of schools in West Virginia, back in 1916, was the first one to use the concept of social capital in advocating the importance of community involvement in the successes of schools. The concept remained obscured, we are told, until Bourdieu and Coleman brought it back into sociological debates. The development of a theoretical body and a research programme around the concept of social capital is attributed to the works. These two sociologists devoted time and effort in defining the concept in terms of its components, features, sources and the way it relates to other types of capital (economic, symbolic and cultural). For Bourdieu and Coleman, the emphasis was on the benefits that social capital yields to individuals and groups. The transitional stretch to the concept of social capital by Robert Putman, a political scientist, made it possible to refer to it as a "stock" possessed by communities and nations resulting in positive developmental outcomes.

Social capital as networks of relationships: Pierre Bourdieu

Bourdieu, a French theorist and philosopher, defines social capital as "the aggregate of the actual or potential resources which are linked to the possession of a durable network of more or less institutionalised relationships of mutual acquaintance and recognition". This definition posits two components of social capital: a resource that is connected with group membership and networks, and its ability to acquire symbolic character given that it is based on mutual cognition and recognition. These characteristics validate relations within networks and symbolic recognition as potential resources that can benefit members socially as well as economically.

Bourdieu was one of the first contemporary sociologists to produce a systematic analysis of social capital. He went to great lengths in re-introducing capital in its different forms (economic, cultural, symbolic and social) into social theory. Bourdieu maintains that the concept "capital" is broader than its monetary notion in economics.

For him, capital is a "resource" that can assume both monetary (tangible) as well as non-monetary (intangible) forms. Other authors refer to this distinction as the material and non-material forms of capital.

All forms of capital in the form of cash savings and liquid assets (economic), social networks and relations of trust and reciprocity (social), material exchange (symbolic) and useful and productive skills (human/cultural) are important assets in all fields found in social structures. Implied here is that, all forms of capital, once manipulated, strengthened and interlocked can bring about sustainable empowerment and social change needed for poverty reduction. As mentioned, access to power and ultimately material wealth depends on cumulative acquisition of proportionate types and amounts of capital.

Bourdieu defines capital broadly as "accumulated human labour" or "the weight of the past on the present". This means that previous cycles of individually and/or collectively accumulated capital create permanent networks of resourceful relationships with potential to produce different forms of capital. Social capital (resourceful connections) is of no significance if it is without an investment of some resources in the form of other capitals. For example, an investment of economic capital is required in order to acquire cultural capital (educational qualifications) as well as symbolic capital (status and influence). The consequent possibility is therefore that people who have accumulated too little capital will have other possibilities closed off to them Bourdieu's stance is that social capital is shaped by power relations. He also insists that social capital is a property of fields. Fields are believed to be autonomous parts of society equated to the notion of institutions that provide settings for competition over allocation of different forms of capital between actors. It simply means that actors occupying these spaces within society are continually contesting for positions. This means that the struggles and conflicts that ensue in a given field get decided by the amount and type of capital actors possess. These different settings for competition highlight the pervasive inequality among actors. It is significant to keep such analyses of capital alive in the field of development as a way of understanding how poverty amelioration and reduction processes can both empower and marginalise actors to get out of or remain trapped in deep poverty. According to Bourdieu (2012), it follows therefore that the four types of capital are reducible to economic capital which is at the root of all types of capital.

Social capital and useful social relationships: James Coleman

James Coleman, an American sociologist from the University of Chicago, defines social capital as "a variety of entities with two elements in common, consisting of some aspect of a social structure and facilitating certain actions of actors within that structure". Coleman defines social capital by its functionality; not by what it is, but by what it does. He sees the value derived from social relations as potential resources that can be used beneficially in the future. Coleman's explanation of social capital identifies its three forms: obligations, expectations and norms. Coleman contends that while obligations and expectations depend on trustworthiness of the social environment and information flow capability of the social structures, norms are accompanied by sanctions. The social capital that inheres in social relations of rational actors not only provides the basis for action, it is also used for the acquisition and flow of information.

For Coleman, social capital is a collective good produced to benefit actors in a network, including those unknown to them. What is implied here is that social capital is conceptualised as resources inherent in relations between actors and among actors, a capital asset that is not lodged in individuals per se, but in relationships they belong to. Coleman's implied resourcefulness of social capital is of a stock, a store and a foundation from which other actions, individually or collectively, might be undertaken to meet mutual interest. Coleman maintains that social capital is the source of social control, hence his particular concern about the disintegration of "primordial" social ties that guarantee the observance of norms. Coleman posits that network structures of families, friends or neighbours have "closure" if they know each other well, share the same values, have mutual trust and meet regularly to ensure common norms for social control. In addition, the degree to which a particular group forms and not just becomes an aggregate of individuals signifies closure Similarly, closure is important not only for the existence of effective norms but also for trustworthiness that allows proliferation of obligations and expectations in the group. Coleman has demonstrated statistically that network structures that have closure possess larger stocks of social capital and enjoy benefits from reciprocal obligations, expectations and norms.

Coleman posits that social capital has evolved from rational choice and structural functionalist foundations. For Coleman, rational choice is a fundamental requirement of sociological analysis; social actors with roles of internalised norms of trust and sanctions within family and community networks will have strong interests and will consciously seek to plan and execute strategies to fulfil these. Coleman uses the process of negotiating a sale in the wholesale diamond market to illustrate mutual confidence among economic agents acting in accordance with collective interests Here social capital allows individuals with close ties (through family, community and religious affiliations) to secure deals. A diamond merchant would hand over a bag of stones that could be worth thousands or hundreds of thousands of dollars to another merchant for inspection at leisure, without insurance or deposit charges. At that time, such free exchanges were regarded as important to the functioning of the market and were carried out to avoid transaction costs. This indicates the capacity of social capital in reducing transaction costs on the basis of network structures that link individuals with ties that are trusting, reciprocal and involving positive emotions. From what have been said so far, Coleman regards social capital as a producer of public good by shaping actions of rational agents who purposefully establish relations and maintain them for as long as they are beneficial.

Social capital as collective action: Robert Putman

Putman, a political scientist, is regarded as the third key author who contributed substantially to recent social capital debates and literature Unlike Bourdieu and Coleman, Putman makes social capital operational at a different social scale, pitching his interest at how social capital supports democratic institutions and economic development at regional level.

Fine and Lapavitsas maintain that Coleman's approach to social capital would have remained less noticed, had it not been for Putman's efforts to make it popular through his publications and seminars. For example, his theoretical conclusions about civil society in his book Making Democracy Work: Civic Traditions in Modern Italy not only contributed compelling arguments, it also initiated research agendas that generated more discussions and debates than any work in political science of recent years. Putman was not the first writer to bemoan the disintegration of civic culture and the corrosive influence of materialism in the USA. He, however, almost achieved celebrity status with his use of the metaphor "bowling alone" when he characterised the transformation of the American social and political life in the post-war era.

Putman conceptualises social capital in three components: moral obligations and norms, social values like trust, and social networks (especially voluntary organisations). Seemingly, the three components are what informed his definition of "networks, norms and trust, which facilitate co-ordination and cooperation for mutual benefit". Putman advocates social capital as the collective value of all social associations with different social capital building capacities as well as different implications for cooperation. Although his definition effectively follows that of Coleman and Bourdieu, his focus and concern about the positive outcomes of social capital is on the behaviour at system and civil society levels and not at the level of individuals and groups; - hence, his theorising that a successful accumulation of social capital is needed for a region to have a well functioning economic system as well as a high level of political integration. Putman's analysis of social capital avoids sociological issues like social stratification and socialisation as discussed by Bourdieu and Coleman respectively. His analysis focuses mainly on networks of civic engagement found in neighbourhoods and voluntary associations, choral societies, cooperatives, sports clubs or mass-based parties. He sees these as essential elements of social capital because they foster robust norms of reciprocity. These norms of reciprocity are believed to fuel social trust among network members, with resultant altruistic actions that contribute to the welfare of others.

What type of community can be classified as civic, one may ask? According to Putman, a community that is civic is identifiable by the public activities of its citizens, such as taking part in voting polls, reading of newspapers to stay informed, participation in sports clubs and voluntary cultural associations, as well as cooperating for mutual benefits in social networks. The characteristics of a civic community as strong social networks, positive institutional performance, and norms of trust and reciprocity that are fostered among members of networks and community associations. An informal savings institution called 'a rotating credit association' (a stokvel in most South African townships) serves as a brilliant example of spontaneous cooperation facilitated by social capital. Members selected based on reputation for honesty and reliability meet regularly to make a small capital contribution to a common fund, portions of which are loaned to members on rotational basis. Although it sounds risky, members continue to make contributions as a result of mutual trust. Naturally, this type of association uses enforceable trust, what Coleman referred to earlier as 'internal sanctioning capacity' using credible sanctions like ostracism.

Voluntary associations are a source of mutual trust and reciprocity, with members acting for the general (public) good, not because they know other actors. This is because members 'generally' trust that their actions will be rewarded or reciprocated, what Putman refers to as generalised trust. However, he chooses to ignore the effects of possible distrust between members of the in-group.

Putman's main argument is on a pervading sense of civic malaise and disengagement and he believes that it is because of 'eroded' social capital. His emphasis is thus on civic engagement and associational life that offer a positive version of how individual and organisational social capital is formed and sustained at group and institutional levels.

REFERENCES

1. Cornforth, Chris. "The Governance of Cooperatives and Other Forms of Enterprise." Routledge, 2017.
2. Doherty, Bob, and Benjamin Gidron. "Social Economy: International Debates and Perspectives." Policy Press, 2010.
3. MacPherson, Ian. "Co-operative Principles Today and Tomorrow." International Co-operative Alliance, 2013.
4. North, Peter. "Local Governance, Economic Development and Institutions." Springer, 2015.
5. Spear, Roger. "Essential Cooperative Wisdom: What Every Worker Needs to Know about Cooperatives and Collectivism." CooperationWorks!, 2006.
6. Vanek, Jaroslav. "The Economics of Workers' Management: A Yugoslav Case Study." Penguin Books, 1977.
7. Whyte, William Foote. "Making Mondragon: The Growth and Dynamics of the Worker Cooperative Complex." ILR Press, 1991.

2 LEGAL AND ORGANIZATIONAL STRUCTURES

INTRODUCTION

Legal and organizational structures play a vital role in shaping the operation and governance of businesses, including community enterprises and cooperatives. These structures define how entities are established, managed, and regulated within the legal framework of a given jurisdiction.

For community enterprises, legal and organizational structures often reflect their commitment to social and environmental objectives alongside economic sustainability. Common legal forms include social enterprises, which blend profit-making with social impact, and nonprofit organizations, which prioritize mission-driven activities over profit distribution.

Cooperatives, on the other hand, are typically structured as member-owned entities governed by democratic principles. They may adopt various legal forms, such as worker cooperatives, where employees collectively own and manage the business, or consumer cooperatives, where customers have ownership rights and participate in decision-making processes.

These legal and organizational structures influence aspects such as ownership rights, decision-making processes, taxation, and liability. They also impact the ability of community enterprises and cooperatives to access funding, engage in partnerships, and achieve their social and economic objectives. As such, careful consideration of legal and organizational structures is essential for ensuring the effectiveness, sustainability, and social impact of these alternative business models.

BUSINESS LEGAL ORGANIZATIONAL STRUCTURES

Business structure refers to the legal structure of an organization that is recognized in a given jurisdiction. An organization's legal structure is a key determinant of the activities that it can undertake, such as raising capital, responsibility for obligations of the business, as well as the amount of taxes that the organization owes to tax agencies. Choosing the proper legal, organizational structure for your business is one of the most important decisions you'll make.

It might not have much of an impact on the day-to-day operations of a small business, but it can have a huge impact come tax time, when you want to borrow money or attract investors, or in the unfortunate event that you're sued or taken to court.

It's possible to change your structure at a later date, but it can be a difficult and expensive process. It's best to make the right decision in the first place, but you have to understand how each structure works in order to do that.

Business Legal Structure

A business legal structure, also known as a business entity, is a government classification that regulates certain aspects of your business. On a federal level, your business legal structure determines your tax burden. On a state level, it can have liability ramifications.

Why is a business legal structure important?

Choosing the right business structure from the start is among the most crucial decisions you can make. Here are some factors to consider:

- **Taxes:** Sole proprietors, partnership owners and S corporation owners categorize their business income as personal income. C corporation income is business income separate from an owner's personal income. Given the different tax rates for business and personal incomes, your structure choice can significantly impact your tax burden.
- **Liability:** Limited liability company (LLC) structures can protect your personal assets in the event of a lawsuit. That said, the federal government does not recognize LLC structures; they exist only on a state level. C corporations are a federal business structure that includes the liability protection of LLCs.
- **Paperwork:** Each business legal structure has unique tax forms. Additionally, if you structure your company as a corporation, you'll need to submit articles of incorporation and regularly file certain government reports. If you start a business partnership and do business under a fictitious name, you'll need to file special paperwork for that as well.
- **Hierarchy:** Corporations must have a board of directors. In certain states, this board must meet a certain number of times per year. Corporate hierarchies also prevent business closure if an owner transfers shares or exits the company, or when a founder dies. Other structures lack this closure protection.
- **Registration:** A business legal structure is also a prerequisite for registering your business in your state. You can't apply for an employer identification number (EIN) or all your necessary licenses and permits without a business structure.
- **Fundraising:** Your structure can also block you from raising funds in certain ways. For example, sole proprietorships generally can't offer stocks. That right is primarily reserved for corporations.
- **Potential consequences for choosing the wrong structure:** Your initial choice of business structure is crucial, although you can change your business structure in the future. However, changing your business

structure can be a disorganized, confusing process that can lead to tax consequences and the unintended dissolution of your business.

Choose the Best Legal Structure for Your Business

There are many choices and factors to consider when you›re setting up the structure of your business. Many of the advantages of incorporating can be gained in other ways for sole proprietors, such as purchasing liability insurance. And the paper legalities are often outweighed by real-world practicalities.

For example, a corporation shields its owners from personal liability for its debts, but it's unlikely that you'll even be able to get business credit during the first two to three years. At least without personally co-signing as a guarantor. And you'll forfeit that protection if you do so.

Your business's legal structure has many ramifications. It can determine how much liability your company faces during lawsuits. It can put up a barrier between your personal and business taxes – or ensure this barrier doesn't exist. It can also determine how often your board of directors must file paperwork – or if you even need a board.

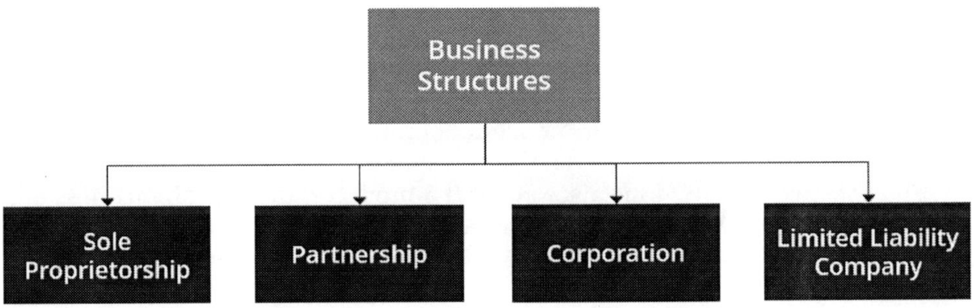

Figure 1. Business Legal Structure.

Source: https://cdn.corporatefinanceinstitute.com/assets/business-structure.png

A Sole Proprietorship

The major advantage of a sole proprietorship is that it's the simplest and least expensive structure to form. There's really nothing to set up and maintain, except perhaps a fictitious business name, referred to as a DBA, or "Doing Business As" name.

An individual owner of an unincorporated business operates the business as an extension of themselves. The profits and losses of the business are reported on the tax return of the owner, and that owner is personally responsible for any liabilities of the business. A court can directly levy the personal bank account and other property of the owner if anyone successfully sues the business for breach of contract, personal injury, or to collect a debt.

A sole proprietorship is the simplest business entity. When you set up a sole proprietorship, one person is responsible for all a company's profits and debts.

"If you want to be your own boss and run a business from home without a physical storefront, a sole proprietorship allows you to be in complete control," said Deborah Sweeney, vice president and general manager of business acquisitions at

Deluxe Corp. "This entity does not offer the separation or protection of personal and professional assets, which could prove to become an issue later on as your business grows and more aspects hold you liable."

Proprietorship costs vary by market. Generally, early expenses will include state and federal fees, taxes, business equipment leases, office space, banking fees, and any professional services your business contracts. Some examples of these businesses are freelance writers, tutors, bookkeepers, cleaning service providers and babysitters.

A sole proprietorship business structure has several advantages.

- **Easy setup:** A sole proprietorship is the simplest legal structure to set up. If you – and only you – own your business, this might be the best structure. There is very little paperwork since you have no partners or executive boards.
- **Low cost:** Costs vary by state, but generally, license fees and business taxes are the only fees associated with a proprietorship.
- **Tax deduction:** Since you and your business are a single entity, you may be eligible for specific business sole proprietor tax deductions, such as a health insurance deduction.
- **Easy exit:** Forming a proprietorship is easy, and so is ending one. As a single owner, you can dissolve your business at any time with no formal paperwork required. For example, if you start a day care center and wish to fold the business, refrain from operating the day care and advertising your services.

The sole proprietorship is also one of the most common small business legal structures. Many famous companies started as sole proprietorships and eventually grew into multimillion-dollar businesses. These are a few examples:

- eBay
- JCPenney
- Walmart
- Marriott Hotels

Pros

- *Simple Setup:* Sole proprietorships/partnerships are among the easiest organizational structures to set up.
- *Few Fees and Oversight:* Sole proprietorships/partnerships don't require much in the way of fees or regulations.

Cons

- *Minimal Liability Protection:* Sole proprietorships/partnerships do not have liability protection. Therefore, if the business fails, the personal assets of you (and your partners) can be used to satisfy the business' debt.

A General Partnership

An advantage of a partnership is that, like a sole proprietorship, no state filings are required to create the business entity. Nor are there any ongoing reporting requirements. Two or more people own the business jointly in a general partnership. They share the profits and losses of the business as spelled out in the partnership agreement. Each partner is potentially responsible for the full amount of the business's liabilities. A creditor of the business can collect the full amount of a partnership debt from the partner that's easiest to collect from.

Distribution of profits and losses is determined by the partnership agreement and passes through to the individual partners. It doesn't have to match the ownership percentages. The partnership itself isn't subject to any income or franchise tax.

A partnership is owned by two or more individuals. There are two types: a general partnership, where all is shared equally, and a limited partnership, where only one partner has control of operations and the other person (or persons) contributes to and receives part of the profits. Partnerships can operate as sole proprietorships, where there's no separation between the partners and the business, or limited liability partnerships (LLPs), depending on the entity's funding and liability structure.

"This entity is ideal for anyone who wants to go into business with a family member, friend or business partner – like running a restaurant or agency together," Sweeney said. "A partnership allows the partners to share profits and losses and make decisions together within the business structure. Remember that you will be held liable for the decisions made as well as those actions made by your business partner."

General partnership costs vary, but this structure is more expensive than a sole proprietorship because an attorney should review your partnership agreement. The attorney's experience and location can affect the cost.

A business partnership agreement must be a win-win for both sides to succeed. Google is an excellent example of this. In 1995, co-founders Larry Page and Sergey Brin created a small search engine and turned it into the leading global search engine. The co-founders met at Stanford University while pursuing their doctorates and later left to develop a beta version of their search engine. Soon after, they raised $1 million in funding from investors, and Google began receiving thousands of visitors a day. Having a combined ownership of 11.4% of Google provides them with a total net worth of nearly $226.4 billion.

Business partnerships have many advantages.

- **Easy formation:** As with a sole proprietorship, there is little paperwork to file for a business partnership. If your state requires you to operate under a fictitious name ("doing business as," or DBA), you'll need to file a Certificate of Conducting Business as Partners and draft an Articles of Partnership agreement, both of which have additional fees. You'll usually need a business license as well.
- **Growth potential:** You're more likely to obtain a business loan with more than one owner. Bankers can consider two credit histories rather than one, which can be helpful if you have a less-than-stellar credit score.
- **Special taxation:** General partnerships must file federal tax Form 1065 and state returns, but they do not usually pay income tax. Both partners report their shared income or loss on their individual income tax returns. For example, if you opened a bakery with a friend and structured the business as a general partnership, you and your friend are co-owners. Each owner brings a certain level of experience and working capital to

the business, affecting each partner's business share and contribution. If you brought the most seed capital for the business, you and your partner may agree that you'll retain a higher share percentage, making you the majority owner.

Partnerships are one of the most common business structures. These are some examples of successful partnerships:

- Warner Bros.
- Hewlett-Packard
- Microsoft
- Apple
- Ben & Jerry's
- Twitter

A Limited Partnership

The basic structure and tax implications of a limited partnership are the same as for a general partnership, but a limited partnership allows for one or more limited partners called «silent partners» to own a portion of the business. Silent partners can›t participate in the management of the business.

This type of partnership must also have a general partner who has personal liability for all liabilities of the partnership. This structure allows a partnership to have outside investors without subjecting them to the liabilities of the business.

A Limited Liability Partnership (LLP)

The LLP came about as a result of demand from attorney and accounting firms who wanted to be able to limit the liability between partners. These firms were not allowed to incorporate at one time. An LLP is taxed like a partnership, but it limits the liabilities of all partners, much like an LLC. Limited liability partnership laws can vary significantly from state to state. California and New York allow this form of business structure only for attorney and accounting firms. Partners in an LLP only have a "limited shield" in other states and aren't afforded the same protection they would enjoy in an LLC or corporation.

A Limited Liability Company (LLC)

An LLC is a hybrid of a corporation and a partnership, and it›s rapidly becoming the most popular structure for small businesses due to its flexibility. Its cost to create and maintain is low, while it still offers most of the advantages of a corporation. The ownership percentages, profit and loss distributions, and voting powers of each member are determined by the LLC Articles of Organization, rather than by stock ownership.

An LLC can choose to be taxed as a partnership or as an S Corporation with profits and losses flowing through to the owners' tax returns, or taxed as a C Corporation, filing its own return. The owners, officers, and directors are protected from the liabilities of the company, as in a corporation.

A limited liability company (LLC) is a hybrid structure that allows owners, partners or shareholders to limit their personal liabilities while enjoying a partnership's tax and flexibility benefits. Under an LLC, members are shielded from personal liability for the business's debts if it can't be proven that they acted in a negligent or wrongful manner that results in injury to another in carrying out the activities of the business. "Limited liability companies were created to provide business owners with the liability protection that corporations enjoy while allowing earnings and losses to pass through to the owners as income on their personal tax returns," said Brian Cairns, CEO of ProStrategix Consulting. "LLCs can have one or more members, and profits and losses do not have to be divided equally among members." According to Wolters Kluwer, the cost of forming an LLC comprises the state filing fee and can vary depending on your state. For example, if you file an LLC in New York, you must pay a $200 filing fee, a $9 biennial fee, and file a biennial statement with the New York Department of State.

Although small businesses can be LLCs, some large businesses choose this legal structure. The structure is typical among accounting, tax, and law firms, but other types of companies also file as LLCs. One example of an LLC is Anheuser-Busch, one of the leaders in the U.S. beer industry. Headquartered in St. Louis, Anheuser-Busch is a wholly owned subsidiary of Anheuser-Busch InBev, a multinational brewing company based in Leuven, Belgium.

Here some other well-known examples of LLCs:

- Pepsi-Cola
- Sony
- Nike
- Hertz Rent-a-Car
- eBay
- IBM

Pros of LLCs

There are a number of advantages to forming your company as an LLC.

- *Protection of Personal Assets:* Your business becomes its own entity, protecting you and any partners from personal liability. Any debts incurred by an LLC belong to the LLC itself, rather than to the owners of the company.
- *Flexible Structure:* An LLC can be run like a corporation (with a board of directors who make decisions), but it also can be run as a partnership, where each member has a say in the day-to-day decisions.
- *Flexible Profit Distribution:* With an LLC, you're at liberty to make your own choices regarding the distribution of profits; this is not tied to the amount of "stake" a member has in your company.
- *Easier Taxes:* LLCs offer pass-through taxation, which effectively means you simply claim your business profits (or losses) on your individual income tax return, which means an LLC requires less record-keeping than an S-corp.
- *No Ownership Restrictions:* The LLC structure carries no ownership restrictions. Foreign entities, individuals, and even other LLCs can all be named as owners. However, you don't have to have other owners at all: you can operate an LLC as a single member.

Cons of LLCs

- *No Owner Wages:* You cannot actually pay yourself "wages." Your income comes as a portion of the LLC's profits.

- *Investor Limitations:* Taxation of partnerships like LCCs is overly burdensome for investors, involving specialized tax forms, and some investors can't even invest in LLCs in the first place because of tax-exempt statuses. So if you plan to seek outside investment, an LLC structure may be less attractive than a corporation.

Corporation

The law regards a corporation as separate from its owners, with legal rights independent of its owners. It can sue, be sued, own and sell property, and sell the rights of ownership in the form of stocks. Corporation filing fees vary by state and fee category.

There are several types of corporations, including C corporations, S corporations, B corporations, closed corporations, and nonprofit corporations.

- **C corporations:** C corporations, owned by shareholders, are taxed as separate entities. JPMorgan Chase & Co. is a multinational investment bank and financial services holding company listed as a C corporation. Since C corporations allow an unlimited number of investors, many larger companies – including Apple, Bank of America and Amazon – file for this tax status.
- **S corporations:** S corporations were designed for small businesses. They avoid double taxation, much like partnerships and LLCs. Owners also have limited liability protection. Widgets Inc. is an example of an S corporation that operates very simply: Employee salaries are subject to FICA tax (as are all employee salaries), while the distribution of additional profits from the S corporation does not incur further FICA tax liability.
- **B corporations:** B corporations, otherwise known as benefit corporations, are for-profit entities committed to corporate social responsibility and structured to positively impact society. For example, skincare and cosmetics company The Body Shop has proven its long-term commitment to supporting environmental and social movements, resulting in an awarded B corporation status. The Body Shop uses its presence to advocate for permanent change on issues like human trafficking, domestic violence, climate change, deforestation and animal testing in the cosmetic industry.
- **Closed corporations:** Closed corporations, typically run by a few shareholders, are not publicly traded and benefit from limited liability protection. Closed corporations, sometimes referred to as privately held companies, have more flexibility than publicly traded companies. For example, Hobby Lobby is a closed corporation – a privately held, family-owned business. Stocks associated with Hobby Lobby are not publicly traded; instead, the stocks have been allocated to family members.
- **Open corporations:** Open corporations are available for trade on a public market. Many well-known companies, including Microsoft and Ford Motor Co., are open corporations. Each corporation has taken ownership of the company and allows anyone to invest.
- **Nonprofit corporations:** Nonprofit corporations exist to help others in some way and are rewarded by tax exemption. Some examples of nonprofits are the Salvation Army, American Heart Association and

American Red Cross. These organizations all focus on something other than turning a profit.

Corporations enjoy several advantages.

- **Limited liability:** Stockholders are not personally liable for claims against your corporation; they are liable only for their personal investments.
- **Continuity:** Corporations are not affected by death or the transferring of shares by their owners. Your business continues to operate indefinitely, which investors, creditors and consumers prefer.
- **Capital:** It's much easier to raise large amounts of capital from multiple investors when your business is incorporated.

This structure is ideal for businesses that are further along in their growth, rather than a startup based in a living room. For example, if you've started a shoe company and have already named your business, appointed directors and raised capital through shareholders, the next step is to become incorporated. You're essentially conducting business at a riskier, yet more lucrative, rate. Additionally, your business could file as an S corporation for the tax benefits. Once your business grows to a certain level, it's likely in your best interest to incorporate it.

These are some popular examples of corporations:

- General Motors
- Amazon
- Exxon Mobil Corp.
- Domino's Pizza
- JPMorgan Chase

A C Corporation

The term "corporation" generally refers to a C corporation. A corporation is owned by one or more stockholders. It's managed by a board of directors who are elected by the stockholders and it's run day-to-day by officers who are appointed by the board of directors. A single individual can be the sole stockholder, director, and officer of the company. The stockholders, directors, and officers are protected from the liabilities of the company, including liabilities for their own negligence when acting in their corporate role, except in certain extraordinary circumstances.

The profits and losses of the corporation typically are not passed through to the tax returns of the owners. The corporation files its own tax return and it pays its own taxes. It may also be subject to state franchise taxes or other annual fees. Corporate income tax rates are graduated based upon the taxable income as they are for individual taxpayers, but the rates and levels of the brackets are different.

C-Corp Pros

- *Flexible Ownership:* C-corps offer more flexibility than an S-corp in terms of ownership, functioning much more like an LLC in this area.
- *Single Stock Class:* C-corps can have multiple stock classes, whereas an S-corp is only allowed one.

C-Corp Cons

- *Double Taxation:* The major C-corps drawback is that they are taxed twice; once on the corporation's net income, and again when the profits of the corporation are distributed to its shareholders.

An S Corporation

The Stockholders can elect "S Corporation" status after the corporation has been formed by making a filing with the IRS. An S Corporation is taxed as a partnership, and its profits and losses flow through to the federal tax returns of the owners in proportion to their stock ownership.

The S corporation structure is generally preferred over a standard corporation when most of the shareholders are employed by the corporation or are otherwise involved in its day-to-day activities. The corporation distributes most of its income to its shareholders each year.

Pros of S-Corp

- *Long-term Stability:* Some states actually require LLCs to list an ending date (called a dissolution date) when paperwork is filed to form the LLC. So, for instance, you might say that your LLC will dissolve in 20 years. However, an S-corp's designation will remain in perpetuity, which is a better fit for a business that plans to be in it for the long haul.
- *No Business Taxes:* No taxes are paid at the business level (however annual tax filing is still required).
- *Save on Taxes:* An S-corp allows owners to effectively pay themselves (and reduce taxes) by determining a reasonable salary and taking the remaining profits as dividend pay. This cuts down on your self-employment tax obligations, which can save you thousands of dollars a year. You can calculate how much you can save on your own self-employment and payroll taxes by choosing an S-corp.

An S-Corp is preferable to an LLC in specific situations, particularly when it comes to taxation. S-corp owners' salaries are often self-determined and taxed as income, however dividends are paid—and thus taxed—separately. This can save 10% to 15% in taxes over the course of the year, though bookkeeping and related costs will be higher than they are for an LLC.

Cons of S-Corps

- *Limited Shareholders:* The number of shareholders is capped at 75, whereas an LLC can have unlimited shareholders.
- *Restricted Ownership Rules:* For c-corps, ownership restrictions are also tighter: all owners in an S-corp must be U.S. citizens. Additionally, S-corps must have a board of directors who manage at the corporate level, then appoint officers to manage the daily activities.
- *Profit Distribution Rules:* An S-corp must tie its profit distribution to a stakeholder's share: a 30% stake in the company mandates an entitlement to 30% of the profits.
- *Financial Tracking Requirements:* These come along with the S-corp's hefty tax advantages, including quarterly IRS payments and some pretty stringent rules and regulations. This includes filing a business tax return, despite there being no taxes at the business level.

S-corporations are useful for business owners who wish to pay themselves salaries, take advantage of the tax savings that come with a dividend structure, and/or want to make their companies permanent entities.

The S-corp structure also simplifies the steps required to transfer ownership or shut down the business.

The Non-Profit Corporation

A non-profit corporation may be an industry association, a social organization, a research firm, or even a consulting group. It can sell products or services. The difference is that there are no owners, and any "profits" are simply retained by the corporation to be reinvested for whatever the purpose of the corporation may be. A non-profit can have employees, and these employees can be paid fair market value for their services. There are *many* restrictions on non-profits that make it a challenging choice, but it›s an option if you›re interested in seeing your vision come to life.

Pros of Nonprofits

- *Tax Exemptions:* The primary draw of this structure, because a nonprofit provides a public service, it is exempt from federal, state, and local taxes.
- *Organizational Profits Allowed:* Contrary to popular belief (and the name itself), nonprofits are allowed to make a profit in order to pay for things like overhead and employee salaries.

Cons of Nonprofits

- *Strict Operational Requirements:* Nonprofits' tax exemptions only come if the company's main purpose directly benefits the public.
- *Personal Profit is Limited:* The income cannot act as profit for any officer or director of the company.

Cooperative

A cooperative (co-op) is owned by the same people it serves. Its offerings benefit the company's members, also called user-owners, who vote on the organization's mission and direction and share profits.

Cooperatives offer a couple main advantages.

- **Increased funding:** Cooperatives may be eligible for federal grants to help them get started.
- **Discounts and better service:** Cooperatives can leverage their business size, thus obtaining discounts on products and services for their members.

Forming a cooperative is complex and requires you to choose a business name that indicates whether the co-op is a corporation (e.g., Inc. or Ltd.). The filing fee associated with a co-op agreement varies by state.

An example of a co-op is CHS Inc., a Fortune 100 business owned by U.S. agricultural cooperatives. As the nation's leading agribusiness cooperative, CHS reported a net income of $422.4 million for fiscal year 2020. These are some other notable examples of co-ops:

- Land O'Lakes
- Navy Federal Credit Union
- Welch's
- REI
- Ace Hardware

FACTORS TO CONSIDER BEFORE CHOOSING A BUSINESS STRUCTURE

For new businesses that could fall into two or more of these categories, it's not always easy to decide which structure to choose. Consider your startup's financial needs, risk and ability to grow. It can be challenging to switch your legal structure after registering your business, so give it careful analysis in the early stages of forming your business.

Here are some crucial factors to consider as you choose your business's legal structure.

Flexibility

Where is your company headed, and which type of legal structure allows for the growth you envision? Turn to your business plan to review your goals and see which structure best aligns with those objectives. Your entity should support the possibility for growth and change, not hold it back from its potential.

Complexity

When it comes to startup and operational complexity, nothing is more straightforward than a sole proprietorship. Register your name, start doing business, report the profits and pay taxes on it as personal income. However, it can be difficult to procure outside funding. Partnerships, on the other hand, require a signed agreement to define the roles and percentages of profits. Corporations and LLCs have various reporting requirements with state governments and the federal government.

Liability

A corporation carries the least amount of personal liability since the law holds that it is its own entity. This means creditors and customers can sue the corporation, but they can't gain access to any personal assets of the officers or shareholders. An LLC offers the same protection but with the tax benefits of a sole proprietorship. Partnerships share the liability between the partners as defined by their partnership agreement.

Taxes

An owner of an LLC pays taxes just as a sole proprietor does: All profit is considered personal income and taxed accordingly at the end of the year.

"As a small business owner, you want to avoid double taxation in the early stages," said Jennifer Friedman, principal at Rivetr. "The LLC structure prevents that and makes sure you're not taxed as a company, but as an individual."

Individuals in a partnership also claim their share of the profits as personal income. Your accountant may suggest quarterly or biannual advance payments to minimize the effect on your return. A corporation files its own tax returns each year, paying taxes on profits after expenses, including payroll. If you pay yourself from the corporation, you will pay personal taxes, such as those for Social Security and Medicare, on your personal return.

Control

If you want sole or primary control of the business and its activities, a sole proprietorship or an LLC might be the best choice. You can negotiate such control in a partnership agreement as well. A corporation is constructed to have a board of directors that makes the major decisions that guide the company. A single person can control a corporation, especially at its inception, but as it grows, so does the need to operate it as a board-directed entity. Even for a small corporation, the rules intended for larger organizations – such as keeping notes of every major decision that affects the company – still apply.

Capital Investment

If you need to obtain outside funding from an investor, venture capitalist or bank, you may be better off establishing a corporation. Corporations have an easier time obtaining outside funding than sole proprietorships.

Corporations can sell shares of stock and secure additional funding for growth, while sole proprietors can obtain funds only through their personal accounts, using their personal credit or taking on partners. An LLC can face similar struggles, although, as its own entity, it's not always necessary for the owner to use their personal credit or assets.

LEGAL FORMS AND STRUCTURES OF ORGANIZATIONS

The organization's structure, or design, is the overall arrangement of the organization's various roles, processes, and relationships in the organization. The design of an organization is a *means* to accomplishing the organization's overall goal — the structure is not an end in itself. In systems theory terms, the design ensures that the appropriate inputs go through the necessary processes to produce the required outputs to produce the intended outcomes.

Figure 2. Legal forms.

Source: https://management.org/wp-content/uploads/2022/09/Person-Holding-Gray-Twist-Pen-and-White-Paper-on-Brown-Wooden-Table.jpg

Broad Overview of Primary Legal Forms of For-Profit Organizations

For-profit businesses are usually of three primary legal forms, including unincorporated, corporations and limited liability companies. There are other forms of businesses, too, for example, nonprofits, franchises, government-owned corporations, cooperatives, limited liability corporations ("L3C"), etc. The three primary forms are explained below.

A corporation is a *privately owned corporation* or a *publicly held corporation*, depending on whether the corporation is owned privately or by the public at large.

Business people should seek the counsel of a lawyer when determining what legal form of business they should choose.

1. Unincorporated (sole proprietorships or partnerships)

Most small for-profit businesses are unincorporated. As an unincorporated organization, you can be a sole proprietor or in a partnership. A sole proprietorship is owned by one person or a marriage. Business activity is viewed by the IRS as your personal activity, for example, business income and taxes are viewed as your personal income and taxes. The sole proprietor is personally liable for the business.

A partnership can be a general partnership or a limited partnership. A general partnership is viewed by the IRS essentially as two or more sole proprietors equally responsible for the business. The terms of sole proprietorship apply fully to each partner. In limited partnership includes one or more general partners and one or more limited partners. Limited partners are liable for activities of the business to the extent of their investment.

2. Corporations (C Corporations and S Corporations)

A corporation is formed as its own legal entity, apart from the individuals who own and/or formed the organization. (The corporation can be either for-profit or nonprofit.). The principals of a for-profit business decide to incorporate mostly to shield themselves from personal liability for activities of the business and/or to sell stock in the business. A corporate *Board of Directors* oversees policy and strategy for corporations, whether for-profit or nonprofit. Principals and board members of for-profit corporations typically have little or no liability for the operations of the corporation, unless the owners or board members broke federal and/or state laws in running the corporation.

Theoretically, the for-profit and nonprofit corporation exists forever, past the death of its owners. For-profit corporations can be C Corporations or Subchapter S Corporations. More about these in the topic Enterprise Law.)

3. Limited Liability Companies (LLC)

The LLC is a relatively new form that combines the advantages of a corporation (minimum personal liability, selling stock, etc.) with those of a sole proprietorship and partnership (sharing management decisions, profit, etc). The LLC is an increasingly popular form of organization.

Broad Overview of Primary Legal Forms of Non-Profit Organizations

As noted above, for-profit businesses are usually of three legal forms, including unincorporated, corporations and limited liability companies. There are other forms of businesses, too, for example, nonprofits, franchises, government-owned corporations, cooperatives, etc. The following link provides more information about nonprofits, including their many legal forms.

Traditional Organizational Structures and Design in Businesses

See the organization charts depicted in Traditional Organizational Structures and Design in Businesses.

Functional Structure

Most organizations start out with a functional structure or a small variation of this structure. This is the basic "building block" for other structures. It is useful because it recognizes that there are different types of recurring management functions (Manufacturing, Sales, Marketing, etc.) in the organization and it also ensures coordination of these activities by a central office.

Divisional Structure

This structure is typically for well-established organizations that have multiple and often complex products such that each product requires its own functionally designed structure. Similar to the functional structure, it recognizes that there are different types of product lines, each of which requires different its own functional structure of different management functions.

Matrix Structure

This is referred to as a matrix because it is essentially a grid with rows and columns. The different rows represent different management functions and the columns represent different products. In this structure, highly skilled personnel in each management function are shared across different product lines. Thus, each person reports to a functional manager and a product manager.

Traditional Organizational Structures and Design in Nonprofits

Functional Structure With Non-CEO

New nonprofits often start by having no paid staff, including no paid CEO. The CEO might even be a member of the Board of Directors — a practice that is often frowned upon by key stakeholders because a CEO reports to the Board of Directors and, thus, there is an inherent conflict of interest in having a CEO on the Board. Thus, the CEO usually is not on the Board later on. Staff members are all volunteers.

Functional Structure With a CEO

The CEO reports to the Board of Directors and is not on the Board. Staff members are paid as is the CEO. In this structure, different employees might begin being associated with certain different programs.

Program-Based Structure With a CEO

In this structure, the nonprofit has different programs each of which has employees dedicated to operating a certain program for the nonprofit's clients. The manager of each program reports to the CEO. If the nonprofit continues to expand with each program expanding as well, then it might evolve into a divisional structure.

New Structures of Organizations

Driving Forces Causing New Structures

In organizational design, there is a guideline that "form follows function". In other words, the structure of the organization is a strategy to work toward the purpose and priorities of the organization. There are numerous driving forces that are causing organizations to re-think their priorities, for example, driving forces such as increasing diversity in the workforce, expanding markets around the world, and the public's increasing demands for more transparency and accountability for how organizations operate. In addition, to become more adaptable to the rapidly changing environments outside and inside of organizations, organizations are resorting to different structures in how they operate.

B-Corporations

From the B-Corp website "Certified B Corporations are a new kind of business that balances purpose and profit. They are legally required to consider the impact of their decisions on their workers, customers, suppliers, community, and the environment. This is a community of leaders, driving a global movement of people using business as a force for good."

ORGANIZATIONAL STRUCTURE

An organizational structure is the grouping of resources at different levels depending on their responsibilities, power, and position. It helps various departments in a company exchange data, coordinate, and work together to achieve business goals.

A company devises an organizational structure to ensure that suitable employees with the right set of skills occupy each position in the company. The OS reveals the accountability and authority of each role. This removes any uncertainty with regard to task performance and reporting and enhances employee productivity.

A company must clearly define its objectives before creating an OS. Then, group similar activities together to create departments, identify resources for each unit, and establish a hierarchy of employees based on their duties.

Thus, an OS of a company:

- Forms the basis of employee reporting and relations
- Decides the post of employees in their administrative divisions
- Formulates a system of coordination and interdependence in an organization
- Establishes a well-defined workflow aimed at attaining organizational goals

Every OS contains the following six essential elements:

- Work design: It defines the nature and job description of a particular position.
- Administrative division: It involves the grouping of jobs into departments to facilitate the coordination of work.
- Deputation: It means the power conferred to each employee and department in the organization.

- Management ratio: It refers to the number of employees that are reporting to a supervisor.
- Hierarchy: It creates various levels of authority arranged in the order of delegated powers in the organization.
- Centralization or decentralization: It presents the mode of operation followed in an organization.

Basic Elements of Organizational Structure Design

An organizational structure is based on a range of elements, including:

- Work specialization
- Departmentation
- Chain of command
- Span of control
- Centralization/Decentralization
- Formalization

Work specialization

Work specializations define how responsibilities are split between employees based on the job description. It's used to split projects into smaller work activities and assign digestible tasks to individual employees. The most common results of improper specialization are low efficiency and burnout.

Documentation

Documentation is an act of grouping specialists on the basis of the job description, skills, location, or other factors that connect them. The biggest challenge is choosing the criteria for departmentation. In many cases, it's no more enough to apply functional departmentation – where employees are grouped based on the tasks they perform. Startups often go for matrix departmentation that involves combining two types of departmentation and takes the best out of both worlds. For instance, functional departmentation can be joined by geographical departmentation to better serve clients in different locations.

Chain of command

Chain of command represents a system for passing instructions and reporting within an organization. Ideally, it distributes the power, supports knowledge sharing, and encourages employee accountability. The traditional chain of command makes decision-making more complex and does not allow for much flexibility. On the contrary, modern approaches strive to enhance employee autonomy and avoid micromanagement.

Span of control

Span of control regulates the number of direct reporters managed by a single supervisor. It heavily depends on the three aforementioned elements of organizational structure. Furthermore, to identify the right span of control, you need to evaluate your leaders' capacity, workplace size, and experience level of employees.

Centralization and decentralization

Centralization and decentralization are the concepts defining how managers, as well as employees, give input on company goals and strategy. While centralization gives leaders the ultimate control over decision-making processes, decentralization allows employees to impact business decisions. We'll dive into centralized and decentralized organizational structures in the further section.

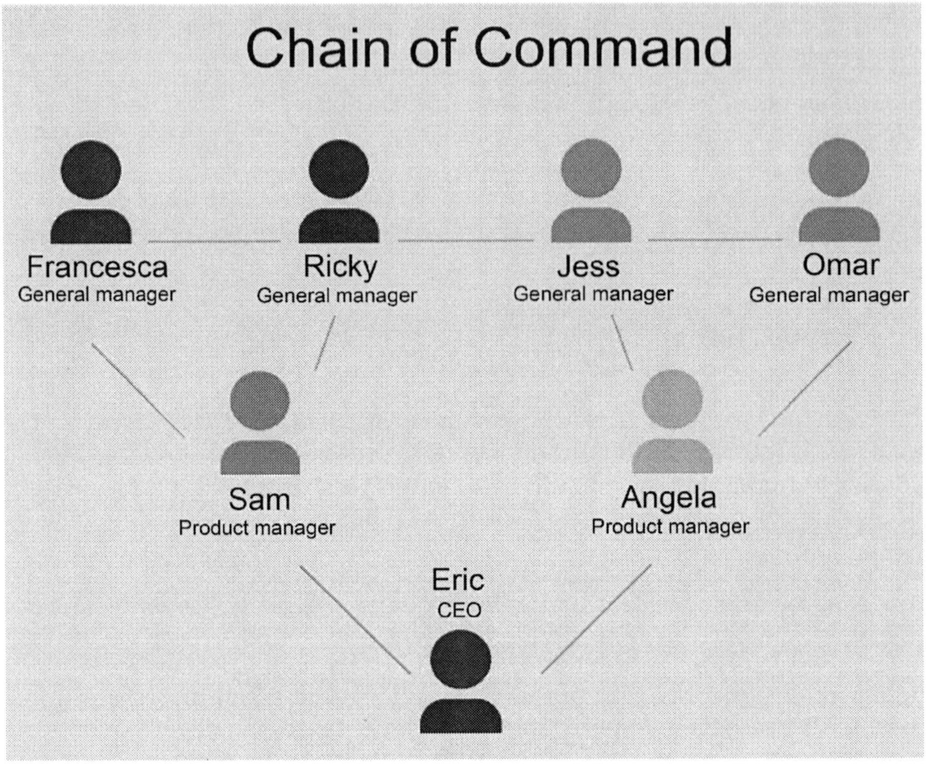

Figure 3. Chain of command.

Source: https://whatfix.com/blog/wp-content/uploads/2022/03/Chain-of-command.png

Formalization

Formalization determines to which extent business processes, policies, and job descriptions are standardized. It may regulate communication between employees and managers, workplace culture, operational procedures, etc.

Centralized vs. Decentralized Organizational Structures

Back to centralization and decentralization. When designing an organizational structure, you'll need to choose a side. Do you want to implement top-down or bottom-up management?

Centralized organizational structure

As has been said, in a centralized organizational structure, decisions are made by top managers and are distributed down the chain of command.

For sure, the structure has a range of advantages. It ensures greater control over business processes. But most importantly, it only includes highly experienced professionals that are able to foresee the effect of decisions made in the long run.

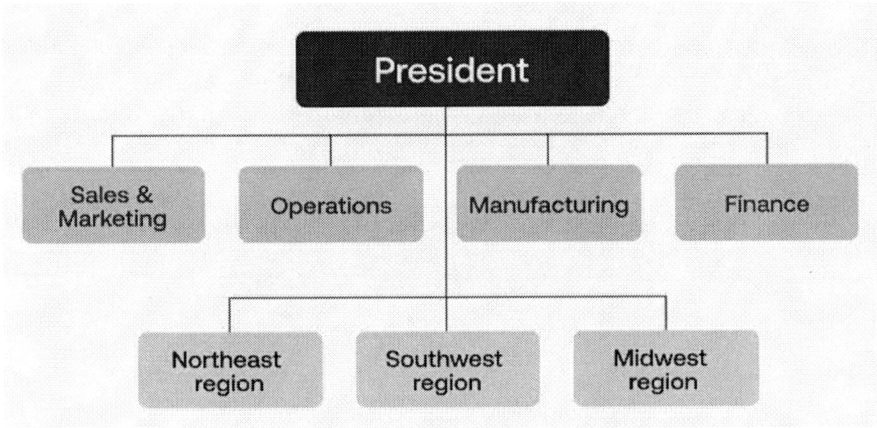

Figure 4. Centralized organizational structure.

Source: https://whatfix.com/blog/wp-content/uploads/2022/03/Cetralized-chart.png

The biggest drawback of a centralized organizational structure is the amount of time the decision-making process takes in large companies. Imagine a customer support manager being asked to implement an exclusive package for a high-ticket customer. To get permission, they'd need to run the request up the chain of command and wait for it to be processed by top management. When the request is approved, a high-ticket customer might no longer be there.

Decentralized organizational structure

To avoid this issue, large organizations turn to decentralization. In a decentralized structure, lower-level employees pinpoint issues and make decisions before communicating it to upper management. Greater autonomy not only empowers employees but also eliminates process delays, which are common for centralized systems.

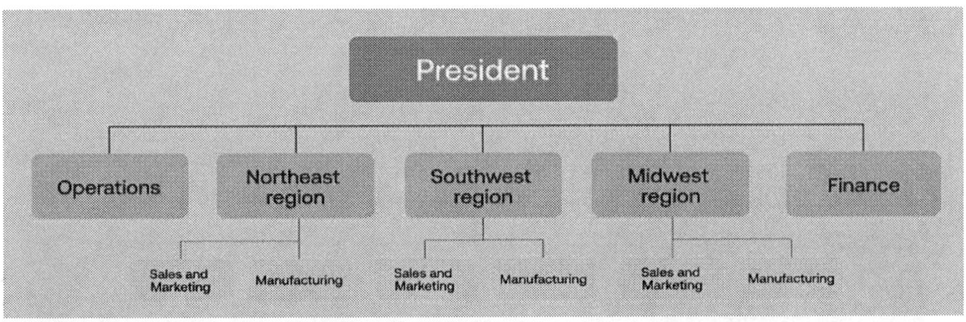

Figure 5. Decentralized structure.

Source: https://whatfix.com/blog/wp-content/uploads/2022/03/De-Cetralized-chart.png

However, decentralization also brings coordination challenges and higher expenses. Often, it's recommended that early-stage startups and small businesses go after a centralized organizational structure. Fast-growing companies and enterprises usually choose a decentralization framework.

Types of Organizational Structures

The key purpose of any organizational structure is to make the processes more straightforward. However, there are many ways to achieve that.

Let's look into the seven common types of enterprise organizational structures to help you decide how you want to develop your company and its various departments and teams.

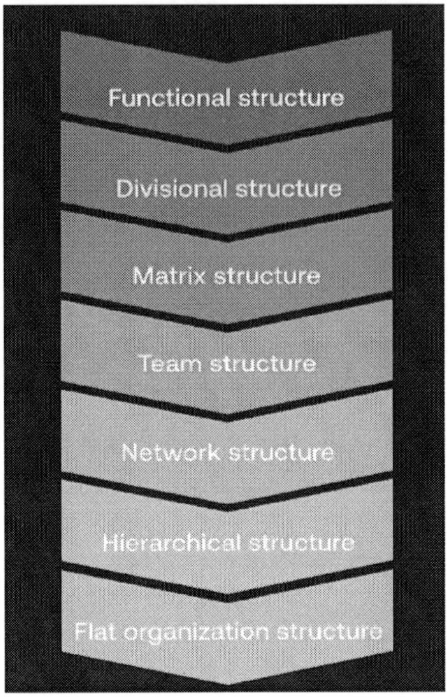

Figure 6. Types of enterprise organizational structures.

Source: https://whatfix.com/blog/wp-content/uploads/2022/03/7-stages-of-organisational-structure.png

1. Functional structure

A functional structure groups employees into different departments by work specialization. Each department has a designated leader highly experienced in the job functions of each employee supervised by them.

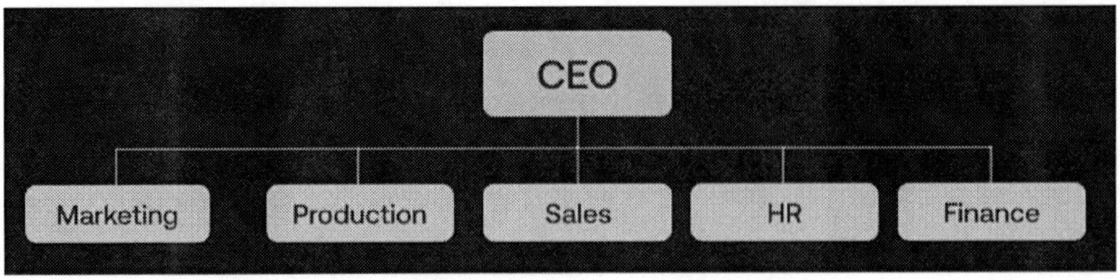

Figure 7. Functional structure.

Source: https://whatfix.com/blog/wp-content/uploads/2022/03/Functional-Chart.png

Most often, it implements a top-down (centralized) decision-making process where department managers report to upper management. Ideally, leaders of different teams communicate regularly and coordinate their strategies while lower-level employees have little idea of the processes taking place outside their department. The main challenge companies with a functional structure face is the lack of coordination between departments. Employees may lose the larger company context when focusing on very specific tasks and failing to interact with members of other departments.

To create a functional organizational structure that works, you'll need to train leaders to foster collaboration across departments. Examples of organizations with a functional structure include: Amazon, Starbucks.

Pros and Cons

- Scalable.
- Operational efficiency.
- Encourages employees to specialize their skillsets.
- Empowers employees to focus on their specific role and responsibilities.
- Empowers teams and departments with clear, specific goals that they can work towards.

2. Divisional structure

A divisional structure organizes employees around a common product or geographical location. Divisional organizations have teams focused on a specific market or product line. Examples of companies applying a divisional structure are McDonald's Corporation and Disney. These brands can't help but split the entire organization by location to be able to adjust their strategies for audiences representing different markets.

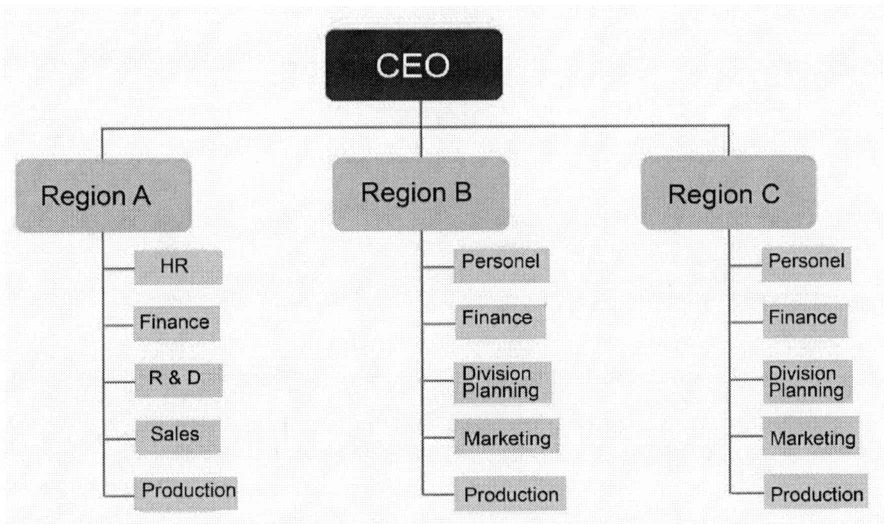

Figure 8. Divisional structure.

Source: https://whatfix.com/blog/wp-content/uploads/2022/03/Divisional-section.png

These smaller groups are relatively independent and mainly follow a decentralized framework. Still, the leaders of each department are likely to operate under centralized corporate management. It means that company culture is dictated by top management, but operational decisions can be made by each division independently.

Giants such as McDonald's and Disney also add functional units to their structure for better control.

Examples of organizations with a divisional structure include: Disney, GM, McDonalds.

Pros and Cons

- Understand individual markets better.
- Promotes flexibility.
- Faster responses to changes or needs that are locality or regional-based.
- Autonomous approaches lead to team experimentation and allow organizations to test multiple strategies, driving innovation.

3. Matrix structure

Within a matrix organizational structure, team members report to several managers at once. Wait, what's the point?

Having multiple supervisors allows for company-wide interaction and faster project delivery. For instance, when answering to functional managers and project managers, employees have a chance to collect experience outside their team. While functional managers can help to solve job-specific issues, project managers can bring in knowledge or talents from other departments.

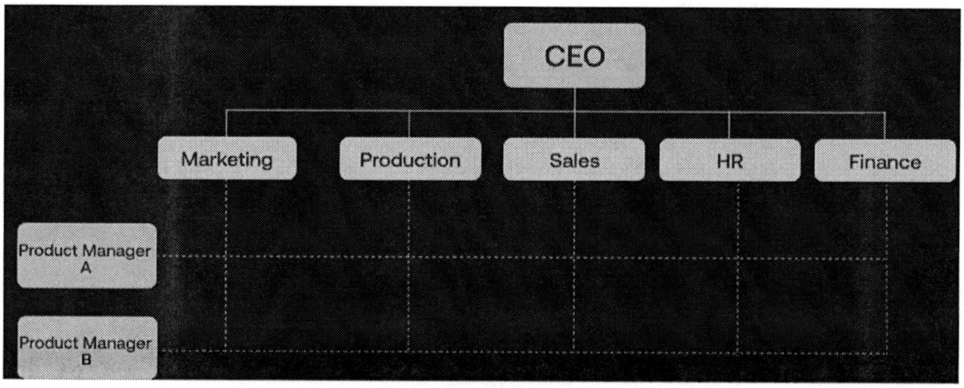

Figure 9. Matrix organizational structure.

Source: https://whatfix.com/blog/wp-content/uploads/2022/03/Matrix-Structure.png

If you go after a matrix organizational structure, you'll need to find a way to avoid authority confusion and prevent conflicts between managers.

Examples of organizations with a matrix structure include: Caterpillar, Phillips, Texas Instruments.

Pros and Cons

- Flexibility to pull employees into more important projects at will.

- Empowers employees to build and test skillsets outside of their pre-determined roles.
- Faster project deliverables.

4. Team structure

A team-based organizational structure creates small teams that focus on delivering one product or service. These teams are capable of solving problems and making decisions without bringing in third parties.

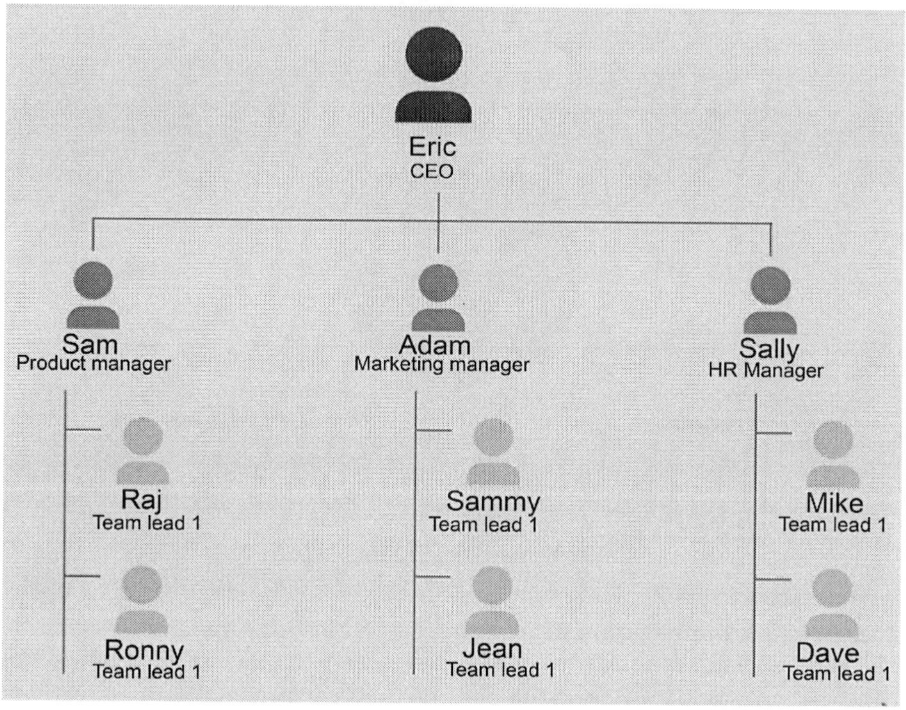

Figure 10. Team-based organizational structure.

Source: https://whatfix.com/blog/wp-content/uploads/2022/03/Team-Structure.png

Team members are responsible for managing their workload and have full control over the project. Team-based organizations are distinguished by little formalization and high flexibility. This structure works well for global organizations and manufacturers.

Examples of organizations with a team-based structure include: Apple, Cisco, Google, Whatfix.

Pros and Cons

- Drives growth and innovation.
- Promotes lateral career moves.
- Provides experiences across departments and teams.
- Experience is valued over seniority.
- Less emphasis on management.
- Is more agile.

5. Network structure

A network structure goes far beyond your internal company structure. It's an act of joining the efforts of two or more organizations with the goal of delivering one product or service. Typically, a network organization outsources independent contractors or vendors to complete the work.

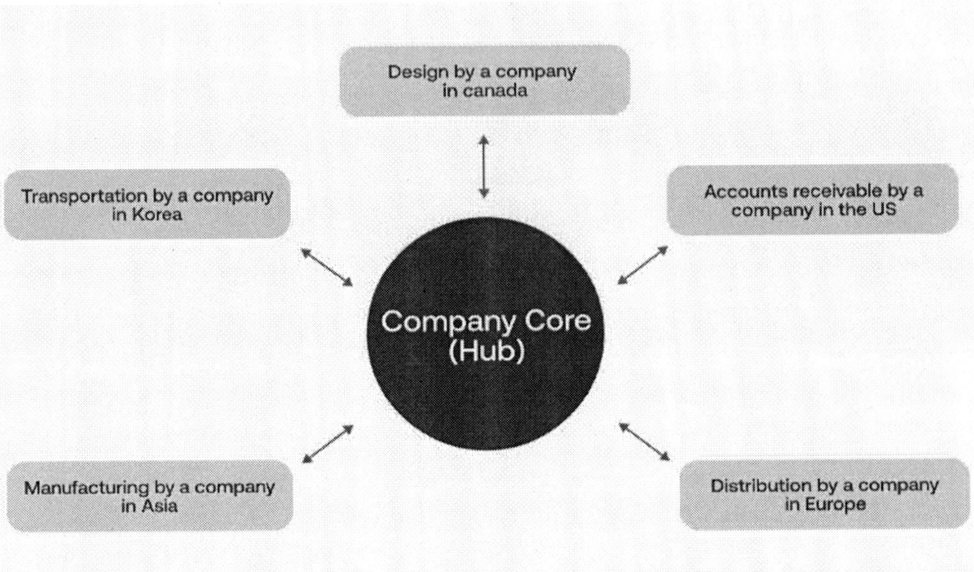

Figure 11. Network structure.

Source: https://whatfix.com/blog/wp-content/uploads/2022/03/Network-Structure.png

In a network organization, teams are built from full-time employees as well as freelance specialists – this way, in-house workers can spend most of their time focusing on the work they specialize in. Such an approach allows companies to adapt to market changes and obtain the missing skills fast.

Working with individuals that aren't integrated into your company culture results in lower formalization and higher agility.

Examples of organizations with a network structure include: Dow Chemical, H&M, IBM

Pros and Cons

- Promotes organizational agility and flexibility.
- Fosters collaboration across employees.
- Breaks down silos.
- Cultivates better understanding of industry, products, and customers.
- Creates a web of work-related relationships.
- Creates highly-specialized skillsets in employees.

6. Hierarchical structure

You must already have an idea of what a hierarchical structure is. It's the most common organizational structure type that follows a direct chain of command.

A chain of command, in this case, goes from senior management to general employees through a range of executives on the departmental and team level. The highest-level executive has the highest power over the decision-making process.

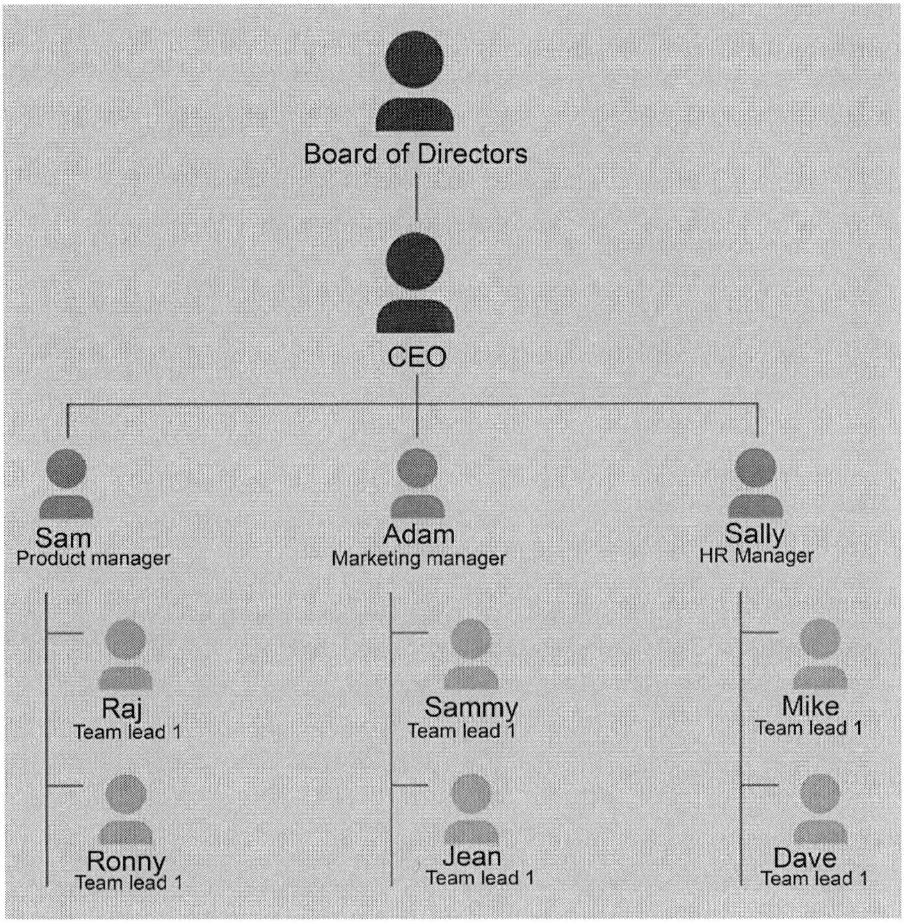

Figure 12. Hierarchical structure.

Source: https://whatfix.com/blog/wp-content/uploads/2022/03/Hierarchical-Structure.png

On one hand, this structure enables organizations to streamline business processes, develop clear career paths, and reduce conflicts. A company hierarchy leaves no place for challenging managers' authority, which can be good in some cases. On the other hand, a hierarchical structure slows down decision-making and may hurt employee morale.

Examples of organizations with a hierarchical structure include: Amazon, Sony

Pros and Cons

- Obvious chain-of-command.
- Clearly defined reporting structure and individual responsibilities.
- Sets clear career path growth.

- Builds niche skills and specialities.
- Departments and teams create a sense of "we're in this together".

7. Flat organization structure

In a flat organizational structure, there are few middle managers between employees and top managers. The structure requires less supervision, increases employee involvement, and boosts trust in the workplace.

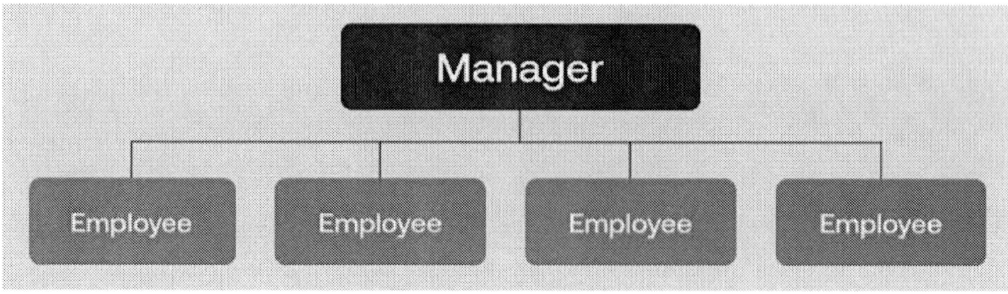

Figure 13. Flat organizational structure.

Source: https://whatfix.com/blog/wp-content/uploads/2022/03/Flat-organisation-Structurs.png

Due to its simple nature, a flat organization structure, also called a "flatarchy", is typically used by small businesses and startups. Examples of organizations with a flat structure include: Value, most small businesses.

Pros and Cons

- More responsibility for employees.
- Open communication.
- Clear path of approval.
- Implementation happens fast.

How to Design Your Organization's Structure

Whatever structure you choose, you'll need to make an effort to implement it. Here are eight simple steps towards designing an organizational structure from scratch.

1. Create a charter

First of all, you need to prepare documentation.

You need a project charter outlining the purpose of building a clear structure, key stakeholders, and their responsibilities. This is your rough plan for implementing an organizational structure that should give you a direction for your next steps.

When creating a charter, you'll be able to answer the following questions:

- Why do we need to design (or re-design) an organizational structure?
- When do we start?
- Who are the key stakeholders in this project?
- What should we do first?
- Where is the company headed? Will our organizational structure be relevant in a year?

2. Build your strategy

To build a structure from scratch, you'll need to start by outlining a long-term strategy and mapping out goals. Your future vision of your company determines which type of organizational structure will work best for you.

3. Assess your internal processes & systems

If your business has already been operating for quite some time, take a look at your current strategy and try to highlight the areas of improvement. Do you need to revisit your core ideology and company culture? You can only answer this question by talking to your employees and managers.

When you know where you stand and have a clear vision of what you want to achieve, creating an organizational direction shouldn't be a problem.

4. Design your structure

A clear understanding of your company's strategy lets you filter out irrelevant organizational structure types and pick the one that fits with your core values, mission, and goals.

Choose one of the seven organizational structures and use it as a template for designing a custom organizational chart. This chart is also known as *an organogram* – it's a diagram used to visualize the relationships between individuals, teams, and departments within an organization.

5. Create a transition plan

Next, it's time to design an optimal workflow for implementing or switching to a new structure.

Talk to the stakeholders and decide on the deadlines for establishing a brand new organizational structure. Prepare a list of recommendations for top managers and team leaders that will help to communicate the change to the rest of the organization.

6. Implement your new structure

From there, leaders should create an implementation plan that includes training their teams to adopt new roles and skills, as well as how to follow a new decision-making and reporting framework. Week by week, employees will become accustomed to their new organizational structure and adapt to the change.

7. Monitor the impact

The transition process might take months, and it's very likely that the performance of individual employees or even entire teams will go down at some point. However, you can assess the impact of a new structure in action only after the transition is complete. With a new organizational structure in place, run the performance review and talk to executives. It's important that you monitor the contribution of each individual department – chances are the changes don't work equally well for everyone at the company.

8. Gather feedback & improve

Again, once you implement an organizational structure, it's never too late to make adjustments. Alongside performance checks, survey your employees to learn how they feel about a new structure. It can be that their input will help you fine-tune the organizational design without extra cost and effort.

LAWS OF ORGANIZATIONAL STRUCTURE

There's a saying in architecture and design that "form follows function." Put another way, the design of something should support its purpose. For example, take a minute and observe the environment you're sitting in, as well as the objects in it. Notice how everything serves a particular purpose. The purpose of a chair is to support a sitting human being, which is why it's designed the way it is. Great design means that something is structured in such a way that it allows it to serve its purpose very well. All of its parts are of the right type and placed exactly where they should be for their intended purpose. Poor design is just the opposite. Like a chair with an uncomfortable seat or an oddly measured leg, a poorly designed object just doesn't perform like you want it to.

Even though your organization is a complex adaptive system and not a static object, the same principles hold true for it. If the organization has a flawed design, it simply won't perform well. It must be structured (or restructured) to create a design that supports its function or business strategy.

What actually gives an organization its "shape" and controls how it performs are three things:

- The functions it performs, or the core areas or activities in which the organization must engage to accomplish its strategy (e.g., Sales, Customer Service, Marketing, Accounting, Finance, Operations, CEO, Admin, HR, Legal, PR, R&D, and Engineering)
- The location of each function, or where each function is placed in the organizational structure and how it interacts with other functions.
- The authority of each function within its domain, or each function's ability to make decisions within its domain and to perform its activities without unnecessary encumbrance.

A sound organizational structure will make it unarguably clear what each function (and ultimately each person) is accountable for. In addition, the design must both support the current business strategy and allow the organization to adapt to changing market conditions and customer needs over time.

When you know what to look for, it's pretty easy to identify when an organization's structure is out of whack. Imagine a company with an existing cash cow business that is coming under severe pricing pressure. Its margins are deteriorating quickly and the market is changing rapidly. Everyone in the company knows that it must adapt or die. Its chosen strategy is to continue to milk the cash cow (while it can) and use those proceeds to invest in new verticals. On paper, it realigns some reporting functions and allocates more budget to new business development units. It holds an all-hands meeting to talk about the new strategy and the future of the business. Confidence is high. The team is a good one. Everyone is genuinely committed to the new strategy. They launch with gusto.

But here's the catch. Beneath the surface-level changes, the old power structures remain. This is a common problem with companies at this stage. The "new" structure is really just added to the old one, like a house with an addition—and things get confusing. Who's responsible for which part of the house? While employees genuinely want the new business units to thrive, there's often a lack of clarity, authority, and accountability around them. In addition, the new business units, which need freedom to operate in startup mode, have to deal with an existing bureaucracy and old ways of doing things. The CEO is generally oblivious to these problems until late in the game. Everyone continues to pay lip service to the strategy and the importance of the new business units but doubt, frustration, and a feeling of ineptitude have already crept in. How this happens will become clearer as you read on.

An organization's structure gets misaligned for many reasons. But the most common one is simply inertia. The company gets stuck in an old way of doing things and has trouble breaking free of the past. How did it get this way to begin with? When an organization is in startup to early growth mode, the founder(s) control most of the core functions. The founding engineer is also the head of sales, finance, and customer service. As the business grows, the founders become a bottleneck to growth—they simply can't do it all at a larger scale. So they make key hires to replace themselves in selected functions—for example, a technical founder hires a head of sales and delegates authority to find, sell, and close new accounts. At the same time, founders usually find it challenging to determine how much authority to give up (too much and the business could get ruined; too little and they'll get burned out trying to manage it all).

As the business and surrounding context develop over time, people settle into their roles and ways of operating. The structure seems to happen organically. From an outsider's perspective, it may be hard to figure out how and why the company looks and acts the way it does. And yet, from the inside, we grow used to things over time and question them less: "It's just how we do things around here." Organizations continue to operate, business as usual, until a new opportunity or a market crisis strikes and they realize they can't succeed with their current structures.

What are the signs that a structure isn't working? You'll know it's time to change things when inertia seems to dominate—in other words, the strategy and opportunity seem clear and people have bought in, yet the company can't achieve escape velocity. Perhaps it's repeating the same execution mistakes or making new hires that repeatedly fail (often a sign of structural imbalance rather than bad hiring decisions). There may be confusion among functions and roles, decision-making bottlenecks within the power centers, or simply slow execution all around. If any of these things are happening, it's time to do the hard but rewarding work of creating a new structure.

Here are five rules or laws of organizational structure, along with the most common mistakes that companies make by not following them. As you read on, see if your organization has made any of them. If so, it's a sure sign that your current structure is having a negative impact on performance.

Rule #1: When the Strategy Changes, Change the Structure

Every time the strategy changes—including when there's a shift to a new stage of the execution lifecycle—you'll need to re-evaluate and change the structure. The classic mistake made in restructuring is that the new form of the organization follows the old one to a large degree. That is, a new strategy is created but the old hierarchy remains embedded in the so-called "new" structure. Instead, you need to make a clean break with the past and design the new structure with a fresh eye. Does that sound difficult? It generally does. The fact is that changing structure in a business can seem really daunting because of all the precedents that exist—interpersonal relationships, expectations, roles, career trajectories, and functions. And in general, people will fight any change that results in a real or perceived loss of power. All of these things can make it difficult to make a clean break from the past and take a fresh look at how the business should be now. There's an old adage that you can't see the picture when you're standing in it. It's true. It also means that when restructuring, you need to help your staff look at things with fresh eyes. For this reason, restructuring done wrong will exacerbate attachment to the status quo and natural resistance to change. Restructuring done right, on the other hand, will address and release resistance to structural change, helping those affected to see the full picture as well as to understand and appreciate their new roles in it.

Rule #2: Don't Allow Functions Focused on Efficiency to Control Functions Focused on Effectiveness

Efficiency will always tend to overpower effectiveness. Because of this, you'll never want to have functions focused on effectiveness (sales, marketing, people development, account management, and strategy) reporting to functions focused on efficiency (operations, quality control, administration, and customer service). For example, imagine a company predominantly focused on achieving Six Sigma efficiency (doing things "right"). Over time, the processes and systems become so efficient and tightly controlled, that there is very little flexibility or margin for error. By its nature, effectiveness (doing the right thing), which includes innovation and adaptation to change, requires flexibility and margin for error. Keep in mind, therefore, that things can become so efficient that they lose their effectiveness. The takeaway here is: Always avoid having functions focused on effectiveness reporting to functions focused on efficiency. If you do, your company will lose its effectiveness over time and it will fail.

Rules #3: Don't Allow Functions Focused on Short-Range Results to Control Functions Focused on Long-Range Development

Just as efficiency overpowers effectiveness, the demands of today always overpower the needs of tomorrow. That's why the pressure you feel to do the daily work keeps you from spending as much time with your family as you'd like. It's why the pressure to hit this quarter's numbers makes it so hard to maintain your exercise regime. And it's why you never want to have functions that are focused on long-range development (branding, strategy, R&D, people development, etc.) reporting to functions focused on driving daily results (sales, running current marketing campaigns, administration, operations, etc.). For example, what happens if the marketing strategy function (a long-range orientation focused on branding, positioning, strategy, etc.) reports into the sales function (a short-range orientation focused on executing results now)? It's easy to see that the marketing strategy function will quickly succumb to the pressure of sales and become a sales support function. Sales may get what it thinks it needs in the short run but the company will totally lose its ability to develop its products, brands, and strategy over the long range as a result.

Rule #4: Balance the Need for Autonomy with the Need for Control

There is an inherent and natural conflict between autonomy and control. One requires freedom to produce results, the other needs to regulate for greater efficiencies. The design principle here is that as much autonomy as possible should be given to those closest to the customer (functions like sales and account management) while the ability to control for systemic risk (functions like accounting, legal, and HR) should be as centralized as possible. In addition, the autonomy to sell and meet customer needs should always take precedence in the structure because without sales and repeat sales, the organization will quickly cease to exist. At the same time, the organization must exercise certain controls to protect itself from systemic harm (the kind of harm that can destroy the entire organization).

Rather than trying to make these functions play nice together, this design principle stems from a recognition of their inherent conflict, plans for it, and creates a structure that attempts to harness it for the overall good of the organization. For example, if Sales is forced to follow a bunch of bureaucratic accounting and legal procedures to win a new account, sales will suffer. However, if the sales team sells to a bunch of under-qualified leads that can't pay, the whole company suffers. Therefore, Sales should be able to sell without restriction but also bear the burden of underperforming accounts. At the same time, Accounting and Legal should be centralized because if there's a loss of cash or a legal liability, the whole business is at risk. So the structure must call this inherent conflict out and make it constructive for the entire business.

Rule #5: Put the Right People in the Right Functions

Your structure is only as good as the people operating within it and how well they're matched to their jobs. Every function has a group of activities it must perform. At their core, these activities can be understood as expressing PSIU requirements. Every person has a natural PSIU style. It's selfevident that when there's close alignment between job requirements and an individual's style and experience then they'll perform at a higher level.

In the race for market share, however, companies make the mistake of mismatching styles to functions because of perceived time and resource constraints. For example, imagine a company that just lost its VP of sales who is a PsIu (Producer/Innovator) style. They also have an existing topnotch account manager who has a pSiU (Stabilizer/Unifier) style. Because management believes they can't afford to take the time and risk of hiring a new VP of sales, they move the account manager into the VP of sales role and give him a commission-based sales plan in the hope that this will incentivize him to perform as a sales person. Will the account manager be successful? No. It's not in his nature to hunt new sales. It's his nature to harvest accounts, follow a process, and help customers feel happy with their experience. As a result, sales will suffer and the account manager, once happy in his job, is now suffering too. While we all have to play the hand we're dealt with, placing people in misaligned roles is always a recipe for failure. If you have to play this card, make it clear to everyone that it's only for the short run and the top priority is to find a candidate who is the right fit as soon as possible.

Structure Done Right

Below is a picture of how realigned the company's structure to match its desired strategy. Here are some of the key things to recognize about this new structure and why it's superior to the old one. Each box represents a key function that must be performed by the business in its chosen strategy. Again, this is not an org chart. One function may have multiple people such as three customer service reps within it and certain staff may be wearing multiple hats. So when creating the structure, ignore the people involved and just identify the core business functions that must be performed. Again, first we want to create the right structure to support the chosen strategy. Then we can add roles and hats.

How to Read this Structure

At the bottom of the structure you'll see an arrow with "decentralized autonomy" on the left and "centralized control" on the right. That is, your goal is to push decision-making and autonomy out as far as possible to the left of the structure for those functions closest to the customer. At the same time you need to control for systemic risk on the right of the structure for those functions closest to the enterprise. There is a natural conflict that exists between decentralized autonomy and centralized control. This structure recognizes that conflict, plans for it, and creates a design that will harness and make it constructive. Here's how.

Within each function, you'll see a label that describes what it does, such as "CEO," "Sales," or "Engineering." These descriptions are not work titles for people but basic definitions of what each function does. Next to each description is its primary set of PSIU forces. PSIU is like management shorthand that describes the forces of each function. For example, the CEO function needs to produce results, innovate for changing demands, and keep the team unified: PsIU.

Identifying the PSIU code for each function is helpful for two reasons. One, it allows a shared understanding of what's really required to perform a function. Two, when it's time to place people into hats and roles within those functions, it enables you to find a match between an individual's management style and the requirements for the role itself. For example, the account management function requires following a process and displaying a great aptitude towards interaction with people (pSiU). Intuitively, you already know that you'd want to fill that role with a person who naturally expresses a pSiU style. As I mentioned earlier, it would be a mistake to take a pSiU account manager and place them into a sales role that requires PSiu, give them a commission plan, and expect them to be successful. It's against their very nature to be high driving—and no commission plan is going to change that. It's always better to match an individual's style to a role, rather than the other way around.

The General Manager (GM) Function

The first and most important thing to recognize is that, with this new structure, it's now clear how to scale the business. The green boxes "GM Vertical #1 and #2" on the far left of the structure are called business units. The business units represent where revenues will flow into the organization. They're colored green because that's where the money flows. The GM role is created either as a dedicated role or in the interim as a hat worn by the CEO until a dedicated role can be hired. Each business unit recognizes revenue from the clients within their respective vertical. How the verticals are segmented will be determined by business and market needs and the strategy. For example, one GM may have authority for North America and the other for Asia/Pacific. Or one might have authority for the entertainment industry and the other for the finance industry. Whatever verticals are chosen, the structure identifies authority and responsibility for them. Notice that the code for the GM/PsIU is identical to the CEO/PsIU. This is because the GMs are effectively CEOs of their own business units or can be thought of as future CEOs in training for the entire organization.

Underneath each green business unit is a Sales role, responsible for selling new accounts and an Account Management role, responsible for satisfying the needs of key clients. Essentially, by pushing the revenue-driving functions to the far left of the structure, we are able to decentralize autonomy by giving each GM the authority and responsibility to drive revenue, acquire new customers, and meet the needs of those customers. Each GM will have targets for revenue, number of customers, and client satisfaction. They will also have a budget and bonus structure.

The Product Manager (PM) Function

To the immediate right of the green business units is a black box called "PM" or Product Manager. The function of the Product Manager is to manage the competing demands of the different verticals (the green boxes to its left) as well as the competing demands of the other business functions (the grey boxes to its right) while ensuring high product quality and market fit and driving a profit. The grey boxes to the right of the Product Manager—CEO, Finance, Operations, Engineering, Marketing Strategy, and Admin—represent the rest of the core organizational functions. Effectively, these functions provide services to the green business units so that those units have products to sell to their markets. The revenue that the business generates pays for those internal services. Profits are derived by subtracting the cost of those services from the revenues generated by the business units. A Launch Manager who helps to coordinate new product releases among the business units supports the Product Manager.

The code for the Product Manager is pSiU. That is, we need the Product Manager to be able to stabilize and unify all of the competing demands from the organization. What kind of competing demands? The list is almost endless. First, there will be competing demands from the verticals. One vertical will want widget X because it meets the needs of their customers; the other will want widget Z for the same reasons (and remember that this particular company's strategy is to run multiple verticals off a single horizontal platform). Operations will want a stable product that doesn't crash and integrates well within the existing infrastructure. Engineering will want a cutting-edge product that displays innovative features. Marketing Strategy will want a product that matches the company's long-range plans. Administration will want a product that doesn't cause the company to get sued. The CEO will want a product that tells a great story to the marketplace. Finance will want a product that generates significant ROI or one that doesn't require a lot of investment, depending on its lifecycle stage. So the list of inherent conflicts runs deep.

The reason we don't want a psIu in the Product Manager is that at this stage of the company's lifecycle, the innovative force is very strong within the founding team, which will continue to provide that vision and innovation in another role, new Vertical Development and R&D under Marketing Strategy (more on this later). Nor do we want a Psiu in the Product Manager function because a big producer will focus on driving forward quickly and relentlessly (essential in the earlier stages of the product lifecycle) but will miss many of the details and planning involved with a professional product release (essential at this stage of the product lifecycle).

It's worth discussing why we want the product P&L to accrue to the Product Manager function and not the CEO or GMs. By using this structure, the CEO delegates autonomy to the GMs to drive revenue for their respective verticals and for the Product Manager to drive profits across all verticals. Why not give P&L responsibility to the CEO? Of course, the ultimate P&L will roll up to the CEO but it's first recognized and allocated to the Product Manager. This allows the CEO to delegate responsibility for product execution in the short run while also balancing the long-range needs of the product and strategy.

We don't give the Product Manager function to the GMs at this stage for a different reason. If we did, the product would have an extreme short-run focus and wouldn't account for long-run needs. The business couldn't adapt for change and it would miss new market opportunities. At the same time, the GMs need to have significant input into the product features and functions. That's why the Product Manager is placed next to the GMs and given quite a lot of autonomy—if the product isn't producing results in the short run for the GMs, it's not going to be around in the long run. At the same time, the product must also balance and prioritize long-range needs and strategy and that's why it doesn't report to the GMs directly.

If the business continues to grow, then one of the GMs will become the head of an entire division. Think of a division as a grouping of multiple similar verticals. In this case, the Product Manager function may in fact be placed under the newly formed division head because it is now its own unique business with enough stability and growth to warrant that level of autonomy. Remember that structures aren't stagnant and they must change at each new stage of the lifecycle or each change in strategy. For this current stage of the lifecycle, creating a dynamic tension between the GMs, the Product Manager, and the rest of the organization is highly desired because it will help to ensure a sound product/market/execution fit.

The Operations Function

To the immediate right of the Product Manager is Operations. This is the common services architecture that all GMs use to run their business. It is designed for scalable efficiency and includes such functions as Customer Service and Technology Infrastructure. Notice how all of these functions are geared towards short-run efficiency, while the business still wants to encourage short-term effectiveness (getting new clients quickly, adapting to changing requests from the GMs, etc.) within these roles and so it gives more autonomy to this unit than to those to the right of it. The code for Operations is PSiU because we need it to produce results for clients every day (P). It must be highly stable and secure (S) and it must maintain a client-centric perspective (U). It's important to recognize that every function in the business has a client whom it serves. In the case of Operations, the clients are both internal (the other business functions) and external (the customers).

The Engineering Function

Going from left to right, the next core function is Engineering. Here the core functions of the business include producing effective and efficient architectures and designs that Operations will use to do their work, such as SW Design, SW Development, and QA. Notice, however, that the deployment of new software is ultimately controlled by the Product Manager (Launch Manager), which provides an additional QA check on software from a business (not just a technology) perspective. Like Operations, Engineering is also short-run oriented and needs to be both effective and efficient. It is given less relative autonomy in what it produces and how it produces it due to the fact that Engineering must meet the needs of all other business functions, short- and long-run. The code for Engineering is PSIu because we need it to produce results now (P); to have quality code, architecture, and designs (S); and to be able to help create new innovations (I) in the product.

The Marketing Strategy Function

The next core function is Marketing Strategy. Marketing Strategy is the process of aligning core capabilities with growing opportunities. It creates long-run effectiveness. Its code is psIu because it's all about long-term innovation and nurturing and defending the vision. Sub-functions include new Vertical Development (early stage business development for future new verticals that will ultimately be spun out into a GM group), R&D, Marketing Execution (driving marketing tactics to support the strategy), PR, and People Development. A few of these sub-functions warrant a deeper explanation.

The reason new Vertical or Business Development is placed here is that the act of seeding a new potential vertical requires a tremendous amount of drive, patience, creativity, and innovation. If this function were placed under a GM, then it would be under too much pressure to hit short-run financial targets and the company would sacrifice what could be great long-term potential. Once the development has started and the vertical has early revenue and looks promising, it can be given to a new or existing GM to scale.

The purpose of placing R&D under Marketing Strategy is to allow for the long-run planning and innovative feature development that can be applied across all business units. The short-run product management function is performed by the Product Manager. The Product Manager's job is to manage the product for the short run while the visionary entrepreneur can still perform R&D for the long run. By keeping the Product Manager function outside of the GM role, New Product Development can more easily influence the product roadmap. Similarly, by keeping the Product Manager function outside of Marketing Strategy, the company doesn't lose sight of what's really required in the product today as needed by the GMs. Similarly, if the R&D function was placed under Engineering, it would succumb to the short-range time pressure of Engineering and simply become a new feature development program—not true, innovative R&D.

The reason Marketing Execution is not placed under the GM is that it would quickly become a sales support function. Clearly, the GM will want to own his or her marketing execution and s/he may even fight to get it. It's the CEO's role, however, to ensure that Marketing Execution supports the long-range strategy and therefore Marketing Execution should remain under Marketing Strategy.

The basis for placing People Development under Marketing Strategy rather than under HR is that People Development is a long-range effectiveness function. If it's placed under HR, then it will quickly devolve into a short-range tactical training function. For a similar reason, recruitment is kept here because a good recruiter will thrive under the long-range personal development function and will better reflect the organization's real culture.

The Finance and Admin Functions

To the far right of the organization are the Administrative functions. Here reside all of the short-run efficiency or Stabilizing functions that, if performed incorrectly, will quickly cause the organization to fail. These functions include Controller (AR/AP), Legal, and the HR function of hiring and firing. Notice, however, that the Finance function is not grouped with Admin. There are two types of Finance. One, cash collections and payments, is an Admin function. The other, how to deploy the cash and perform strategic financial operations, is a long-run effectiveness function. If Finance is placed over or under Admin, the company will suffer from lack of effectiveness or a lack of efficiency, respectively. Allowing one function to control cash collections and cash deployments also creates a tremendous liability risk. It's better to separate these functions for better performance and better control.

The CEO Function

The top function is the CEO. Here resides the ultimate authority and the responsibility to keep the organization efficient and effective in the short and long run. The code for the CEO is PsIU because this role requires driving results, innovating for market changes, and keeping the team unified. By using this structure, the CEO delegates autonomy to the GMs to produce results for their respective verticals. The GMs are empowered to produce results and also to face the consequences of not achieving them by "owning" the revenue streams. The CEO has delegated short-run Product Management to produce a profit according to the plan and simultaneously balances short- and longrun product development needs. At the same time, the CEO protects the organization from systemic harm by centralizing and controlling those things that pose a significant liability. So while the GMs can sell, they can't authorize contracts, hire or fire, or collect cash or make payments without the authorization of the far right of the structure. Nor can they set the strategy, destroy the brand, or cause a disruption in operations without the authority of the CEO and other business units. The goal of structure is to create clarity of authority and responsibility for the core organizational functions that must be performed and to create a design that harnesses the natural conflict that exists between efficiency and effectiveness, short run and long run, decentralization and control. A good CEO will encourage the natural conflict to arise within the structure and then deal with it in a constructive way.

REFERENCES

1. Ambrose, M. L., & Cropanzano, R. S. (2000). The effect of organizational structure on perceptions of procedural fairness.
2. Hollenbeck, J. R., Moon, H., Ellis, A. P. J., West, B. J., Ilgen, D. R., et al. (2002). Structural contingency theory and individual differences: Examination of external and internal person-team fit.
3. Inkpen, Andrew and Ramaswamy, Kannan (2006).Global Strategy (Creating and Sustaining Advantage across Borders). OUP.
4. Lasserre, Philippe (2003).Global Strategic Management. Palgrave Macmillan.
5. Porter, L. W., & Siegel, J. (2006). Relationships of tall and flat organization structures to the satisfactions of foreign managers. *Personnel Psychology, 18,* 379–392.
6. Schminke, M., Ambrose, M. L., & Cropanzano, R. S. (2000). The effect of organizational structure on perceptions of procedural fairness.
7. Shad Morris, James Oldroyd & Ram Singh (2021): International Business, Wiley India Pvt. Ltd.
8. Sine, W. D., Mitsuhashi, H., & Kirsch, D. A. (2006). Revisiting Burns and Stalker: Formal structure and new venture performance in emerging economic sectors.
9. Stonehouse, George, Hamill, Jim, Campbell, David and Purdie, Tony (2001).Global and Transnational Business: Strategy and Management. John Wiley&Sons Ltd.

3 COOPERATIVE FINANCE AND CAPITAL

INTRODUCTION

Cooperative finance and capital represent the financial mechanisms and resources utilized by cooperative organizations to support their operations, growth, and sustainability. Unlike traditional corporations, cooperatives are owned and democratically controlled by their members, who contribute to and benefit from the organization's activities. Cooperative finance encompasses various sources of funding and capitalization tailored to the unique needs and principles of cooperatives.

Cooperatives typically raise capital through member investments, where individuals contribute funds to become members and participate in the cooperative's decision-making processes. These investments may take the form of membership fees, share purchases, or patronage dividends, depending on the cooperative's structure and objectives. Additionally, cooperatives may access external financing from banks, credit unions, government grants, or impact investors to supplement member contributions and support business expansion.

Cooperative finance also involves prudent financial management practices, such as budgeting, accounting, and risk management, to ensure the organization's financial health and resilience. Furthermore, cooperatives often prioritize ethical and sustainable investing, aligning their financial decisions with social, environmental, and community-oriented values.

Cooperative finance and capital play a vital role in empowering cooperative enterprises to fulfill their missions, serve their members, and contribute to sustainable economic development.

COOPERATIVE FINANCE

A cooperative, like any business, requires money, or capital, for start-up, stability, and growth. Cooperatives can use both debt and equity to meet their capital needs. Debt is money that is borrowed and must be paid back to the lender with additional interest payments. Usually these loans come from banks or other financial institutions. While lenders may be financing a significant portion of a cooperative's capital needs, they do not have ownership rights.

Equity is money that is invested in a business without a guarantee of payback or financial return. The "at risk" capital entitles the investor to share in ownership, control, and any business profits or losses. Equity provides businesses with capital without interest expense or fixed payback obligations.

Cooperative members make equity contributions that give them ownership and control rights in their cooperative. These rights enable them to prioritize cooperative operations that meet their needs instead of increasing investment returns.

Sources of Cooperative Equity

Membership equity requirements

Membership in a cooperative requires an equity payment, usually through purchasing common stock or a membership certificate. The stock cannot be traded and does not appreciate. Each co-op determines the cost of becoming a member and must balance its need for capital with the members' ability to pay.

Retained earnings

When a business is profitable, the owners may decide to retain all or a portion of the earnings and reinvest them in the business. In a cooperative, profits may be allocated to members based on their use, or patronage, of the cooperative. These patronage allocations may be distributed to the member as a refund, retained as allocated equity in the member's name, or a combination of both. A portion of net profits may be retained and collectively held as unallocated equity in the cooperative. Typically, unallocated equity is the profit from business conducted with non-members.

The board of directors makes decisions annually about profit allocations and redemption of past retained patronage allocations. The board considers the co-op's capital needs, its members' needs, and its tax position.

Per unit retains

Per unit retains are often used by producer co-ops. The co-op retains a percentage of each financial transaction with a member for products that it receives or purchases. The retained payments are credited to member equity accounts.

Preferred stock

Wisconsin co-ops may raise equity capital by selling preferred stock to members and non-members. Preferred stock offers a dividend but does not grant member voting rights. Dividends are paid out of the cooperative's net profits, but are not guaranteed and are made at the discretion of the board.

Other Approaches to Cooperative Financing

Cooperative start-ups that are capital intensive may require more equity than members can provide. Accumulating the retained earnings needed for new capital-intensive investments may be difficult for cooperatives, which operate to benefit members rather than to maximize profits. Some states, including Wisconsin, have adopted hybrid cooperative laws that allow both investor and patron members. Patron members determine whether non-patron members may vote and receive a portion of net profits based on investment. In Wisconsin, these hybrid cooperatives are called Unincorporated Cooperative Associations.

Cooperative Profit Distribution and Taxation

Cooperatives are taxed differently than other types of business. A cooperative pays taxes at the corporate rate on the net profit that is retained as unallocated equity. Members pay taxes on the net profit that is allocated to them on the basis of patronage. Allocated patronage can be designated qualified or nonqualified.

Members pay taxes on patronage allocations that are retained and designated as qualified. At least 20% of the qualified allocation must be distributed to members in cash to help pay the taxes they owe on the entire patronage allocation. This method provides a way for members to make ongoing equity investments in the co-op in proportion to their patronage. There is an expectation that the retained allocations will be redeemed over time, since the member has paid taxes on them.

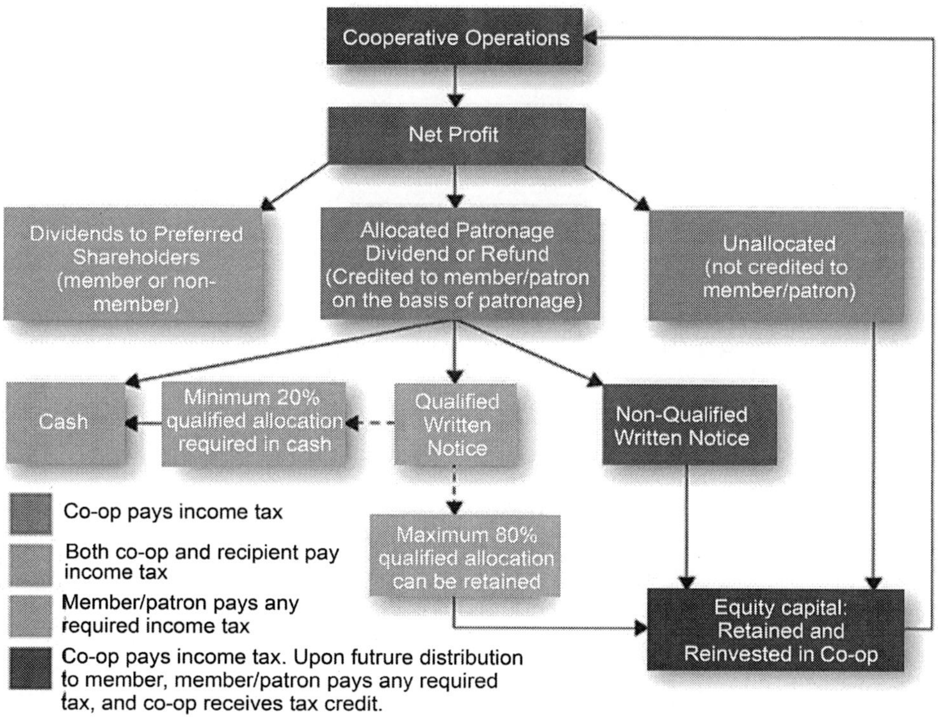

Figure 1. Cooperative oprations.

Source: https://uwcc.wisc.edu/wp-content/uploads/sites/242/2019/03/Net-Profit-Distribution.png

If patronage allocations are retained and designated as nonqualified, the co-op initially pays the taxes at the corporate rate. When nonqualified retained allocations are distributed to members at some point in the future, the member pays the required tax and the cooperative receives a tax credit. Since the member has not paid taxes on nonqualified retained allocations, there is less pressure to redeem this type of retained equity. In consumer cooperatives, where members conduct business for personal use, patronage allocations are treated like refunds and are not subject to income tax.

FINANCING THE CO-OPERATIVE BUSINESS

Raising the funds you need to start a new business isn't easy. If you want to open a store, for example, that could require a big chunk of money – especially if you need to pay for the construction of a new building.

Beyond possible building costs, entrepreneurs often need to pay for things like a business plan, start-up inventory, or legal fees. This tool provides some guidance for groups who want to know how to finance a co-operative business.

Loan from a Financial Institution

First, we recommend that you avoid long-term debt for as long as possible. This might be difficult, but it's a good idea to explore other, non-repayable options first to keep monthly expenses low. That said, loans are a common way to finance a new business. A loan can be amortized based on the co-op's business plan. To qualify for a commercial loan, your co-op will need to have a strong proposal to assure the lender that you'll be able to repay the loan. A solid business plan can help with this.

Membership Shares and Fees

Most co-operatives build their membership by selling membership shares (sometimes called "common shares"). When someone buys a membership share in a co-op they become an *owner* of that business — they can vote, run for the board, and (in some co-ops) get a share of the profits. The co-op's steering committee/first board of directors decides how much membership shares cost when they first incorporate the co-op. They choose the value based on its needs and goals. For example, if a co-op wants to have a large membership, selling shares for a smaller amount (e.g. less than $20) may be the way to go. If the co-op will need a lot of capital, and/or could provide significant benefits to members (like with a community investment co-op), it might be practical to charge a higher cost for that share. It may be a good idea to offer different classes of membership shares that are open to different interest groups. For example, a theatre that is co-operatively owned by movie-goers and staff could have two share classes. This may be a useful strategy for raising capital and creating a specific governance structure.

Some co-ops require annual membership fees — these are separate from membership shares (which you only pay for once). This is common in non-profit co-ops that don't raise a lot of capital from selling shares. Requiring members to pay an annual fee is a good revenue stream, and also weeds out inactive members.

Member Loans

Co-operatives have the unique ability to borrow funds from their members. To do this, they should create an agreement between the lender (member) and the co-op that outlines specific arrangements both parties agree to. Also, in the co-op's bylaws, outline the maximum interest it will pay on member loans, based on provisions in co-operative legislation.

Investment Shares

Selling *investment* shares is one way for co-op businesses to raise a larger amount of capital. These shares usually cost much more than membership shares and are purchased by people who want a return on their investment. Investors will normally enter into an agreement with the co-operative that outlines their investment's rate of return, payment schedule, and other stipulations. Investment shareholders can hold multiple share, but they still have to purchase a membership share to be an owner and gain things like the right to vote. Once a co-operative is in a stable financial position, it can buy investment shares back from its investors. Also, investment shares can be issued while the co-op is operating, if it needs to raise capital for a special project.

Fundraising

Co-operative businesses tend to be connected to their communities. This gives them the ability to raise money through donations from residents or local businesses.

If your co-op is a non-profit and wants to be able to issue tax-deductible receipts to people who give donations, it can get *charitable status*. You can also consider non-financial donations, like volunteer time and in-kind services that can help build the business. A co-op's leaders should make the co-operative's services and benefits clear to people in their community to encourage them to get involved.

Another option is using online fundraising tools like Kickstarter or Indiegogo. These will work better for innovative, new business ideas that get the public excited. These platforms allow individuals, businesses, or groups to raise funds, usually for a start-up, with the intention of providing donors a product/reward once they're in business. Using these platforms requires a very good understanding of your budget and capital requirements to ensure you can follow through on delivering the promised product.

Grants

In some cases, co-operative businesses may qualify for financial assistance from granting agencies. These grants are often ideal for the exploratory stages of a business, and can help finance things like early legal fees or developing a business plan. The grant process will often require an application to a government, NGO, or large enterprise. Big credit unions or co-operatives often fund business or community development initiatives. Co-operatives first can help you find the right funding agency for your business.

Group Discussion

Raising money for a co-operative is an ongoing process in the early stages, with different steps requiring more funds than others. Depending on the type of co-operative you are forming, the sources of capital may be very different; this is especially true for non-profit co-operatives versus those that issue share capital. The following development steps provide some insight into the cost that may emerge when developing a co-op:

- Community engagement and bringing people together
- Incorporation and registration fees; high if working with consultants

- Business planning (cost of time); higher if working with consultants
- Purchasing equipment, supplies, leasing, building, and hiring staff

In these early stages, many costs can be covered by volunteer time and member fees or sale of shares. It is also common to access grants or donations to help cover the costs of the business plan, especially if you seek out an expert to do it. Depending on the capital requirements of the co-operative's business, a loan may be required to get operational, but this should always be a last resort.

How can cooperative activities be financed?

The greater the amount of capital held by the cooperative, the greater its ability to purchase more efficient technology, invest in staff training and education and make other improvements to the running of the business.

Capital for the operation and improvement of the cooperative business can come from three main sources:

- directly from members themselves
- from retained surpluses generated by the cooperative business
- from outsiders.

Figure 2. Cooperative finance.

Source: https://www.fao.org/3/w5069e/w5069e04.jpg

Directly from Members

Members help finance the operations and growth of the cooperative through:

- one-time or annual membership fees
- member contributions with no individual ownership attached, such as service fees.

- member share capital
- individual member deposits with the cooperative which may be used for business
- deferred payment to members for part or all of their produce delivered to the cooperative

Member share capital represents individual member commitment to the cooperative form of business. It also identifies the individual member's financial stake. It is withdrawn only when the member leaves the cooperative. Some other forms of member contributions, usually related to patronage, are more variable but once given cannot be withdrawn and hence are a particularly useful form of cooperative capital.

From Cooperative Business Surpluses

Funds created through the retention of cooperative business surpluses that are not directly allocated to members are another important source of cooperative capital. This is a long term source of funds since most cooperatives' rules allow these funds to be distributed only when a cooperative is liquidated. Unlike loans, or individual member deposits, the cooperative does not have to pay interest to use these funds. Of course, retaining such funds by the cooperative also represents a cost to the individual members who otherwise would have had that portion of the surplus allocated to them. Members willingly accept this cost when the benefits it creates for them are clear and worthwhile.

This source of funds from retained surpluses is often called "institutional capital" and represents the collectively-owned wealth of the cooperative.

From Outsiders

In addition to institutional capital and member capital, cooperatives often make use of external sources of funds to run their operations or to finance investments. These non-member sources of funds may include cooperative or commercial banks, suppliers, government or donor agencies. External funding may be provided in different ways:

- as a grant
- as a short-term loan
- as a long-term loan
- as trade credit offered by a supplier.

Commercial providers of funds, such as banks, generally provide credit or loans that are legally secured by collateral (pledged assets of the cooperative). They are motivated by profit and seek to minimise risk. Non-commercial providers, such as governments or donors, generally provide credit on more generous terms at below market rates of interest or provide grants. Their motivations may be social, political or economic - often a mixture of all three.

The gearing ratio

The more assets the cooperative owns and has fully paid for - buildings, equipment, stock and financial reserves - the more others are willing to lend additional funds. Also, the greater the amount of the cooperative's institutional plus member capital, the higher the amount that can safely be borrowed from outside sources. Financial leverage, or gearing, is expressed by a percentage ratio which gives an indication of the amount of risk involved in borrowing funds. The higher the gearing ratio, the higher the risk the cooperative runs in losing their assets in the event of inability to repay a loan.

The gearing ratio relates the amount of externally borrowed capital to the total capital employed by the cooperative (institutional and member capital plus funds borrowed).

Gearing = funds borrowed ÷ (institutional and member capital plus funds borrowed) × 100

For example, a cooperative might have $900 of assets that it has fully paid for If it borrows $900 from a bank, it would have a high gearing ratio (50%)[2]. If on the other hand, the cooperative borrows only $100, the low gearing ratio of 0% indicates a much lower level of risk.

i.e. gearing ratio = 900 ÷ (900 + 900) × 100 = 50%

i.e. gearing ratio = 100 ÷ (100 + 900) × 100 = 10%

The gearing ratio and hence the level of risk involved in borrowing a given amount will vary according to the type of business a cooperative conducts. A consumer organization with a high level of turnover but relatively low investment in fixed assets (such as buildings and machinery), may be able to safely take on relatively high short term debt in proportion to its total assets. The same gearing ratio would represent a higher level of risk for an agro-processing society with relatively large investment in fixed assets.

Institutional and member capital are lower risk than outsider funding since they are provided by the members and hence the assets of the cooperative are less at risk. In most situations, therefore, they are often a preferred form of funding. Institutional capital, in addition, is the cheapest form of capital since generally no interest needs to be paid.

Which kind of funds are best?

Institutional and member capital are the lowest risk, safest forms of funding and hence should be the first choice in most cases. However these types of funding are sometimes not enough, or are not available at the time when they are needed. Funds may, for example be needed to cover running costs until a harvest is sold. In this case, a short term loan from an outside source may be taken and repaid after the harvest. In other cases, funds may be required for a longer period. This may be the case when the cooperative decides that the purchase of a new piece of equipment is economically justified. The group may then decide to obtain a long term loan.

In all cases, borrowing from non-members, such as banks and suppliers, is a good strategy only when the returns from such borrowing are larger than the cost of borrowing.

The type and source of capital is important because they determine the terms and conditions attached. For example, share capital which can generally be withdrawn by the member-owner only upon leaving the cooperative, is a relatively stable and long-term source of funds. The cost of share capital is low because of the cooperative practice of making low (or in some cases no) payments to the members based on their share holdings. It is also low risk since no collateral is required to secure the funds. Commercial loans from banks are higher cost as interest has to be paid on them. They are also higher risk since cooperative assets used as collateral may be forfeited to the lender in the event of inability to repay the loan and interest.

Equipment suppliers may also effectively provide a loan to a cooperative by allowing payments to be spread over a period. Again, the lender may be protected against risk through cooperative assets pledged as collateral.

Short term seasonal loans from a bank to finance the purchase of a harvest by a marketing society for example, have to be repaid within a few months of the harvest. These funds are also generally relatively expensive. However as this example suggests, such short term loans can be very useful for a cooperative.

Legal Framework and Support

Many of the regulations governing the operation of cooperatives were established before the recent changes in the world economy mentioned in the introduction (declining donor support, globalization of markets and increasing privatisation) began to take effect. Some of the regulations are still appropriate, others less so.

Many laws and regulations, for example, tend to restrict cooperatives in their business activities. For example:

- a specified percentage of the sales revenue of the cooperative may have to be returned to members within a specified short period of time, regardless of the financial condition of the cooperative.
- payouts of patronage refunds may have to equal a specified minimum percentage of the surplus, regardless of the wishes of members.
- a certain portion of the surplus may have to be placed in reserve with a government authority or an apex cooperative organization, or dedicated to community improvement such as maintenance of parks or roads, regardless of alternatives that would otherwise be available and possibly of greater use to members.
- some cooperatives may be required to deliver their produce to government agencies at prices that are not attractive, or to sell government-rationed goods at mark-ups that are not remunerative.

Financial support and privileges for cooperatives are decreasing and cooperatives are obliged to operate in competition with conventional businesses. Without the former associated privileges, many of the above regulations put cooperatives at a competitive disadvantage in the market place.

Many current business laws and regulations are however also appropriate and benefit cooperatives, such as those:

- that guarantee that business contracts will be enforced.
- that permit land and property to be confiscated on non-repayment of loans and hence allow them to be used as collateral.
- that promote greater transparency in business transactions, and
- that require accounts to be periodically audited.

A review of government laws and regulations governing agricultural cooperative businesses is needed in many countries to enable farmer cooperatives to successfully participate in increasingly competitive markets.

How can mobilization of member funds be improved?

Cooperatives need to find ways to increase member funding, since this provides the lowest cost, lowest risk form of capital for operations and investment. As government and donor support continues to decline, increasingly this also becomes the only practical source of funding for cooperatives. Even where outside support is still available, the advantage of increased reliance on member funding is that it gives greater autonomy to the cooperative and lowers the risk of eventual withdrawal of outside funding.

The strategy for increasing member funding depends on the particular circumstances of the cooperative, the type of activity it is engaged in and its scale of operation. Among the strategies to consider are:

Improving member services and patronage

Most strategies for cooperative development require increased funds. The strategy for developing the cooperative so that it maintains or expands its market position should focus on operational efficiency and on patronage, on how the cooperative can maintain existing business and attract more business and new members. Increased patronage provides an important source of member capital. However, it also usually requires more working capital for the operation of the business of the cooperative and may require more investment in fixed assets such as buildings and equipment.

Consider use of outside funding

In simple terms, the higher the institutional and member capital, the more outside lenders such as banks and suppliers will be willing to loan funds to the cooperative. Care should be taken in borrowing, however since the higher the outside funding as a proportion of funds used, the higher the risk if something goes wrong. (This risk is measured by the gearing ratio - an increased gearing ratio meaning a higher risk). If more funds are required, a low gearing ratio can be maintained if member contributions are also increased. For example, if the cooperative owns $1000 and needs an additional $1000, it will be highly geared (50% gearing ratio) if all funds come from a loan. Alternatively, if the cooperative raises an additional $500 from member funding, the sum to be borrowed would be lower The gearing ratio would then be 25% representing a considerably lower risk. It is also easier to find a bank or other lender willing to provide the less risky loan. The interest rate will also often be lower

i.e. gearing ratio = 1000 ÷ (1000 + 1000) × 100 = 50%

i.e. gearing ratio = 500 ÷ (1500+ 500) × 100 = 25%

Improving operating efficiency

Improving efficiency can be important for the mobilization of funds. It enables a cooperative to offer more competitive prices, securing and keeping member loyalty.

Funding and efficiency are related. Cooperatives with sufficient funds are able to invest in training and technology to reduce costs, and to increase or improve production. Well managed, technologically efficient cooperatives are generally more likely to accumulate capital.

Promoting patronage

The more members use the cooperative's services - that is by selling through or buying from the cooperative - the more funds the cooperative will receive. It is therefore important for the cooperative to promote patronage. This is most easily achieved when cooperatives provide services valued by members, offer competitive prices and prompt payment.

Giving priority to mobilizing member funds

Most cooperatives will have to rely on member generated funds to finance their operations. Members' financial stakes in the cooperative enforce greater accountability of the cooperative to members, build member participation in decision making and strengthen cooperative financial self-reliance and operational autonomy.

There are a number of ways in which member funds are obtained. In many cases, increased levels of funding can be achieved through adjusting these methods:

- Non-refundable membership fees upon joining

These fees are often small, but they need not necessarily be so if new members are buying into a successful business that provides valuable services.

- Member shares

All members are required to purchase shares, which are usually the primary source of member capital. Shares purchased should earn interest and are refundable to the member upon withdrawal from membership or to his/her heirs in the event of the member's death.

Shares in some cooperatives can be paid for over time through check-offs from a member's transactions with the cooperative. The members share account is credited with the amount of the deduction.

Many changes in cooperative financing are underway in Europe. These have included the issue of new classes of shares in addition to member shares, that are weighted on the basis of one share, one vote, providing control and governance incentives that result from cooperative solidarity but not necessarily by the traditional ownership structure. This technique can attract additional members and capital from those who would otherwise not be willing to contribute their capital due to their relative lack of control when capita entitles each member to only one vote regardless of the members' investment in the cooperative. Other changes involve the use of limited company forms of organization for certain activities undertaken for the benefit of cooperatives and their members. These activities may include wholesale or other large scale marketing activities.

- Retention of surplus

A surplus arises when the cooperative is able to retain some of the proceeds from sales of members' produce or from members' purchases from the cooperative. This surplus can either be retained by the cooperative as institutional capita, or paid out in patronage refunds to members following the close of each year In practice, cooperatives often offer prices more favourable than those prevailing in the market, creating little surplus and making it impossible to offer patronage refunds. In other cases, cooperatives are protected by governments and do not operate in competitive markets, making any surplus unrelated to competitive performance.

Whenever possible, these practices should be altered either to build up surpluses or increase patronage refunds and attract new members.

- Deferred payments

A surplus creates two opportunities for increasing capital available to a cooperative. One is the surplus retained, and the other is the patronage refund that is allocated but not immediately paid out in cash. During the period between the realisation of the surplus and the cash pay-out of patronage refunds, the cooperative has the use of the cash. Pay-out may take the form of a share or of an obligation to pay the member in the future.

Cooperatives in North America have been particularly creative in finding ways of retaining cash while allocating surpluses. The usual procedure is to issue notes payable over several years, such as five or seven. The member receives a portion of the allocation each year, while the cooperative is able to rotate its capital over the same period.

- Making member delivery rights transferable

In certain new processing and marketing cooperatives in North America the founder-members can purchase delivery rights which guarantee that the cooperative will purchase a given amount of produce each year. They also oblige the member to provide a certain amount of produce. These rights are freely transferable, which gives them a market value. This feature gives members an incentive to behave in a manner that maintains and increases the market value of their rights.

Too much institutional capital?

For the majority of cooperatives in developing countries, the possibility of accumulating too much institutional capital any time soon is small. However, members should be aware that it is actually possible for the original purpose of the cooperative to be lost if the amount of institutional capital becomes too large.

This may result in the exclusion of new members, because present members do not want others to benefit from the services provided and surpluses produced by the capital accumulated. It may lead to strategies for intentional losses so that the capital accumulated returns to the members in the form of unrealistic prices for services. It may also lead to the conversion of the cooperative to another legal form, such as a limited company While this may benefit existing members by providing them with higher incomes, the members should be aware that many of the ideals of a cooperative may be lost in the process.

Cooperatives have always been referred to as "member-owned" organizations, yet in countries where cooperatives have depended too heavily on outsiders for financial support, that sense of ownership and personal financial stake has been lost. It is not uncommon to hear farmers and shareholders refer to their cooperative as the "government's cooperative" instead of their own cooperative. This is largely because the financial stake or contribution of the membership of the cooperative is small relative to the non-member stake. In spite of the one-member-one-vote principle, the major suppliers of capital, in this case non-members, have the largest say and tend to determine the main priorities of the cooperative business. Cooperative member participation drops and the cooperative promise is weakened.

FINANCING METHODS

The cooperative itself is not in business to make profit of its own, but to increase the profits or reduce the expenses of the individual members. Since the cooperative is run by members, is natural that a major share of this capital comes from them.

Obtaining Capital from Members

The function of the cooperative is to serve the members, and this can best be achieved if members have final control over the operations of the association. For this reason it has long been a principle in cooperatives that equity capital be owned by members or patrons alone, and that there is a limit to the percentage of the stock that can be owned by each member. At present the limit on stock held by an individual member is set at 5 percent of the outstanding common stock. The purpose of this limitation is to maintain democratic control of the cooperative.

Cooperatives also 1imit the amount of dividends paid on capital stock. When farmers invest in a cooperative, their main purpose is to have an agency which can sell their products or purchase supplies for them. The importance of the cooperative to them is that it may reduce their marketing and purchasing costs and consequently increase their net income. Such savings are more important to members than the return on the investment they have in the cooperative.

As a rule, cooperatives do not obtain capital from the investing public. The limitations on dividends on capital stock have also discouraged outside investors f r o m putting past instances when private investors bought stock in cooperatives, they eventually obtained control of the association.

In general, cooperatives have found it desirable to obtain most of their capital from their own members. This capital can be obtained by direct means through sale of stock or membership fees, or by borrowing from members, or by indirect means such as retaining patronage refunds.

Sale of Stock. Purchase of stock is a condition for membership in many cooperatives. In some, one share of stock is enough; in others prospective members may be required to buy more than one share. Sometimes the amount of stock required depends on the size of the farm enterprise. This has been particularly common in creameries. In most cases the amount of direct investment through purchase of stock is limited. Par value of stock generally varies from $10 to $10 0. In this study the most common par value was $25.

The total amounts which can be obtained through sale of capital stock to members is small in comparison with the capital required for acquiring facilities and for daily operations. A cooperative of 400 members would obtain only $10,000 if each member purchased one share of stock with par value of $25, and $40,000 if the par value was $100. This is clearly insufficient for many cooperatives.

Certificates of Indebtedness. Funds can also be obtained by borrowing from members. Some cooperatives issue certificates of indebtedness which bear interest. This is a method which so far has been little used, and may have possibilities.

The advantage of certificates of indebtedness is that members with surplus funds may be willing to invest when they know that they receive a good return on their funds. These usually have a definite rate of interest and a due date.

Consequently , this method may obtain funds which would not be invested in capital stock. One disadvantage in comparison to capital stock is that certificates of indebtedness are liabilities, and they do not solve the problem of a cooperative which has insufficient equity capital.

Preferred Stock. As an alternative some cooperatives have sold preferred stock with a fixed dividend. Preferred stock is equity capital, but the cooperative may have to pay income tax on the amount paid in dividends. In contrast, interest on certificates of indebtedness is considered a business expense.

Occasionally cooperatives borrow money from directors. This is usually not considered good business practice and should be unnecessary if the members take any interest in their cooperative.

Deferred Patronage Refunds. In the last 25 years, cooperatives have been obtaining an increasing share of their capital from members indirectly by deferring patronage refunds. Instead of paying patronage refunds in cash, cooperatives have allocated them to members but keep them for a period of years before payment is made. Such decisions are usually made by the members at the annual meeting. By doing this, cooperatives have been able to build up their capital to meet the needs of the business. In this method, member investment is in direct proportion to the amount of business they do with the cooperative.

Although the principle of this method is fairly simple there are some problems in its use. One problem which immediately arises is whether deferred refunds are to be considered part of the members' equity or a 'claim against the ·cooperatives. Many cooperatives issue capital stock or stock credits for deferred refunds, and if this is done, it is clear that they are members' equities. In other cases, there is a question whether to consider the deferred refunds as equities or liabilities. The practice among cooperatives vary in this respect. Legal clarification is necessary.

Another important problem is whether the deferred refunds are to be included in permanent capital or in short term or temporary capita l. This is of great importance to management in its planning of the enterprise. Some cooperatives do not have any clear- cut policy in this respect, and probably even f ewer of the members know what the policy of their cooperative is. Ordinarily, cooperatives defer refunds for expansion or f or securing the financial position of the business. When enough has been obtained they may begin paying out. Even if members receive capital stock f or the patronage refunds, it is desirable to have some plan f or paying it out.

This problem of when and how patronage refunds are to be paid in cash is an important one. As mentioned before, some cooperatives have given no attention to this question. Others have set up certain plans, but some of these are not satisfactroy either from the viewpoint of management or members.

Revolving Funds. Among methods used in paying off patronage refunds, use of revolving funds has become common in recent years. In a revolving fund, patronage refunds are held back f or a certain number of years and when cash payments are made the oldest are paid first.

An example will illustrate the principle of this method. If a cooperative uses a·3 -year period and starts its operations in 1954, payments would run as in the schedule below, assuming the same net savings each year. In this case it would always have $15,000 in its revolving fund. Unfortunately such stability in savings is seldom found. If the volume of business and saving s both fluctuate, the cooperative may have to pay large amounts in cash in years when savings are low. Again, using a 3 - year period the following situation could occur.

To protect against such situations, sinking funds are used. This difficulty can also be avoided by not having a due date. In the revolving fund in order that the cooperative is not obligated to pay a certain amount in a specified year. Revolving funds are used both when deferred refunds go into capital stock and when they are treated as a liability. The practical importance of a revolving f und without a due date is that the oldest refunds are always paid first.

Some cooperatives pay a percentage of each member's total refunds in cash each year at the discretion of the board of directors or members. This would operate in the following manner, using 20 percent cash payment.

This method is preferable f or the beginning farmer since he receives some cash payments without waiting as he would have to in the ordinary revolving f und plan.

The difficulty of this method is that it is hard to explain to members, and that it involves a considerable amount of extra bookkeeping. Also management can never have a good picture on future commitments under this plan. Of course, it may not be necessary to make any cash payments in years when savings are low.

Some cooperative leaders have recommended that deferred patronage refunds be divided into two parts. One part to go into capital stock as permanent capital, and the other part to be paid out in cash either immediately or at some future date. The advantage of this is that funds would be clearly designated as permanent capital instead of being a commitment at some in.: definite future time. A clear-cut policy such as this can also be easily explained to members.

Deferring of patronage refunds has proved to be an effective method of obtaining capital from members. However, lack of definite policy about the handling of the deferred refunds has weakened the financial position of many cooperatives and created problems in membership relations. In contract law it is an essential point that both parties to a contract understand its meaning. Deferring patronage refunds is a form of contract between management and members. All too often the terms of this contract are not clear to any of the parties.

Self-flnancing

To a limited extent cooperatives can us e their savings to build up contingency reserves. Usually they are required by law to do so. The reserves are built up to provide a cushion against price declines or temporary losses. Any cooperative which wants to maintain a good financial status has to build up reserves for this purpose.

Tax exempt cooperatives need not file income tax return s, but have to fulfill certain requirements to maintain their status. At present, this provision is not of great importance to most cooperatives, and about half of the cooperatives in the United States do not apply for tax exempt status. It should be made clear that if patronage refunds have been allocated to patrons and patrons have been notified, they are not, at present, considered income to the cooperative. This is true regardless of whether the cooperative applies for tax exempt status or not. Cooperatives which are not tax exempt can treat part of their savings as a business profit and enter it in the books as surplus. In this case, the savings need not be allocated to· members, but the cooperative is required to pay income tax on it.

Borrowing from Non-members

As any other business enterprise, cooperatives may at times have to borrow money. They may borrow from banks and other lending institutions, or from their business connections. When a cooperative belongs to a regional organization the regional may be a source of credit.

The Bank for Cooperatives, which was established in accordance with the Farm Credit Act of 1933, is an important source of credit for farmers' cooperatives. This bank gives three types of loans.

1. Commodity loans are made to marketing associations chiefly for the purpose of making advance payments to patrons on products delivered, and secondarily to pay the costs of marketing.
2. Physical facility loans are made for financing of buildings and other physical property.
3. Working capital loans are made to finance current operations.

CO-OPERATIVE PRINCIPLES ON CO-OPERATIVE CAPITAL

Why do we co-operatives circumscribe our access to capital by rendering shares withdrawable and limiting their compensation? The rudimentary answer is that this is the result of Principles laid down in the International Co-operative Alliance's (the Alliance) Statement on the Co-operative Identity. Below is a brief narration on specific Co-operative Principles that set co-operative capital apart from company share capital:

Principle 1 – "Voluntary and Open Membership" and "Definition" of co-operatives

The voluntary nature of co-operatives allows a member to resign from the co-operative at any time – usually taking his/her share capital with him/her. Even if the co-operative can delay the withdrawal for reasons of solvency or liquidity management, it would ultimately have to redeem the shares if they are not transferred to another member. Company share capital, however, cannot be "forcibly" redeemed in the same way; the very nature of a limited liability commercial company is that of a permanent entity with permanent capital, until and unless it is brought to dissolution.

The open doors of a cooperative also implies that new shares will be issued to new members as a matter of course and usually at nominal value if share subscription is a condition of membership, unlike in companies where existing shareholders have the right to reject new share issuance out of dilution concerns.

Principle 2 – "Democratic Member Control"

One member, one vote – or other democratic forms of organisation – means that members who contribute more share capital do not have greater control than those who contribute less. This is diametrically opposed to the "one share (or unit capital), one vote" system of control in commercial companies.

Principle 3 – "Member Economic Participation"

This Principle introduces several aspects of co-operative capital:

1. At least part of the capital is "common property" and the establishment of "indivisible reserves" is encouraged. Where this is practised, co-operative members have no claim on the net asset value of the co-operative beyond their withdrawable membership capital. In contrast, a company share represents a claim on the net asset value of the company.
2. Membership capital receives limited compensation, if any at all. It would appear that capital, on its own, is not necessarily entitled to compensation. This runs counter to the prevailing commercial company's core purpose of maximising shareholder return and shareholder value.
3. Benefits to members should be in proportion to transactions with the co-operatives, not in proportion to shareholding as in companies.

Principle 4 – Autonomy and Independence

The raising of external capital (e.g., issuing debt) elicits concerns from co-operatives on the preservation of democratic control. This is sometimes translated into national legislation requiring membership approval for incurrence of external debt, but not for issuance of new shares. In contrast, most company shareholders are happy to allow management to use leverage insofar as it increases return to equity without adversely impacting the credit or regulatory standing of the company, but would definitely be concerned about issuance of new shares.

The Philosophy behind the Principles

The main Principles on voluntary and open membership, democratic member control, limited interest on capital, and transaction-based distributions have persisted throughout modern co-operative history. This indicates that there are deep and distinct convictions and beliefs that underpin the co-operative movement's treatment of capital.

We find out a clue about the underlying philosophy of co-operative capital in the very same Statement on the Co-operative Identity, in the section on Co-operative Values. Cooperative Values are listed as: "self-help, self-responsibility, democracy, equality, equity and solidarity." We might say that these combine elements of a socially and community oriented philosophy and those of a self-help movement. In Britain – the birthplace of the Rochdale Principles – socialism and co-operation were not so far apart. In Europe, many of the traditions that inspired co-operatives were religious – centred on the belief of the brotherhood of humankind – and the founders aimed to improve the wealth of co-operative members by empowering them in the market.

Indeed, at the root of the complexity of co-operative capital is a tension of philosophies and values. While modern co-operation has always had strong social and community underpinnings, co-operatives operate and are regulated within a global economic and financial system that is largely framed by market-oriented principles, which some may also term "capitalist".

Co-operative philosophy believes in the possibility of a more egalitarian world. It is grounded in a worldview that human beings are social creatures who are willing and able to co-operate with one another for a greater good. Human relationships, community, and association are emphasised over property relationships. As a factor of production, labour has dignity and precedence over capital. Capital, if it enters the picture, should be a servant to labour.

Market-oriented thought, in contrast, emphasises individualism and competition. The pursuit of self-interest is natural and normal, and the market's "invisible hand" will ensure the most efficient outcomes. Inequality is a natural reflection of the condition of humankind and not necessarily a bad thing. Any effort to reduce inequality should be philanthropic in nature and handled separately from the economic system. In this philosophy, the focus on individualism means that property relationships are core. Capital is the master that hires labour.

From this lens, we can see why co-operatives redeem the capital of a resigning member, curtail financial return to shareholders, and make distributions mainly in proportion to a member's transactions. Co-operation is first and foremost about people coming together to meet common aspirations and needs; that a business enterprise is involved and that the business might need financial capital are ancillary. In fact, one of our authors has pointed out that it was not always the case that businesses needed capital to be started: many European financial co-operatives were started on the basis of the collective guarantee of a community. The "founding energy" of a co-operative, as he puts it, is thus not necessarily in a provision of funds but in their desire to work together. Contribution of financial capital, along with other types of resources, is a responsibility of membership, not a claim to individual ownership.

For a co-operative, the cardinal relationship is that of membership of a community of "real" people. The manifestation of a co-operative's meaning for existence is the active participation of people as producers, consumers, and/or workers – stakeholders who have some organic relationship to the "real" business. A co-operative will thus maximise benefits to the group of stakeholders for which it is formed. For a market-oriented company, the cardinal relationship is that of shareholding, and it does not matter if these are faceless people or institutions whose identities change all the time because the share capital remains paid up. A shareholder need not have any organic relationship with the company's business, and the meaning for a company's existence is the maximisation of value for the shareholders, whoever they might happen to be at that point in time. Other stakeholders' demands are to be "managed" as inconveniences and costs and as a matter of regulation, except where serving them well also contributes to shareholder value.

From this philosophical lens, we can also better understand why a gulf remains between co-operatives and regulators on the issues of withdrawability of capital. Co-operators fundamentally believe that their fellow members are capable of looking beyond self-interest. This includes allowing their capital to absorb actual losses or opportunity costs and providing for indivisible reserves for intergenerational use, i.e., co-operators think of the community of future members and not just current ones. In one of the chapters, the authors gave the example of how members – being contributors of "philosophical capital" – had practised "altruism" in the history of their insurance co-operative when it ran into difficulties. In another chapter, we read arguments to the Basel Committee about the availability of co-operative capital to absorb losses. In yet another piece, we read that the author has argued to the accounting standards boards that co-operative shares should be recognised as equity because the turnover of membership in industrial co-operatives is actually very low.

For regulators schooled in the dominant market-oriented framework, however, the worst case scenario of each man looking out for himself must always be considered: if a financial institution is failing, which reasonable person would not withdraw his shares if he is able to? The Basel Committee also does not understand how an instrument with a limited return can be loss-absorbing equity. In this frame of mind that atomises and distributes risk, it is unthinkable that an investor would accept "fixed income" if he was taking equity risk.

CAPITAL BUILDING IN INDUSTRIAL AND SERVICE CO-OPERATIVES

A first key consideration considering co-operative capital is that, according to the third Cooperative Principle, "member economic participation", capital in one same co-operative includes both nominal capital and common reserves. The two types of capital reflect the fact that the co-operative combines the individual interest of the distinctive members and the latter's common interest. The simultaneous existence of these two types of capital is a fundamental element in the financial management of industrial and service co-operatives across the world.

However, a discussion on co-operative capital, at least from the point of view of industrial co-operatives, would not be complete if it did not also include considerations on capital generated by the co-operative movement itself as a community of co-operatives in close relation with the capital in the individual co-operatives.

We analyse capital in the co-operatives themselves: both the nominal capital (often referred to in English as "share capital") that "[m]embers contribute equitably to, and democratically control" and the co-operative reserves. In the second section, we analyse the capital in the co-operative movement aimed at strengthening the capital in individual co-operatives.

The Capital in the Co-operatives

Nominal capital contributed by members

The nominal capital contributed by each member in industrial and service co-operatives can oscillate from very low to very high amounts. The average amount contributed responds to different co-operative traditions rather than to regulatory provisions, even though some provisions can help leverage higher amounts as we will see in the second section below. In the same country, one finds industrial or service co-operative SMEs where each member contributes the equivalent of a few hundred USD, whereas in others such contributions can reach several tens of thousands of USD. Co-operatives with such a high level of members' equity logically tend to be more sustainable economically, especially in capital-intensive activities, such as those that the Mondragon group deliberately decided to develop since its inception. Logically, their members also tend to show a particularly high level of concern for and participation in shared management. The nominal capital in co-operatives is clearly a different type of financial instrument compared to ordinary share capital in the hands of shareholders. To avoid such confusion in this chapter, we are neither using the term "share capital" nor "share" as far as co-operatives are concerned. Notably, in a number of other languages than English, a different term is used. The third Co-operative Principle itself does not mention the term "share capital": instead it stipulates that "[m]embers contribute equitably to, and democratically control, the capital of their co-operative", and that this capital is "subscribed [by members] as a condition of membership". Let us first try to clarify the intrinsic differences between the two types of capital.

A first fundamental difference between members' nominal capital and shareholders' shares has to do with the fact that the people and/or entities owning and controlling the co-operative are stakeholders (in general workers or producers in the case of industrial and service co-operatives) rather than shareholders: by this we mean that the key reason why they become members of the co-operative is not to invest capital in it to profit from, but to solve specific needs or aspirations linked to their stakes as stakeholders – in the case of industrial and service co-operatives, such stakes usually have to do with employment, production, and/or community services. The "capital subscribed as a condition of membership" (excerpt from the third Co-operative Principle) is thus secondary to the fact that the co-operative gathers persons "united voluntarily to meet their common economic, social and cultural needs and aspirations" (excerpt from the Co-operative Definition).

A second fundamental difference, which is a corollary of the first one because it reinforces the role of co-operative members as stakeholders and not as shareholders, has to do with the fact that "[m]embers usually receive limited compensation, if any, on capital subscribed as a condition of membership" (excerpt from the third Co-operative Principle). This latter provision is generally well abided by in industrial and service co-operatives: cooperative members do not normally invest in their co-operative for the purpose of having high yields on their investment, but rather to make their jobs or production more economically sustainable, which is the key mission of their co-operative. If they just want to get high yields from an investment, they will normally opt for other options.

As a further confirmation of this second difference, members generally do receive variable returns as a part of the co-operative's surplus, but such returns are aimed at "benefiting members in proportion to their transactions with the co-operative" (excerpt of the 3rd co-operative principle). The transactions that members have with the co-operative can be of three kinds (from the point of view of the member): purchase in the case of usermembers, e.g., in consumer co-operatives, sale in the case of producer-member in producers' co-operatives that deal with the commercialization of the producers' products, and remuneration in the case of worker-members (in worker co-operatives and social co-operatives). Thus, co-operative returns to members are to be seen as an adjustment of the transaction price (of purchase, sale, or remuneration) and not as dividends.

As a consequence of the two above-mentioned fundamental differences (stakeholder nature of the members and limited return on the capital invested) comes a third one, namely that the nominal capital contributed by members is not tradable: it is not a financial instrument that can be bought and sold from one member to another member, and even less so, of course, from a member to a non-member. The nominal capital is redeemed to the member through a board or general assembly decision according to a series of statutory conditions which the member agreed upon when entering the co-operative (e.g., gradual redemption over a period of time). This practice is well abided by in industrial and service co-operatives, where one of the main issue has to do with the redemption period after the worker-member or the producer-member leaves the co-operative, especially when his/her contribution to the co-operative's nominal capital is substantial.

Differently from shareholders' share capital, co-operative capital should be considered as equity and not liability for the enterprise. After the International Accounting Standards (IAS) Board published IAS 32 on equity instruments in 2003, it published the International Financial Reporting Interpretations Committee (IFRIC) interpretation for co-operatives, which considers that co-operative members' nominal capital could be considered as equity provided that the co-operative's general assembly has the power to (at least in theory) uphold its redemption to a member. The rationale behind the IAS Board's interpretation is, seemingly that if the general assembly is able to uphold the redemption of any part of the co-operative's nominal capital, it effectively exercises control on it in its entirety.

Since the publication of IAS 32 and IFRIC 2, the IAS Board and the US Federal Accounting Standards Board (FASB) have made it increasingly clearer that the most important criterion concerning the distinction between equity and liability has to do with control rather than ownership. Nevertheless, as CICOPA communicated to the IAS Board within the framework of the latter's consultation on the "Review of the Conceptual Framework for Financial Reporting", in which the concepts of equity and liability stood out prominently, it is not necessary for the co-operative to have the power of withholding redemption in order to consider that the co-operative capital is equity and not liability. Indeed, in the case of co-operatives, the very fact that the enterprise is "jointly owned and democratically controlled" (excerpt from the Co-operative Definition) by members ensures that there is both ownership and control over the enterprise by a community of members whose turnover is very slow. It is particularly slow in industrial and service co-operatives, where members are comparatively few but where a worker or a producer usually remains a member for many years or even decades. In users' co-operatives (such as consumer co-operatives, housing co-operatives, or co-operative banks), the turnover may be quicker, but this is compensated by the fact that members are comparatively far more numerous: in both cases, the turnover between old and new members remains marginal; therefore, the vast majority of members remains stable over time and we usually find basically the same community of members from one year to the next controlling the cooperative. Such stability and constancy in the community of members ensures that effective control by the latter over the co-operative's overall strategy and management remains thorough, and that if as the IAS Board itself claims the main criteria to define equity is control, the co-operative nominal capital is indeed equity and not liability for the co-operative.

Over the last decades, we have observed a debate in a number of countries on whether or not to open up the co-operative nominal capital to external investors, to what extent, and with or without voting power. The basis for such discussions has invariably been the need for further capitalization. This debate was particularly lively in France, Italy, and Spain in the late eighties and early nineties when legislation was passed to make it possible to partly open up the co-operative capital to external investors provided that the cooperative's general assembly so decides and always keeping the co-operative members with a strong majority both in terms of ratio of the nominal capital and in terms of voting power. Twenty years later, the results of this regulatory wave in terms of capitalization has not reached the expected results while it has reportedly brought about other interesting outcomes: the so-called external investors that have invested capital have often done so because they in fact had another stake than financial being clients, providers, or entities linked to the co-operative through joint ventures or other network arrangements.7 This phenomenon actually reinforces the fact that the co-operative is a stakeholders' enterprise, because such investors invest as stakeholders (clients, providers, partners) to build value chains rather than as shareholders seeking financial yields.

Co-operative Reserves

The third Co-operative Principle stipulates that "[m]embers allocate surpluses for ... developing their co-operative, possibly by setting up reserves, part of which at least would be indivisible".

As we can read, the idea of setting up reserves is instrumental to the purpose of developing the co-operative. Again, the development of the co-operative is linked to it being a stakeholder-based enterprise: it must develop in such a way that the "persons united voluntarily to meet their common economic, social and cultural needs and aspirations" (excerpt from the Co-operative Definition) through the co-operative can do so even better qualitatively (e.g., through safer jobs or a more stable activity for producers) and/or quantitatively (e.g., by generating more jobs or welcoming more producers in the co-operative).

When they are able to do so, co-operatives by and large dedicate part of their surplus to financial reserves and use their accumulated financial reserves to invest in the type of entrepreneurial development described above. But what are exactly the "indivisible reserves" mentioned in the third Co-operative Principle?

Let us first try to clarify what divisible reserves are. Divisible reserves are non-nominal assets (thus not part of the members' nominal capital), which the members of a cooperative being closed down are entitled to share among themselves after payment of any outstanding debt.

This possibility is, instead, totally excluded in an indivisible reserve regime: indivisible reserves can never be distributed among co-operative members, even after dissolution and payment of all outstanding debt. National or regional legislation making indivisible reserves mandatory (e.g., France, Italy, Quebec, or Uruguay) have actually created a sui generis type of property, clearly distinct from both individual private property and from public property, and more akin to the "commons" discussed by late economy Nobel Prize winner Elinor Ostrom in "Governing the Commons". This is also why specific tax regimes have been established for the percentage of results earmarked for indivisible reserves. These laws oblige co-operatives to earmark to such reserves a minimum percentage of their year-end results, e.g., 30% in Italy. Beyond this legal minimum, though, co-operatives are free to earmark a higher percentage of their year-end results to indivisible reserves: e.g., in Italy, even after a drastic decrease in fiscal advantages in 2003, industrial and service co-operatives have continued to reinvest a significant amount of annual results to indivisible reserves with an average of 86.8% of net profits reinvested in the firm and only 10.2% distributed to members in 2005. By 2009, the average share of profits allocated to indivisible reserves did not see any decrease in the accumulation of indivisible reserves.

Where are indivisible reserves channelled after dissolution? In some cases, e.g., Argentina, they are channelled towards the governmental fiscal system but must be used to promote co-operatives.

In other countries, such as France or Italy, when co-operatives are affiliated to a federation, they are systematically channelled towards that organization or another one linked to it, which normally redistributes it for the development of co-operatives (start-ups, conversions, or development projects in existing co-operatives) in that country. Since the 1990s, the Italian legislation has established development funds under each of the three main co-operative confederations, which, among other mechanisms, channel all assets from dissolved co-operatives within their membership whereas a similar fund under the government has the same function for all non-affiliated co-operatives. We will return to these development funds in the second section.

The philosophical rationale behind indivisible reserves is that a co-operative is seen as an intergenerational enterprise, namely meant to last several generations, established among the same category of stakeholders (such as workers, producers, or users) who remain the same category of stakeholders, with a constant generational turnover. Under this vision, the reserves accumulated by former members in older co-operatives do not legitimately belong to the present members only; at the same time, the reserves accumulated by the present members are also not the exclusive property of the latter but are an investment for future members as well. Thus, if the present members decide to get hold of reserves accumulated by their predecessors and/or to destroy an entrepreneurial instrument meant to serve future generations of members, this is considered unfair towards predecessors or future generations.

It is widely considered that this type of reserves is particularly decisive for the survival and development of enterprises in the case of co-operative SMEs in industry and services. SMEs in general have a low survival rate in their first years of operation, e.g., 50% of French SMEs die after 5 years, as we can observe in the table below. Co-operative SMEs in countries where indivisible reserves are mandatory have shown a substantially higher survival rate than the average for SMEs, e.g., in France 66% of industrial and service cooperatives are still alive after 5 years, as also shown in the table below.

As far as industrial co-operatives in the CICOPA network are concerned, the density, average sustainability, and long-term development of such co-operatives, and of the jobs therein, appear to be substantially higher in countries and regions where indivisible reserves are mandatory by law. This has caught our attention as a key criterion for the development of co-operative SMEs in the most varied industrial and service sectors. Indeed, such characteristics can be found in particular in Argentina, France, Italy, Quebec, Spain, and Uruguay where indivisible reserves have been mandatory for years or decades. There certainly are other criteria by which co-operatives in these places have developed strongly (such as a good network of business support entities providing training, consulting and non-banking financing; the existence of co-operative groups; or a strong intersectoral integration at the level of representative organizations) but we find no other key criterion that would be common to all of them in such a significant way.

The main advantages of indivisible reserves that have been identified are the following:

- They stimulate the development of the firm beyond the individual interests of its members: as we saw above, the co-operative aims at combining both the individual and common interests of its members; the proper balance between these two elements seems to be best attained through the existence of indivisible reserves.
- They allow members to enter and leave the enterprise without destabilizing it, because they gradually become more important than the nominal capital: in some industrial cooperatives that are a century old or older, they can reach 90% of all the co-operative's assets. This is of strong importance to industrial and service co-operatives, where the need for stable capital is strong and the number of members is low. As a corollary, they gradually become a more important part of the enterprise's equity than the nominal capital for investment projects and as collateral for bank loans.
- They have proved to be a very strong incentive towards intensive capital investment, as in the co-operatives of the Mondragon group.
- They provide a particularly strong anchor in times of crisis, giving time and space to rethink present and future strategies
- They act as a powerful deterrent on any aggressive or speculative potential buyer who would never be able to get hold of such assets: the amount to acquire the business of the co-operative (once members decide to close down the co-operative and sell the activity or assets) includes the value of indivisible reserves, but the latter will never be under the control of acquirers. Internationally known co-operative legislation specialist Hans Münkner says in this respect that in indivisible reserve regimes, "hostile takeover of co-operatives is excluded. Where these rules are abandoned: plural voting, investor-members, transferable shares and other participation certificates, preferred non-voting stock etc., co-operatives and co-operative groups lose their special character as member-oriented self-help organisations and become ordinary commercial (i.e. investor-driven, shareholder value-oriented) enterprises for which the commercial law rightly applies".
- They also act as a powerful deterrent on the members themselves, who would have to think twice before closing their business, especially when indivisible reserves have become substantial assets;
- They help prevent or limit corruption, e.g., managers' corruption that can endanger the existence of the co-operative: as they are clearly regulated by law, nobody can run away with them.

Interest in indivisible reserves among industrial and service co-operatives in countries where they do not exist yet or exist only partly is on the rise. For example, the draft Japanese worker co-operative law also introduces the idea of indivisible reserves. Some of the UK worker co-operatives have instituted indivisible reserves, which are optional in that country. And the Canada Worker

Co-operative Federation (CWCF), a CICOPA member, has tabled a recent general assembly resolution promoting optional indivisible reserves in other provinces than Quebec, where they are mandatory as we have seen above.

Coming back to the above-mentioned sentence from the third Co-operative Principle, now that we have clarified the meaning of indivisible reserves, the expression "setting up reserves, part of which at least would be indivisible" may still appear partly unclear because of the term "would". The fact that only part of the reserves should be indivisible is not a problem per se, since even in countries where indivisible reserves are mandatory, it is possible to also earmark part of the surplus to divisible reserves once the minimum legal percentage earmarked for indivisible reserves has been attained. As for the term "would", it is softer than "should", and is clearly aimed at leaving the option open for national legislation not to make indivisible reserves mandatory, even though the text is drafted in such a way that such reserves are clearly recommended.

A SYSTEMIC APPROACH TO CAPITAL IN THE CO-OPERATIVE MOVEMENT

Co-operative capital - be it members' nominal capital or reserves – should not be seen as purely limited to the co-operative itself, and this is even more the case in industrial and service co-operative SMEs. The evolutionary trend of these co-operatives, wherever density is strong and the development history long, is built at a "meso" level, by using innovative financial instruments.

Members' nominal capital in co-operative SMEs can be boosted by instruments of "quasi equity", such as the French "titre participatif" (participation certificate): a type of bond that provides the buyer with a remuneration that includes minimum fixed remuneration and a variable additional amount indexed to the enterprise's results and which is subscribed mainly by investors in the social economy (co-operatives, mutual etc.). This instrument is considered as equity and not liability for the issuing co-operative, because the latter can retain this bond without redeeming it as long as it deems fit. The average redemption period is between 7 and 10 years, making it "patient" capital. The participation certificates invested by French specialized financial institutions such as SOCODEN or ESFIN-IDES in co-operatives that issue such bonds are usually invested according to a matching contribution to the members' aggregate nominal capital, often 1 to 1. They thus encourage further capitalization by co-operative members. The substantial increase in equity, which this system brings about, creates a tangible leverage on banks, and first of all on co-operative banks, which tend to be sensitive to the dynamics of trust that is generated.

This mechanism has been widely used in cases of business transfers to the employees under the co-operative form, in which business plans often have to be elaborated within weeks. A similar mechanism exists in Italy through other forms of equity within the framework of the 30-year old Marcora Law, also in great part for business transfers to the employees. Through a sophisticated matching contribution system – which sees on the one hand the workers invest part of their unemployment benefits cashed in as a three-year lump sum, and on the other a financial co-operative called Cooperazione Finanza Impresa (a CICOPA associate member) provides matching venture capital – several thousand jobs have been saved in a sustainable manner over the last 25 years in industrial enterprises that were about to close down. The Italian development funds that channel indivisible reserves from dissolved co-operatives to re-invest them in other ones, as we saw in the first section, also (and predominantly) channel contributions by Italian co-operatives corresponding to 3% of their results. The mechanism involves all Italian co-operatives, but many of the beneficiaries are industrial and service co-operatives (worker and social co-operatives). In France, a mechanism limited to the worker co-operative system channels one per thousand of the turnover of all French worker co-operatives affiliated to the French confederation of worker co-operatives (over 90% of them) to a similar solidarity fund.

Another mechanism being used at the "meso" level and in which the building of indivisible reserves in single co-operatives is a key element is the use of guarantee consortia. For example, the 2009 annual financial statement of Cooperfidi Italia (a consortium of 9 co-operative guarantee consortia) showed that it had built up a good level of capital funds equivalent to 28.8 million Euros, 18.5% of which was held as nominal capital and 13.8% in indivisible reserves with the remaining 67.7% composed of the accumulated risk funds. On the basis of these capital funds, the company issued guarantees for a value of close to 78 million Euro, with a ratio of guarantees issued and capital funds of slightly more than one to three.

When they are generated within the framework of co-operative groups, indivisible reserves help in bidding public and private contracts: In Italy, for example, the Consorzio Nazionale Servizi (CNS) – a large horizontal consortium of service co-operatives with over 200 cooperatives active in the fields of facility management, catering, logistics, the environment, tourism, and cleaning – has been allocating high amounts of group-level surpluses to indivisible reserves since its inception in 1977. Through accumulated indivisible reserves plus the introduction of successive processes to increase its capital stock (with the support of the Coopfond development fund), CNS has managed to gather enough financial resources to support its smaller members and has been able to shorten the public administration's payment terms, which are particularly lengthy and inconvenient. The CNS was created in 1977 by 11 worker co-operatives in the service sector with the aim of obtaining contracts from private customers or public bodies for work that would then be carried out by the member co-operatives, particularly in the sectors of cleaning, logistics, maintenance, ecology, catering, arts and cultural services, reception and caretaker services, and finally, facility management services. The CNS has been so successful that it is now one of the leaders in its field at the national level. Similar mechanisms have been developed within the Mondragon group where, additionally, the returns to members are capitalized till the latter leave the co-operative.

MANAGING CAPITAL STRUCTURE

All of the assets in a cooperative must be financed by some forms of debt and equity. Those assets include the fixed assets such as the plant, building, equipment and rolling stock as well as the short term assets such as accounts receivable and inventories. When we discuss capital structure we are referring to the choices that the cooperative made in creating the capital to fund all of its assets. Capital structure impacts the profitability and return on investment of the firm and also has major impacts on risk.

Financial Leverage

There are two primary sources of funding a business: debt capital and equity. The degree to which the cooperative is funded by debt is measured by either the debt to equity ratio or the debt to asset ratio. Both ratios are measures of financial leverage. A firm that funds a greater portion of its assets with debt is said to be more highly levered. Financial leverage amplifies the effect of profit or loss on the owners return. When the firm is highly leveraged (has a higher portion of debt financing) a profitable situation will result in greater impact on the owners return on investment relative to a similar firm that experienced the same profits but was funded only by equity. On the other hand, when the firm is highly leveraged an unprofitable situation will result in greater losses to the owners relative to that of an unlevered firm. Debt financing also involves obligations to make scheduled principal and interest payments. If the firm is unable to make those payments on schedule the lenders can force the firm into bankruptcy. For those reasons higher leverage (higher ratios of debt to assets) increases the risk of the firm. Debt capital only increases the owners return when the internal rate of return of the cooperative is greater than the interest rate. Cooperatives with higher profits are therefore more likely to have higher leverage.

Debt Financing

Debt is money borrowed from a lender with a promise to pay the principal and interest on a set schedule. Almost all loans involve a loan contract which gives the lender certain rights. Failure to make the scheduled payments can result in the lender exercising those rights. The most extreme case would be for the lender to force the firm into bankruptcy and liquidate the assets. In that case the value of the firm would be distributed to the lenders holding claims on the firm, in the order of the priority of those claims. Any residual value would then go to the owners of the firm. It is that structure of debt financing that creates both the returns and risk of leverage. Because debt payments are fixed, if the firm is able to use the funds or project that create profits in excess of the loan payments, then that excess flows to the owners and increased their return. On the other hand, if the firm is not profitable the firm must still pay the lenders at the agreed on schedule and the burden of those payments falls on the owners.

There is generally a rationale for a cooperative, or any other firm, to take on debt financing. First, as described, debt financing creates the opportunity for the owners to increase their return on investment. Second, the owners of the firm often have difficulty in providing the funds to finance all of the firm's assets. This is particularly true in agricultural cooperatives. The cooperative members are financing their own farming operations. The equity that they provide to the cooperative therefore competes for the funds they need to finance their farming operations. Cooperatives are also unique in that they are usually limited to obtaining equity capital from their user members.

Open membership cooperatives typically create that equity out of the profit stream by distributing a portion of profits in the form of stock. That means that they can only create equity when they are profitable. Closed membership cooperatives create equity by selling membership stock during their formation period. That membership equity is typically linked to a usage right. Equity drives in a closed membership cooperative are complex and costly. Those sources and structures for raising equity in cooperative firms are in contrast to investor owned firms that can sell equity at any time. Most large investor owned firms are publically traded meaning that they can raise equity capital by selling stock on public stock exchanges. It is easy to see that cooperatives do not have unlimited access to equity capital and have a rationale for some degree of debt financing.

A third rationale for debt financing is that interest payments are tax deductible. Cooperatives can reduce their taxable income by issuing cash and qualified stock patronage to members and by redeeming previously issued nonqualified stock. Because of those tools to reduce taxable income, deductible interest expenses are not as important for cooperative firms. Still, most cooperative have non-member business which creates taxable income. When a cooperative has taxable income equal or greater to its interest expense, the interest expense is reduced by the tax savings. For example a cooperative paying 5% interest with a 30% tax rate would have an after tax interest rate of 3.5%.

Cooperative's Use of Debt

According to the most recent USDA Agricultural Cooperative Statistics (2017) agricultural cooperatives financed 54% of their total assets with some form of debt. Larger cooperatives tend to have higher portions of debt financing. The smallest category of cooperatives (under $5 in annual sales) had a debt to asset ratio of 36%. For all size categories of cooperatives, short term financing represented more than 50% of total debt. Short term financing is typically used to fund inventories, accounts receivables and other short term assets.

Sources of Debt

Commercial Banks

Cooperative banks (discussed below) are an important source of both short term and long term debt financing for cooperatives. Like other firms, cooperatives can also borrow from commercial banks. Historically, banks have not been active in financing cooperatives because they do not understand the business model. Commercial banks have a particularly difficult time in understanding cooperative's structure of patronage refunds and equity redemption. The dynamic nature of cooperative equity is troubling to bankers that are used to dealing with permanent equity capital.

Cooperative Banks

The greatest real advantage cooperatives have in the acquisition of debt capital is that they can borrow from their own cooperative lenders. Agricultural cooperatives have access to CoBank in the Farm Credit System. Non-agricultural cooperatives can use the National Cooperative Bank, and rural utility cooperatives can use Cooperative Finance Corportation. Because these lenders are themselves cooperatives, they understand cooperative finance better than other lenders. CoBank is part of the Farm Credit System (which is itself a cooperative) and has a national charter to serve cooperatives. By its original authorizing legislation, the Farm Credit System had 13 banks for cooperatives that were established regionally around the U.S. In the late 1980s, CoBank was formed through the merger of 11 of the original 13 banks. By mid-1999, all the original banks had joined CoBank which now has the sole Farm Credit charter to serve cooperatives. The funds that CoBank lends cooperatives are borrowed from the government-sponsored-enterprise market through the Farm Credit Funding Corporation. In essence, CoBank sells bonds in national capital markets and then lends those funds to its cooperative borrowers. While the Farm Credit Funding Corporation bonds are not backed by the federal government, the agency is associated the U.S. government. For that reason, investor perceive the bonds to be low risk and will purchase them at slightly lower interest rates, relative to corporate bonds. This source of funding provides a relatively low cost source of financing for cooperatives CoBank is owned by the cooperatives that borrow from it. When a cooperative obtains its first loan from CoBank, it must purchase stock just like any member joining a cooperative.

Ultimately, the borrowing cooperative must make an investment in CoBank in proportion to the size of its loan. The borrowing cooperative most often acquires its equity via retained patronage refunds. The relationship between CoBank and its member cooperatives is equivalent to that between other cooperatives and their members. For this reason, it also has some of the same challenges in its relationships with borrowers that cooperatives have with their member patrons. Based on the legislation authorizing the Farm Credit System, CoBank has strict policies that regulate borrower eligibility for its loans. In order to eligible to borrow from CoBank a business must:

(1) Do 50% of its business with members,

(2) Have 80% of its equity owned by producers and

(3) Operate on a cooperative basis with respect to voting and profit distribution.

Cooperatives borrowing from CoBank must also meet the financial requirements established by the bank. These requirements vary according to prospects for individual cooperatives. CoBank evaluates applications in much the same way as do other lending agencies. Such factors as repayment ability, collateral, balance sheet, and income statement changes or trends, quality of management, and member support enter into approval of a loan. CoBank makes seasonal and long-term loans.

The former are used to finance short-term seasonal needs such as inventories, which, in agribusiness, may represent a relatively large portion of total liabilities at certain times during the year. Long-term loans are used to finance long-lived assets such as land, buildings, and equipment.

The National Cooperative Bank

The National Cooperative Bank (NCB) was established by Congress in 1978 and then was privatized in 1981. NCB serves organizations that are defined as cooperatives, as well as those having similar organizing principles. The scope of its membership is quite large, including independent grocery cooperatives, Employee Stock Ownership Plans, housing cooperatives, purchasing cooperatives, and other similar groups. NCB goes directly to the capital markets for debt financing as well as sells pools of cooperative loans into the market.

The National Rural Utilities Cooperative Finance Corporation

The National Rural Utilities Cooperative Finance Corporation (CFC) is a cooperative banking entity created by rural electric cooperatives in 1969 to supplement government lending programs. Today, CFC offers a full range of financial products and services to member utility cooperatives. Like NCB, CFC is a conduit for its members to the private capital markets. In addition to serving rural electric cooperatives, CFC operates several affiliated organizations—the Rural Telephone Finance Cooperative and the National Cooperative Services Corporation. All of the cooperative banks, CoBank, NCB, and CFC, share one thing in common—they have special insights into the financial needs and challenges of the cooperatives who are their members. Member cooperatives know that they can count on these institutions when other private sources of borrowed capital may not come through with required funds or may not understand the needs of cooperative organizations.

Loans from Members

Cooperative can potentially borrow funds from their members. Member financing raises numerous issues. One question is whether the cooperative will be considered to be selling a security. If so the firm may have to register the offering with the Securities Exchange Committee. That registration process is complex and may cost hundreds of thousands of dollars. Member financing also exposes members to an additional source of risk from the cooperative. The attractive aspect of member financing is that the interest rate that the cooperative is paying is often higher than what members can obtain in their bank savings accounts. That creates the opportunity for the cooperative to obtain funds at a lower interest rate while giving members higher rates, relative to their local bank. Historically, many local cooperatives made the mistake of issuing demand notes to patrons. The notes functioned like certificates of deposit in a local bank except that the members could cash them in at any time. When the economy took a down turn, the members all rushed in to redeem their notes at the exact time the local cooperatives were struggling to obtain funds.

Trade Credit

Just like other business, cooperatives often finance a portion of their current assets with trade credit. When a cooperative purchases fuel, fertilizer and other inventories they often have a short period of time to make the payments. Those obligations show up as accounts payable on the cooperative balance sheet and are a source of financing. Regional cooperatives may be particularly willing to supply trade credit to local cooperatives.

Cooperative Equity

Equity is the investment that member-patrons make in the cooperative. According to cooperative principles, members have a key responsibility to provide equity. Cooperative equity can be allocated (issued in the specific name of a member) or unallocated (a general reserve fund that is collectively owned). Cooperative equity can also be revolving, semi-permanent or permanent. Revolving equity can be qualified or nonqualified. The distinction between qualified and nonqualified equity relates to the taxation of the patronage distributed as equity. Both qualified and nonqualified equity are forms of revolving equity and are similar in terms of the cooperative's capital structure or equity management system.

Because cooperatives distribute profits based on use, and not in proportion to equity ownership, there is little incentive for members to invest equity capital. Open membership cooperatives often create equity out of the profit stream by issuing a portion of patronage in the form of equity. Closed membership cooperatives often link each unit of equity with a usage right. Members hold equity in a closed membership cooperative order to use the cooperative and receive patronage in proportion to their use.

Equity in any firm is risk capital. Equity holders have the right to the residual returns. In other words the owners of any firm have a claim on what is left over after all of the creditors have been paid. When a cooperative is profitable and retains a portion of the profits as equity then the equity value of the cooperative increases. If the cooperative loses money then the equity value of the firm decreases. Lenders like to see a strong equity base because it enhances their collateral position and makes the loan less risky. When a substantial portion of the assets are financed by equity the lender knows that if the cooperative is unable to make the loan commitments and is forced into bankruptcy it is likely that the assets can be sold to generate enough funds to pay off the creditors. The cooperative equity is the basis for its borrowing capacity. Agricultural cooperatives have historically financed between 40% and 50% of their assets with equity.

Direct Investment

Direct investment is equity created when a member makes a cash contribution or investment in exchange for equity. Direct investment is allocated equity since it is held in the names of specific patrons. Direct investment is semi-permanent. It is typically not redeemed by the cooperative until the death of the member. The most common form of direct investment is the membership share of stock that a member must purchase as a condition of joining the cooperative. In an open membership cooperative the membership share is often a nominal amount ranging from $100 to $1,000. In closed membership cooperatives direct investment shares of equity have associated usage rights and members have to purchase shares in proportion to their use of the cooperative. For example, when Dakota Growers Pasta was formed, members bought shares of stock in the cooperative for $3.85 a share. Each share purchased required the member to deliver one bushel of durum wheat each year. The cooperative raised $12.5 million in equity in this manner and secured for itself nearly 3.25 million bushels of durum. For new generation cooperatives, the vast majority of their equity is in the form of direct investment.

Direct investment is usually the only option available to raise the equity to start a cooperative. The equity drive to obtain the direct investment helps to determine if there is enough interest and commitment to establish the cooperative. By raising direct investment the incorporating board can ensure that the cooperative has the proper level of equity. In terms of existing cooperatives, direct investment or membership stock ensures that members have some "skin in the game" before they are granted the right to vote and use the cooperative's assets. As the amount of direct investment is increased, the cooperative has less need to retain profits as equity and can issue higher portion of cash patronage. The major disadvantage of direct investment is that because cooperative profits are distributed in proportion to use, there is no return linked to investment. In an open membership cooperative equity does not appreciate and it cannot be bought and sold. Because of that, members have little interest in investing in cooperative equity. In a closed cooperative, there may be a limited market for the cooperative equity because of the usage rights. Direct investment is not generally a recurring source of equity capital since it takes a special effort to develop an equity drive and that often requires careful compliance with security laws and regulations.

Retained Patronage Refunds

Retained patronage refunds are portions of the net income allocated to members but paid in the form of equity rather than cash. Retained patronage refunds creates allocated equity since it is held in specific patron accounts. Retained patronage refunds is typically revolving equity meaning that it is eventually redeemed for cash by the cooperative at its original face value. Traditional, open membership cooperatives have traditionally raised the majority of their equity through retained patronage refunds.

The advantage of retained patronage from the member's perspectives is that it created from the profit stream and members to not have to make cash investment. Members essentially "earn their way into ownership". Retained patronage is well suited for supply cooperatives and for grain marketing cooperatives. In those instances, producers have other options for purchasing inputs and selling their commodities. While they might be interested in joining the cooperative in order to be eligible for patronage, they are unlikely to make a large up front direct investment. Retained patronage is a systematic method for the cooperative to build equity and one that it is relatively painless for the member.

The disadvantage of retained patronage from the cooperative's standpoint is that it is dependent upon the profitability of the cooperative. If the cooperative has a loss year the equity value of the cooperative is reduced. That creates a need for more equity but the cooperative obviously cannot created retained patronage equity until it is profitable. The revolving fund aspect of retained patronage also creates challenges for the cooperative board of directors. When they redeem equity the cooperative is using cash and also reducing (destroying) equity. That creates the need to create more equity and cash through retained patronage. Revolving equity creates a complex balancing act for the board of directors. Another disadvantage of retained patronage and revolving equity is that members may expect the cooperative to revolve equity regardless of its financial condition. Members only realize value for the share of profits distributed in the form of equity when that equity is redeemed for cash. That causes members to want the cooperative to revolve equity as rapidly as possible and to keep the revolving cycle constant or increasing.

Per Unit Capital Retains

Per unit capital retains, also called per unit retains, are equity that is deducted from the member's commodity payment for each unit of commodity handled. Some marketing cooperative operate as pooling cooperatives. All of the commodity delivered by the patrons are pooled and then processed, packaged and marketed by the cooperative. The patrons often receive an intermediate payment to cover their production expense and then receive a final distribution when all of the commodity is sold and the pool is closed. While one can think of the intermediate payment as a commodity payment and the final payment as patronage there is really no dividing line because there is no defined price for the commodity. Pooling cooperative therefore do not have patronage and cannot make retained patronage distributions (stock patronage). The per-unit retain is an alternative means for the cooperative to create equity. Per-unit retains differ from retained patronage in that they are based solely on the units of commodity handled and not on profits.

Per unit retains create a stable source of equity for the cooperative since they are not based on profitability. The disadvantage of per unit retains from the member's standpoint is that the cooperative deducts equity even when commodity prices are low. Some members may also feel that the stable source of equity, regardless of profitability, places less pressure on the cooperative to operate profitably and efficiently. Because per unit retains are deducted from the commodity payment, some members perceive that the cooperative is not price competitive. Per unit retains creates allocated equity and it can be allocated as either qualified or nonqualified equity. They are taxed in a similar way to patronage refunds except that a cooperative issuing qualified per unit retains does not have the requirement of issuing at least 20% cash patronage, which is a requirement for qualified patronage refunds.

Unallocated Equity

Unallocated equity, also called unallocated retained earnings is a general reserve fund that is collectively owned by the members but not individually owned. As the name implies unallocated equity is unallocated and it is the only permanent category of equity in a cooperative since it is never revolved or returned to the members. One of the purposes of unallocated equity is to create a reserve fund that can be reduced if the cooperative experiences a loss. In the absence of unallocated equity the cooperative would have to write down the value of the member's stock in any year that a loss occurred. If the cooperative returned to profitability new retained equity would be created but the value of the stock that was written down would not change. Stock write downs create a member communication challenges and also lead to confusion among members as to the value of their allocated equity. Unallocated equity is often created from the profits on non-member business. In that case, it is logical since non-member profits cannot be allocated to patrons and the cooperative must always pay tax on those profits.

A more controversial source of unallocated equity is when a portion of member profits are retained as unallocated equity. The disadvantage of retained member profits as unallocated equity (from the member perspective) is that unallocated equity are never revolved by the cooperative and the member never receives those profits. If a cooperative is liquidated, the residual value of the firm, after all creditors are paid, is distributed to members in proportion to past use during some defined "look back periods", typically around 6 years. Active members therefore still have a claim on the assets funded by unallocated equity. However, once a member becomes inactive they eventually leave behind any claim on the unallocated equity. High levels of unallocated equity can therefore create an incentive for members to liquidate a cooperative in order to capture the value of the unallocated equity. That phenomenon is know as "demutualization". High levels of unallocated equity are rarely the direct cause for members to vote for liquidation, but it can be a contributing factor.

Unallocated equity reduces the member's return from the cooperative since the profits retained as unallocated equity are never returned to the member. It therefore violates the principle of distributing profits in proportion to use. It may also reduce the member's sense of ownership in the cooperative since it is not reflected in the stock amounts held in the owners name. Despite those facts the portion of unallocated equity in agricultural cooperatives has been increasing. According to USDA cooperative statistics, allocated equity represented approximately 60% of cooperative equity in 2017 with 40% being unallocated. Many boards of directors are attracted to retaining profits as unallocated equity since it avoids the need for future equity redemption payments.

Preferred Stock

Most cooperative bylaws permit the cooperative to sell preferred stock to either members or non-members. Preferred stock owners do not have voting rights. If the cooperative is liquidated, the preferred stock holders have a claim on the residual value ahead of the common stockholders. That is the origin of the term 'preferred". There is typically no market for preferred stock in a cooperative and, as we know, cooperative profits are distributed based on use, not stock ownership. Because of those facts, cooperative preferred stock typically carries a dividend rate. The maximum dividend is often limited by law to 8%. The board has discretion not to pay the dividend if the cooperative does not have the financial resources. That is what makes preferred stock equity and not debt. However, the board cannot pay patronage unless the preferred dividends have been paid. Because there is no public market for cooperative preferred stock, cooperative typically establish some system where members can petition the board to have the preferred stock redeemed.

In recent years, some progressive cooperative have redeemed revolving equity by converting it to preferred stock. The effect is that after some period of time, the cooperative begins to pay dividends on patron equity. That can be beneficial to the cooperative since they don't have to expend the cash to revolve the equity (only to make the dividend payment). Many members may also be happy to hold the equity since they are receiving a dividend. The cooperative can also use the profits from non-member business to pay the dividend payment. The preferred stock dividend is often higher than the cooperative's interest rate. It is therefore not a cost effective alternative for the cooperative, but since the funds are going to members and to outside lenders it may still be considered to be in the member's interest.

Nonmember Sources of Equity

One limitation of the cooperative business model is that it generally does not lend itself to raising capital from nonmember investors. Cooperatives can sell preferred stock to non-members. As mentioned previously the dividends on cooperative equity are often limited to 8% either by law or by the cooperative's bylaws. In low interest rate periods of time cooperative preferred stock could be attractive to nonmembers. However when interest rate rise investors have alternative investment choices which would be considered lower risk and providing a higher rate of return. Regional cooperatives are able to justify the security registration costs and issue preferred stock that is publically traded on stock exchanges. Local cooperatives cannot justify that process which means that there is no formal market for their preferred stock. That makes the preferred stock an illiquid investment which also limits the interest from nonmember investors.

The hybrid member-investor cooperative form has two classes of members. Investor members receive a share of profits based on their ownership while user members receive a share of profits based on patronage. That creates a direct incentive for nonmember investment and addresses some of the limitation in raising nonmember equity. However, unless the cooperative is large enough to afford to register with the Security Exchange Commission there will probably not be a formal market for the investor member stock. The investor members may also be concerned that the user members will manipulate the price paid for commodities or charged for inputs such that the users benefit while reducing the profits paid to the investors. For those reasons, the member-investor model has not been particularly successful as a vehicle for attracting nonmember investment.

Classification of Cooperative Equity			
	Allocated or Unallocated	Revolving, semi-permanent or permanent	Qualified or non-qualified
Direct investment	Allocated	Semi-permanent	NA
Retained patronage	Allocated	Revolving	Can be either
Per Unit Retains	Allocated	Revolving	Can be either
Preferred stock	Allocated	Semi-permanent	NA
Unallocated Retained Earnings	Unallocated	Permanent	NA

Equity Redemption

Equity redemption is the process of returning cash to members who had been previously issued equity patronage. Equity redemption is unique to cooperatives. Because cooperatives distribute profits in proportion to use there is no direct rationale for holding equity. Because of that there is no market for cooperative equity. (The exception would be if the cooperative equity has an associated usage right.) Because cooperative equity typically has no market value, the cooperative must establish a system to eventually redeem the equity for cash. It is only through equity redemption that the member realized any benefit from the patronage distributed as equity. Due to the time value of money the member's return is increased when the cooperative revolves equity more rapidly. Shorter equity revolving periods reduce the cooperative's cash flow and thus create another tradeoff between the cooperative's financial stability and member benefit. The process of equity redemption, or equity management is also important to keep the member's investment proportional to their use of the cooperative. If a cooperative fails to revolve equity or has a long equity revolving period, many older members may have high equity balances but have slowed or discontinued use of the cooperative. Those members are over-invested in the cooperative. On the other hand, younger members may be using the cooperative but have relatively little equity and hence be underinvested. Ideally, a cooperative board would like to manage equity so that equity investment is roughly proportional to use. Failing to redeem equity reduces the member's return from the cooperative and also results in members perceiving little or no value on stock patronage. State statues generally require a cooperative to redeem equity if the patron dies. A systematic system of equity redemption therefore helps the cooperative to avoid the unpredictable timing of estate settlements.

Equity Redemption Systems

For the reasons just mentioned, equity redemption is important to maintain the member's return from the cooperative, to help keep equity in proportion to use and to eliminate unpredictable outflows to estates. On the other hand, equity redemption reduces the cooperative's cash flow and also reduces equity which increases its debt to equity ratio. Equity redemption is therefore a complex balancing act for the cooperative board of directors. An equity redemption system is an established plan for redeeming equity. Most cooperative have systematic systems which include age of stock, age of patron, percentage of all equities and base capital. The cooperative can also have a nonsystematic program such as having members petition for equity redemption in the case of hard ship. Estate settlements are also often categorized as a non-systematic program.

Factors Affecting the Choice of Equity Redemption Systems

Cooperative boards consider a number of factors when selecting an equity redemption system.

- They would like the system to be fair to members. In general, that means that the system keeps equity investment proportional to the use of the capital. It is logical that cooperatives that are using the cooperative to a greater extent should have higher levels of equity investment and that the cooperative should redeem the equities of inactive or low volume members.
- The equity management system should encourage members to contribute equity or at least support the structures which create equity. Members are more likely to support equity management systems that redeem equity more rapidly and on a consistent basis.
- The cooperative needs to consider if it has the cash flow to support the plan. A cooperative needs a high level of profits to be able to consistently revolve equity under a rapid cycle. A cooperative's profit and cash flow also change year-to-year due to weather and other conditions. The cooperative board must consider if the equity redemption system provides enough flexibility for the cooperative to adjust redemption payments according to available funds.

- Local cooperatives would like the equity management system to be compatible with that of the federated cooperative. When the local cooperative receives patronage from the regional cooperative that patronage is a combination of cash and regional cooperative stock. That become part of the local cooperative's profits which are passed on to members in a combination of cash and stock. In essence the cooperative is issuing stock patronage to the members some of which is really pass through stock patronage from the regional cooperative. The local cooperative already faces cash flow issues if the cash and stock percentage does not match that of the regional cooperative. The same issue occurs when the local cooperative redeems equity. If the local cooperative redeems equity more rapidly than the regional cooperative then it is issuing its members cash for regional equity which it is still holding on the balance sheet. Similar problems occur if the local cooperative is on a different equity management system relative to the regional cooperative.
- Fifth, and finally, the cooperative would like the equity redemption system to meet the requirement of the lenders. The cooperative's creditors require it to maintain a minimum equity to asset ratio and also a minimum cash balance. Redeeming equity reduces both cash and equity. Equity redemption programs that are not tied to the cooperative's financial condition can therefore hinder a cooperative's ability to repay loans and limit future borrowing ability. Ideally, the cooperative board would develop an equity redemption budget that is based on the cooperative's financial situation. They would then apply that budget to the specific equity management program. In reality, some types of equity management systems are more compatible with the concept of a redemption budget relative to others.

Age of Stock (Revolving Fund)

Under an age of stock plan, also called a revolving fund, the cooperative redeems the oldest equity on a first-in, first out basis. For example if the cooperative was on a ten year age of stock plan it would redeem the equity that it issued in 2009 in the year 2019. Cooperatives using an age of stock plan can attempt to maintain a fixed revolving schedule or can accelerate or slow the cycle according the financial condition of the cooperatives. Cooperatives can also revolve part of a year or multiple years. For example if the cooperative was very profitable in 2009 and issues a large amount of stock patronage they might have to revolve that year over a 2 or 3 year period. At other times they might have the funds to revolve two or three previous years in a single year.

Illustration of an Age of Stock (revolving fund) Plan				
Year	Beginning equity	Patronage refund retained	Amount redeemed	Years redeemed
1	0	500	0	
2	500	500	0	
3	1000	500	0	

4	1500	500	500	1
5	1500	1000	100	2 and 3
6	1500	500	500	4

Percentage of all Equities

Under the percentage of all equity system the cooperative redeems a percentage of every patron's equity balance each year. The board would establish the percentage based on the financial condition and balance sheet goals for the cooperative. For example the cooperative might consider how much new equity is was creating through equity patronage and establish a percentage to redeem such that the total equity in the cooperative remained constant. The percentage of all equities programs rewards new members because every member with an equity balance receives some redemption. One problem with the percentage of all equities program is that it delays the time for a new, under invested member to build equity in proportion with their use. Some rural electric cooperatives use a percentage of all equities programs because they feel it helps new members understand how the equity system will work. When the new member receives a small redemption payment after one year, they may see how the redemption payments will increase as they build equity. The percentage of all equities program never completely retires equity since the member only receives a portion of the balance each year. It therefore often needs to be combined with some sort of lump sum payment to close out the balance.

Illustration of Percentage of All Equities Program

Beginning Equity	2000
Retained Patronage	500
Equity Available	2500
Target level of Equity	2300
Equity to be Redeemed (2500- 2300)	200
Redemption Percentage (200/2000) Redemption divided by beginning balance	10%

Age of Member

Under an age of member system, the member has all of their revolving equity redeemed when they reach the specified trigger age. Some cooperative specialist describe the age of member system as a systematic program since it establishes a plan for revolving equity. Some classify as a non-systematic program since an individual member only receives a redemption when a specific even (achieving the trigger age) occurs. Many agricultural cooperatives were formed in the 1930's and 1940's. Their memberships tended to be young farmers who saw the need for the cooperative and were content to build equity to fund the cooperative's growth. The concept that the equity would be redeemed when they reached a retirement age was acceptable. Now that those cooperatives have matured, many of them struggle with the cash flow and equity implications of their age of patron systems. A high percentage of their memberships are now nearing the redemption trigger age creating challenges in meeting the redemption cash flows. Members also often come to expect redemption at a specified age to be a right or a contractual obligation of the cooperative. That makes it very difficult for the board to adjust the trigger age to manage redemptions within a specified budget.

Base Capital

The base capital system is conceptually very simple but can be complex to implement. Under the base capital system the patron's percentage of the total equity in the cooperative is matched with the patron's percentage of the cooperative's business volume. In other words, a patron that did 5% of the cooperative business would be required to hold 5% of the cooperative's equity. Underinvested members have to invest more equity while over invested members receive equity redemption. The base capital system is therefore the best system for keeping equity investment in proportion to use. A base capital system is not attractive to new members since they would have to make an immediate investment to bring their equity balance up to the required level. A beginning farmer may not have the funds to invest the equity required under a base capital system.

In practice, many cooperative using base capital do not require an under invested member to make a direct investment but instead eliminate their cash patronage until they build the required equity level. Because those cooperative do not instantaneously receive equity from under invested members they also cannot instantaneously redeem the equity of over invested members. They therefore do not keep equity in exact proportion to use but keep equity balances adjusting towards that level.

Illustration of Base Capital Plan

Member	Beginning equity	Patronage (5 year average)	Share of business	Equity Obligation	Over invested (-redemption) or under invested +paid in
A	1685 (9.2%)	120,208	11%	2035	-$350
B	3345 (18.3%)	207,631	19%	3515	-$170
C	2805 (15.4%)	152,991	14%	2590	+$215
D	5515 (30.2%)	327,839	30%	5550	-$35
E	4550 (24.9%)	284,127	26%	4810	-$260
F	350 (0%)	==	—	0	0
TOTAL	18250	1,092,796	100%	18250	$0

Nonsystematic Methods

A nonsystematic plan, also called a specialized plan, is one where equity is redeemed only if a special situation occurs. One special situation, that has already been mentioned, is the death of the member. Less frequent situations would be when the member moves away or is in a hardship situation. Aside from estate settlements which are often required by statute, cooperative board consider special situations on a case by case basis. Relying on a nonsystematic system would have a low financial burden for the cooperative. However, they provide a poor financial return to members and result in unpredictable cash outflows. They also do a poor job of keeping equity in proportion to use. Nonsystematic or specialized systems generally do not meet any of the goals of a desirable equity management system. They tend to occur as the end result of not implementing a systematic program.

Advantages and Disadvantages of Equity Redemption Systems

System	Advantages	Disadvantages
Age of Stock (revolving fund)	Easy to understand, moderately proportional if revolving period is short, easy to match to the budget by extending or shortening the revolving period	Length of revolving period tends to creep upward and members place low value on stock if revolving period is long
Percentage of all Equities	Rewards new members, easy to understand	New members are already underinvested and percentage redemptions expand the time period for them to become adequately invested
Base Capital	Most Proportion, only method that forces under invested members to contribute additional capital	Difficult to explain and complex to implement, new members may be unable to meet equity obligations
Age of Member	Seemed logical when new cooperatives were being formed and all members were young and a similar age, Some cooperatives sell the concept as retirement income	Not attractive to young producers, difficult to manage within a redemption budget, members expect redemption regardless of cooperative's financial condition

Alternatives to Redemption

While redeeming revolving equity is the method by which a member receives value for their stock patronage, it does create management challenges for the cooperative board. It is also difficult to design an equity management program that is attractive to the members and meets the cooperative's needs for financial stability. Cooperatives have experimented with alternatives to equity redemption.

Redemption at a Discounted Rate

Under certain circumstances, some cooperative have redeemed a member's equity before they would have otherwise received a payment but redeemed the equity at a discounted rate. In essence they paid the member the present value of the equity and not the future value. One situation for discounted redemption would be when a member of a cooperative with an age of stock program dies. In that case the estate could wait and receive the equity over a number of years as each year of stock becomes eligible. In order to close the estate, the executor may ask if the cooperative could pay the future redemption payments immediately but at a discounted rate to reflect the time value of money. If the equity balance is not large the cooperative may be interesting in complying in order to simplify recordkeeping.

Establishing a fair discount rate for discounted redemptions can be difficult and some members do not understand the concept of the time value of money and may consider the payment unfair. Most cooperatives describe the face value of the retained patronage as a benefit flowing to the member. They are therefore reluctant to discuss the present value of the revolving equity since it would be perceived as diminishing the value of stock patronage. A cooperative that was implementing discounting would obviously want to carefully specify the procedures and limitations in the bylaws or policies since it would not have the funds to retire everyone equity.

Conversion to Preferred Stock

One alternative to redemption is to convert the equity to a dividend-paying preferred stock. That reduces the cooperative's immediate cash outflow and the member may be content to hold the equity since they receive dividend payments. Unless the dividends can be paid with non-member profits the cooperative is reducing patronage based profit distribution to distribute a portion of profits to the preferred stock holders. The cooperative must also establish some system to eventually redeem the preferred stock or allow it to be sold to another member. Otherwise they will eventually have to redeem the equity as an estate settlement.

Exchange of Equity among Members

Closed membership cooperatives often allow members to sell their equity an associated usage rights to another eligible producer. The price for the equity is negotiated between buyer and seller although the cooperative board typically has to approve that the buyer is eligible for membership. Under that structure the value for the equity and usage rights is determined by the anticipated amount of future patronage. It therefore tracks the profitability of the cooperative. The possibility of exchange between members creates the potential for cooperative equity to appreciate in value. It also increases its liquidity since a member may have the opportunity to sell it at any time. Of course by selling the equity the member loses the right to use the cooperative. Also, since the exchange is limited to other qualifying members the market for the equity might be thin and not result in a fair price.

A few open membership cooperatives have experimented with equity exchange between members. Similar to the concept of discounting, a member who desires immediate redemption could sell his equity to another member at a privately negotiated discounted rate. Again, another problem is that the market for the equity is thin. The member purchasing the equity also bears the risk that the cooperative expands the revolving period or writes down the value of the equity due to a loss.

REFERENCES

1. "Cooperative Banking: Innovations and Developments" edited by Vittorio Boscia, et al. Springer, 2009.
2. "Cooperative Capital: Re-Thinking Democratic Money and Ownership in the Age of Finance Capitalism" by Pat Conaty and Christopher Houghton Budd. New Economics Foundation, 2011.
3. "Cooperative Finance in Developing Countries: The Case of African Countries" by Yitbarek Takele. LAP Lambert Academic Publishing, 2015.
4. "Co-operative Financial Institutions: An Introduction" by Johnston Birchall. Routledge, 2014.
5. "Co-operative Financial Institutions: Issues in Governance, Regulation, and Supervision" edited by R. Varatharaj and A. Sasidharan. New Century Publications, 2011.
6. "Co-operative Financial Institutions: Issues in Governance, Regulation, and Supervision" edited by Gershon Feder and David E. Grosh. World Bank Publications, 2008.
7. "Cooperative Financial Institutions: Issues in Governance, Regulation, and Supervision" by D. Narayana. Routledge, 2018.
8. "Cooperative Microfinance: A Sustainable Alternative for Development" edited by James Copestake, et al. Routledge, 2014.
9. "Financial Cooperatives and Local Development" edited by Alberto Zevi, et al. Palgrave Macmillan, 2020.
10. "The Co-operative Advantage: Creating Shared Value in Financial Services" by Johnston Birchall and Szilvia Borbáth. Edward Elgar Publishing, 2018.

4 COMMUNITY ENTERPRISE DEVELOPMENT

INTRODUCTION

Community enterprise development focuses on fostering economic growth and social well-being within local communities through the establishment and support of businesses and organizations owned and operated by community members. This approach emphasizes collaboration, participation, and sustainability, aiming to address local needs and challenges while harnessing local resources and talents. Key aspects include capacity building, entrepreneurship training, access to finance, and the promotion of inclusive decision-making processes. By empowering communities to take control of their economic destiny, community enterprise development contributes to building resilient, self-reliant, and thriving communities. It serves as a catalyst for local development, job creation, poverty reduction, and the enhancement of community cohesion and resilience.

OVERVIEW OF COMMUNITY ENTERPRISE DEVELOPMENT

Community enterprise development is a multifaceted approach aimed at empowering and supporting communities to establish and manage their own businesses or enterprises for collective benefit. At its core, it embodies principles of local ownership, participation, and sustainability, fostering an environment where communities take charge of their economic destinies. Central to this process is community engagement, involving active participation of local residents in all stages of enterprise development. Through inclusive decision-making processes, community members identify needs, set goals, and determine the direction of their entrepreneurial endeavors. This ensures that enterprises are rooted in the realities and aspirations of the community, leading to greater relevance and ownership.

Moreover, community enterprise development prioritizes capacity building, providing community members with the necessary skills, knowledge, and resources to initiate, manage, and sustain enterprises successfully. This may involve training programs, mentorship, and access to technical assistance, equipping individuals with the tools they need to navigate the complexities of entrepreneurship. By investing in human capital, communities can unlock their full potential and seize opportunities for economic advancement.

Resource mobilization is another critical aspect of community enterprise development, as it involves facilitating access to financial capital, infrastructure, and networks necessary to establish and grow enterprises. This may entail forging partnerships with financial institutions, philanthropic organizations, and government agencies to secure funding and support. By leveraging external resources while also tapping into local assets and networks, communities can overcome barriers to entry and scale their enterprises more effectively.

Market analysis plays a pivotal role in guiding community enterprise development efforts, helping communities identify viable business opportunities that align with their resources, skills, and market demand. Through thorough research and assessment, communities can identify niche markets, assess competition, and develop strategies to position their enterprises for success. By understanding the needs and preferences of their target audience, communities can tailor their products or services to meet market demand, thereby increasing their competitiveness and profitability.

Furthermore, networking and collaboration are essential elements of community enterprise development, as they enable communities to tap into external expertise, resources, and opportunities. By forging partnerships with other organizations, businesses, and stakeholders, communities can access valuable insights, mentorship, and market linkages that can accelerate their enterprise development efforts. Collaboration also fosters collective action and solidarity, enabling communities to tackle common challenges and achieve shared goals more effectively.

Sustainability lies at the heart of community enterprise development, as it entails promoting business models that are environmentally sustainable, socially responsible, and economically viable in the long term. By adopting practices that minimize environmental impact, promote social inclusion, and generate sustainable profits, communities can build resilient enterprises that contribute to long-term prosperity and well-being.

In conclusion, community enterprise development offers a holistic approach to economic empowerment, enabling communities to harness their collective potential and drive sustainable development from within. By fostering local ownership, participation, and sustainability, community enterprise development empowers communities to create thriving businesses that not only generate economic value but also foster social cohesion, resilience, and self-reliance. Through strategic investments in capacity building, resource mobilization, market analysis, networking, and collaboration, communities can unlock opportunities for inclusive growth and prosperity, ensuring a brighter future for generations to come.

Community Enterprise Development process

At Community Owned Enterprises, our primary objective is to build stronger regional and remote communities. We do this by identifying and creating enterprise opportunities, then work in close collaboration with local leaders, to facilitate the development of community operated, and ultimately owned, enterprises.

We take a unique approach to enterprise development, our 5 Step Process is outlined below:

1. Identification & Approval of Concept

The initial stage of the Enterprise Development process involves our Enterprise Development team working closely with key stakeholders in regional and remote communities to identify potential opportunities.

Enterprise opportunities typically present as either locally grown business ideas or via an upcoming tender opportunity that can be facilitated by local community members. All enterprise opportunity concepts go through a detailed screening and approval process to assess viability.

If the opportunity concept is approved, our Enterprise Development team prepare a full business plan, which is reviewed before being approved to proceed, or declined.

Key Operational Objectives

- Identify viability and potential sustainability of proposed enterprise
- Identify if proposed enterprise aligns with Community Owned Enterprises' Strategic Plan
- Identify alignment to Community Owned Enterprises' Core Values
- Identify level of community support
- Identify potential for community & individual empowerment
- Identify existing market conditions

2. Enterprise Development

Once a sustainable business model is approved by Community Owned Enterprises, in close collaboration with local leaders, our Enterprise Development Team commence the Enterprise Development phase of the process. Here we work to develop and understand the vision/ goals of the business, and establish critical relationships with potential contractors, suppliers, stakeholders, service providers and customers.

Creating a business strategy, registering a business name and developing an appropriate logo to represent the business would also be undertaken at this time. The Enterprise Development Team work to arrange business essentials; establishing partnership & lease agreements, setting up bank accounts, sourcing funding, developing operational systems and processes. The final critical component coordinated at this time, is the recruitment and training of local employees to work within the enterprise.

Key Operational Objectives

- Understand business vision, goals & objectives
- Establish critical relationships
- Develop business strategy
- Source business essentials
- Recruit & train local employees to work within the enterprise
- Implement start-up processes

3. Enterprise Operation

Upon completion of the Enterprise Establishment Phase, we move into actively operating the enterprise. The Enterprise Development Team coordinates all facets of business management, ensuring the enterprise's operations align to the business plan objectives and day-to-day contract obligations are being met.

Throughout this phase, the Enterprise Development Team also focus heavily on building the capacity of staff to ensure they have the skills and knowledge required to successfully complete their role within the enterprise. At this time, any stand-out employees are identified as potential future owners of the enterprise.

Key Operational Objectives

- Cement relationships with staff, partners, stakeholders and contractors
- Positive employee engagement and capacity building
- Identify business growth opportunities
- Resources and supplies are maintained
- Administration procedures are adhered to
- Inventory is managed effectively

4. Building Capacity of Employees

Building the capacity of the enterprise and its employees is at the core of Community Owned Enterprises' service model.

The first step we take in building capacity is to undertake a Skills Gap Analysis of both the enterprise itself and the employees working within the enterprise. This allows us to understand what critical skills are required in order for the enterprise to continue being viable once the ownership transition phase is implemented.

Any missing skills or qualifications that are identified throughout the Skills Gap Analysis will form the foundation of a Development Plan. This simple model ensures the Development Plan is tailored to both the business and individual employees working within the enterprise.

Key Operational Objectives

- Complete Skills Gap Analysis of enterprise and employees
- Create Development Plans for employees who show business ownership potential
- Employees commence implementing their Development Plans – learning new skills to be used to enhance the functionality of the enterprise
- Once employees have completed their Development Plans, the enterprise's future owner/s are identified.

5. Ownership Transition

Once the operational processes are established, staff are fully trained and the enterprise is functioning effectively, work can commence to prepare for transition. The Enterprise Manager will identify that the business has potential to transition and present the case to Community Owned Enterprise's General Manager for assessment. Enterprises being assessed for transition will require financial statements as well as a full transition plan. Once transition has been approved, a transition handover checklist must be completed.

Key Operational Objectives

- Identify potential for transition phase to commence
- Provide financial statements and a full transition plan for assessment
- Approve or decline ownership transition
- If approved, transfer business name, assets, leases, suppliers, credit applications into name of the employee who has been identified as the future owner
- Identify level of support required with regard to back-end services: Payroll, HR, WH&S, Marketing and/or Finance
- Connect enterprise new owner/s with assisting intermediaries including Indigenous Business Australia & Many Rivers

Key Components of a Community Development Project

A community development project aims to improve the well-being, social cohesion, and economic opportunities of a specific community or group of people. Successful community development projects require careful planning, collaboration, and a focus on sustainable solutions.

Here are some key components that are crucial for the success of such projects:

- ***Needs Assessment*:** Conducting a thorough needs assessment is the first step in understanding the challenges and opportunities within the community. It involves gathering data, engaging with community members, and identifying their priorities, strengths, and areas for improvement.
- ***Community Engagement*:** Active involvement and participation of community members throughout the project are essential. Engage them in the decision-making process, solicit feedback, and ensure their voices are heard and respected.
- ***Clear Objectives and Goals*:** Establish clear and measurable objectives for the project. Define what the project aims to achieve and set specific, achievable, relevant, time-bound (SMART) goals.
- ***Project Planning*:** Create a comprehensive project plan that outlines the steps, timelines, and resources needed to achieve the project's objectives. This plan should take into account potential risks and challenges and include strategies to mitigate them.
- ***Collaboration and Partnerships*:** Community development projects often involve multiple stakeholders, such as local government agencies, non-profit organizations, businesses, and residents. Building strong partnerships can bring diverse expertise, resources, and support to the project.
- ***Capacity Building*:** Empower community members by providing training and support to develop skills, knowledge, and leadership abilities. Capacity building helps the community take ownership of the project and ensures its long-term sustainability.
- ***Resource Mobilization*:** Identify and secure funding and resources required to implement the project. This could include grants, donations, government funding, or in-kind contributions from partners.

- ***Implementation and Monitoring***: Execute the project according to the established plan, and regularly monitor progress towards the defined goals. This allows for timely adjustments and ensures the project stays on track.
- ***Evaluation and Learning***: Assess the impact and effectiveness of the project upon completion. Learn from both successes and challenges, and use this knowledge to improve future community development initiatives.
- ***Sustainability and Exit Strategy***: Plan for the long-term sustainability of the project beyond its initial implementation phase. Develop an exit strategy to ensure that the benefits of the project continue even after direct involvement ends.
- ***Cultural Sensitivity***: Respect and consider the cultural norms, values, and beliefs of the community. Cultural sensitivity fosters trust and enhances the relevance and acceptance of the project.
- ***Communication and Transparency***: Maintain open and transparent communication with all stakeholders. Regularly update the community on progress, challenges, and decision-making processes.
- ***Social Inclusivity***: Ensure that the project is inclusive and considers the needs and perspectives of all community members, including vulnerable and marginalized groups.
- ***Environmental Considerations***: Address any potential environmental impacts of the project and promote sustainable practices to minimize negative effects on the environment.

By incorporating these key components, community development projects can have a more significant and lasting positive impact on the targeted communities.

BASIC FUNDAMENTALS AND PRINCIPLES OF COMMUNITY DEVELOPMENT

For every concept, theory, or method, there are certain basic fundamentals that determine its very nature. These facets are referred to as principles and they act as the key identifiers for a concept down to its simplest state. They are similar to the materials that are used in the construction of a building; the building blocks that individually play a role in the overall structure and function of the final product. Analysis of these principles can offer a person further insight into the concept they are trying to understand. Key principles that feed into the structural design of community development. Understanding each piece will provide further understanding of the concept as a whole, as each one is necessary for the process to be successful. Those listed in this are the major principles that have the most significant purpose, although there may be smaller, less frequently applicable principles that are present when the process is used. In those cases, those additional principles will be pertinent to the specific situation and its circumstances instead. Thus, the larger presence of those discussed here will mean that they will be applicable for all instances of community development.

Empowerment

From a psychological standpoint, people are more likely to do things that they are motivated to do so and feel like they have come level of control over their actions. Not only does this give them the sensation and satisfaction that what they are doing is of their own free will, but that their actions actually have some value in the long run. This empowerment acts as a motivator in society and it holds a great deal of importance in community development. Members of a community who are empowered to take action for improvements are going to have genuine cause to do so, rather than because they were told to by others.

As a key principle of community development, empowerment often is what prompts things to get done in the first place. There needs to be a reason for people to want to improve things in their community for themselves and others; it can't just be a facet of social or public duty. Empowerment is a powerful motivator because of it, as there is usually a personal source involved. Newer models of empowerment suggest that it is not a feeling that causes people to act, but rather evidence from their surroundings that influence them. Parents, for example, typically want their children to be able to be safe as often as possible-regardless of if it's at home, at school, or just walking down the street to the local playground. If there is something within their surroundings that prevents or otherwise impedes upon their children's safety, the parents will make attempts to remedy the situation. Their own children do not necessarily have to directly be in danger, as even the possibility of a threat to their child's safety is enough to raise some parent's concerns in most cases. Those who see that something is missing or lacking in their surroundings, regardless of the degree that they are impacted by it, will often be empowered to do something about it.

Character and Appearance

While some may think that focusing on the physical appearance of something can be rather shallow, principles of character and appearance are actually important components of community development. Many communities and neighborhoods have a distinct appearance and sensory association that are clear identifiers for them. These features set the tone within the community and are a strong influence for the community's public reputation. Since many people who are active participants in community development have a clear visualization of what they want for their community, things like character and appearance are incredibly important.

The character-the overall sense of a place-of a community is typically set and introduced through the appearance of the community. It's an ingrained habit-or an instinct, in some instances-for people to judge or come to a conclusion about something based on a quick observation. A community will have a positive or a negative association attached to it based on what people perceive about it, and that can impact things like how residents and members view or care about it, the resources available, and what influences those resources to be there in the first place. Resources, like new businesses, are not going to make themselves available in communities that have a poor sense of character where they may not be able to sustain themselves long enough to have an impact.

Inclusion and Diversity

Many people have heard about inclusion and diversity in recent years as individual topics. Their growing involvement in society and their connection to each other make them necessary parts of successful community development. Diversity typically refers to the traits present in a group-gender, race, socioeconomic status, religion, political views, etc.-and it's a term that almost everyone is familiar with in some way. The world is a very diverse place, so it's not uncommon for a single community to have a fairly healthy level of diversity even when the group at large is built upon a specific focus or interest. Everything in a community needs to be addressed during the community development process, so it's important to pay attention to even the smallest degree of diversity in a community.

Inclusion, however, is not a term that everyone is familiar with. From a social or community-based perspective, inclusion is best defined as actions taken to make sure that everyone is equally valued and has equal access to resources. It's basically a way to put everyone in a community on a level playing field, regardless of what it is that makes them different from their peers. One of the main points behind community development is to make improvements for those within the community; it doesn't make a lot of sense if those improvements only benefit certain people while putting others at a great disadvantage in the process. It would be like giving instructions to a crowd, but you're whispering instead of shouting or talking loudly. Those closest to you are probably going to pick up on what you're telling them to do, but those furthest away are going to have no idea what is going on.

Planning and Preparation

Since community development is a process that can get rather complicated based on the circumstances, planning and preparation are key principles necessary for it to work. The instigators of community development need to be able to take a look at what they want to do and how they want to do it. It's not an easy task to enact widespread changes, so careful consideration and preparation are required to make sure that all needs are being addressed and that there are legitimate reasons behind the actions being taken. The process is a long one, and there's often quite a bit that needs to be done in order to accomplish a single goal.

As one of the key principles, planning and preparation can be greatly beneficial to the community as it goes through the process of community development. The changes made are going to be significant, and there's a good chance that there may be some difficulty adjusting to them within the community. Planning things out gives those within the community a chance to acclimate to the new situation and offers opportunities for feedback to be given to those leading the changes before moving on to the next step. It can also allow a community to gather the necessary resources for changes to be made, especially if those resources have certain requirements for access (e.g. funding). Since there's little possibility that the process will be perfect, planning and preparation can help provide a community with a bit of a safety net against problems and errors.

Collaboration and Participation

Like its name suggests, community development isn't really something that is done on an individual level or by a single person. In order for it to actually accomplish something, the members of the community itself need to get involved and work together. As mentioned before, it can take a lot of work to implement the desired improvements through community development so it's best not to do it alone. Collaboration helps bring together people of different backgrounds who may have access to different resources that can be of benefit to the community. Each person also has a role that they play within the community, thus it is likely that they will each have a role to play in the process of community development. The interactions that occur through the collaborative efforts of community development can help bolster leaders and the skills they are using to guide the community through the process.

Participation, on its own, is a necessary component of community development in that it helps support the community members involved as they make decisions. It's not just their peers and leaders that they're supporting during the process by participating, but their own decisions as a member of the community. Participation allows a person to exert any influence they have in that moment during the process-they're able to offer input and provide feedback on things that are going to directly impact them as a member of the community. This can tie together with empowerment as well, as the two principles will often feed into one another during the process.

Awareness

To be fair, it's hard to take action to improve upon something if you are unaware that something needs improvement in the first place. Awareness is a key principle of community development because it allows communities to identify things like resources and needs within their own space. A potential issue that's causing harm to a community and/or its members isn't going to have a giant sign saying "FIX THIS!" with an arrow pointing at it. Most likely, the problem(s) may not even be initially recognized as problematic until there's a significant enough impact on the community at large. Actively paying attention to things in the community and how they are affecting the community can help catch those issues early on and allow the community development process to handle them effectively. It allows the community to take ownership of their problems when they are aware of it, which can prompt them to take action on their own.

Awareness in the community development process can do more than just identify problems, it can also monitor the progress of the process and the improvements that are implemented. Just as you can't identify a problem if you're not paying attention, the same can be said for the solution to the problem. If the improvement or solution that has been put in place by the process isn't working as it should-it's causing more problems, it's not affecting the right people, etc.-then that can be caught before it causes further issue if the community is actively aware of it.

Transparency and Trust

For anything to work in a community of any type, there needs to be some level of trust and transparency between those involved. This applies to the leadership, those who are participating in the community development process, those who are being directly impacted by improvements, and anyone else in the community who may be indirectly affected. The process can result in major changes in a community, so there can be significant backlash if those implementing the changes are not completely honest about what is being done and why. People become comfortable and use to how things are when that's been the norm for so long; some resistance is going to be expected as people acclimate to the new circumstances, even if it's to their benefit.

As not everyone in the community is going to be able to fully participate or have their say in the community development process, there's going to be a degree of trust placed on those who are actively making decisions. Those in those leadership and decision making positions during the process will need to be transparent in their actions or risk losing that trust. Betraying that trust-especially if the actions taken are not universally beneficial for community members or if they are done in bad faith-can generate more problems in the community and make it difficult for future improvements to be made.

COMMUNITY DEVELOPMENT RELATIONSHIPS TO CORPORATIONS (CDCS)

A community development corporation (CDC) is equally a part of the community development process. Its usage is as common as CBOs and they do have a similar role. Their involvement with community development warrants a further look into CDCs in order to provide information to those who need it.

This article will discuss CDCs and their relation to community development. Topics will include their legal standing, their similarities and differences with CBOs, and what purpose(s) a community may have for them. Information on active CDCs in the U.S. and abroad will also be available.

Community development corporations, or CDCs, are institutionalized non-profits designed to assist communities in any kind of improvement efforts. As a corporation, they tend to have a wider range of services that they can offer to a wider audience. To some degree, CDCs act more like a regular business than a typical non-profit due to the scope of the services they offer and how those services are managed. Many CDCs are associated with government agencies and will work in tandem with them, but they themselves are not government-operated.

The prevalence of individual CDCs has decreased in recent years. It was estimated that there were 4,600 CDCs operating nationally as of 2006, with no clear numbers as to how many were active solely on the state level. Each CDC can have multiple businesses and services under their control, so their reach may be more than what one may expect from only 4,600 operations. Experts state that CDC services are still in high demand due to the economic difficulties in the last decade or so, despite a more accurate count not being conducted since 2006.

CDCs were the byproduct of the Civil Rights movement and Special Impact Program amendment to the Economic Opportunity Act of 1964. The act itself was one of the first federal community development movements since Franklin D. Roosevelt's New Deal of the 1930s, and was specifically designed as an attempt to curb poverty and the issues associated with it. Many CDCs in the early days doubled as activism groups in addition to focusing on community development; the activism interest is still a part of some CDCs to some degree, but it has largely died out.

Operationally, many CDCs have a demographic focus rather than a location-specified base. This means that a single CDC is most likely going to operate in multiple communities that are similar to one another in particular aspects. They will still work to generate improvements in a community or communities, but their efforts will be more directed towards their particular area of interest(s). An example would be a CDC focusing on poverty-stricken families with young children in urban environments. Improvements in those demographics will still use the facets of community development as they are applicable to their efforts.

- **Are They the Same as CBOs?**-Yes and no. CDCs and CBOs are both classified as a type of non-profit organization and they can have similar roles in communities. Technically, CDCs are an amplified version of CBOs that have more power than their smaller counterparts. They both can be set up by members of a community or by existing groups, but many communities seek out existing CDCs rather than develop their own. CDCs are also harder for community members to control due to their independence from the community and outsider status. Most CDCs are also viewed as being tied too closely to government involvement and funding than CBOs, which means that there's quite a bit of criticism associated with them.

Their Legal Standing

CDCs are legally classified as 501(c)(3) non-profit organizations and are licensed as such by the federal government. That status also identifies them by another name, economic development organizations-which is much more applicable as they tend to not be isolated to a particular community. Like any other non-profit organization, this means that they have tax-exempt status and will not have to pay federal taxes in accordance with the law. The formation of a CDC will follow the same steps that a standard non-profit would, as it doesn't have any specialized classifications that make it a separate operation type. The only legal variations that there would be in the creation process would be if there are any extra state requirements or regulations.

As a non-profit, CDCs have all the protections and regulations afforded to them that any other non-profit organization would have. This means that they have to meet all of the requirements for their creation and the must adhere to any and all state and federal laws applicable to non-profits. Failure to do so can cost a CDC it's non-profit status and cause it to face repercussions for its actions. Since most CDCs operate in multiple states at once, there may be rules that apply to one branch but not another based on where they are located. Before a CDC registers to operate or fundraise in a state, they should thoroughly research what requirements there are before officially setting up operations.

Do Communities Need A CDC For Community Development?

Like with CBOs, CDCs are not a requirement for community development, but rather an option available should the community need it. Communities that want to use a CDC have the option to enlist the services of one that is already formed or create their own if they are so inclined. As many who use the services offered by CDCs, deciding to use one depends on what services are available and what the community needs. Finding a CDC, if a community chooses to do so, depends on what is in the area and what area of focus the CDC has. Remember: CDCs often focus their efforts on specific demographics rather than the whole of the community. Just because there is one operating in the area does not mean its services are going to be applicable to what the community wants or needs.

Communities that are actively going through the community development process may be approached by organizations like CDCs that offer assistance. They operate independently so there is a possibility of unsolicited assistance depending on the circumstances. In some cases where a community is not actively engaging in the community development process-whether by their choice not to or their inability to do for whatever reason-a CDC can still offer its services to community members. Most of them are going to be on the look-out for areas where their services are needed the most, even if the community itself is not doing anything to address problems. There is also the possibility that community members may seek out services that are associated with a particular CDC but not be aware of it. Many CDCs have other organizations and businesses that they offer their services through, whether it's through a partnership with that particular organization or because they own the business. In that regard, communities should do some research on what is available to them in their area before they seek out the assistance of a CDC.

National and International CDCs

There are quite a few options available when it comes to CDCs. In addition to the 4,600 nationally operating CDCs in the U.S., there are also international ones that also act domestically in addition to their efforts abroad. In the years since the last count was made of active CDCs, there may be hundreds, if not thousands more currently operating in the country. There is also the possibility of state and local level CDCs that may be available to communities in their operational jurisdictions; a simple internet search of local community development groups will usually turn up some results. There is also the possibility of membership with many of these CDCs, which provides access to certain resources and information that isn't necessarily available publically. Membership requirements are going to vary from group to group, so it's best to check out the rules before submitting an application.

Some of the more well-known and established CDCs, both national and international, include:

- **NCDA-**The National Community Development Association is a Washington, D.C. based group. It's a collective with 400-plus local governments and communities that use their community development services, including housing initiatives and economic development. They've been in operation since the late 1960s and work closely with a lot of federally funded community development programs, like HUD's CDBG program. In addition to their regular services, NCDA offers training conferences in different parts of the country where attendees can learn about new development initiatives that they can use in their own communities.
- **NACEDA-**NACEDA, or the National Alliance of Community Economic Development Associations, is also a collective of 45 multiple governments and communities. It's currently operational in 28 states and Washington, D.C. on the state and local levels. Through its membership, NACEDA

has a network with around 4,000 different non-profits that focus on community development. It doesn't have a specific area of focus in its services, but rather addresses all the elements of community development.

- **NCDS-**In operation for 40 years, the National Community Development Services offer fundraising resources for different community needs. Their focus is on fundraising campaigns specifically, and they offer services that are designed to generate the best results for their clients' efforts. They pride themselves on offering a better return on investment (ROI) for those that use their services. The tactics that they use focus on analyzing all factors involved in community development funding and using strategy to generate the best results.
- **IACD-**The International Association for Community Development is a Scottish-based community development network that operates on a global scale. They are funded by membership fees-which vary based on location and duration (one or three years) for groups and individuals-as well as grants from the Scottish government. It is accredited by the United Nations and takes a sustainable approach that is backed up by practice and experience. As a global group, it has worked in a variety of communities with a wide range of development factors involved. It offers training and educational conferences like the NCDA, but they are often located in the UK and Ireland.
- **NADO-**NADO is the National Association of Development Organizations. In addition to advocating and offering education and training, NADO also does research into community development strategies and resources. Both its operational and research division include multiple affiliate programs on national and state/regional levels. It offers a range of program focuses for community development, with some of its affiliates specializing in certain specialties. NADO has a unique membership system, offering different tiers that grant members different degrees of access to its resources, services, and training. The fees are a bit on the higher end, ranging from $500 to $6000 depending on the level chosen.
- **ADC-**The Association of Defense Communities is a CDC that specializes in services for military communities and communities closely associated with the military (e.g. towns near bases). Based in Washington, D.C., ADC has about 300 communities and organizations affiliated with it since it started in 1976. The unique circumstances that communities face due to military association means that a specialized approach is sometimes needed for community development. The ADC works with those unique features that military communities have in order to ensure that their uniqueness remains. They offer support and specialized services to military members and their families. Because of its military focus, the ADC does collaborate with other programs offered through the U.S. Department of Defense.
- **UEDA-**UEDA or the University Economic Development Association is another specialized group that has been operating since 1976. It focuses on community engagement and development with higher education institutes, and many of its efforts are based in research and resources

development. UEDA's approach is more along the lines of studying and learning about community development, which can make it a valuable informational resource. They host an annual summit in different parts of the country where members can look at current and new community development practices, as well as connect through UEDA's vast network.

MEANINGS OF COMMUNITY MEMBERS TO COMMUNITY DEVELOPMENT

Community development is one of the things in society that can do a lot for people when it's introduced and properly carried out. It is, by design, intended to improve the lives of members in the community that it is implemented in. The goal is for there to be a positive change for the community and its members, which provides flexibility for the details of those changes and the methods used to reach that endgame. It doesn't matter if the changes are massive improvements that have a widespread effect or small alterations that cause a gradual upgrade in particular areas; both are acceptable.

How is it that they benefit from the process, even when the improvements and changes are not being directed specifically at them and their impact is more indirect? There are dozens upon dozens of ways that a person can benefit from community development in their community, through multiple different avenues. This is because each community, and each of its members, are unique and are going to be as varied as the objectives they have in the community development process are.

Some of the major ways that community development can be of value and be beneficial for community members. These are most likely going to be universally applicable to some degree regardless of the circumstances surrounding the community and its members. Keep in mind that the information listed in this article is just a sampling of the ways that community development can be beneficial and should not be treated as a finite list or guarantee.

On A Personal Level

One of the most noticeable and significant ways that a community member may find value in community development is on a personal level. Those who have been directly impacted by the issues present in the community-whether it's in the form of poverty, education, safety, infrastructure, or anything really-are going to personally benefit from any actions taken to remedy those problems. The people in the community ARE the community, so of course any actions taken to improve the conditions within the geographical confines of the space the community occupies will impact them. The effects of community development's impact on a personal level will be different for each member of the community, as people can be impacted differently based on their association with the issues being addressed and their own personal circumstances.

Health

A pretty significant way that residents can benefit and may find value in community development is through the impact it has on their health and well-being. When a person has their life negatively impacted by things in their surroundings-quite possible things that may not be entirely in their control-there's going to be an effect on their mental and physical health. Chronic stress is usually a common response in these cases and it can wreak havoc on a person's health. Mental and physical exhaustion, extended muscle tension, increased heart rate and blood pressure-which can impact cardiovascular health and a person's heart attack risk-gastrointestinal ulcers, raised blood sugar-problematic for diabetics-and reproductive health issues are known side effects of chronic and prolonged stress. Causes of stress within the community can be removed to some degree through community development, such as the introduction of missing but necessary resources.

Community development all tends to identify health issues in the community and attract the appropriate services. A lack of mental health services and resources in a community, for example, tends to put an undue strain on existing resources and can prompt further issues for residents. Organizations like the World Health Organization (WHO) that use community development techniques globally has documented many cases where the introduction of mental health services has greatly improved community conditions, including lessoning social stigma and abuse. Substances abuse, which can have devastating effects on a person and on a community, is often tied to mental health, as many people will attempt to self-medicate with legal and illicit substances. Several studies have supported this, suggesting that community development can be a fantastic way to address and offer solutions to mental health issues within a community, including education and support.

Economically

Since community development often tackles issues related to poverty, many of the improvements target the economic aspects of the community. Actions taken to improve the community's economy and stabilize it, directly or indirectly, are most likely going to have a ripple effect throughout the community. Many attempts to generate character and a positive appearance of the community will often generate business or retail attraction and retention as a byproduct. Communities with a positive reputation are going to attract more attention from potential businesses as a place to open a location at than communities with a negative reputation.

A stable economy in the community means that resources are going to be coming in for the benefit of the community members. Some of those resources can include jobs and skills training, goods and services, financial flow, networking connections, and tourism. This can create an economic base that the community can build upon for further improvements. It doesn't necessarily have to be focused on a single industry or type of business either, as a lack of variety in the economy can lead to stagnation over time. In communities that have become economically stagnant, attracting new business and industry that is different than what is already present can provide a significant boost for the community. Community development can address and seek solutions to any issues that may be impeding the economic aspects of the community, and then provide the community with the tools to maintain any economic improvements that are made.

Safety and Security

One of the values and benefits of community development that many experts tout is that it improves the safety and security within the community. Crime is a serious issue in the United States and community and government leaders are always looking for solutions to decrease the crime rate and improve the safety of citizens. Community development looks at all of the factors and issues that are impeding the community, not just the ones pertinent to the goals the process is trying to achieve. As everything is frequently connected to each other in a community, addressing issues of safety and security is going to be necessary in order to reach those goals and prevent those issues from damaging the efforts made to improve things.

Public safety and security is often considered to be one of the main focal areas for community development organizers. It's often a good indicator of progress, which can help measure the impact and success of improvements as they are being implemented. For members of the community, it's usually a priority concern; this can be especially true for families with children. Improvements in safety within the community will also be one of the more noticeable changes that community members will pick-up on sooner than others. There are tangible effects from improved public safety measures that can be felt quickly, depending on what actions are taken.

Ownership

It's normal for people to have some degree of pride in the community they are a part of; they are invested in what goes on and they want to have a say in things because of the impact it can have on their lives. For members who truly appreciate their community, community development can provide them with a sense of community ownership. The community development process requires engagement with community members in order for it to be successful, which can provide a voice to those who may not have had one before in regards to actions taken by the community. It validates them as members and gives them as a way of having a role within the community without forcing them to take on positions of leadership-which everyone isn't necessarily able to do.

That ownership also provides continuous benefit for the community and its members. By allowing members a voice and a place in the decision making process, they are going to want to make sure that things continue to improve. There's going to be an increased effort in maintaining established positive changes to ensure continued success, which can include people keeping an eye out for new issues that may spring up. In that regard, it can help protect the community from things that can cause harm or otherwise impede its progress. Community ownership also generates feedback for the benefit of the community as a whole, so there's a continuous discussion and flow of information being used to address matters. There's a degree of trust that develops when there's open dialog in a community, which is going to have its own benefits for the community and its members so long as it's maintained.

Leadership

Some of the changes that are made through the community development process are going to impact the community's structure and leadership. Occasionally, that's where the problems that need to be addressed are located to begin with and improvements there can cause results to spread through to other areas the community. A feature of the process identifies and develops effective leaders within the community, whether they were in a position of leadership beforehand or not. Efficient leaders found through community development are more likely to have an authentic following, as they tend to prove that they are invested in the community and are paying attention to the needs of its members. There is more trust and accountability with such leaders, and this provides a mutual benefit between the community's leadership and its members.

With improvements in leadership, there tends to be more attention paid to services that are made available in the community. Leaders take a closer look at what policies are made, how they're implemented, and what effects they have. If a policy should have adverse effects on a service in the community, such as public transportation like a bus line, it's the responsibility of the leadership to address that. Leaders who have participated in the community development process will also be able to recognize what services are needed but may not be currently present in the community. Implementing such services where and when they are needed will undoubtedly be of value to community members who will be using them.

Food

There has been quite a bit of attention paid to food-related issues in communities in recent years, particularly in regards to what are known as food deserts. These are areas where there isn't enough access to affordable fresh, healthy foods for residents, usually due to a lack of sources like grocery stores. What is available in these areas is usually heavily processed and loaded with sugar and fat that contributes to health issues like obesity and malnutrition. This can compound other issues, as many food deserts are in areas with a high poverty rate and a lack of viable resources. There also tends to be geographic barriers, like a distance and a lack of transportation, that prevent members of these communities from accessing nutritious food sources. As a result, it's been a priority issue for communities and one of the more common objectives in the community development process as of late.

Actions taken to alleviate food deserts through community development have involved attracting new grocery stores to areas that lack them and improving the offerings at existing stores. While this has shown to offer substantial benefits for the community and its members, including from an economic perspective, it's not the only solution(s) available. Many efforts have included the organizing of community gardens-which are maintained by members of the community on their own time and at a reduced cost-and education on nutrition and diet. In some areas, things like farmers' markets and food share services have been set up in order to bring these outlets directly to the community. It's an ambitious effort-there's around 23.5 million people living in food deserts around the country-that can have significant benefits to communities when the proper actions are taken.

IMPACT OF COMMUNITY-BASED ORGANIZATIONS

With community development, there can be multiple forces and sources of action to implement changes and improvements. A community seeking to improve itself is not limited to what is directly within its reach. It is possible for the average citizen to be the primary participant in the community development process, but they often have help from larger groups within and outside of the community. While this can include federal organizations and government assistance, it also includes community-based organizations.

Community-based organizations and what they can do for those going through the community development process. The basics about community-based organizations and what makes them different from any average non-profit organization. The different types of community-based organizations and the advantages and disadvantages of the concept in regards to community development will also be discussed. Additional information will include how a community can develop its own community-based organization, should they choose to do so.

Community-Based Organizations

Community-based organizations, or CBOs, are local non-profit groups that works to generate improvements within a community on the local level. They are basically the community development process in the form of a formal organization. They are usually locally formed, locally staffed, and their actions are specific to the location they operate in. Most CBOs are mainly volunteer organizations, with few paid positions as most of their funding is delegated towards completing the group's objectives. Their local status also means that they may be limited in what resources they have access to, depending on the geographical location of the CBO and the community it serves.

Since they are so localized, a CBO is only going to tackle issues within the community they operate in. This does not mean that CBOs only focus on minor things; large scale issues like crime and poverty are common areas of interest for CBOs. These groups are free to look at issues that exist outside of their community that are affecting the community itself, but they will just look at how those issues impact things within that particular space. In some instances, a CBO may collaborate on an issue outside of its community with another CBO. This usually happens when there is some overlap in regards to their areas of interest, such as shared geographic boundaries between the two communities. They may also look at how a larger issue is being handled in other communities and by other CBOs in order to find guidance or alternative solutions. Otherwise, it will remain within a specific community and not venture outside of it.

It should be noted that will most CBOs are considered to be a type of non-profit and may operate similarly, they are not the same thing. Non-profits are usually large operations that have a particular area of focus and methodology that they are addressing through multiple projects and actions. A CBO is far more limited, usually handling a single project pertaining to an area of focus purely within the community they are present in.

Aside from the collaboration exception mentioned previously, a CBO will not exist outside of the community they act in. They can be a part of or connected to a larger organization like a regular non-profit, but they will not act as a branch of that organization outside of their geographic focus. This does not mean that communities going through the community development process are limited to working with either a CBO or a larger non-profit; they can work with both if they so choose.

Role Do CBOS Play in Community Development

Within community development, CBOs tend to serve primarily as the middleman for resources and actions. Many larger groups, like non-profits, and intersecting communities use CBOs as a way of interacting with those who are already at work on issues within the community. A CBO is often how volunteers find public service projects that they can participate in, as CBOs tend to be in the thick of things within the community. In a way, an established CBO can attract and filter resources necessary for the community development process.

CBOs also have a role in community development as the public voice of the community. One of the best features of a CBO, due to their localized focus, is that it is a wealth of information regarding the issues it is focused on within the community. They highlight issues that need to be addressed and then include every relevant piece of data regarding those issues for those that will be working on them. This includes details about what is wrong in the community, what should be done to remedy the situation, what needs to be done, the resources available, and the effects the issue is having on the community. For anyone who is attempting to instigate the community development process in their community, including a CBO in the process can help make things go smoothly.

Types of CBOS

Just as with any organization, not all CBOs are alike. The localized nature of a CBO means that each one is going to be unique to the community it serves and to the interests it has within that community. However, there are certain categorical types that these varied CBOs tend to fall under. Each type usually dictates the structural and legal features of the CBO and impacts its operations. The most common include:

- ***Common Interest Groups***-Also referred to as CIGs, these are usually organizations that involve community members who have shared goal(s) and interest(s). These can be rather simple and are flexible enough to be modified while still retaining its core structure. As a result, CIGs are a fairly common CBO type present in communities and community development.
- ***Micro-Finance Institutions***-These are CBOs that are focused on financial elements in the community, like lending and savings. MFIs are not banks, per se, but they do offer similar services for poor communities.
- ***Village Development Committees***-VDCs tend to be CBOs that act as a collective governance in villages. They have a set of rules that govern not only the VDC's actions, but the community as a whole. A VDC can also be set up in addition to a village's current government, and the two can work in tandem.
- ***User Associations***-Technically a type of CIG, user associations are similar to clubs where the resources they provide to the community are applicable primarily to the association's members. They can operate, maintain, and fund facilities using resources and money obtained publically and/or privately.
- ***Faith-Based Organizations***-FBOs are CBOs and non-profits with a religious twist to them. They can have similarities to other types of

CBOs, depending on how they are initially set up. There is quite a bit of controversy and criticism regarding FBOs, which does mean that some of the disadvantages listed later in this article many be more of an issue for this type than others.

There are far more variations when it comes to CBOs than what is listed here. CBOs can be formal or informal, public or private. Their features can range along an entire spectrum and back, so a CBO can take on any form that it needs to in order to accomplish its goals for the community.

Advantages

A CBO offers a lot of advantages in the community development process when one is included. Since a CBO is a type of non-profit organization, and the two will often be associated with one another, several of the following are advantages that are also applicable to the inclusion of a non-profit.

- **Tax-Exempt Status-**CBOs are legally defined as a nonprofit organization, and thus have a similar legal standing. Not having to pay taxes for the actions taken by the group can actually help if there is limited funding in the first place. Any money that the CBO earns on its own-e.g. through fundraising-can be used to fund its efforts in full. Tax-exemption status also as additional financial advantages, such as access to public service announcements (a.k.a. PSAs), advertising discounts, and reduced mail rates.
- **Direct Benefits-**A CBO is designed specifically for the community it operates in, thus ensuring that any benefits the organization offers goes to those it is intended for. Because the CBO's efforts are not going to those that don't necessarily need it or are being divided in any way, the community is getting help in full. It makes it easier to make sure that the issues in the community are getting as much attention as they need in order to find and administer a solution.
- **Perpetuity-**Since a CBO is an established organization, it is separate from any one individual and is eligible for organizational perpetuity. Even if the person who initially began and operates the CBO leaves for whatever reason-quits, retires, dies, etc.-the organization isn't going to necessarily end because they are gone. It's a kind of immortality that allows it to continue so long as it has a purpose.
- **Liability Protection-**The separation that CBOs have from individuals as organizations means that they have some built-in liability protection in place. If a member's personal actions lead to consequences like fines or lawsuits, the CBO isn't going to be impacted on a legal standpoint. Should a CBO be sued directly or have any kind of legal consequences for its actions, they it is able to have its own liability insurance coverage to protect it as it is considered a type of non-profit.

Disadvantages

Just as there are advantages, there are also disadvantages for CBOs. Again, these are similar to what would be applicable for a standard non-profit due to the connection between the two formats. Some of these disadvantages may be more applicable for certain CBOs due to their type and other details.

- **Financial Restrictions-**Money is often going to be an issue for any CBO, as their actions are going to be dependent on the funding they have. Progression towards the group's goals and their movement through the community development process can be delayed if there are any financial issues at hand, like a lack of money. Fundraising and donations are often the only source of money for a CBO, and that can restrict their abilities if there isn't enough.
- **Workforce-**CBOs are dependent on people being involved in the organization, and their workforce is primarily made up of volunteers. While this can be a good thing-volunteers tend to have a genuine passion for their cause(s)-it can backfire if there isn't enough volunteers to get things done. People are busy, they have other responsibilities, and that may mean that they don't have enough spare time to offer. They are a necessary resource for CBOs and community development, and one person can only do so much.
- **Social Pressures-**Even when there is support within the community for CBOs and community development, there can also be resistance. The goals and/or methods of a CBO may not have widespread acceptance in the community. It is incredibly important in this regard for a CBO to pay attention to the atmosphere of the community and the attitudes of its residents when it takes action. This is often the case with FBOs, as the religious tenants of these organizations are not necessarily going to mesh with the beliefs of everyone in the community.

How to Create a Community-Based Organization?

Depending on what it is you want to accomplish with a CBO in the community development process, setting one up is actually a rather straight-forward process. The simple way to create a CBO includes the following:

- **Identify Needs and Goals-**Why are you creating a CBO in the first place? What is it that you hope to accomplish? What needs are there in the community that need to be met? This is the purpose of the CBO, so you need to establish that before you can do anything else. You may want to put together a mission statement detailing the CBO's purpose and goals.
- **Choose Type, Structure-**Consider how the CBO is going to be set up. You can have an informal or formal group, which can impact things like the CBO's legal status and operational reach in the community. It's best to choose the structure that fits the needs and objectives you wish to fulfill. Take into account how you wish to accomplish those things, not just what you want/need to accomplish.
- **Paperwork-**If you are creating a CBO with a formal structure and are seeking legal status as a non-profit, then you need to fill out and submit the proper paperwork. Check with your local and state laws to determine what is needed to do so
- **Management-**A CBO needs some kind of leadership in order for it to work, so the details of its management need to be determined. Even a simple setup of a single leader plus volunteers needs to be decided upon first.

- **Resources-**Before the CBO can really do anything, resources need to be identified and acquired. This means funding, volunteers/staff, and other materials necessary for the CBO's operations.

THE PROCESS OF IMPLEMENTING CHANGE WITH COMMUNITY DEVELOPMENT

Community development has been described as a process that is done to implement change. This suggests that there are a particular set of steps and requirements that a community needs to follow in order for their efforts to be successful. To some degree, this is true. There are certain things that need to be done in order for any actions to be taken within the community and for there to be any real results from them. However, the process isn't something that is completely set in stone due to the circumstances surrounding each community and social progressions that impact things. In a way, the community development process is more of a series of guidelines or a checklist that communities should consult as they make improvements. It can be adjusted as needed and still be successful, so long as the key principles are met.

This will look at the community development process and the basic steps that a community should consider. Each of the steps discussed can be modified to fit the needs and goals of the community going through the practice. For the most part, the following is what needs to be addressed as changes are implemented through community development.

Collect and Analyse Data

No improvements can be made through community development if you have not identified what needs to be improved. To some degree, this might require more work than any other stage in the process. The size of the community, and the issues present in it, may mean that there is a lot of information to gather and sort through before taking action. Depending on how many people are involved in the community development process at this point, it could take some time to do so.

So how does one go about collecting and analyzing data for community development? Some methods can include:

- **Learning-**Take a look at the community and learn as much about it as possible. Familiarize yourself with what the details about the community, including the issues, needs, and resources available there. Some of this information can be obtained through simple observation and participation in the community; attend a local event, for example. It may also be documented through things like newspaper articles, reports, and social media.
- **Get Feedback-**When there's a problem in the community, people are going to be vocal about it in the hopes that something is done. This feedback can be incredibly valuable because not all of the information you obtain about the community is going to come through formal channels. Surveys, open forums, and even talking with your peers in the community are all good methods of getting honest feedback. So long as the dialog between development organizers and the community members remains open, information should be able to flow.

- **Consider Motivations-**Why are YOU choosing to take action to improve the community? Why is anyone doing so and why are they choosing now to do it? The motivations of those who are leading the process in a community often can be sources of information as members of the community. Perhaps they were directly impacted by the issues in the community, or they witnessed the effects first hand. Such information may not be found elsewhere and can provide a different perspective on the issues already identified.
- **Compare and Contrast-**Take the information about the community and compare it to what is known about other communities that lack those issues. The differences can help identify what is missing and what needs to be done, which can be helpful later on in the processes when actions need to be taken. The data can also go through a SWOT analysis-Strengths, Weaknesses, Opportunities, and Threats-to identify pertinent information and discrepancies in the data.

Set Goals and Objectives

Using the information collected, determine what goals and objectives you seek to achieve through community development. These can be long-term, short-term, or whatever it is necessary to generate improvements. In the early stages of the process, it's best to set a few tentative goals for the community, as things can change as the process continues. Some things to consider as you set goals:

- **Practicality-**It's admirable to set an ambitious goal, but it can backfire if it isn't practical. In many cases where community development fails, the goals are unrealistic and the leaders lack a real understanding of the situation. This may be a result of visibility issues or a lack of information, but it could also be due to a misinterpretation of the data.
- **Time-**Goals often have a deadline attached to them, which can provide some restrictions. There's only so much that can be done in a set amount of time and that will impact the fail/success rate for the community development process. Prioritize what needs to be done based on the demands of the community and any time constraints.[5] It may be helpful to break up goals into stages that can be completed in batches over time, rather than one giant goal with a final deadline.
- **Resources-**The ability to meet goals on time will depend on what resources are needed to do so. This is one of the reasons why analysis of information is important, as it identifies what the community already has and what it needs. A goal can't be met if the community does not have the necessary resources to achieve it, or if they don't know what resources they need in the first place.
- **Commitment-**Goals can't really be achieved if no one is actively working on them. Community development's success is dependent on people being committed to doing the work that is needed; nothing's going to get done if they quit half-way through. The goals need to be something that the community is willing to commit to or little will be accomplished.

Address Options

Basically, once you know what it is you're trying to achieve and why, you need to consider how you're going to do it. Every community is going to have different options for the actions it can take for community development. Some are going to be better than others, depending on the circumstances. Not every available option is going to work, either, so it's best to address and consider each one in regard to what it is that the community wants to accomplish. Again, this is another step that is going to require some information analysis and collection in order to find the solutions that are going to fit best. Determining what options are at your disposal requires a bit of research and brainstorming; look at the details of the community's issues and goals, as well as your available and needed resources. Weigh each option carefully and consider the different factors that can impact a particular action's effectiveness. Some of the same factors that affect the goals in the previous step, such as practicality and time, can also affect what actions and methods can be used. If there are too many factors working against an option, then it will most likely have a high possibility of failing-and possibly even cause additional problems that can worsen the situation. It may be necessary to consider back-up options, just in case, in addition to the primary actions and methods being planned.

Make a Written Plan

Once the details have been nailed down and smoothed out, they need to be written out into a comprehensive plan. Putting it in writing creates a record of it that can be referenced throughout the process and accessible to participants. The process is a rather long one and can continue until well after the goals have been met. Having a detailed written plan can help ensure that everyone involved is literally and figuratively on the same page.

The written plan can also serve as the formal documentation and collection for all of the information that has gone into the process thus far. It solidifies the reasoning that went into the actions being taken, which can help later on if an action is questioned. Citing the written plan may also be required if there's a need for formal application for resources, like grants and other funding-it's information that helps the sources of those things determine if the recipient is truly deserving of those resources and if they are going to use them responsibly. One community's community development plan can also serve as a reference for another community, so putting some genuine effort into the written plan can be beneficial to more than just its authors. A formal written plan can be made by anyone involved in the process, but whomever does write it should have full access to all of the necessary information. If something changes during the earlier planning stages, then they need to know. For communities that are using professional services for their community development, keeping those that were hired in the loop can impact the overall costs of those services. Failing to inform such professionals can also lead to mistakes being included in the plan, leading to a ripple effect later on when action is actually taken.

Implementation

So you've decided upon what you're doing, why you're doing it, and how, and you have it formally laid out-it's time to take action! The implementation part of the community development process takes everything that has been done during planning and puts it into motion. It's a good idea to make sure that everything is ready to go *before* going ahead and acting. If there are elements missing-resources, funding, volunteers, etc.-then things are not going to go along as intended. This is why planning and preparation are key principles of community development and why they are so important to the process. Taking the time to make sure things are ready is going to help save time that may go to fixing mistakes once the implementation stage begins and is going to make it more effective for the community development process.

During the implementation stage, actions should be monitored to make sure that they are having the intended effect(s). If something doesn't work, then you want to make sure that you catch it before it impacts future actions. Evaluating as you go may take up some additional time, but it will help ensure that things are progressing as intended. Monitoring will also assist in making sure that the plan is being followed as it should. Unexpected delays due to screw-ups or failure to do what needs to be done can result in a waste of resources, funding, and time. This can be especially important when there's a deadline in place or some kind of restriction or limitation involved. One solution would be to use the written plan made in the previous stage as a checklist for each task that is needed to implement the improvements and keep things on track. Breaking things down into stages or phases can also help; until everything is done in one phase, the next phase cannot begin.

Continued Progression

The community development process doesn't end when all of the goals are met and the last part of the plan is complete. Even the best community development plan isn't going to be self-sustaining-at least not from the start. In most cases, some degree of maintenance is going to be needed. This may mean that the entire community development process-or certain parts of it-is going to need to be repeated to keep things going. In this way, the process is a cycle that doesn't really have a true end.

A cyclic community development plan isn't necessarily a bad thing. Being able to go back to an earlier stage means that there is always an option to fall back on when things go wrong. Circumstances change and new issues are bound to arise within the community that can lead to new problems. Society and the world are ever evolving and the communities that want to successfully exist in such a place need to have that flexibility if they want to survive.

MEMBER INTERACTIONS AND COMMUNITY DEVELOPMENT

The idea that community members need to be involved to some degree in the community development process is an important element to the process' success and the community's continued progress. The people in the community are integral parts of the system, so of course they should do what they can to have a part in improving their community. Sitting back and letting someone handle things isn't going to help matters, and it makes it harder for your voice to be heard in the community forum. The role that the members of the community have in community development. Topics will include engagement, participation, and the value that people hold in their community. There will also be information on how community leaders can improve engagement and participation to better benefit the community during the development process.

What Is Engagement?

Community engagement is a term that gets thrown around a lot in community development and leadership practices. It has multiple meanings, depending on who you talk to and what the context is, but community development treats it as the method of connecting people with the intent of ensuring that their needs are met within the spaces of the community. For many community leaders, it can be a way to check on the value the community and its facets have for the people who reside there. It's a connection that allows for a relationship between the different parts of the community and makes it so people feel like they belong.

- ***Does It Matter?***-Due to the variations of view regarding community engagement, there is some question as to whether or not its inclusion is really worth it. Should community leaders dedicate their time and resources in the community development process towards measuring and instigating engagement with residents? To some degree, yes, it matters and it should totally be included. There are a ton of benefits that engagement can offer a community, including solutions to problems, increased project success rate, and the development of healthy community partnerships. There are very few downsides and those really only occur when engagement is poorly done. The only circumstances where engagement does not have any role in a community is with smaller communities, where there are fewer factors that can impede connections amongst residents.

It's Value in Community Development

The concept of engagement is both a process and an outcome, so its value for communities and community development can be rather extensive. There is so much that is changing in today's society that engagement is one of the few tried-and-true tools that community leaders can use with little modification. The effects and importance of engagement in community development will depend on the factors involved. Namely, how it's used, why it's used, and the demographics of the community. For example, engagement tactics in rural communities are going to be slightly different than those used in more urbanized areas, usually much more direct and attentive in order to reach their intended audience.

Universally, engagement does have some value that will be of benefit to the community development process regardless of the circumstances it is used in. They include:

- ***Opens Communication***-Engagement usually encourages dialog between the different parts of the community. This is crucial for information and feedback to be able to spread throughout the community. Open communication lines makes it easier for community leaders to understand the gravity the effects of their actions have on the community and its residents. It also gives those same residents the chance to have a real shot at providing input and having a voice when it comes to decisions made in their community that can affect them.

- ***Prompts Interest***-In order for engagement to work, you need to catch people's attention first. Residents are more likely to engage with their peers in the community if they have an actually interest in what's going on. The little bits of information that community leaders first through out to start the engagement process act as bait, which prompts people's interests enough to paying attention or at least start to pay attention. If the issues occurring in a community are enough for a person to get involved and have a genuine interest, then they are going to seek out others in the community who feel the same way and bring the situation to the attention of their peers.
- ***Attracts Resources***-Since engagement brings people's attention to certain aspects of the community and gets conversations going, it often allows for news about what the community needs to spread. This can, in turn, alert those in and outside of the community who have access to certain resources of those needs. Such information routes can prompt donations and offerings of those resources that are needed the most, simply because people are talking about them. There are less resources used in the process, which can make such efforts a much more sustainable and budget-friendly option for the community. It's not going to be something that happens all the time-it would be perfect if it did-but the occasional occurrence can make it a valuable commodity.
- ***Improves Decision Making***-To put it mildly, engagement's ability to prompt more people to get involved in their community means that there is going to be a wider variety of viewpoints and problems solving abilities present. Everyone has a different perspective on things and knowledge that allow them to provide different solutions to the same problem. The more information a community has about a particular issue, the more likely they are going to find an efficient solution that has the best results. In community development, where the biggest task is problem solving, that can be a very valuable resources in and of itself. Decision making is one of the aspects that guides the community through the process, so anything that can improve it improves the community.

Participation

The role of member participation, especially in regards to community development, is just as equally debated and valued as engagement. The two often play off of one another, with engagement prompting participation and participation improving engagement. However, its importance in the community development process is something that people are unsure about. Sure there are instances in every community where community development still worked despite a lack of participation, but it's necessity to the process is still heavily documented throughout history. There's no requirement stating that everyone needs to participate in community development in order for it to work, just that there needs to be a significant amount of participants. There are options! A person can say 'no' to participating in something that they have no time or interest in participating in. Forcing yourself or someone else to participate isn't going to accomplish anything, and may just end up sabotaging the efforts of those that willingly participate.

- ***It's Value for Community Members***-When it's done correctly and willingly, participation can be rather valuable for community members. For the most part, it can offer them a sense of fulfillment and belonging as a member of the community. It also allows them to be in the thick of the community development process, which means they have options and power in the process that they wouldn't have otherwise. Things that they want to see in the community-certain improvements, resources, or services-can be suggested in the planning stages and actually considered as a real option. They will most likely be more invested in their community if they feel like they have actually contributed to it in a meaningful or helpful way.
- ***Limitations and Obstacles***-As wonderful as participation can be, it's not perfect. There are limitations in place that can prevent it from working as well as it should and curb the progress of community development. Aside from people not wanting to willingly participate and there not being enough people involved to get things done, there can also be too many participants. It can overload the process and make it too difficult for things to get accomplished due to the sheer amount of people jockeying to get their own agenda into plans. There are also administrative positions that need to be filled in order to manage the amount of people involved, which can get to be an issue when participation turnout is high. For those in leadership positions in the community development process, it can be overwhelming.

How to Improve Engagement Efforts

When engagement efforts fail-and it's always a possibility that they can-different methods need to be used. It is entirely possible that the wrong means are being used in the wrong environment, or that the effort being put into generating engagement is simply not enough. When engagement isn't working as well as it should, you often need to take steps to improve the method(s) being used. Some things that can be done to improve engagement include:

- ***Focus on Empowerment***-As one of the key principles of community development, empowerment can help with almost anything in the process. Empowerment can be strategic in helping people identify what interests them in the community and what motivates them to seek them out. Appealing to the wrong interests through engagement doesn't get results, and it can even alienate members of the community if the community's interests are presented as opposite of theirs. Empowerment can help the leadership and members reevaluate what it is that they want for the community, and allow for engagement to act with that in mind.
- ***Address Obstacles***-Certain obstacles can impede engagement's success, just like they can impede community development. Even if you are appealing to the right interests, there can still be something that you are doing wrong. Looking at what it is exactly that is being done to generate engagement or participation can help pinpoint issues that are preventing success. The smallest of issues can still have a large effect, so it's best not to overlook anything just because you think it may be insignificant.

Addressing obstacles of any kind early on can help stop any damage that they cause from developing.

- ***Get Creative***-In recent years, there has been a boom in the use of creativity and art to engage members of the public in community development efforts. Creative measures have been shown to offer more strategies that can be used to engage with others and have a wider appeal. The various details in the backgrounds of community members means that anything that can work on a large-scale to engage the public is a valuable tool. There's more attraction and interest when people get creative with their pitch and come up with something unique. More options means that there are going to be more people reached. That creativity can also be continued to retain engagement and participation, as the same old thing isn't going to work for long.
- ***Prioritize***-Engagement isn't going to work if people think that there are better issues that need to be addressed than the ones that the leadership is focusing on. The members of a community may view a certain issue as being more of a priority than whatever the leadership is focusing on. In some cases, this can translate as community leaders being out of touch with the needs of the community. That in turn can alienate potential participants who may think that their opinions won't matter. Prioritizing projects based on what the community members want means that there will be more enthusiasm and likely more responses to engagement efforts.
- ***Apply Resources***-Resources are not just for the improvements in the community development process. Successful engagement requires putting some effort and using whatever you got to catch the attention of community members. In some cases, there may be resources available that can make it easier to reach those members. Technology, for example, has become the go-to resource for community engagement, with nearly every community connecting with members through social media. It's fast and it allows community leaders to measure engagement responses in real time.

EXPLORING STRATEGIC FACTORS OF COMMUNITY DEVELOPMENT

There have been several factors that can influence community development. These factors can have as much of an impact on the community development process as they do on the community itself. They may even be contributing to the issues being addressed, or be a central part of the problem. In many cases, the influence these factors have can greatly shift a community's ability to succeed or fail in the community development process. They are broken into four categories: human elements, social factors, environment and geography, and resources. Each factor discussed in the article is only a factor that may possibly be present in a community that can contribute towards community development. Depending on the circumstances present in a community, some may have more of an influence than others and some may not even be present.

Human Elements

The human elements of a community are by far one of the more important aspects of community development. Communities are based upon the people that make up their memberships; without them, communities wouldn't exist. It's no wonder then that factors related to the people can be so influential on community development. The diversity in human populations largely contributes to this, and many of these factors are rooted in the human nature of community members. Some human factors include:

- **Participation-**Participation is something that is repeatedly brought up in regards to community development because it really does play a significant role in the process. The human element of community means that participation is practically mandatory on some level in community development. However, this does not mean that participation should be forced upon the community and its members; such paternalistic actions can backfire and are damaging to the process's results. Quite possibly, forced participation can lead to resentment and sabotage regarding the efforts being made.
- **Interest-**To put it plainly, the success of a community development plan is going to hinge on how much people care about their community. When there is considerable interest, community members are going to willing put the work in for improvements. Little to no interest means it's unlikely that anything will get accomplished any time soon.
- **Leadership-**It's the leadership that guides the community through things. The actions of a community's leader and their abilities are going to determine the outcome of the community development process. Poor or ineffective leadership, especially when there's a lack of communication, can be especially devastating and can destroy trust and credibility with community members. Strong, positive leadership, on the other hand, can bring the community together and set them on the path towards success in their efforts to improve themselves.
- **Attitude-**Just because community members willing participate and have a genuine interest in community development doesn't mean that their attitude will match. People do things that they don't necessarily like all the time, usually out of necessity, duty, morality, or other influence. Attitudes can impact the effectiveness of the efforts made in community development, and can be especially influential when there are conflicting attitudes involved.
- **Errors-**People are, well, human. They're not perfect beings and they're going to make mistakes at some point. Even the most cautious person is eventually going to make an error. It shouldn't be something that is viewed as surprising in any situation, even community development. To some degree, human error should be expected and treated with the same regard as any other factor that may influence a situation. If it happens, it happens-and there's no reason that it should be treated as an absolute guarantee of failure either.

Social Factors

Social factors present in the community are often going to act as a negative influence rather than a positive one. This is because the sociocultural elements tend to be deeply ingrained in society, and it can be difficult to take action that may deviate from those values. It's not just an issue for community development either; economically, social factors can affect what business actions and decisions are acceptable in the public eye. Social factors can have one of the strongest impacts on community development because it can impact other factors on multiple levels.

- **Discrimination and Prejudice-**Beliefs, misconceptions, and stereotypes are ingrained into society and they can dictate people's actions without much effort. This leads to prejudice towards others and instances of discrimination, which can both generate problems and block solutions. In a community setting, discrimination can be widespread if the rationale behind it is shared amongst the majority of the members. Because discriminating practices tend to be habitual in these communities, it can be quite a powerful obstacle to community development efforts.
- **Expectations-**Every society has a set of expectations placed upon those who are active in it. They can dictate what is acceptable regarding actions, appearance, beliefs, and behavior in the public sphere. This extends into communities, which are essentially samples of society and may have additional expectations of their own. Actions taken in the community development process often need to meet the social and community expectations in order to have any support or success.
- **Culture-**Many social elements are a part of the culture(s) present in the community. They bring their own belief systems, moral codes, expectations, and attitudes into the mix with varying degrees of effect. Elements of culture in a community can dictate how efforts of the community development process progresses, simply through the ways in which those efforts translate via the cultural norms.
- **Religious Beliefs-**Religion is one of the tenants of society and community, with shared religious beliefs being one of the interests that communities have developed around for centuries. It can be a powerful catalyst for change and an equally powerful opponent, depending on the interaction between religious beliefs and the proposed changes. For community development, religion in the community should not be taken lightly.
- **Political Views-**Everything as of late seems to be political, even things that have nothing to do with politics. This is because politics set policy, and the political beliefs of those in charge of a situation-such as community development-can dictate everything from management to decision making. Political problems, like corruption, are often behind many of the issues that are being addressed through community development. Political power in the community can also impede any actions that go against the political views of the leadership, which can stagnate the entire process.

Environment and Geography

- The geographic location and the environment that a community is physically a part of are always going to impact whatever actions the community takes as a whole. There are going to be advantages and disadvantages to the community's physical location, and not all of them are going to be controllable. On a global scale, location is a pretty significant factor for pretty much anything. Throughout history, environmental and geographic factors related to a particular location have often been the key contributors for the level of development that occurs there. Those factors present in a community, whether they are controllable or not, are often going to impact the progression of community development efforts.

- **Legal Restrictions-**Laws are in place for a reason, but that doesn't mean that they are not problematic for development. In most cases, legal restrictions on community development are there to prevent an overstepping of boundaries and to ensure that social rules are followed. Any legal restrictions that are in place in a community will often help development leaders determine what changes and efforts are going to be feasible and beneficial to the community.
- **Government Involvement-C**ommunity development does include some government involvement. This can vary based on existing laws and what it is that you are trying to accomplish with the process. Large-scale actions may require more government involvement than smaller actions. Event or building permits, for example, usually need approval from local government agencies in order to obtain them. Government involvement may pose some restrictions on the community development process, but it can also act as a guiding force.
- **Economics-**The local economic factors are going to impact quite a bit when it comes to community development. Anything from community members' socioeconomic status to available resources, to their willingness to participate in the process can be tied to the economy. Poverty is one of the most common issues that community development is used to improve. Economies that are heavily impacted by poverty are often the ones that need community development the most, but their instability make it that much harder for the process to work.
- **Natural Disasters-**Certain community development efforts are going to be centered on what goes on in the community's environment. This includes things like climate and weather. Geography plays a heavy role in how natural disasters like tornadoes and earthquakes impact communities, but not all community development efforts take such things into consideration. Depending on a community's location, many of the issues the process is setting out to address may be a byproduct of the damage caused by natural disasters common to those areas.
- **Impediments-**Location-based obstacles, like geographic structures, can influence what community development efforts are needed and what will work. An island-based community is going to have different geographic impediments than a community that is inland. Such features can impact the availability of resources, and what elements of culture, social expectations, and belief systems are present in the community. These can be harder obstacles to face due to the fact that you cannot always remove or replace them through conventional means, if at all.

Resources

Probably more so than any other factor listed in this article, the impact that resources have on community development is going to be substantial. They are one of the key ingredients for the process to work and a lack of quality necessary resources is almost always going to cause problems for a community. Obstacles regarding resources can be especially troublesome as a result, and may cause significant delays in a community's efforts to improve itself. Even the most imaginative and creative person can only do so much with nothing, so resources really are a valuable factor in community development.

- ***Costs and Budgeting***-Money is already going to be an issue for some communities, but it is definitely going to be a factor in what can be done in the community development process. For many communities, access to the necessary financial resources are essential for them to reach their goals for improvement. Even when there is money to use for community development, if it isn't used wisely and budgeted, then it's not going to be around for very long. Factors surrounding costs and budgets are largely going to impact the planning stages of the community development process, so some care is needed.
- ***Availability***-It's really difficult to accomplish anything in community development when the availability of your necessary resources is limited. This is applicable for financial, material, human, or social resources, as areas that are lacking tend to put added strain elsewhere. Many community leaders will shape their community development efforts around the resources they already have access to, which can cut down on any availability issues that can arise later on in the process. However, a lack of resources isn't the only way that the process can be impacted; an abundance of resources can be an issue because it can lead to waste.
- ***Sustainability***-The sustainability of the resources used by the community during the community development process can carry a lot of influence over other factors. Unsustainable resources can have damaging effects on the community's environment and can drain other necessary resources in their handling and acquirement. They also tend to have limited usage-mostly once and then that's it. Sustainable resources, on the other hand, can often be used repeatedly before being discarded and they have a lower environmental impact. In some cases, such resources can be introduced to the community and flourish on their own for later usage. Depending on what it is that the community wants to accomplish, addressing the sustainability of their resources may be necessary.

PARTICIPATORY APPROACHES TO PLANNING COMMUNITY INTERVENTIONS

In its simplest terms, a participatory approach is one in which everyone who has a stake in the intervention has a voice, either in person or by representation. Staff of the organization that will run it, members of the target population, community officials, interested citizens, and people from involved agencies, schools, and other institutions all should be invited to the table. Everyone's participation should be welcomed and respected, and the process shouldn't be dominated by any individual or group, or by a single point of view.

That's the ideal. The reality may often be quite different. Some people might not want to be involved - they may feel it takes too much time, or they don't have the skills needed. Particular individuals or groups may feel left out and disrespected if they're not invited to participate. The planning process may be a rubber stamp for ideas that have already been developed. Some people's opinions may be listened to more carefully than those of others. In some of these situations, a participatory process can cause as many problems as never involving people at all.

The important thing to remember here is the word participatory. The use of that term implies not just that you'll ask for someone's opinion before you do what you were going to do anyway, but rather that each participant becomes an important contributor to the planning process.

A true participatory approach is one in which everyone's perspective is considered. That doesn't mean that people can't challenge others' assumptions, or argue about what the best strategy might be. It does mean, however, that everyone's thoughts are respected, and it isn't necessarily assumed that the professionals or the well -educated automatically know what's best. Everyone actually gets to participate in the planning process, and has some role in decision-making.

Advantages of a Participatory Planning Approach

- *Participation carries with it feelings of ownership, and builds a strong base for the intervention in the community.* If people are integral to the planning of a community intervention, then that intervention will be theirs. They have a stake in it not only as its beneficiaries or staff or sponsors, but as its originators. They›ll do what they can to see their work succeed.
- *It ensures that the intervention will have more credibility in all segments of the community* because it was planned by a group representing all segments of the community. If people know that others with the same point of view and experience as theirs were instrumental in making the intervention happen, they›ll assume that their interests were attended to.
- *Bringing a broader range of people to the planning process provides access to a broader range of perspectives and ideas.*
- *A participatory planning approach avoids pitfalls caused by ignorance of the realities of the community or the target population.* If, for instance, Muslims are part of the planning process for an intervention in a community which includes many followers of Islam, they›ll know that lunch meetings during Ramadan, the Islamic month of daytime fasting, are not likely to work. Long-time community members will know what has failed in the past, and why, and can keep the group from repeating past mistakes.
- *It involves important players from the outset.* If the intervention needs the support of a particular individual, or that of a particular agency or group, and they›ve been part of the planning from the beginning, their cooperation is assured.
- *It can provide an opportunity for often-disenfranchised groups to be heard,* and teach the community that they have important things to say.
- *It teaches skills which last far beyond the planning process,* and can help to improve the community over the long term. People learn to run meetings, to analyze data, to construct strategic plans - in short, to become community resources and leaders.
- *It can bring together and establish ties among community members who might normally have no contact.* Such relationships - between low-income

people and business leaders, for instance - are not only supportive of the intervention, but may help to create long-term relationships and break down barriers in the community.

- *A participatory planning process builds trust,* both between your organization and the community and among the individuals involved. This trust can serve as a foundation for future community development and community action.
- *A participatory planning process generally reflects the mission and goals of grass roots and community-based organizations.* With its underpinnings of collaboration, inclusiveness, and empowerment, a participatory approach embodies the ideals that form the foundations of most grass roots and community-based organizations.
- *It implies respect for everyone in the community,* and thus sets a standard for community participation and empowerment that other organizations - and the community at large - may feel compelled to follow.
- *Logically, a participatory planning approach should be effective.* The fact that it includes the views and perspectives of everyone affected by the intervention should work to assure that all assets and needs are identified and addressed, and that unintended consequences are minimized.
- *Finally, it does things the way they should be done.* It respects everyone's intelligence, values everyone's ideas and experience, and affords everyone a measure of control. By empowering the community, and particularly the target population, rather than just superimposing its own ideas on a social structure that already exists, your organization can give substance to its ideals. In the final analysis, some level of participatory approach is almost always the most ethical way to plan a community intervention.

Disadvantages of a Participatory Planning Approach

It's crucial to understand and anticipate these considerations, and to decide when and how a participatory planning approach can work in your situation.

- *A participatory process takes longer.* A diverse group always takes longer to make decisions and come to conclusions than does an individual or small group.
- *Members of the target population or the community may not agree with the "experts " about what is needed.*
- *Education may be needed, for community members and the organization.* Members of the target population and the community may not have important technical knowledge or experience, and may need to understand some theory or past practice in order to see what the organization is trying to do. Some may need new skills in order to participate fully in the planning process. The organization, on the other hand, may need to learn more about local culture, political issues, and community history in order to tailor the intervention to the community and avoid past errors. Education takes time.
- *One determined individual can wreck the whole process if he's not handled well.* Someone who has a particular axe to grind, or who's convinced that only he knows what's right for the community can make a participatory

process very difficult. Handling this situation can take both tact and toughness.

- *It may be difficult to assure that all the right people get to the table.* Some key people may simply not want to participate. Factions in the community, a history of failed attempts at communication or at dealing with problems, ignorance of which groups or individuals are important, or just basic mistrust may complicate the task of creating a participatory planning process. Overcoming this barrier, however, can have profound positive consequences in the community over the long term.
- *A participatory planning process takes patience and commitment on everyone's part.* People have to maintain their commitment over time, remain civil while discussing issues about which they may have strong feelings, and be willing to compromise. A few misplaced words, or one or a small number of key people losing interest can upset the whole process.

While these disadvantages present potential or real challenges to the success of a participatory planning process, overcoming them may tremendously increase the possibility of designing and carrying out an effective community intervention.

Levels of Participatory Planning

There are a number of ways to consider participatory planning. As demonstrated in the discussion above of advantages and disadvantages, this kind of process always presents, even at best, a trade-off between efficiency and inclusiveness. Time pressure, the needs of the community, the skills and experience of those participating, and the nature of the intervention, among other factors, all help to dictate the actual shape of the planning process.

The following as a model of the different possible levels of participation:

- *Information* - The least you can do is tell people what is planned.
- *Consultation* - You offer a number of options and listen to the feedback you get.
- *Deciding together* - You encourage others to provide some additional ideas and options, and join in deciding the best way forward.
- *Acting together* - Not only do different interests decide together what is best, but they form a partnership to carry it out.
- *Supporting independent community initiatives* - You help others do what they want - perhaps within a framework of grants, advice and support provided by the resource holder.

Each of these levels may be appropriate in different circumstances, or with different groups, although only at "deciding together" and above do they really begin to be fully participatory.

Participatory Planning Appropriate

Information-only may be appropriate when:

- The course of action has already been decided - by a funder, for instance
- You're simply reporting on something that's already in progress
- You're keeping people informed so that they'll have the information to be part of a participatory effort later

Consultation-only may be appropriate when:

- You want to evaluate or improve existing services
- There are limited options, and you're trying to choose among them
- There are technical reasons - again, perhaps because of a funder - why only certain people or groups can be officially involved in the planning process

But remember, if you consult with people in the community, you have to pay attention to what they tell you. If you're simply going to ignore their ideas and recommendations, you shouldn't consult at all. Being asked for an opinion and then ignored is much more insulting and infuriating than never being asked in the first place. At the very least, people deserve an explanation of why their advice isn't being followed.

Deciding together may be appropriate when:

- It's important that everyone feel ownership of the plan
- You want fresh ideas from as many sources as possible
- You can pull in people whom the intervention will directly affect
- There's a commitment to provide support through the process for those who need it
- There's enough time

In reality, as mentioned earlier, a planning process often is time-limited by proposal deadlines, the severity of the need (if teenagers are dying every day by gunfire, a violence prevention program needs to get under way quickly), the requirements of other partners or funders, etc. The trick is to balance participation and time restraints, and to try to use the highest level of participation possible under the circumstances.

Acting together may be appropriate when:

- The intervention will be more effective than if it were run by a single entity
- There is a funder's requirement for community oversight
- There is commitment to the development of a real partnership
- Everyone benefits from acting together
- One goal of the intervention is the eventual assumption of leadership or the learning of leadership skills by the target population and/or others in the community

The word "partnership" implies a relationship of equals, where everyone has an equal voice, and where power and responsibility are equally shared. Forming such a relationship, even in circumstances where everyone truly desires it, is not a quick or easy task.

It takes time, commitment both to the process and the end product (the partnership), and the willingness to air and work through disagreements and philosophical differences. If you're not willing to give yourself to the development of a real partnership, acting together may be only a future goal for your organization and its community.

Supporting local initiatives may be appropriate when:

- There is a commitment to community empowerment
- The community has the desire and at least some of the tools to start and run a successful intervention

- There is a commitment to provide training and support where needed
- Your organization can only provide support, or can only run an intervention for a short time

Participatory Planning Not Appropriate

There are also some general guidelines for when a participatory planning process may not be appropriate at all, including:

- A grant may have to be written immediately, for instance, or a situation - youth violence, perhaps - may have reached such crisis proportions that it must be addressed immediately. In such a circumstance, it may be possible to do some participatory planning after the fact, either to adjust the intervention before it begins, or to plan its next phase.
- When a community is so brutally divided, it's impossible to get all - or even any - of the rival factions to the same table.
- When there's no way to provide proper support - facilitation, structure, etc. - for the process.
- When the target population is simply not interested in participating, and just wants the organization to take care of it. One goal may be to get them interested, but that may have to be part of the intervention, rather than part of the planning process.
- When the intervention rests on technical knowledge of a kind that the target population and community members simply don't have.
- When involving all or most stakeholders simply isn't logistically possible, because of distance, time, or other issues.
- When funding constraints or funders' regulations don't allow it.
- When there is no trust between your organization and the community. This may be because the organization is new and unproven, or because of past history. In the latter circumstance, it is important to reestablish trust, but it may not be possible to do this before the intervention needs to be planned.

Involvement in a Participatory Planning Process

The ideal answer here is everyone who is affected by the proposed intervention, but that's seldom possible, or even desirable. You may be talking about thousands of people, too many for an effective planning process. In reality, there should be strong and effective representation for everyone involved, including:

Targets of Change

Targets of change are the people at whom the intervention is aimed or whom it is intended to benefit. That could be very specific (e.g. teen mothers, for a job training program aimed at teen parents) or very general (the community as a whole, for a smoking prevention and cessation initiative aimed at everyone in the community).

There are really two groups to be considered here:

- Members of the target community, both those on whom the intervention is specifically focused, and others who share their culture, age, language, or other characteristics.

- People whom the target community sees as significant opinion makers. They may be members of the target population itself, or outsiders - clergy, advisors, former community members who now move in circles of power, politicians, etc. - whom people in the target community trust and rely on.

Agents of Change

Agents of change are the people who make or influence policy or public opinion. These include actual policy makers, but also encompass people influential in the community at large, who can help or block an intervention by their support or opposition.

Policy makers

- Local elected or appointed officials
- State or federal elected or appointed officials who have influence in the community or over the issue at which the intervention is aimed.

If elected officials agree to be involved in your planning, they›ll often send aides to represent them. This can be preferable to the officials themselves attending, since the aides often have a great deal of influence over their bosses, and are also more likely to have the time to participate fully.

- Local public agency heads (welfare, e.g.) who actually administer policy in the community. If they're involved from the beginning, they may be able to bend rules or otherwise alter their procedures to smooth the way for the intervention.
- Local university professors or researchers who are viewed as experts on the issue in question.

Influential People in the Community

- Members of the business community. There are a number of good reasons to try to involve the business community: They tend to be practical, often a helpful trait. They also tend to be conservative, so that if they support the effort, their credibility - and, as a result, that of the intervention itself - may be high among other conservative elements in the community. They are often directly affected by such issues as illiteracy, employee health, insurance, the environment, etc., and so may be quick to see the need for an intervention. Last but not least, they often have access to money, which may be important to sustaining the intervention over time.
- Clergy and the faith community. In many communities, clergy wield great influence, and many see involvement in community issues as part of their spiritual mission. Faith-based groups, because of their cohesiveness, their sense of purpose, and their moral standing, can be powerful forces in a community.
- Natural leaders, those whom others respect and listen to.
- The media, or others who have a public platform.
- Directors or staff of other organizations affected by the problem or issue. Many of these people may be highly respected or well known in the community.

A community intervention may involve a number of organizations, public agencies and services, and other groups. A community initiative to offer treatment to substance abusers, for instance, could involve, among others:

- Schools
- Police
- Local hospitals, clinics, and health maintenance organizations
- Services for youth
- Mental health centers
- Private therapists
- Employers
- United Way

Interested Members of the Community

These might include parents, youth, or school personnel, for instance, for an intervention dealing with youth. Many seniors have the time, the desire, and the experience to be excellent community volunteers. People with a personal or professional interest in the issue may also want to participate - parents whose children have had drug problems, graduate students, retired teachers or doctors.

Members of the Organization Itself

Administrators and line staff, volunteers, current participants, board members, and supporters.

REFERENCES

1. "Creating Rural Wealth: A Guide for Local Leaders." Southern Rural Development Center, 2002.
2. Baum, Joel AC, and Christine Oliver. "Institutional Embeddedness and the Dynamics of Organizational Populations." American Sociological Review, vol. 64, no. 4, 1999, pp. 540-566.
3. Brown, L. David, and Michael H. Miller. "The Community Economic Development Movement: Law, Business, and the New Social Policy." University of California Press, 2001.
4. Brown, L. David. "Building Sustainable Communities: Tools and Concepts for Self-Reliant Economic Change." Kumarian Press, 2007.
5. Center for Rural Entrepreneurship. "Building Sustainable Communities: Tools and Concepts for Self-Reliant Economic Change." Community Development Investments, vol. 17, no. 1, 2005, pp. 15-21.
6. Community Development Society. "The Community Development Society." Taylor & Francis.
7. Dees, J. Gregory. "The Meaning of 'Social Entrepreneurship'." Stanford University, 1998.
8. Institute for Community Economics. "Starting a Community Land Trust: Organizational and Operational Guidelines." Institute for Community Economics, 2003.
9. Pearce, Diana. "Communities, the State and Market Enterprise: A Solution to the Crisis of Urban Economies and Welfare." Policy Press, 2002.
10. Peredo, Ana María, and Murdith McLean. "Social Entrepreneurship: A Critical Review of the Concept." Journal of World Business, vol. 41, no. 1, 2006, pp. 56-65.

5 A MULTIFACETED RELATIONSHIP

INTRODUCTION

The relationship within cooperative enterprises is a multifaceted interplay of diverse stakeholders, including members, employees, management, and external partners. This intricate dynamic encompasses various dimensions, such as governance structures, participatory decision-making, social responsibility, and economic sustainability. Cooperative enterprises, unlike traditional business models, prioritize democratic principles and shared ownership, fostering a sense of community and solidarity among members. This unique approach not only empowers individuals within the organization but also enables cooperatives to fulfill broader societal goals, including promoting economic development, supporting local communities, and advancing social justice. Understanding this multifaceted relationship is essential for comprehending the distinctiveness and resilience of cooperative enterprises. A cooperative enterprise, as we have seen, must operate in the same free market as other firms with different ownership structures. The cooperators cannot withdraw from the market, but will try to improve their position in the market by putting the communal cooperative enterprise between themselves and the market. This creates an "internal market" between the cooperative enterprise and the members' businesses, or the primary enterprise. The primary enterprise of the cooperative will either be purchasing or sales if the members formed the cooperative to provide those services. At the same time, purchasing or sales are not the primary enterprise of the members. Hence, an internal market develops. The internal market is, by nature, a market of negotiation or a market of agreements. A forum is created for the various interests of the members and the cooperative itself in which the various interests must be weighed against each other. The member users of the forum can bring influence to bear on that forum. Meanwhile, the cooperative enterprise is there for all members and belongs to them.

MEMBERS AS A USERS—THE ESSENCE OF RELATIONSHIPS

Cooperative enterprises revolve around three issues: user-owned, user-controlled and user-benefitting. This means that members are users of the cooperative. They have certain interests that they want their cooperative to mind. This is important in the multifaceted relationships between members and the cooperative. As a result, the relationships can be described in this way:

1. ***A transaction relationship.*** Depending on the type of cooperative, the members will either be the suppliers of raw materials or the buyers of the product of the cooperative enterprise. The transaction relationship is at the core of the "use" that members make of the cooperative. This is where they derive their user-benefit, and that is quite different from profit. Anyone who, as a consumer, is a member of a cooperative bakery will expect to get bread there and not be told the bakery has no bread left. It won't help to say the bakery made a good profit.
2. ***A financial relationship.*** The member-users provide the cooperative's capital. That makes them owners. The cooperative enterprise is thus user-owned. From this relationship, members derive their influence on the cooperative, and have a vantage point to check that their interests are being served. The substance of that relationship is determined by the members' objectives. It could well be that the cooperative bakery could produce bread much better, more quickly and cheaply if investments were made. But if the members, or most of them, do not have the funds for such investments, then the investment is probably not even desirable.
3. ***A control relationship.*** The cooperative is an association in which the memberusers have a voice. The cooperative enterprise is therefore user-controlled. That means the members must be able to monitor and influence the cooperative's activities. Shareholders in a publicly traded company can rely on the market, carrying out a reasonable degree of monitoring. Members of a cooperative have to manage this monitoring themselves, using whatever resources they have available.

Two-Layered Enterprise

All this means the cooperative enterprise has less freedom in its market function than other enterprises with different ownership structures. On the member side of the equation, there is the primary market with the threefold relationship. The cooperative enterprise is considered to be a dependent, or at least not a wholly independent enterprise. This seems at first glance to be a disadvantage, or an exceptional handicap, especially in a world of free-market advocates. But that overlooks the reality that every enterprise is dependent on a market, be it suppliers, buyers and/or financiers. More important still, if it draws a tight circle around the enterprise and uses the input of its members, the cooperative is in fact truly independent.

The essential difference is that a cooperative is a two-layered enterprise. There are two departments, in a sense, and the departments are just as dependent on each other as two departments in any other enterprise. Goods and services are exchanged between the departments. When one department observes new opportunities in the market, it is dependent on the question of whether the other department has seen the same opportunities. Fine-tuning and consultation remain of utmost importance.

It must also be borne in mind that one of the departments is actually the "boss," which is the department formed by the members. They determine the framework of the business strategy and judge the other department—the cooperative enterprise—on its merits. It ponders questions, such as, "Does the cooperative enterprise serve the entrepreneurial goals of the members? Does it add the expected value? Does it provide the goods and services that are needed by the members?

This can become a sticky problem, especially as the one department (the cooperative enterprise) becomes bigger. Staff within the cooperative enterprise can probably see plenty of opportunities to make extra profits, and they begin to view the bosses (the members of the cooperative board) as a millstone around the neck of their enterprise. Those members are seen to have insufficient interest in the enterprise, have insufficient funds, or simply don't understand the nature of the cooperative; but the staff will complain they must talk to their members and persuade them until they are blue in the face. When this attitude sets in, the cooperative enterprise would rather get on with its business independently of the members.

We cannot ignore that independence of this nature can sometimes be prudent. Any healthy company—cooperative or not—will discuss issues of this nature. The point to remember here is that it would turn the world upside down to declare a cooperative enterprise independent of its members. In principle, the firm is no more than a service division of a larger whole.

THE TRANSACTION RELATIONSHIP

Cooperators establish a cooperative with the intention of achieving a specific, shared goal. This common approach is often mandated in national legislation. This is done through enabling legislation, spelling out conditions and requirements of enterprises seeking legal stature by incorporation under various national business codes. It can also be done through tax legislation that distinguishes between cooperative enterprises and other investor-owned firms. The United States of America, for instance, does both—primarily through its Capper-Volstead Act which is often called the "magna carta" for American cooperatives. Denmark is the most notable exception. It doesn't have a separate cooperative business code; rather, it merely accepts cooperative members as another form of investors regardless whether the investment comes from payment for shares or from use. Dutch legislation, meanwhile, speaks of the "material needs" of the members. This underlines recognition that the goals are not idealistic. At the same time, it confirms that the primary aim of the enterprise is not to accrue profit from invested capital. There must be more than a purely idealistic goal and more than a purely financial relationship. That makes the transaction relationship the core reason for cooperating, and it explains why influence and funding are linked.

The collective interest in cooperation can express itself in four aspects of the transaction relationship. The first can be that the cooperative makes certain transactions possible. Other important issues are price, quality and volume. Before we consider these points in more detail, we shall first consider the differences in the intensity of members' involvement in the cooperative.

Intensity

There can be great differences in the intensity of cooperation. The interest that anyone has in the cooperative or transactions with the cooperative vary widely within different cooperatives, and by individual members. We shall look at just a few examples:

- ***Emotional involvement.*** Involvement is the lubricant of any association. It influences how much the member is inclined to put into his membership of the cooperative, both in terms of labor and money and in terms of collegial benevolence. This involvement can take many different forms. Members take pleasure in helping other members. Members can be fanatical because they want to prove themselves among their peers, or because they have a substantial vested interest. Members can also be passionate because they feel that the cooperative's mere existence is of fundamental importance. All these forms of involvement can contribute to a feeling of belonging to a group, a feeling that can inspire others. Not only does this perpetuate emotional ties to the cooperative or group; it reinforces emotional ties to the group because a successful club is more inspiring. In reverse, an underlying feeling of belonging can contribute greatly to emotional involvement. Historically, group feelings (the farmers, the village, the church) and ideological considerations (anger at exploitation and injustice, the desire for a "better world") have always been the driving force behind the founding of cooperatives.1 In the case of consumer cooperatives, a striking distinction between the various socio-religious groups. In Socialist circles the emphasis seems to be on "Forwards!" and "The Future" (which will rule the world tomorrow). In Protestant circles, the emphasis is on helping, both you and each other.
- ***Individual dependence.*** The economic interest that members have in the cooperative depends on their own situation. Specialized members may well conduct 100% of their transactions through the cooperative, while it might be a sideline for others. The latter group will have fewer vested interests and less influence in the cooperative, and they will likely feel less involved. This aspect affects nearly all consumer cooperatives. No matter how well the cooperative is functioning, whether a bakery, a shop or a bank, for many members it may simply be one of the many transactions they make in the course or their work or lives.

  The individual dependence can also be shaped by the role the cooperative plays in providing market access or professionalism for the member. While some members would succeed on their own, others are utterly dependent on the cooperative. The cooperative represents graduated benefits for the first group, but it is crucial for the success of the second.
- ***Collective dependence.*** Another question arises over what extent the members—- collectively—need the cooperative. The added value of the cooperative is proportionate to those economic interests. For one member, it can mean a slightly improved position in the market. For another, it can

represent the sole opportunity to obtain a particular service or an opportunity to continue operating the member's private business. As the market changes over the years, so does the members' dependence on the cooperative. One example is Avebe, a large potato starch cooperative based in Veendam, which is the only channel through which farmers in the fenland district of Groningen can sell their industrial potatoes. The same applies to sugar beet cooperatives in Minnesota and North Dakota, in the United States of America, and specialty crop cooperatives throughout the world where there is no independent market except that made by the members themselves. Without these market-making cooperatives, there would be no market. And this represents the extreme form of collective dependence.

Delivery and Supply

The first thing cooperators want from their cooperative is the opportunity to conduct certain transactions. They want to sell their own products or buy a particular product or service. That can be an absolute requirement. For fruit growers in remote African villages, where there is no local demand for fresh fruit, a market cooperative with means of transport can make markets reachable. The reverse is also true. A cooperative purchasing organization, also with transport, can bring means of production, food and other requirements back to the village. Cooperation can also be the answer if certain products or services cease to be available. If insurers no longer cover a particular risk, potential clients can set up a mutual association. When a village factory is threatened with closure, local people can decide to continue operating it as a cooperative venture. Examples of this are the potato growers' Avebe and sugar beet growers' American Crystal Sugar Co., mentioned above, when no other market alternative exists. Generally, the market situation isn't that black and white. There are usually alternatives, at least in appearance, and people start cooperating in search of a better price, better quality, or better volume. There is also a fourth aspect to cooperating for people seeking assured delivery or supply. By joining forces to buy or sell, cooperative members can be assured of regular deliveries or sales. They will no longer be dependent on the right seller or buyer at the right moment. This is an issue that is particularly important to the producers of perishable commodities. At the same time, even a cooperative cannot offer 100% assurance. The cooperative also has to go to the market. It is probably more accurate to think of cooperatives as mutual delivery insurance. Members share the risk that they incur when buying or selling their products and services. Every cooperative becomes a mutual association

Price

The benefit of cooperating is usually measured on the basis of the price that cooperators pay or receive for their transactions. That benefit stems from the cooperative adding market power, or savings on costs, or because cooperation leads to a better quality that is worth more in the market.

Price Leadership

Cooperation leads to a better price if the cooperative can influence the market. When the market is working well and there is sufficient competition between buyers and sellers, cooperation does not have much to add. At the same time, the comments made earlier about the relevance of the size of the business continue to apply. Whatever the case, most cooperatives try to obtain a price advantage for their members, an advantage that becomes manifest in the transaction relationship. As soon as the cooperative is able to obtain a better price for its members, competitors in the market are forced to respond by offering their suppliers better prices as well. The mere presence of a cooperative can therefore determine the distribution of profits between players in the supply chain, from cooperative members on through to end users, and from the cooperative enterprise and its peers and competitors.

A curious example of price leadership from the former Dutch colony of New Guinea in the 1960s. Chinese traders bought copal, a resin-like substance, for 50 cents a kilo while the world market price was 140 cents. The government established a "cooperative" that would pay 100 cents. The traders quickly increased their offer. And when the cooperative offered a price of 140 cents, the traders offered more again. They wanted to be rid of the cooperative. The government realized this, and did not increase its offer. Producers turned once again to the traders. But the cooperative continued to exist. The cooperative buying office demonstratively opened its doors for a couple of hours a week. It continued to be a market-correcting device by its mere presence. This was a small investment by government and cooperative members to force the traders to pay a fair price. The example illustrates that price leadership calls for perseverance. In this case, it was made possible because the government was behind the plan. In most cases, however, what is needed is insight and solidarity.

That is because cooperatives often attach great important to transparency in their efforts to provide market corrections. If prices are clear to everyone, especially the relationship between price and quality, then third parties will find it more difficult to cheat suppliers and buyers, or to play them off against each other. The cooperative auctions and countless purchasing and sales cooperatives were established with the express purpose of creating a fair and transparent market price.

In some sectors, the cooperative's price leadership has led almost all players to become members. Examples are frequently found among specialty crop producers or narrowly defined service providers and professionals for whom a negligible market exists. Specialty nut and exotic fruit producers from California and Mediterranean areas are prime examples. Another example is the cooperative for Dutch veterinarians, AUV, which was established as a purchasing cooperative in 1969 with 100 members. Nearly all veterinarians in the Netherlands had become members within 25 years. Problems can arise, however, when competitive firms hold out against the cooperative. The members then no longer see an advantage in cooperation, as nonmembers are getting the same price. This skepticism is difficult to refute because the cooperative must then try to explain that market prices would be far less favorable without the cooperative, a point that is virtually impossible to prove after the fact. This has proven to be a problem with the grain marketing "pools," or cooperatives in the western provinces in Canada, and to a lesser extent for CHS Inc., the large grain marketing cooperative in the United States. To appreciate both the price leadership and market-correcting roles of their firms, current members must have a clear image of market imperfections overcome by grandparents when they formed those cooperatives.

Free Riders

Apart from the above problems, many non-members believe they can take advantage of the success of the cooperatives—sometimes consciously and at other times unconsciously. This is often frustrating for members. The complaint is "We make the effort, and they get just as much benefit". But it is even more frustrating when members themselves start to exhibit free-rider behavior. When they no longer see the benefits of the cooperative, members will try their luck elsewhere, sometimes occasionally and sometimes permanently. If that happens on a large enough scale, it can seriously undermine the position of the cooperative, including its price leadership. A side effect is that the cooperative will have fewer options in its own actions. When members cannot see a clear difference between themselves and non-members, it becomes more difficult to fund new investments. This can lead the cooperative to pursue a protective and defensive policy, weakening its ability to add value for members and impose price leadership.

It occurs mainly in sectors where members have relatively more chance to obtain an incidental advantage for themselves. The meat and livestock sectors are good examples in most developed countries. On the other hand, we find that sectors in which cooperatives have been particularly successful, such as dairy and horticulture, are far less susceptible to free riders. These sectors produce perishable products that cannot be stored for any length of time and must be marketed quickly and regularly. In such cases, producers prefer to rely on a well-organized marketing agency rather than risk their relationship with the cooperative for the sake of a quick profit.

Price Competition

Even though the cooperative is the price leader, members will still be subject to competition in terms of price and other aspects of their market. The cooperative can act as a buffer and achieve a better price, but if members cannot meet the standards of the market, they will still fail on a personal level.

No Redistribution

Although cooperatives have been eager to promote members' social capital—the feeling of solidarity and involvement—they have insisted on strict business-like practices from the start. Even at Rochdale, one of the first basic rules was that members paid cash and paid the prevailing market price for products or services. That may seem heartless in retrospect, considering that so many members were poor and unemployed. But experience shows that deviation from business practices inevitably leads to the failure of the cooperative. That led to the rule that members should first pay the market price and later, once the cooperative had financial success, they could share the success through a proportionate value of their transactions with the cooperative.

The price members receive is part of the financial relationship within a cooperative. At this point, we shall look at the linkage between prices and the transactions with members. The price paid must be the same for all members. Any suspicion about unequal treatment undermines solidarity and puts the cooperative concept at risk. Another basic rule is that the personal treatment of one member must not be detrimental to other members. The ideas of the Rochdale Pioneers and all subsequent philosophies can be expressed in the maxim, "Every man for himself, and the cooperative for all of us." In this case, self-help serves solidarity. A cooperative is not an instrument for redistribution. The organization ceases to be sustainable the moment it becomes an instrument for redistribution, whether it falls under the guise of charity, social policy or a replacement for government. This creates inequality among members and is a potential and continual source of discontent.

The principle of equal treatment forms one of the pillars on which the democratic structure of the cooperative is based. The fact that the cooperative is democratic presupposes that equal treatment can be discussed internally. An organization that wants to maintain unity must take into account minorities. But the argument for mutuality will take precedence over self-interests.

In most national experiences, a business-like attitude has always held sway, especially where it is understood that the cooperative must maintain its competitive position within markets. But there is opportunity for social welfare policies on the margins. Methods have included advice and sanctions to protect members from disasters. The Raiffeisen Banks and the Farm Credit Banks in several countries are proud of rarely being the instrument causing member bankruptcies. The effort these banks put into helping members and avoiding bankruptcies is easily justified to other members. It is a mutual insurance in terms of pure profit and loss. Bankruptcies cost a bank a great deal of money.

Over the years, there seems to be a noticeable shift from the concept of mutuality to a better-understood concept of self, or own interest. Business-like dealings are gaining the advantage, especially in agriculture. Cooperatives are inclined to strip social aspects from their budgets. This is undoubtedly linked to increased competition at the cooperative level and to increased competition at the member level. It is remarkable that a number of definitions of cooperatives state that members are not in competition with each other. But in reality, they were, are and will remain competitors. This recognition is gaining greater prominence today. It becomes a question of what gives the individual a better chance at success, working together to create added value or eliminating competitors.

Allocation of Income and Expenses

The 'solidarity versus own interest' debate still plays an important role with regard to allocation of income and expenses to individual members. Advocates of solidarity always emphasize the principles of proportionality whereby the cooperative enterprise pays in proportion to the volume of transactions. Advocates of a more business-like approach prefer a slight modification: the cooperative enterprise pays in proportion to the volume of transactions, which are considered to be of equal value as they arrive at the cooperative's premises. This is sometimes referred to as the performance principle.

Transport costs are a useful example. Per kilo or pound of goods, it is much cheaper for the cooperative enterprise to collect or deliver a container full of a product rather than one sack or basket. It also makes quite a difference to costs whether the member lives next door or in some remote place. These days, transport costs of this nature are invariably allocated to the individual member, but that has not always been the case. In the earliest days, the problem hardly ever arose. This was because the members were expected to bring their goods to the factory, or to collect their purchases themselves. As these were usually local factories, especially in the dairy produce sector, this was not a big problem. Transport costs were not high between the members and the cooperative enterprise. Even when the factory worked with bulk milk collectors, members were usually charged a standard or average price for transport. In the earliest stages, in particular, when the feelings of solidarity are emphasized, a cooperative would be reluctant to embark on the discussion of such a difficult and relatively unimportant subject. It would, in fact, have been very difficult to calculate and charge the exact costs for each individual member.

Nonetheless, there are cooperatives that ultimately decided to allocate these individual costs. They often started with quantity surcharges and discounts. This grew to a more refined and almost exact system of allocating costs. Needless to say, this policy also led to emotional discussions within the cooperative. The term 'quantity discount' itself suggested that larger members were getting an 'unfair' advantage. From the point of view of the cooperative entity, however, it can be seen as a form of equal treatment. The principle that everyone receives the same treatment must also apply at the doors of the cooperative. If one member has to incur expenses for another, this is effectively a transfer of costs.

A system whereby transport costs were not allocated to the members individually was used by Cosun, the Dutch sugar processing cooperative. When discussions were held about the location of a new factory, the question of transport costs threatened to swamp all other issues. The members eventually selected a location that was the most favourable economically on the condition that members would pay the cost of collecting sugar beets from all members jointly. In essence, this became a businesslike argument for solidarity. But this example demonstrates how every decision can give rise to conflicts of interest. One consequence of mergers is that distances to processing sites change, and with it the costs for individual members.

Quality

Price and quality are closely linked. A cooperative will also need to develop its quality in order for its products to remain marketable and obtain the best market price. Conversely, many cooperatives were established for the purpose of ensuring members they would have access to high quality products or services.

Good Means of Production

We have already seen that the first buying cooperatives were created for the express purpose of assuring members of good quality and reliable products. The market correction was not only aimed at price. It was intended to ensure that traders could not exploit any lack of skill or ignorance on the part of individual customers. The Rochdale Pioneers, for example, felt that members should feel secure to send their children to the store to make purchases. Following the same rationale, the fertilizer cooperatives joined together to hire experts to check the composition and soundness of the offered products. The relatively recent veterinary cooperative was founded specifically to assess and monitor the quality of medication purchases. Even the credit cooperatives can be seen as a response to quality issues. The actual cost of credit was one consideration. But members also wanted transparency of the credit system to preclude arbitrariness and exploitation. The financial products offered also had to serve the target group. Farmers, for example, needed long-term credit. Workers formed cooperative credit unions primarily for short-term credit. In fact, quality of credit services is an important aspect in nearly all consumer and service cooperatives.

That brings us back to the issue of homogeneity. Members needed to agree on the question of which qualities were necessary and in which qualities they should invest.

As the wishes of the members become more individual, there is more emphasis on individual transactions whereby each member must pay for each service separately.

Quality and Market

Quality was also an important factor behind the founding of marketing cooperatives. Members were either looking for a way to market their special quality products, or inadequate quality was seen as a communal handicap preventing them from gaining a foothold in far-away markets. Many well-known regional wine and cheese brands from France can be traced back to cooperative initiatives, and we already saw how quality was a central motive for establishing dairy cooperatives. Successful dairy farmers had vested interests in quality transparency. The price differentiation between good and poor products should be visible in the market.

In fact, while striving to achieve market correction, many marketing and consumer cooperatives have contributed to the raising of average quality standards. You could say that they not only played the role of price leader, but also that of "quality leader". If they placed a premium on quality, the competition would have to follow suit. Messing around with butter, fertilizer, cattle feed and credit was banished slowly but surely.

National legislation and government controls have also played an important role in establishing quality standards, but the influence exerted by the cooperative sector is also generally acknowledged. As noted before about market leadership, a problem arises when that leadership becomes less visible because the competition falls into line.

Instilling Discipline

The importance of maintaining quality places considerable demands on internal democracy. Mutual control is necessary. It is in everyone's interest for members to fulfil established standards. When a cooperative is first founded, you can agree on standards in advance, but as the market and technology changes, member products can become subject to new requirements. Those requirements can affect various aspects. For instance, the product might need to be more attractive, larger, smaller, tastier or healthier. When the cooperative wants to present itself as the supplier of such new qualities, this will invariably have consequences for the members' businesses and their production processes. That raises a thorny problem. It seems that the cooperative is elbowing in on the independence of the members. As long as the changes are not drastic and there is transparent collective benefit, new quality requirements can generally be discussed productively in a cooperative context. Anyone who finds it difficult to adapt can probably receive assistance and be persuaded to remain part of the group. It might take quite a lot of time and energy, but you could look upon it as one of the added values of the cooperative buffer. It becomes more difficult when the impact on the members' businesses is of greater economic consequence.

Quality requirements for member businesses can put great pressure on the internal democracy of a cooperative. It will inevitably lead to the formation of "parties" or factions. Members who can easily fulfil the new requirements will see an opportunity to improve their position, while those same requirements can mean leaving the business for others. This makes a precarious and painful discussion within the enterprise. Everyone realizes that the signals sent by the market will, sooner or later, affect the individual members of the cooperative. But in the cooperative they face these facts in public, eye to eye with fellow members. It is quite different when the invisible hand imposes change or exodus anonymously.

It should be noted that the horizon of the members plays a dual role in these discussions. Older members will be reluctant to make further investments in quality, which is particularly important for younger members. On the other hand, the simple fact that many members are approaching the end of their working lives makes this a good moment to establish new quality parameters. The only thing that is needed is to agree on a transition period for the older members.

Whatever the case, it will always be difficult for an existing cooperative to continually maintain and live up to its quality leadership role. The conflict of interests can be substantial, and the members will only be prepared to alter their working methods if they can see good economic reason to do so. Unfortunately, the necessity will only become evident when it is too late. An extra complication arises with the possibility of the loss of members through resignation. That can happen when it isn't clear that profit made from enhanced quality will compensate for the loss of market power or economies of scale for the members.

Homogeneity

It is generally acknowledged that major differences in the quality of members' product can give rise to significant solidarity problems. This is one of the reasons why sales or marketing cooperatives are usually found in the domain of bulk products. Bulk products, or commodities, are homogenous by nature. The individual producer can do little to add extra quality. Sugar is sugar, and milk is milk. Insofar as there is a difference between the product of farmer A and farmer B, the difference disappears by the time the cooperative factory has bottled the milk or made the cheese. If there is a clearly discernible difference in the quality of product produced by the members, and that difference is relevant for the market, it would be less sensible to throw all those products into one basket or tank. That is why market gardeners derive their power from the auction as a communal market place, rather than from communal marketing and sales.

At the same time, the solidarity problem we have sketched out here seems to have contributed to a culture in which there is more emphasis on price and quantity—on saving costs—than on quality. This becomes a culture of "same is better". This translates itself, for the members, in a quality standard formulated in terms of minimum requirements for protein content and purity. Over the years, those requirements are gradually raised (cell count, germ count, etc.), but there is little incentive to encourage the members to really improve their product.

Where possible, most quality requirements become differentiated. A sugar beet grower is paid in proportion to the sugar content of his beets, less a reduction for the amount of sand and other pollution attached to the beets. But even this differentiation is prompted more by the principle that income and expenditure should be allocated to the individual member than by any desire to improve quality. This phenomenon has always been carefully restricted to easily measured aspects of production and processing and can objectively be linked to the costs or revenues of the cooperative.

Differentiation

Different quality classes were formulated early on in the fruit and vegetable sectors that produce consumer products, often in consultation with traders. Independent inspectors classified the products: shiny apples in A, slightly damaged apples in B, overripe apples in C. The apples came to auction pre-sorted, and prices were then determined by the buyers. This process effectively makes quality differences more transparent. But that is not so welcome for the members whose products end up in the lower categories. They worry that they will receive a permanently lower price, once again creating a clear conflict of interest between group members.

This sort of issue also regularly prompts discussions at auctions. Those who deliver the best quality products know that they are in the minority. They can threaten to leave—literally a loss of quality for the cooperative—but if they do, they in turn will lose the channels, the market power and probably even the price leadership offered by the cooperative. Conversely, the remaining members will have to be careful not to chase away any more quality producers. Only the lesser producers would remain.

Besides the difference in interests, the collective interests as a whole also play an important part in the considerations. It becomes a matter of weighing benefits derived from the power of the cooperative in the market against costs. The more classifications and separate product flows, the greater the costs. This theme is understandably unpopular in cooperatives that are focused on reducing costs.

Members have to fight to get new quality initiatives adopted within cooperatives. But such initiatives often depend on other members' willingness or reluctance to invest in the initiatives of others.

Quality in the Chain

The impression that there is no room for quality in sales cooperatives. Nothing could be further from the truth. Up to now we have been looking at the opportunities for the member businesses to earn more by delivering better quality to the cooperative. For the cooperative as a whole, however, the situation is different.

The process seems to be ongoing: extra quality and production innovation are expected from the cooperative enterprise, but not explicitly from the members. This seeming ambiguity does not need to be a problem. It depends on where the members have drawn their circle.

Most farmers are happy with a successful cooperative that tells them what the market wants. They can then channel their creativity and skills to fulfilling those requirements. But there is less space for the creativity necessary to discover for themselves what the market wants. The same phenomenon can also be seen in retail cooperatives. The stricter the "format" imposed by the cooperative, the less scope there is for creativity on the part of the individual retailer.

Quantities

One of the main interests that members have in a cooperative is the opportunity to extend their market for selling or for buying, including the number of transactions they can complete. This applies in both absolute terms (without a cooperative there is no supply or no demand), and in relative terms. A member business can develop by growing or by increasing productivity. But then you have to be able to sell the extra produce or buy more raw materials. Thanks to the cooperative, members can tap into markets further afield from their core business. This, typically, is a marketing activity that could not be undertaken by a single business, both because it requires special expertise and members already have their hands full developing their own business.

Free Admission and Transaction Obligation

Surprisingly, the aforementioned individual member's objective accords well with a cooperative that clusters purchasing, sales and/or processing on behalf of its members. More production gives economies of scale and hence lower costs. In a market where countervailing power counts, more production can even lead to a better price. This is a situation where collective strength really applies. This probably also explains why free admission and the right to deliver unlimited quantities of product have always been more the rule than the exception for cooperatives, so much so that many manuals mention free admission as an essential characteristic of cooperation.

Incidentally, it is not the case that free admission is balanced out by free withdrawal. When investments have been made in a cooperative and production capacity has been created, the co-operators need to be able to rely on each other to ensure sufficient volumes of deliveries or sales. Otherwise, the remaining members will have to cover the cost of under-utilization. In other words, members have to be subject to an obligation to deliver their products. The more capital-intensive cooperatives have quite strict resignation procedures based on compensating the losses that the other members would suffer. Some have even imposed an additional financial penalty.

In more recent years, the necessity for a resignation (or exiting) penalty has been tempered by the fact that cooperatives now have equity capital that is accrued by the members themselves and which is not repaid on resignation or retirement. That "capital in the dead hand" is effectively an implicit resignation penalty. We saw earlier that a purchasing obligation on the part of the cooperative represents mutual delivery insurance for the member; the obligation to deliver represents a substantial reduction of risk for the cooperative enterprise. An obligation to deliver is also an important factor in combating free-rider behaviour. The disadvantage to such obligations is, of course, that they restrict a member's autonomy.

It could be difficult to reconcile such an obligation with the principle that the cooperative exists to support its members in the realization of their own goals. Moreover, you run the risk that the cooperative enterprise, or its management, will become lazy. After all, there will not be much need to expend energy on maintaining member loyalty. Such arguments have always been pivotal in cooperative practice. Members should not be restricted any more than is strictly necessary. That necessity is greatest in the case of capital-intensive processing cooperatives, but somewhat less acute in capital-intensive marketing cooperatives. It is a less urgent matter in consumer cooperatives such as retail shops, banks and feed producers.

As a general rule, there is less solidarity among members in cooperatives where there are no transaction obligations. The circle around the cooperative enterprise plus the transactions with the members is no longer clear. This becomes especially acute in many consumer cooperatives. Many of these cooperatives are quick to start doing business with non-members. If a feed processing factory is built, and members do not buy all the feed, trade with non-members becomes an attractive prospect and may be necessary for survival. The same happens in many retail cooperatives. In the long run, the only difference between members and non-members was that members received dividend stamps on the basis of which they received a share of the profits. Even Rabobank and other large cooperative banking systems have evolved to where they are no longer just credit cooperatives and have become cooperative financial services providers.

Transaction Rights

A transaction obligation implies no more than that members are obliged to exercise their transaction rights. It is important to make that clear. The primary reason to become a member of a cooperative is to acquire transaction rights. The word "right" indicates that membership of the cooperative has some value. It is because of the value of that right that people are prepared to become members, to invest and even to give up a degree of autonomy in exchange for a transaction or other obligation. The first value element of a delivery right is the obligation to purchase on the part of the cooperative enterprise. We have already pointed out that the value of this right represents a mutual delivery insurance. The value of such a delivery right becomes more explicit as the cooperative has a more exclusive position within the market. It can make good "profits" for the members, or it represents the members' sole channel for sales. The position of the cooperative can, however, change over the years. If its operations are weak, or if it has strong competition, the members might decide to leave the cooperative. Their transaction right with the cooperative then has no further value. But if the cooperative has become the only real option, or becomes an ever-stronger partner for the members in some other way, then it can literally cost more money to become a member. Good examples of this are the agricultural processing cooperatives where delivery rights (membership portions) are negotiable. This means that members must buy into the cooperative.

New Generation Cooperatives (NGCs)

Many cooperatives have been started in which members have to purchase delivery rights in advance. These are being called New Generation Cooperatives

(NGCs). The delivery rights go hand in hand with delivery obligations. But that doesn't mean that non-producers may not purchase delivery rights. If members do not deliver, the raw materials are then purchased from the market at the expense of the member in question. Members who do deliver raw materials receive a normal market price. If the cooperative makes a profit, this is shared among all members in proportion to the delivery rights they own.

In fact, this is exactly the opposite of what the classic or traditional cooperative does. The older-model cooperatives work according to the Rochdale Principles, with a market-matching return on invested equity and the distribution of profit on the basis of transaction volumes. In that case, the transactions are settled at market prices and the profit is distributed on the basis of capital equity. In most established cooperatives, the order is of little importance as long as the proportionality between investment and amount of delivery product—i.e. between the financial and the transaction relationship—remains intact. The order of business does become important when there are external shareholders.

NGCs are built out, or as an extension, from the members' original objectives. In general, they are primarily aimed at stimulating the regional economy by keeping more of the production value at home. The suppliers do so with capital and raw materials, the investors with capital and by covering their share of the necessary raw materials. Such a communal interest frequently arises in remote areas where the benefits of cooperation are visible to most, if not all, community residents. If no cooperative existed, suppliers would be in a less favourable situation, located too far from buyers. In addition, employment opportunities would be lost. The communal interest lies in the presence of a local cooperative enterprise that offers employment, and when it produces something that local people need or has a higher marketplace value that enhances the local economy. At the same time it contributes to the continuing presence of the member-suppliers. The investment in the cooperative enterprise is the core issue for both objectives. That investment forms the criterion on which any profit will be distributed. Thus, the enterprise leads to profits for investors and for the "regional family": the local community.

The future will have to show whether dissimilar communal objectives are robust enough to be sustainable. There are already examples of NGC failures, but their failure rate in the decade from the mid-1990s to 2005 was less than 10% in the midwestern U.S. states of Minnesota, Iowa and North Dakota. In contrast, there is a 50% failure rate for all new forms of enterprise, cooperative or not, within three years of starting up.

Transaction or Investment

We will end this section with a special case of "premium membership". This is a situation that involves cooperative enterprises' activities that have no direct link with the transaction relationship with members. We will first give a few examples.

Avebe is a cooperative enterprise that extracts starch from its members' potatoes. It does so in the name of its members: farmers in the fenland communities who have little choice other than to grow industrial grade potatoes. It is surprising enough that Avebe can keep going, because potato starch has lost out to competition from cheaper varieties of starch in nearly all markets. One of the secrets of Avebe's continuing success was the forward strides the company made in the starch markets. It started to produce other varieties of starch itself, cheaper and more competitive varieties such as tapioca starch. It already had starch-extracting technology; the company could now take a wider variety of starch derivatives to the market for both the food and the non-food industries and it made good profits. Now that Avebe is a leading player in the world market for starch products, it continues to be able to sell its members' products.

Avebe and many other cooperatives decided for marketing reasons to extend their activities beyond their core business. Fruit and vegetable markets, for example, were quick to ensure that more exotic varieties of fruit and vegetables were available. Royal Friesland Foods started to make lemonade alongside its traditional milk and chocolate milk products. Land O'Lakes and most other major North American dairy food cooperatives began processing and distributing fruit juices to assure their niche in the supply chain, allowing them to supply refrigerated supermarket cases for both milk and juice products. Along another path, wider use of its skills and available knowhow enabled Campina to set up a division that uses milk protein for the fabrication of computer monitor screens.

Another form of "expansion" is the trend for cooperatives to begin international operations, prompted by increasing international competition. This often takes the form of mergers with foreign businesses. Finally, there are the increasing investments in sales, in the development of consumer products and their marketing. All of these business expansions emphasize the added value that can be created in the cooperative enterprise even though success is not dependent on transactions with the members.

This development can lead to a curious situation in which cooperatives are busy creating extra added value while they have no need for extra transactions with their members. In situations like that, the right of delivery is more important than the obligation to deliver. In addition, the right of delivery becomes a costly one. Many extra investments must be made on the supply side of the cooperative. Also, new investments must be made on the demand side. Members are allowed to receive a share of the added value that is generated without regard to the member transactions, at the same time that they are still being rewarded in proportion to those transactions.

Thus, there are two problems in need of solutions. The first is the incentive problem. Members are receiving a higher reward than their transaction is worth to the cooperative enterprise. This will send out false signals. A second problem is that the transaction relationship increasingly becomes an investment relationship. The delivery right becomes expensive because of the high investment component, and this can be a great drawback for the transaction-dependent members. This is often overlooked because, for the member business, the transaction remains the central issue for membership.

THE FINANCIAL RELATIONSHIP

A cooperative enterprise must be funded. This is done in most investor-owned, public stock companies by issuing shares that are bought by people who: (a) clearly have capital at their disposal, and (b) want this capital to earn as much as possible for them. It's all about the potential profit per unit of capital. The case is frequently different for private individuals who set up a business. They are not passive investors who only want to see a return on their capital. They are trying to make as much profit as possible on their proposed business activities while building an enterprise that is durable and sustainable. They see funding as a straightforward cost item. If they do not have the required funds themselves, they can try to persuade the bank to lend them money. If that fails or proves to be too costly, they can try to persuade third parties to invest in their business. They may well have to give up some of the profits, but if the business is dependent on risk-bearing capital, they won't begrudge it. Where the interests are homogeneous, there could be no objection to drawing investors into the business. It might mean sharing the profits, but the investors have the same basic interests as the entrepreneur: earning the best possible profit from the economic activity. After all, more profit on the economic activity means better returns on the invested capital. Nonetheless, there is a catch. Problems can arise when the external investor decides that the capital is not bringing sufficient returns. He can walk away or demand that the business strategy be changed. In doing so, he is interfering in the activity of the original entrepreneur and the latter will probably not like that idea: "Come on, Van Gogh, those paintings aren't bad, but why don't you start creating something that there's actually a demand for?"

In the case of a cooperative enterprise, profitability-induced interference would be absolutely undesirable since the concept of profitability has a different meaning for members of a cooperative than for investors. At this point we must remind the reader of the dual objective of the cooperative. True, a cooperative must operate as well as possible as a business, but the interests of the members remain the primary consideration. These are not the interests (or the profit) of the cooperative enterprise itself. Such member interest is served via the transactions with the members and this is therefore the central activity.

In principle, the external investor is not interested in the members' interests. If more profit can be made from other activities or transactions, or from more or fewer transactions, then he will opt for that. He is only interested in the profit of the cooperative enterprise itself. As far as he is concerned, the cooperative must simply make a profit. To do so, the enterprise must provide added value to its customers or its suppliers (members, for example), but that is simply a means to an end: making a profit.

And that brings us to an even greater problem: how much profit does a cooperative enterprise actually make? If you consider only "user benefit", and see the cooperative only as a means to achieve a better transaction price for the members, then the cooperative enterprise itself makes no profit at all. It is a task-oriented organization. Before we go on to consider the funding of a cooperative enterprise, we shall first consider the cooperative surplus and its allocation to the cooperative enterprise. In doing so, we shall briefly consider relevant the fiscal aspects.

The Cooperative Surplus

Cooperatives are often described as "not-for-profit organizations". Draheim (1952) used the descriptive term Kostendeckungsbetrieb (business covering costs): the cooperative enterprise should be seen as an extension of the members' businesses. It is, as it were, a department of the member business that must provide a particular service at the lowest possible cost. The cheaper that can be done, the more profit the primary business (i.e. the member business) can make. In the case of a marketing cooperative, for example, the members entrust their products to the cooperative enterprise. The cooperative must then do something with that product (package, adapt, process), and sell it in the market on behalf of the members. Any costs incurred are deducted from the earnings from those sales, and the difference—the net result—is divided among the members in proportion to their deliveries to the cooperative. We have previously seen that account is taken of costs and earnings which can be directly attributed to the individual member, but that does nothing to diminish the principle that this surplus is allocated to the members in its entirety and in proportion to their own transactions.

This surplus actually consists of two components: a reward for the members' product and the value added by the cooperative enterprise itself. The members are entitled to share in the first component as producers of the delivered product, and in the second component as owners of and investors in the cooperative enterprise. For most of the members of the cooperative, this distinction will be of little interest, at first sight at least. Call it price, cooperative profit, or dividend, they receive it anyway, and what they receive is proportional to the value of their transactions with the cooperative. The result usually means that success of the cooperative enterprise is tied to the difference between the price members receive and the price non-members receive. But we can still add some notes in the margin concerning such a carefree attitude:

- In the first place you can never be sure what the market price would have been if there was no cooperative. We have already discussed the phenomenon of price leadership: if the effect of the cooperative is that other buyers also start to offer higher prices, the cooperative will seem to have no added value.
- Secondly, the "profit" from cooperation can lie in the fact that new markets have been accessed, by organizing exports for example. This is a volume effect, one that cannot be seen directly in the price received. It is quite possible that other buyers pay their suppliers the same price or even more, but they may not do so for the volume of products that can be sold to the cooperative.
- Finally, members have to ask themselves what membership in the cooperative costs them. The member may receive the same price as other suppliers, but might have had to invest more to get it. These costs are not only measured in money investments, but also in terms of organizing the cooperative, making agreements and complying with long-term contracts. In other words, the member incurs transaction costs and has every right to expect something extra in return. On the other hand, being a member of the cooperative means making those agreements with a voice in the conditions and in having a contract in the first place, and thus, the certainty of selling products. That is a benefit in itself, a profit if you will, of the cooperative enterprise. It might even be a reason to be satisfied with a slightly lower price.

This just shows how difficult it can be in practice to attribute the surplus to the members or to the cooperative enterprise. It is difficult to define exactly what performance has been provided by the cooperative and what by the members. But it is precisely that point that becomes the focus of discussions when cooperatives become involved with external investors. What profit should be allocated to the investors, and what to the members? Nevertheless, it remains worthwhile—with or without external investors—to determine as accurately as possible what added value the cooperative realizes. It becomes particularly important when members want to assess how well the cooperative enterprise is performing. What return or benefit is it offering? How does that compare to the returns of other cooperatives or competitors?

Benchmarking like this is relevant, for example, when attempting to assess the management of the cooperative. Conversely, it also forces the members to formulate the criteria they wish to use to define how "successful" their cooperative is. That, in turn, is in the interests of the management, as they will then know how they will be judged. When the members need to approve substantial investments, it is even conceivable that the rate of return on invested assets should be an important criterion. Members, after all, have to decide whether they are better off investing in their cooperative, in their own business or in something different altogether.

A warning note is appropriate here. It is important to keep the dual objectives of the cooperative in mind when developing assessment criteria. Fixation on the profitability of the cooperative enterprise alone can lead to the subordination of the central objective, i.e. the interests of the members. Conversely, fixation on the prices to be received in the short-term can obscure the necessity to ensure that the cooperative enterprise remains strong.

Fiscal Aspects

Another party that is interested in the difference between "member profit" and "cooperative profit" is the tax authorities. How much profit does the cooperative make, and how much corporation tax do the members have to pay as a result? The cooperative answer is simple, as we have already seen. A cooperative does not make a profit. It realizes a better price for its members. So any tax burden falls on the members' businesses. But the taxman is not always satisfied with this answer. This book is not the place to go into the specifics too deeply, in part because cooperative taxes are applied and administered differently in different countries. But we shall make a few general comments.

For the taxman, the central question revolves around to what extent the cooperative enterprise is truly an extension of the members' businesses and to what extent it is an independent enterprise. If the latter is dominant, then the cooperative may be expected to pay taxes like any other independent enterprise. The taxman will also want an answer to the question of what earnings can be attributed to the cooperative enterprise (the "independent" profit) and what earnings can be attributed to the members (the "extension" profit).

Dutch law tries to make a distinction by determining a "market price" for the members and then attributing part of the business profit to the members as "extension" profit on the basis of a special formula. The cooperative must pay corporation tax on the remainder. In the cooperative setting, it is generally beneficial for as much fiscal profit as possible to be attributed to the members. The members are generally liable to pay tax at a tariff lower than corporation tax rate.

Non-cooperative competitors keep a close eye on this issue, as they will not want cooperative enterprises to pay less tax or to have any other fiscal advantage. For that reason, the question of tax and cooperatives is a regular topic of discussion which is easily nurtured.

Variations of the above apply in most developed or industrialized countries. Part of the friction between ownership structures of business entities comes from cooperatives having separate codes of incorporation and separate tax codes. This is especially so in the United States with its Capper-Volstead Act that clearly defines cooperatives as for-profit ventures, not non-profit organizations, and then extends "single" or one-time taxation on most profits that are cash "patronage" payments, or dividends, that are returned to members. Critics of cooperatives, however, ignore that American cooperatives do pay corporate income taxes on the "retained earnings," or profits, which are not distributed to members but are retained as unallocated funds for future enterprise activities.

We have already seen that there is plenty to be said about the "market price" paid to the members. In practice this is a price that has to be "estimated" and is not exactly an objective method. Another question that can only be answered subjectively is to what extent the cooperative is an extension of the members' own businesses. If the cheese produced by cheese-making farmers is delivered to a cooperative cheese factory, you could indeed say that part of the members' business has been incorporated into a cooperative enterprise. But can you still say the same thing if the cooperative makes new types of cheese? Or low-fat butter? Or vanilla custard? The tax authorities must decide where to draw the line.

As already mentioned, Dutch law uses a standard formula that considers the percentage of overall costs that relate to the efforts of or on behalf of the members. In practice, these "member costs" are usually based on the sale of basic products and first-line processing. The same percentage of the cooperative's profit is then designated "extension" profit. It will be clear that this simply moves the goalposts of the discussion. What specific costs can actually be said to relate to member performance?

A subsequent problem arises in most countries as the extension profit is only deductible for the cooperative enterprise as it relates to the current financial year. That means that if cooperative A disburses all the calculated extension profit to the members, it may deduct the entire amount from the cooperative's profit, and so will pay no corporation tax on it (although the members will of course pay income tax on their share). But if cooperative B decides to retain the extension profit in the cooperative that year to enable it to make an investment, it will be liable to corporation tax. If, a couple of years later in year X, the cooperative disburses that profit to the members, it will no longer be designated as extension profit as it was not earned in financial year X. The members will pay income tax on their share as usual, but the cooperative will also have paid corporation tax on it as well. This produces a problem of double taxation.

Besides the fact that double taxation will never be "nice", we must mention in the spirit of this chapter that this double taxation is actually a disincentive for the members to put money into the cooperative enterprise. It is as if the member is paying the taxman twice. In other words, tax treatments stimulate short-term thinking. The higher the effective disbursement here and now, i.e. the less money is left in the cooperative enterprise, the lower the burden of double taxation. This makes the arbitrary line between member profit and enterprise profit an important fiscal problem. An unpleasant consequence is that quite often complicated and artificial constructions are designed to avoid undesirable fiscal burdens, especially double taxation: constructions, for example, by which the money may well be disbursed officially, but then made available to the cooperative again in some form or other. This cat-and-mouse game is not good for the transparency of the financial relationship between the members and their cooperative enterprise.

In the United States, cooperatives are only charged an advance on corporation tax, which is then refunded as soon as tax has been levied on the members. Cooperatives in various EU countries also enjoy a relatively accommodating tax regime. Denmark, for example, assumes that cooperatives do not make a profit. Taxation is limited to a levy of 14.8% on the cooperative's equity capital. This favourable treatment does, however, come to an end when more than a quarter of the turnover is realized through non-members. This explains why international merger partners of Danish cooperatives (such as Arla) are keen to choose Denmark as their home base.

Self-financing

From what was said in the introduction to this chapter about the interests of external financiers, it will be obvious that cooperatives—by definition—prefer to be self-financing. They want to be sure that the transaction relationship is at the core of their business and that the capital only serves that relationship. For the same reason, the proportionality principle should also—by preference—be applied to financing. Members contribute pro rata to their transactions with the cooperative. Otherwise, discrepancies will arise between the members other than as a result of the transaction relationship, in the sense that one member will be more of an "investor" than another.

Once more, we would like to emphasize that a cooperative is not a vehicle by which to make capital profitable, as it would be in a limited company. The primary objective is to fulfil "material needs", in order to carry out some communal economic function as an aid to the operations of the members' businesses. Recruiting capital is not an end: it is simply a means. But it remains necessary, so how should it be done?

Pre-financing

A first option is a form of pre-financing. In this case, members put a certain amount in the kitty, preferably in proportion to their intended transaction volume. If the investment is relatively small, as it might be in a consumer cooperative or an ordering association, collecting the subscribed capital or charging a membership fee can achieve it. We have already seen that this was the principle used in Rochdale. In order to prevent the subscribed capital taking on too prominent a role, there was a maximum limit to members' subscriptions and a fixed rate of interest. In the early years, the Rochdale cooperative managed to satisfy its financial needs by buying on credit from its suppliers while demanding cash payment from its member customers. A second option for acquiring working capital is to get members to lend funds to the cooperative, in proportion to their transactions.

This can also be done as trade credit, if the members agree to defer payments. In practice, however, a more common method is for members to accept an advance on their price at a relatively low rate and to receive a supplement at a later date once the annual results are known. By analogy, the Rochdale approach can also be seen as being based on buyer's credit. Members pay a predetermined price—in the case of Rochdale, the market price—and receive a retrospective discount once the annual results are known. Those results could, of course, be disappointing. Then the "discount" will be negative, and members will have to make an additional payment. In cooperative practice, it has always been the custom to make cautious calculations. That is important for the cooperative's financial situation, and also so that members are not confronted with financial setbacks after the event.

A third method of acquiring funds is to borrow on the capital market. To do so, the cooperative enterprise will have to provide the lender with the necessary guarantees. The fewer guarantees provided, the more expensive the loan. If the risks are too great, no banker will be willing to provide the necessary capital. A new cooperative that has not yet accrued any equity capital to serve as collateral can channel the guarantee through its members. Members will have to accept liability for the debts of the cooperative. Liability in this case is a provisional obligation to furnish capital. The members do not need to deposit funds in the cooperative immediately, but they accept guarantor status in the event that something goes wrong. That is why the term 'potential equity capital' is used here. Once again, it will be obvious why agriculture, in particular, has spawned so many cooperatives. With their land, buildings and livestock, farmers have fairly substantial assets, and together they are quite capable of taking on the role of guarantor.

Liability

Dutch law demands that the question of liability should be arranged in the articles of association. In principle, there are three options:

- ***W.A.—statutory liability.*** If the articles of association do not provide otherwise, the cooperative will have statutory liability. This is unlimited, and applies to each member in equal proportions. That means to say that in the event of dissolution or liquidation, the liability will be shared among all members equally. The members' liability applies to the entire value of the deficit. If redress cannot be obtained from any member, then the other members' liability will be increased by an equal share of the amount not obtained from that member. Statutory liability expires one year after a member withdraws from the cooperative, so that members cannot avoid liability simply by pulling out when a financial crisis looms.
- ***G.A.—modified/adjusted liability.*** It is possible for a cooperative's articles of association to deviate from this general rule. In such a case, we say that the cooperative has modified liability. In the first place there might be a particular reason for sharing liability among the members in another way, pro rata to their participation. Then the members have unlimited liability for unequal proportions. A second possibility is the unlimited joint and several liabilities of the members (this is also known as 'several liability'). In this case, if the cooperative cannot meet its obligations, each member can be sued for the entire deficit. The members named in the suit must

themselves arrange how they will obtain money from the others. This option was often used in new cooperatives that enjoyed little external confidence. It hardly needs to be said that the more wealthy members in particular were not very happy with this liability arrangement. In practice, they will be the first to come under fire. These days, unlimited member liability is hardly ever found. As long ago as 1925, amended legislation allowed liability to be restricted or even excluded altogether. In the case of a limited liability cooperative (beperkte aansprakelijkheid, B.A.), the member liability is limited either to a specific amount or to a percentage of the annual turnover (again, in equal or unequal proportions). This now seems to be the pattern in most developed countries.

- ***U.A.—excluded liability.*** Members of cooperatives that exclude member liability can never be held liable for the cooperative's debts. At most they can lose any money they have contributed (subscribed capital, the balance on member accounts, or loans provided).

It is not only necessary to specify the chosen form of liability of association under Dutch law; it must also be quoted in all correspondence. If that is not done, liability will revert to statutory liability (W.A.). As already mentioned, this liability only means that the members would have to contribute to cover their cooperative's deficit in the event of dissolution or liquidation. If they are also required to contribute to interim deficits, that must be expressly stated in the articles of association.

Generally speaking, providers of capital (such as banks) are not enamoured of liability arrangements. It is far more important to them that the enterprise is healthy and financially sound. They undoubtedly dread the trouble they would have, in the event of liquidation, if they had to collect the debt from all those individual members. Conversely, joint and several liability is not a pleasant prospect for the members themselves. The cooperative is a business that they run at arm's length, and it could all go wrong at any time.

Both considerations have led to the subordination of the importance of liability in practice. The majority of cooperatives these days have excluded member liability: no less than two-thirds of the current top 30 cooperatives have done so. The remainder have some form of limited liability. Some people feel that this might have a disadvantage: the spectre of liability can mean that members feel more involved with the cooperative and follow its economic affairs more closely.

Transaction Liability

In their appraisal of risk, capital providers attach great importance to the opportunities and potential of the enterprise. In this respect, the cooperative holds an interesting trump card: the transactions with the members. In the first place, members have an obligation to deliver. If a group of farmers decide to set up a cooperative sugar factory, for example, and the members undertake to deliver their sugar beets to the factory, this will effectively cover a major potential failure factor. In principle, the cooperative enterprise will have a long-term contract with its members that will safeguard the supply of raw materials (or the purchase of its products or services). What is even more interesting, from a financial point of view, is that these long-term contracts do not mention prices. That means a cooperative enterprise with committed members can permit itself to pay less to its members for their assured input during difficult economic times. It also means the larger the cooperative, the greater the annual payout and the greater the amount of capital that could be retained in the short term.

A cooperative enterprise does not need equity capital to hedge risks if its members have an obligation to deliver. Whether the results are disappointing or favourable, they can be discounted in the members' transaction price. In other words, the cooperative enterprise effectively "uses" the equity capital of the member businesses as its own equity capital. If the cooperative enterprise's results are inadequate, the members will receive lower prices. The members function as a buffer.

The Formation of Equity Capital

From the previous section it will be obvious that there are a number of reasons why a cooperative enterprise should want to have some equity capital. In the first place it needs working capital. It is utterly impractical to have to go hat in hand to members and say that funds are needed "for a while". In the second place you need equity capital as collateral when borrowing from third parties. That aspect becomes even more important as the liability of the members is reduced. Thirdly, it is desirable for the cooperative to have its own equity capital when it needs to accept more risk. The greater the risk, the more expensive (and perhaps more difficult) it becomes to obtain credit. In that sense, the formation of equity capital can also help to reduce costs. Unlike borrowed capital, equity capital does not need to be paid back. Precisely for that reason, it can support more risks. The term 'equity capital' is therefore often used as a synonym for risk-bearing capital.

The most important way in which cooperatives form equity capital is the same way individuals do it. They decide to keep some of the current year's surplus funds in the cooperative as part of a potential disbursement kitty. Members thereby waive their right to part of their "direct and personal claim" to the surplus for the year in question.

The equity which is formed in this way can consist of various components: deposits in the authorized capital of the cooperative (in principle, this is then a "gift" from the members), personal participation in the cooperative's risk-bearing capital, or a short- or medium-term loan on specific conditions. In the first case, the funds are incorporated into the cooperative enterprise's equity capital. In the last case, the funds are actually borrowed: a debt owed by the cooperative to the members. We shall now consider a number of variations on this theme:

- unallocated capital
- debt to members
- members' capital
- cooperatives based on shares
- combinations of the above

Capital in the Dead Hand

Members can agree that part of the money to which they are entitled should be deposited into the general reserves of the cooperative. The capital that is so created is known as the "capital in the dead hand", and has the character of authorized capital. In earlier chapters we saw that the Rochdale cooperative declared this cooperative capital to be "indivisible". Members could no longer lay claim to the capital that the cooperative enterprise had formed. The cooperative's equity capital is subject to collective decision-making and is no longer owned by any specific member. This is possible because the cooperative is a legal entity and the members have no individual title to its capital. If they resign their membership, they no longer have any claim to these reserves and their rights to the capital cannot be devised by will or transferred. In other words, co-operators enjoy usufruct on this capital, but only for the period that they remain members. Each generation adds to this authorized capital.

Depending on the wording of the articles of association, it is possible for the cooperative to eat into the general reserves and draw down the capital in the dead hand. It can do so by paying members a higher price for their products and services—or by charging a lower price—than would be justified from a commercial point of view.

In the period when a cooperative is being built up, the collective will nearly always have a tacit agreement that the cooperative's capital must be spared and kept intact. This is done with the understanding that something was being built up, from the desire to reduce the burden of liability on the individual members, and in the conviction that the communal enterprise should primarily offer the prospect of continuity. This is for the benefit of both the cooperative and the members' businesses as well.

This "unselfish" choice was linked to the collective conviction that capital, and whatever it might yield, should not play a dominant role in the cooperative. The transaction relationship and continuity should be the central consideration. Continuity concerns would be pressing if a majority of the members, or even a sizeable number, were to reclaim their capital. That could mean the end of the cooperative. The "founding fathers" of many cooperatives were well aware of this risk, and rightly so. When young entrepreneurs get together to form a cooperative, there is a good chance that they will reach the end of their working lives more or less simultaneously and will want to withdraw their money from the cooperative simultaneously. In the case of longer-established cooperatives, the ages of members will be more varied.

The apparent "selflessness" of these founding fathers should be seen against the background of their time. Besides their own interests, many cooperatives were also concerned with the emancipation of a particular population group or with achieving a structural improvement of circumstances for that group. In other words, cooperatives were originally endowed with an important social task. The cooperative should serve the sector as a whole, and its future prospects, and should have an open mind to the admission of new members from the sector. Once this aspect became less important, the capital in the dead hand was seen more and more as equity for the existing members. As this idea took hold, so too did the members' desire to at least be able to withdraw the nominal value of their share of the equity on retirement, preferably with a bonus to allow for growth in the value of the enterprise.

In agriculture, another aspect besides the deeply felt sectoral identity also came to the fore. Farmers were well used to capital in the dead hand, namely the land on which their family business was built. This was land that you could not sell, but only pass on to your children. In their minds they held that business literally "in usufruct". You worked the land and the farm, added to it if you could, and in leaner times you could consume some of the assets. Ultimately, you passed it on to the next generation. The inherent nature of succession—thinking in terms of generations—perhaps explains why farmers in particular are so aware of the need for continuity and why cooperatives have always been so popular with farmers.

The phenomenon of capital in the dead hand has become less selfevident in modern times. Members do, of course, enjoy the usufruct, as shareholders enjoy their dividend. But when their membership comes to an end, they want to be able to reclaim some of the assets to which they have contributed over the years, just as shareholders want to be able to sell their shares at some time or other, preferably at a higher price.

To some extent, the declining acceptance of capital in the dead hand can be linked to the general increase in individualism in society. People are less inclined to practice self-denial for the benefit of the future generations of their professional group. On the other hand, the "horizon" of many members has changed. For many farmers, for example, it is no longer self-evident that their children, or even other members of the family, will take to farming or continue to make use of the cooperative in some other way.

A laudable but at the same time dangerous aspect of the capital in the dead hand is that it is ostensibly "free of charge". It was, after all, a "gift" from previous generations. In principle, no interest needs to be paid on it. In that sense it is a very attractive business practice. The cooperative will have a comparative advantage over businesses that have to borrow "expensive" capital. But members who have to appraise the cooperative enterprise on its performance will have the task of ensuring that sufficient benefit is drawn from this "dead capital". If the success of the cooperative is based solely on a lack of interest payments, it is likely that the cooperative has a weakness in comparison with the competition. Members should be aware of this prospect.

Debt to Members

The alternative is to consider the discount on the transaction price as a personal loan from the member to the cooperative. The cooperative then enters the discount as a credit entry on the "member debt account" in the name of the member. At the moment the entry is made, a note is added to show when the cooperative will redeem this debt. Many cooperatives use a revolving fund to operate this member debt system; the amount that was withheld X years ago is disbursed to the members. Normally, some interest payment is included in the disbursement. It goes without saying that with this system the cooperative does not actually accrue any equity capital. But the system does give the cooperative a fairly permanent working capital so that it becomes less dependent on outside funding.

Members' Capital

A more recent alternative is the so-called member capital account, also known as the personal reserves, participation reserves or registered equity. This account is also supplemented by withholding a proportion of the surplus, and the account also has interest added to it. There are, however, two major differences with the debt to members. In the first place, members' capital is only repaid when a member resigns or withdraws on lawful grounds and in a lawful way. But even more important is the fact that the members' capital is under the direct management of the cooperative. This means that the cooperative can, if necessary, withdraw funds from this capital. This means that the members' capital can be seen as part of the cooperative's equity capital. But this is limited to a certain level. If a member resigns, his portion must be repaid.

Cooperatives Based on Shares

Lawmakers throughout the industrial world have been making it explicitly possible to convert parts of cooperative enterprises into another non-cooperative legal form. That gives the option, in principle, of launching or acquiring some particular and often more risky activity in which other investors are involved. Subsidiaries of cooperatives are, of course, sometimes funded with borrowed capital. Sometimes this is done because of a lack of members' capital or equity capital, or because the party selling the acquisition will remain a shareholder for a while, or because the enterprise being taken over is listed on some foreign stock exchange. In most cases, this kind of funding situation is short-lived.

Some cooperatives literally opt to incorporate the cooperative enterprise, or at least part of it, into a so-called corporate cooperative. As a rule, all shares are held by the cooperative association, with the Board of Directors of the cooperative association acting as the Board of Supervisors for the cooperative enterprise. In practice, there is seldom a clear reason for choosing this construction. For the members there does not need to be any great difference with the cooperative's legal form as far as risk or effectiveness is concerned. If the cooperative enterprise is incorporated, however, legislation sets limits on what it considers realistic principles of association. One important reason for opting for incorporation of the cooperative seems to be that a "regular" company is more easily recognizable in international dealings. The cooperative form is slightly less well known and moreover the legal and fiscal regulations for cooperatives are by no means universal around the world. This may well be important in international trade and for attracting international funding.

In general, the shares in corporate cooperatives or in cooperatives based on shares are not freely transferable. The marketability (and then only of depositary receipts for shares) remains limited to the circle of members or is linked to a delivery right and/or an obligation to deliver. We have already pointed out that the earliest cooperatives were heavily focused on keeping admission fees for new members as low as possible.

This was intentional because they were dealing with people who had little money. It was also important to the success of the cooperatives, in terms of market power and economies of scale, that as many people as possible participated. Financial barriers had to be as low as possible. In many cases, subscribers only needed to make a small partial payment on the shares. In other cases, such as grain marketing cooperatives in North America, members only needed to show up and use the marketing services to become a member. In the event of a setback of even liquidation, the liability of the members went no further than the need to pay up their shares. This was a typical form of connecting liability (and/or "shares") as potential equity.

However, at a time when market strategy and added-value strategies are receiving extra attention, shares are considered important as a form of real equity capital. Usually, cooperatives have issued these emphatically as participating preference shares, often tied with delivery rights or delivery obligations. This allows the cooperative enterprise to work with a predetermined volume of raw materials and equity capital, and the members buy the right to deliver those raw materials. These cooperatives are not "open to all". New members have to buy shares (rights) from existing members. Members can also trade their shares among themselves and so increase or decrease their delivery rights or delivery obligations. It is a limited market, one in which supply and demand determine the price. That price is a reflection of the expected or realized returns of the cooperative enterprise. The proportionality between transaction, funding and voice remains unchanged in a construction of this kind.

A new form of registered equity, which closely resembles the equity capital or share capital of an investor-owned company, is the so-called "B share". B shares are risk-bearing, not redeemable, and not compulsory; but they are negotiable (to a degree), and do not need to form part of the current assets of the members: they can form part of the private assets instead. In this way, members have the opportunity to invest some extra funds voluntarily in their cooperative enterprise. Royal Friesland Foods for example offers members this option. B shares may not be traded outside the circle of members, but former members may hold them. On the death of a member, however, they have to be put on the market within one year. B shares carry no voting rights and are not necessarily issued in proportion to transaction volumes.

Such shares can be issued through a subsidiary or a foreign division, and the determination of profit, or the determination of dividend, is usually unrelated to the price paid for raw materials. If the B shares are issued by the cooperative enterprise, the price must be in line with the market. This holds, regardless of whether the enterprise is incorporated as a private or a public limited company, and the valuation must be independent of the parent cooperative's company policies. If not, there is a risk of a conflict of interests between members with B shares and those without, especially when there are substantial differences of proportionality between share ownership and transaction volume.

Many Mixed Forms

The plethora of names used to designate registered equity (i.e. member capital) reflects the fact that there are, in practice, many different ways that capital can be made available by members. Just as the cooperatives found their own way of defining "limited liability", so too have they found different ways of designating this capital. Agreements are made about fixed or floating interest rates, the degree to which the cooperative is at liberty to use the funds, and about redemption conditions. Repayment of registered equity on resignation or withdrawal is sometimes deferred for X years, and the "debt" owed by the cooperative to the member is often subordinated. This means that repayment to members will only be effected after other creditors have been paid. This more or less gives the debt to members the character of registered equity capital. Another variant is that the members buy bonds that are freely negotiable—but sometimes only after a specific waiting period—outside the circle of members. If these bonds are perpetual, this variant can be considered to represent equity capital.

But, taken by and large, the general reserves (the dead hand) and any shares issued form the only true equity capital in the cooperative. While it is true that these are assets that never need to be redeemed, in principle, there is always the chance that members will demand a rather too favourable transaction price for a number of years and that this will deplete the reserves of the cooperative. So even in the case of general reserves, it is still unclear to what extent this is truly "equity capital". All these mixed forms lead to a multifaceted mixture of assets, which sometimes leads to subtle differences on the fiscal front.

Doing the Splits of Finance

As we have pointed out, equity capital is necessary as a basis on which to borrow other capital and also for the funding of risk-bearing investments. Over the years the requirements that cooperatives have to fulfil to receive assistance from banks have become similar to those that private individuals are subject to. It must be mentioned, however, that cooperative banks were not usually insensitive to the "semi equitycapital components" described above. In practice, cooperatives adopted various rules of thumb, such as 25% in the dead hand, 25% registered equity and 50% borrowed capital, and rules to maintain the value of their equity capital. This was done either on the basis of value (the growth of the dead hand reserves to keep pace with inflation) or on the basis of prosperity (to keep pace with wage increases).

Today, however, the hot issue is usually the fact that market conditions change drastically. Competition continues to increase, primarily due to liberalization and internationalization/globalization. However large the cooperative is, there always seems to be even greater competition. And however efficient the cooperative might be, there are always areas—oftentimes vast areas—where it is cheaper to produce, because the production factors of labour and land are cheaper. It therefore becomes a question of distinctiveness besides price. Research, product development, brand policies, patents, advertising and clever marketing strategies are becoming more important. All of these factors are also more capital-intensive and more risky than reducing costs. When the traditional cooperative invests in cost-reduction, it could start earning back those investments within days, at least in principle. But when it comes to creating a market profile, or product development, the cost has to be paid long before any benefit can be reaped. These are long-term investments that literally embody more risk. These investments include running the risk of developing a new consumer product that has little chance of ever making it to the supermarket shelves.

All these problems have meant that processing and market cooperatives, in particular, have found themselves doing the splits as far as finance is concerned. With one leg, their need for risk-bearing equity capital is growing. They need capital to fund high-risk, long-term investments in research and innovation, for example. But their other leg is pointing in another direction, as members have become more critical when it comes to approving investments for types of activities that are far removed from the members' core businesses. That makes it more difficult for members to gauge either the usefulness or the risks involved. This problem is compounded because management doesn't want to openly discuss every strategic investment with the members. More important still, the expected benefit will only be derived at some time in the distant future. Investments of this sort are thus hampered not only by the portfolio problem but also by the horizon problem. Members will have little incentive to support investments when they themselves will not derive the resulting benefit.

One solution for the latter problem can be found in certain types of registered equity that are linked not only to discharge but also to a disbursement of profits. But, as we have already seen, the problem with registered equity capital is that the cooperative cannot really consider it to be risk-bearing capital.

This is not to say that cooperatives find themselves facing financial problems because their members have no wish to invest. A quick scan carried out among the 26 largest European cooperatives showed that the unregistered equity capital of these cooperatives had risen by 70% in the period from 1993 to 2003 (from 1.7 to 2.9 billion euros), while the registered equity had risen by only 30% in that same period. This accounted for an overall reduction of the share of registered equity in the total equity capital from 16 to 13%. During that period, the unregistered equity capital per member rose from 8883 to 21,864 euros. The growth of equity capital kept pace with the growth of borrowed capital (70%) as well. Here, too, there was an overall reduction in the share of registered equity (on designated member accounts and member debt accounts) from 21 to 10%. In comparison, the balance sheet totals increased by 60% during this period, from 6.9 to 11 billion euros.

So members seem to be willing enough to leave extra funds "in the dead hand". There is a rather remarkable inconsistency in the dairy industry, however. The unregistered equity capital in that sector grew by no less than 77% in the period between 1993 and 1998, but by only 3 percentage points in the subsequent five years. Perhaps this was a "correction" to the very heavy growth in the preceding period. Members of dairy cooperatives have always been relatively big investors. The unregistered equity capital in the sector is 40,958 euros (double the average for the Top 26); including registered equity, this averages out at 57,827 euros per member. That comes down to 31% of their turnover, and that is a substantial amount for businesses of this size. For the purposes of comparison, small and medium-sized businesses in the construction sector spend an average of 10–15% of their turnover on marketing and sales activities.

THE CONTROL RELATIONSHIP

A cooperative is first and foremost a democratic association. In legal terms, it is an association whose object is to provide for the material interest of the memberusers. That also applies to the cooperative enterprise, at least as it is accommodated in the legal form of a cooperative. Dutch law, and that of a few other industrialized countries, allows considerable leeway for cooperatives to deviate from these statutory principles in their articles of association and other internal regulations. This can sometimes happen at the expense of the democratic character of the cooperative. The democratic nature of the cooperative often surprises outsiders. It shouldn't, given the multifaceted relationship that the members have with the cooperative enterprise and the specific objective of the cooperative. It is an enterprise, just like a private or public stock company, in the sense that it combines the factors of labour, knowledge and capital to generate added value. But the members are co-entrepreneurs and the added value is a special one that provides the members with material benefit. This objective, which is usually prescribed by law, is of great importance both for the actual day-to-day management (in the material sense) and for the entire administrative organization (in the formal sense) of the cooperative enterprise. In that regard it is normative: board members, officers, managers and supervisors can be judged on how they perform in the fulfilment of their objectives.

First- and Second-Generation Cooperatives

In principle, the cooperative is a closed corporation. This is not only a result of the legally prescribed objective of the cooperative, as already noted, but also a result of the legally prescribed way in which that objective must be pursued. It must be "of, for and by" the members. In that sense, the cooperative can be compared to a partnership. A group of people join together to operate a common enterprise with a view to joint enjoyment of the economic advantages of that enterprise. The main difference as opposed to a partnership is the scale, and hence the form of association. For that reason, national laws of associations are often applicable to cooperatives. Family businesses are also an example of enterprises that are, in fact, closed corporations. Characteristic of these closed corporations is the intertwining of the various relationships that the members—shareholders, employees or other involved parties—have with the corporation. Most enterprises, larger ones at least, are completely independent in the sense that they do not operate for the benefit of a specific interest group. The legislator therefore considers them to be independent entities. That independence is reflected in their economic activities, and in their freedom in all markets (labor, capital, means of production). The cooperative enterprise, on the other hand, is not free in at least one of those markets. It is the market that we previously described as the primary enterprise, the market that exists between the members and the cooperative enterprise. This explains why the cooperative is sometimes described as a non-independent enterprise.

The non-independence of the enterprise is also underlined when the cooperative is deemed to be an "extension" of the members' own businesses. When farmers started to pool their milk and process it themselves, for example, this was a collective activity that was previously undertaken on the individual farms. We find the term "extension cooperatives" used in the literature for those cooperatives that are only involved in communal purchasing. That is the collection and sale of products on behalf of the members, clearly with a view to creating a countervailing power, and in first-line processing. By first-line processing, we mean the processing that makes a product suitable for sale on a large scale, such as packaging, for example. Bottling of milk is a form of packaging. Even the processing of milk to make milk powder could be considered a kind of first-line processing. After all, powdered milk can be kept longer than liquid milk and it has far less volume. This makes it easier to sell in markets further afield. Exactly the same trend could be seen at the other end of the scale because purchasing cooperatives were quick to start processing their products.

One characteristic of this type of cooperative is the fact that these activities are closely linked to the activities of the members. That, in turn, means that they are reasonably equipped for democratic decision-making. The examples of the milk powder and mixed feed are illustrative of a transition towards activities that are further removed from the business of farming itself. When the cooperative moves towards vertical integration and tries to draw on the added value achieved in other links of the chain, we are then suddenly confronted with activities that are truly beyond the scope of the members' businesses.

These are what are known as second-generation cooperatives. (You might be persuaded to think that this is the true meaning of "extension" of the members' businesses, whereas what happens in the first-generation cooperatives is no more than a clustering of activities. But we shall adhere to the terminology currently being used.)

The transition is gradual. Even the earliest dairy cooperatives made cheese, something that had previously been carried out on individual farms. Later they added custard, for instance, which at the time was simply a way to sell more milk. The essence of the second-generation cooperative is that the cooperative enterprise starts making strategic plans for the next link in the supply chain. As a result, the cooperative becomes more detached from the members and, to a certain degree, more independent. This development has far-reaching consequences for relationships with members.

The first change we see in the transaction relationship is the character of the internal market (the primary enterprise). The members' product forms the basis of "extension cooperatives". Selling that product at the best possible price is the cooperative enterprise's challenge. There is a degree of two-way traffic. We have already mentioned that cooperative enterprises sometimes had to persuade members to introduce quality and efficiency improvements, the latter through the principle of "he who causes cost, pays the cost". This is effectively the cooperative enterprise steering the members' businesses to give their product a better chance in the market.

But when the cooperative enterprise penetrates further into the column, its efforts to revalue the product take on a different character. It becomes essential to follow a marketing strategy. The cooperative enterprise examines the requirements of the market and the consumer, and then invests in and markets products, which might first be further processed, and services. The focus of such a strategy is no longer the price, but the added value. It is a subtle harmony of investing in market research, innovation, advertising, qualities and quantities. Demand, not supply, is at the heart of this approach. For the cooperative enterprise, it means that that demand has to be fed back to the members. Certain products or qualities are in greater or lesser demand, and the members need to align their production accordingly.

The cooperative enterprise will thus take a more independent stance in the primary market: "with its back to the farmer and its face to the market", as explained. This process sometimes leads to a choice for a standardized product specification with which all the members' businesses must comply. In other cases, it can lead to the cooperative enterprise acting as a marketing organization for a number of larger or smaller chains in which different groups of members are involved. The most difficult point, however, is often that of quantities. Economies of scale are only one of the factors that need to be taken into account in a demand-driven strategy. Surplus supply is undesirable. At some stage it will become necessary to regulate the total quantity of available product or to restrict access to sub-chains in some way. It can be onerous for the functioning of the internal market and for democratic decision-making, if only because restrictions on production only serve to highlight potential competition between the members. One member will benefit from another member's lower production.

The nature of the financial relationship in a second-generation cooperative also changes. Members are assumed to be willing to invest in activities that are further removed from their actual businesses and that involves greater risks than the activities of the extension cooperative, which are based primarily on reducing the cost price. But as business activities evolve, it is difficult to find a direct link with the members' product in many cases. That can be the case, for example, if the cooperative enterprise engages in mergers so as to provide itself with access to specific domestic or international markets, or if the expertise that is available within the cooperative enterprise is used for other products.

Last but not least, the control relationship is under pressure in the second generation cooperative. Where transactions are concerned, the cooperative enterprise will want the members to grant it more delegated authority so that it can discipline the members (qualities, quantities), as well as to be able to have more flexibility to make business decisions about matters such as acquisitions. The cooperative enterprise will be more demanding in financial terms as well. When it comes to expertise, members will feel that they are less capable of evaluating the cooperative strategy.

For a large part of the membership, the strategy is aimed at a market with which they are not personally familiar. At the same time, it is more important than ever for the member to maintain a vigilant attitude. The risks are indeed greater, and the virtual distance between the cooperative enterprise and the members—and thus between the enterprise's objectives and the members' objectives—can easily become too great. It was not without reason that we described the cooperative enterprise as operating from a different link in the chain. The sounding board and reference point of delegated cooperative managers can all too easily shift from the members to the colleagues and competitors in the next link of the national or international commercial chain. This is not an unreasonable development. That is, after all, the stage on which the cooperative enterprise is a player, and it is from that same stage that new managers and experts will need to be recruited. But a process of this kind requires extra safeguards, that the collective interests of the members, and thus the primary objective of the cooperative itself, do not become subjugated.

Finally, we hasten to point out that speed and flexibility are essential factors in competition and modern business management. It is usually undesirable to publicize tactics in advance. Unfortunately, both these aspects are difficult to reconcile with an open and democratic discussion of, for and by the members.

A state of mutual confidence needs to exist between management, members and board, based on a clear and transparent agreement about the main lines of strategic policy.

ADMINISTRATIVE BODIES

The Members

The cooperative is constituted of, for and by the members. That makes the assembly, or the general membership meeting, the body in which all members have a voice. It is the highest body of the cooperative. The law requires that the one-man-one-vote principle be applied. The situation in practice, however, is usually different. In many diverse cooperatives, in particular, the one-man-one-vote system will sooner or later cause friction. This is mainly the case where some of the members are little more than "hobbyists." These are members who are not really entrepreneurs, but are engaged in some activity whereby the cooperative becomes useful to them. In general, their behaviour will be the same as that of much older members. It will become manifest in a lack of long-term vision, such as the horizon problem we mentioned earlier. Members who are not really entrepreneurs will not look at the future in terms of vested interests, and they will not be interested in investment or improving quality. As the membership ages, a sort of entrepreneurial conservatism can creep in, and that could be disastrous for the future of the cooperative.

For that reason, most cooperatives regulate voting rights according to the member's transactions with the cooperative (the principle of proportionality), while maintaining the statutory basis by giving each member at least one vote. Many also institute an upper limit to a member's voting rights.

Most large cooperatives in Europe make use of the statutory possibility of having what is known as a member council. The membership is then often divided into regional or geographical groups—known as districts, circles, branches or departments—which then appoint one or more members to the member council, thus creating a hierarchal organization. This is a practical solution because otherwise the individual voice would be lost amid the clamour of a thousand or more members' voices (upholding the right to voice an opinion). On the other hand, it remains conceivable that the demands of a significant minority of the membership will not be heard in the highest member council because these members form a minority in each of the divisions or districts. This is an important point to bear in mind in an organization where the members' objectives are the central consideration.

The assembly, or the member council where they exist, has a number of specific governance tasks to perform. In the first place these include the appointment, dismissal and/or suspension of members of the board of directors and/or the board of supervisors. This statutory requirement can be pushed aside, but for the purposes of this chapter we shall consider only the most common organizational structure. In addition, the assembly has the legal authority to dissolve the cooperative, prolong its existence, or decide to merge or split the cooperative. Furthermore, it adopts the Articles of Association, and the amendments to those Articles, and draws up the annual accounts (profit and loss account and balance sheet). It also serves as the body that considers appeals in the case of expelled members, or when a candidate for membership wishes to appeal against the board's rejection of a membership application. Finally, the assembly has what is known as a residual competence. All responsibilities that do not devolve to any other body by law or by the Articles of Association are considered vested in the general meeting. In practice, the assembly operates and checks matters after the fact. When the annual report is being considered, the policies and actions of the board of directors and the board of supervisors are first evaluated and, if found satisfactory, the boards are granted discharge. On the basis of statutory regulations, the law of associations also allows the assembly to be involved in the formulation of policy. The assembly can have the right, for example, to appraise proposed policies or important decisions in advance. It is quite customary for the Articles of Association to determine that the board of directors must submit strategic plans, investment budgets, long-term plans and social plans to the assembly for initial consent. In that case, there is a double preventive check in some countries, as such important matters normally also require the approval of the board of supervisors.

The practice of retrospective checks is, in fact, based on members' confidence in and the delegation of responsibilities to the board members. If the assembly continuously puts itself in the place of the board of directors, that will continuously give rise to difficulties, not least of which is duplicated work. But this does not alter the fact that the assembly (or member council) has the power to determine the main lines of the cooperative's policies, or the identity of the cooperative. This can be clearly seen in the general meeting's right to draw up articles of association and to appoint and dismiss board members.

The Board of Directors

The board of directors is the central body in the cooperative organization and is found as the governing body in almost all countries. National laws require that a board of directors govern the cooperative, and the cooperative enterprise. This board manages the organization. This means representing the legal entity in legal situations, and also conceiving, initiating and implementing strategy and policies, and taking all the decisions involved in those processes. The board can therefore take initiatives that go much further than simply managing day-to-day affairs. The board's management is based on the objectives of the cooperative. Those objectives are usually formulated in a mission statement that also indicates the preconditions necessary for achieving the objectives. In this context, these managers can be equated to entrepreneurs. The board acts as an entrepreneur.

The members, either through the assembly or through the member council, elect boards of directors. It is also possible for some of the board members—but always less than half—to be appointed in some other way than through the Assembly. Generally speaking, there is a limited degree of co-optation: the board can itself propose candidates for seats on the board and the assembly can—if it chooses—propose other candidates; the latter is certainly not unknown.

The rule is that the board speaks as one: a collegiate board. This means that they take decisions as a body. Once a decision has been taken, all members will defend that decision, irrespective of how each individual voted. The ultimate consequence for any "nay" voter who cannot or will not defend a decision is that he would have to resign. While it is not unknown for members to try to lure board members into expressing an opinion that differs from board policy, in principle this is "not the done thing". It certainly makes life uncomfortable for board members. Those who had been put forward as a rival candidate by rank-and-file members will find it especially difficult; they feel that they are representing a particular lobby and will not want to let them down. But this is not desirable in a collegiate board. Members are expected to act as part of an independent body, one that is not bound by instructions. It is not always clear, however, whether this also applies in countries where members are appointed as delegates from a district or branch to a central member council. Some cooperatives seek to avoid problems of this nature by including a passage in the Articles of Association directing members of a member council to act independently and without instructions. This gives the meetings at district or branch levels the status of a sounding board where no decisions will be taken.

Accordingly, the management culture within the cooperative is not one of confrontation but of cooperation. It is a true model of democratic consultation. A culture in which the board can itself propose candidates for seats on the board, and in which board members are also assumed to work without interference or instruction from others, is only possible when the board is well balanced and truly has and retains the confidence of the members.

In the context of board affairs, this balance is achieved by investing a great deal of time and energy in involving members in the policies of the cooperative. The strategy pursued by the cooperative must be transparent, unequivocal, and spelled out. "Sudden" events must not be allowed. Decisions must be in line with general expectations. Members must be kept appraised of what is going on, and the members of the board should communicate this themselves so that they have a chance to pick up signals from the responses of the members. On the whole, discussions with the members will not be limited to the annual members' meetings or other assembly meetings, but will be accommodated in more frequent informative evenings at local and district levels.

This method of management can only be sustained if members are really involved in the cooperative's policies and take an active part. If they are not, the managers can easily become "regents" in the sense that they manage without any feedback from their member base. That is another reason for board members to continue to attend district meetings. It is also important for them to remain active in the recruitment and training of young, interested members.

In general terms, then, the cooperative has a statutory board of directors that has the same tasks as the board of a public or private limited company. The only difference is the way the board is composed. In the case of a limited liability company, board members (with the exception of a number of "quality" posts) are elected by the shareholders, or—depending on the regulations governing the company—by a board of supervisors. An exception is when a designated number of board seats are set aside as "quality" posts, or outside directors. In the case of the cooperative and other associations, board members are chosen by and from the members.

Companies where board members are normally known as directors usually have an executive board or committee consisting of full-time managers and key board members. The managers are usually employees of the company. This can also be the case in cooperatives, certainly in larger ones; but being a member of the board of a cooperative is more often an ancillary position. Most board members, after all, have their own businesses to run.

Executive Board or Managing Board

Both investor-owned companies and cooperatives can employ professional managers. They are responsible for the management and the day-to-day running of the enterprise within the parameters of the strategy determined by the board. They have a derivative function. Strictly speaking, the executive board or committee is not part of the cooperative's organizational structure. Its members are officers of the company. As in any other organizational model, it is important that tasks and responsibilities are clearly defined and demarcated. The board of directors manages the cooperative and they can be held to account if they fail in that task. The manager, on the other hand, has a derivative task and cannot be held accountable in the same way. In the event of non-performance, however, the manager can have a personal liability vis-à-vis the cooperative. This also applies to members of boards of directors and supervisors. Against this background it is therefore imperative to have a clear and formal line of demarcation between the responsibilities of the manager and the board.

Most nations' business codes allow generous scope for delegation of responsibilities, but the responsibilities are explicitly only delegated. The person's own responsibility for the specific tasks, either on the board or as a manager, remains intact. Nowadays, it is becoming common for managers to be part of boards of directors in many countries, although this isn't common or even allowed in most North American cooperatives. This is a deviation from the principles set out in the law. Members of the executive board can be appointed by virtue of their specific expertise, and generally speaking—unlike members of the board of directors—they will be fulltime employees. Partly for this reason, the executive board is usually responsible for preparing and documenting the decisions of the board of directors.

We have already mentioned numerous factors that contribute to management having a more central and independent role in the cooperative enterprise. This was undoubtedly the case in the past as well, especially when the bookkeeper or manager had a strong or dominant personality. But it is a more structural phenomenon these days. The gap between the member and the cooperative has become greater. This is partly due to the growth of the cooperative. It also partly results from management becoming the domain of specialists who are able to respond quickly and flexibly, and are capable of handling complicated personnel and marketing policies.

In that context, agency theory is also important in the context of cooperatives. This theory considers the situation that arises when decision-making within an enterprise is left to an appointed manager, the agent. Classic economic thinking assumes the manager, the owner-entrepreneur and the manager-entrepreneur are each other's equal and that they share the goal of achieving maximum profit. If their roles are disentangled, the risk arises that the manager takes decisions in his own interest that may not be in the interest of the owner or the owner-entrepreneur.

The problem can also arise between the board members, who are also members of the cooperative, and the rank-and-file members. This problem can be lessened by ensuring that there is adequate supervision by the members as a whole and by the members on the board. But that supervision itself becomes more difficult when the agent (the manager) has more information at his disposal than the owners. The importance of this issue increases accordingly as the independence of the management increases.

Supervision

In many countries, especially in northwest Europe, cooperative enterprises had and still maintain a supervisory board. Such boards are used by some cooperatives in Canada, but rarely in the United States. It appears that these are another means of democratic checks and balances. Supervision was considered to be in the interest of the members. Usually, the underlying idea was that there should be some way of forestalling impulsive decisions, and that it could do no harm to subject proposed board decisions to a critical review. There is no standard composition for supervisory boards in cooperatives. Sometimes older and more experienced members who are deemed capable of setting aside day-to-day considerations are appointed, and they are expected to keep an eye on the more general affairs within the enterprise. Sometimes the supervisory board is used as a training ground for younger members to prepare another generation for the board of directors.

Not all cooperatives are actually free to determine the composition, tasks and authority of supervisory boards. Enterprises of all types (limited liability companies, cooperatives and mutual insurance companies), whose assets and workforce exceed certain levels, must have a board of supervisors, in the same way as large public or private limited companies. The law also prescribes the way in which supervisors should be appointed and how the board should function. The rules are intended to ensure that supervision is independent and carried out in the interests of all concerned, including the interests of third parties such as vendors. The law does, however, take account of the specific character of the cooperative, in particular the so-called member dominance. This allows the members to have more influence on their cooperative, and the board of supervisors of a cooperative has fewer powers than its counterparts in limited companies. Nonetheless, this regulation has given rise to some highly critical discussions in the past.

Cooperatives retain a closed character by limiting the number of "outsiders" to no more than one-third of the supervisors. That is exactly what the legislature was trying to avoid when the two-tier regulations were introduced. At the moment, the position and the actual function of the boards of supervisors are receiving great attention by groups of investors, other stakeholders, academics and government officials considering questions of the corporate governance of large companies.

Management/Administrative Hierarchy

Typically, the management/administrative hierarchy of cooperative enterprises consists of either two or three bodies: the board of directors (on behalf of the members), the executive board (or the management team) and, where employed, the board of supervisors. In some situations, the board of directors actually runs the enterprise and there is little scope for the executive board. A board of supervisors can, in principle, restrict its supervision to the board of directors. In most cases, however, the board of directors will have delegated the day-to-day running of the cooperative enterprise to an executive board. That produces a three-layered management structure.

Three-Layered Model

In many cases, the executive board of the cooperative enterprise has a high level of independence. It is in charge of day-to-day operations and—in consultation with the board of directors—it draws up the enterprise's strategic plans. The board of directors is mainly concerned with checks and balances. It represents the members' interests and tests the executive board's proposal against the strategic objectives and the interests of the members. In this model, the board of directors is always superior to the executive board. This power is evident in its ability to determine salaries and propose new appointments, and also because its monitoring role is decisive. The board of supervisors is responsible for supervising not only the functioning of the cooperative as a whole, but also the functioning of the cooperative enterprise as a separate entity. This board is expected to consider not only the interests of the members, but also the interests of the employees. As a result, the board of supervisors must supervise both the board of directors and the executive board.

This can, however, be somewhat confusing for the executive board. It may be forced to account for its policies and actions twice, once to the board of directors and then to the board of supervisors. In addition, the board of supervisors is often relatively under-informed. The day-to-day involvement of the board of directors in the affairs of the organization will give that body far more insight into what is going on. Supervisors, especially the external supervisors, have a tendency to fulfil their supervisory role formally and strictly, or they assume that the board of directors protects the cooperative function of the enterprise. If the organization is to avoid one or other of these bodies, feeling it is continually under attack, it is essential that there should be a good level of understanding among and about the three bodies.

In this context, the board of directors must be member-oriented and monitor the enterprise specifically in terms of the interests and objectives of the members. If the board of directors tends to act like a "general" board of supervisors, this will give rise to irritation because of the double supervision, and it will be more difficult for the board of directors to keep the issue of member interests high enough on the agenda of the two other bodies. Instances have occurred where a board of directors has withdrawn completely from an uncomfortable three-cornered relationship and has allowed the executive board to represent the cooperative as a whole vis-à-vis the board of supervisors.

It is an unfortunate fact of life in the three-layered model that although the board of directors is formally responsible for operations, the actual management and the necessary professional expertise is embodied in the executive board. For that reason, many cooperatives have sought ways to reduce the hierarchy to just two levels.

Two-Layered Model

The most common solution is to achieve a legal separation. The entrepreneurial activities are conducted through a public or private limited company, for example, with the cooperative as sole or principal shareholder. The board of directors of the cooperative promotes the interests of the members and, together with some members from outside the cooperative, forms the board of supervisors of the separate company. This establishes two layers, but it still retains the required three lines of representation.

Sometimes the choice is made to devolve some of the powers of the board of directors to the executive board, with the more legally oriented tasks being delegated to the board of supervisors. This model does have its limitations, because of the requirement of keeping management and supervision strictly segregated. One disadvantage is that the members no longer have a voice at the level of the board of directors. The executive board is effectively the managing board of both the cooperative-as-a-business and the cooperative-as-an-association. The promotion of members' interests may well be delegated to a member council, but this body does not have its own chairman because that would effectively create three layers once again. The chairman of the board of supervisors then acts as chairman of the member council. This chairman would have higher recognition within the cooperative, but it is far from optimum in management terms. The "two-to-three" layered model is therefore often called a hybrid or mongrel model.

A third example is the model in which the chairman of the member council is also chairman of the executive board, creating a personal union at the board level. The decisive factor must be whether this person has the professional qualities necessary to lead the enterprise. The board of supervisors monitors, advises, and explicitly checks how the members' interests are being promoted. This model is found in many corporations, especially in Germany, but not yet in any significant number of cooperatives.

Finally, there are also instances where the member council has a special committee to bring issues affecting the members before the executive board or the board of supervisors.

The management of cooperatives is a question of finding a good balance between the interests that are manifest in any enterprise, plus that extra interest that is unique to cooperatives—the interest of the members.

REFERENCES

1. "Cooperative Social Responsibility: The Differentiated Governance of a Multi-faceted Concept" by Claudio Baccarani and Federica Doni. Corporate Governance: An International Review, vol. 26, no. 1, 2018, pp. 55-70.
2. "Cooperatives and the Social Economy: From the Fringe to the Mainstream" edited by Virginie Pérotin and Andrew Robinson. Routledge, 2013.
3. "Exploring Multi-stakeholder Governance in the UK Co-operative Movement" by Mike Aiken and Jonathan Michie. Annals of Public and Cooperative Economics, vol. 85, no. 4, 2014, pp. 539-556.
4. "Governance and Performance in Publicly Listed, Family-Controlled, and Cooperatives: Evidence from Italy" by Amedeo Pugliese, et al. Corporate Governance: An International Review, vol. 25, no. 2, 2017, pp. 101-117.
5. "The Co-operative Advantage: Creating Shared Value in Financial Services" by Johnston Birchall and Szilvia Borbáth. Edward Elgar Publishing, 2018.
6. "The Multifaceted Role of Cooperatives in Sustainable Development: The Case of Fair Trade" by Marie-Christine Renard, vol. 135, no. 1, 2016, pp. 151-161.

6 COOPERATIVE MARKETING AND VALUE CHAIN

INTRODUCTION

Cooperative marketing and value chain initiatives represent collaborative approaches to enhance the competitiveness and sustainability of businesses within a cooperative framework. In cooperative marketing, member-owned enterprises join forces to collectively promote and sell their products or services, leveraging shared resources, networks, and expertise to access larger markets and achieve economies of scale. This cooperative marketing strategy enables small-scale producers or businesses to compete more effectively with larger corporations while maintaining control over their operations and retaining a fair share of the value generated.

Moreover, cooperative value chain initiatives focus on improving the efficiency, transparency, and fairness of the entire production and distribution process, from sourcing raw materials to delivering final products to consumers. By integrating various stakeholders, including producers, processors, distributors, and retailers, into a cohesive value chain, cooperatives can streamline operations, reduce costs, and ensure a more equitable distribution of profits along the supply chain.

Overall, cooperative marketing and value chain initiatives offer promising avenues for empowering small-scale producers, promoting economic development in rural and marginalized communities, and fostering sustainable practices that benefit both producers and consumers. These cooperative approaches exemplify the principles of cooperation, mutual benefit, and solidarity, driving positive social and economic impacts at the local, regional, and global levels.

COOPERATIVE MARKETING

Cooperative marketing essentially involves understanding or an agreement between two companies aiming to promote or sell the other companies' products. They also sell their products. The companies within the agreement do this to complement each other's services. This provides mutual benefits. Cooperative marketing results because of the combined or joint efforts of two or even more companies. Typically, they bundle and group the products and services in the hope of reaching a common target audience. In cooperative marketing, products can complement or even supplement each other. In some cases, it can cater to different seasonal cycles.

The Latin word *co-operari,* meaning *working together,* is the origin of the word Co-operative. It is a voluntary association or organization of people or entities to promote their interests – usually the common economic ones – based on unity, equality, liberty, and economic principles. For example, cooperative marketing is an association of producers who are ready to help each other market their products as a whole, catering to economies that emerge from a large-scale business.

According to K. R. Kulkarni – "Co-operative marketing is the marketing for the producers and by the producers that aims at eliminating the chain of middlemen operating between producers and the ultimate consumer and thus securing the maximum price for their produce."

Cooperative marketing was necessary for several reasons. Rampant malpractices in what was then the agricultural marketing system, the existence of all manner of intermediaries, and their excessive charges made this necessary. That earlier system, or lack of it, meant farmers owed vast amounts of money to lenders, leaving them, sadly, at the mercy of them. Come harvest time. The farmer was routinely forced to sell whatever product they had to the middlemen at shamefully low prices. Cooperative marketing societies were a step to overcome those pre-existing problems. What is interesting about cooperative marketing is that since it is a voluntary business organization, patrons decide to collectively market products for the benefit of each of them in a system governed by democratic principles. The members share all the revenue and savings depending on their share.

The members are all owners; they operate and contribute to the commodities and become direct beneficiaries of savings. They do not have to worry about intermediaries profiting at their expense. They are assured of the benefits of large-scale business, which would have been difficult for them to achieve individually. Here, each producer/member has one vote, regardless of the number of shares he buys.

Cooperative Marketing emphasizes the concept of commercialization, although the economic motives and characters make them stand apart from other associations. The method of operation often resembles private businesses, but the differences in their respective reasons are essential.

Importance of Cooperative Marketing

In cooperative marketing, where multiple players work in tandem, creating valuable benefits to all parties, what is ensured is that the combined endeavors produce a synergy, and this makes superior products, and the whole eco-system results in immense value-addition, for the members as well as the end customers.

Need for Cooperative Marketing

- ***It ensures better results*** because everyone collaborates and adds their bits, both ideas and produces. In addition, the ability to place bulk orders makes the costs go down substantially.

- ***Advertisements of products*** and the availability of each other's marketing network can be done jointly, resulting in more market penetration. Usually, the typical advertising could be direct mails, online marketing, or even print media. As a result, the total cost of products for all parties involved can be reduced substantially. They also get better bargaining power and can negotiate a price better.
- ***Eliminating malpractices*** – all manner of malpractices that prevail, from very arbitrary deductions to unfair and illegal price manipulation, can be reduced, if not eliminated. There is rampant manipulation of weights and measures, which can be substantially reduced.
- ***Establishing appropriate reward for the endeavors put in*** – the veritable army of intermediaries is very interested in collecting, storing, insuring, and financing rural produce. Their charges are hugely inappropriate and disproportionate. Any cooperative marketing strategy that is efficiently organized reduces the price spread, providing fair returns to all stakeholders.
- ***Concomitant of Integrated Programme*** – cooperative marketing has brought in the system of a vast expansion of credit. Marketing societies act as the agents to collect and recover loans given by the cooperative credit societies.
- ***To Stabilise the Agricultural Price*** – left to its own devices, the will of the private intermediaries would only cause more destabilization and uncertainty. Cooperative Marketing ensures that does not happen, along with price stabilization, and results in a very balanced economic development that does not veer towards a single side. The profit motive stops having the upper hand, and usual market conditions do not deviate from fair practice to uncertainties of pointless speculation, leading to hoarding and architected crisis.

Disadvantages

- It can often lead to a lack of commitment because they are not individually responsible for anything. This lack of commitment even among members in an agreement can substantially reduce the business for all.
- Who is the target audience to whom this can be applied? The marketing strategy could potentially be only applicable to a part of the target audience.
- ***Information sharing***: There might be resistance to sharing information with everyone, especially those who have done individual business historically. Simply agreeing does not change behavior ingrained deep into a person. Trust becomes an issue, which can hamper how the products get marketed.

The Structure of Cooperative Marketing

The cooperative marketing societies have different structures in India and can be two-tiered and three-tiered. NAFED is the apex institution for this at the national level. The primary cooperative societies at the base level are the ones who market the farmers' products particular to that area.

Central Co-operative Marketing unions are there, and their primary function is marketing all the farmers' produce that they bring for sale. Usually, their location is at the secondary wholesale markets. The unions have as their members all those who are there in the primary marketing societies and individual farmer members. In addition, the State level societies function through their offices throughout the state. Right now, there are over 6000 primary marketing societies in India. The District level has around 170 Central Marketing Societies, and the State level has 29 Marketing Federations and 16 particular commodity Marketing Federations. NAFED – National Agricultural Cooperative Marketing Federation and NCDC – National Co-operative Development Corporation are national nodal bodies.

The structure is pyramidal. States usually have two or three-tiered designs, depending on their choice and requirement.

Some Features of Cooperative Marketing Societies

These societies have features that are pretty unique and distinguishable from other organizations involved in rural marketing produce. First, their very existence is to assist in increasing their incomes.

Membership

(i) Ordinary Members:

Ordinary members are usually Individual farmers, cooperative societies, and service societies of the locality. Membership would provide them the right to participate in all the discussions within the society, get a share in the profits, and have a voice in the decision-making process.

(ii) Nominal Members:

Nominal members are those with whom the society has reasons to interact. However, they do not get to participate in any decision-making, nor do they get a share in their profits.

Sources of Finance

The following are the significant sources of finance of a co-operative marketing society:

(i) Share Capital

All the members and even the state government subscribe to the share capital. Members can purchase any number of shares they want and are even encouraged to invest as much as they want and buy as many shares as they wish. Like all share markets, they can also support their dividends, etc.

(ii) Loans

These societies are authorized to take loans and stabilize or raise their finances. They can do the same from commercial banks; they accept pledging and clean credit.

(iii) Subsidy

The marketing societies all get subsidies to buy grading machines and other infrastructural needs. In addition, subsidies are also provided to take care of at least a portion of the cost of staffing etc.

Service Motto

The whole philosophy behind cooperative societies was to provide and extend various benefits and services to the members. Profits were never part of the plan. Consequently, all facilities – procuring seeds, manures, and such things, providing tools for grading and standardization, etc. are all sold to members at favorable and affordable rates.

One Person, One Vote

It does not matter how many shares each member holds in cooperative societies. They all have the right to vote as a single unit. This adhered to the principles of democracy and equal rights and freedom. It ensures that no one person can make his orders the rule in joint-stock companies. This eliminates favor and discrimination and gives everyone an equal voice.

Open Membership

Membership in these cooperative marketing societies is open for all. The only rule is that the member has to produce a product. Entry and exit from such memberships are also dependent on a person's desires and convenience. To encourage more membership, following the process is straightforward too, which helps.

Governing themselves

The entire management of the societies is in the hands of the members. Every member is encouraged to participate in the administration, proceedings, and functioning. The member has the power to exercise his vote. The set-up is very democratic, and everything is off, for, and by the members.

Capital rewards

Equality and fraternity are the cornerstones in Cooperative Marketing – all capital invested by members also earn the same interest rate, making it very risk-free for all the members. Profiting is not the motive, as mentioned earlier.

Co-operation

At the core of these initiatives is the concept of self-help while helping others in tandem. These sorts of societies create a sense of cooperation and mutual help. This is then carried into improved advertising, marketing, ensuring better business and a raised standard and quality of living.

Distributive Justice

When it comes to distribution, the concept of one man, one vote is not employed, and members are given their share of profits depending on their investment in the network. This ensures there is no feeling of unfairness and bitterness. The more they contribute, the better the dividends they will be given and vice versa. There is no gainsaying that profits are a direct consequence of members' contribution. Therefore, it is only fair that their rewards should match up.

Main functions of Co-operative Marketing Societies

Purchase and Sale of Produce – These societies buy and sell members› produce, and they do it in bulk. This makes it easy to reduce marketing costs, earning good returns substantially.

Distribution – Main ingredients – seeds, material, etc., are all provided at reasonable rates. Members can also get credit to procure their material.

Storage facility – Many societies typically have their own or hired warehouses for members to store their material, providing much-needed security.

Supplying implements – Cooperative societies often provide infrastructural needs to their members. This helps in raising both the quality and quantity of their produces. Market information – Often, individual members do not have the money to access the latest news and techniques to increase production or benefit in other ways. This information helps members properly assess and ensure they get the correct price of their products.

Stability of prices – The societies can adjust the supply of items based on market demand. This is an excellent way of stabilizing prices and ensuring the members do not face the adverse effects of price fluctuations based on external factors.

Taking part in foreign trade – Participation in export trade initiatives of the country can happen more quickly, promising better prices for the members. The marketing cooperatives open the markets wide for both the members and their customers.

How to Develop a Cooperative Marketing Campaign?

Co-op marketing is a great way to increase your brand's exposure while keeping low marketing costs. It's also extremely cost-effective, so it's a good idea to consider this strategy during your next marketing campaign.

There are three steps for cooperative marketers to develop such a campaign: identifying your target audience, choosing the best partners (such as retail businesses) for your campaign, and creating an effective marketing plan.

1) Identify your Target Audience

First, you'll need to identify your target audience. Who are you trying to reach? What problems does your company solve? What unique value do you provide? Once you know this information, you can start looking for potential partners who will benefit from working with you.

2) Choose the Best Partners

Next, choose the right partners for your campaign. You want companies that offer complementary products or services or have a large customer base in common with yours. You'll also want partners who are willing to promote themselves alongside yours—otherwise, there's no reason for them to join forces with you.

3) Create an effective marketing plan

Finally, create an effective co-op program that outlines how each partner will contribute to the campaign and what they'll get out of it (e.g., increased sales). Then implement it! Also, regularly check the campaign performance analytics and marketing materials to properly use your co-op funds and establish your cooperative branding.

Type of Companies should Implement Cooperative Marketing

Cooperative marketing is beneficial for any company looking to increase its reach and exposure with minimal cost. It can also be used by companies that have trouble finding the right partner to help them reach their goals. Whether you're a start-up, small business, or established company, it is an affordable and effective way to get your message out.

For example, Walmart and Coca-Cola have a long history of working together to promote their respective products. In a new partnership with Coca-Cola, Walmart is expanding its usage of drone delivery. Another example can be seen between Nestlé and Starbucks, which work together to provide customers with a variety of coffee options. Affiliate marketing also offers companies the opportunity to cooperate with other businesses. Affiliates are typically compensated for referring customers to a brand and can help build visibility for both parties while allowing customers to benefit from a variety of products and services. Amazon affiliate program is a great example of this.

Hence, whether you want to grow your business or just want to expand its reach, a cooperative strategy is the way to go! Cooperative marketing works with a well-crafted strategy and the right partners, and you can maximize your marketing efforts while saving time and money by using it strategically.

Examples of Cooperative Marketing Campaigns

To better understand co-op marketing programs, let's take an example of how singers work and also how farmers work.

The singers usually work in a group so that they can play in a scene/event together. This diminishes the expenses of renting the place as the rent is divided among all the singers. But at the same time, all artists gain exposure to the audience from that single platform.

Similarly, farmers bring all their produce to a common market to sell their products. This ensures that the customers all have to come to one spot. Plus smart farmers can package their product and supply multiple options at lower rates.

A Starbucks coffee shop can often be encountered in many of the big malls or shopping centers around the world. These malls then market the Starbucks and at the same time, Starbucks also markets the malls in their ads which promote their locations.

Another cooperative marketing example is the meal deals offered by KFC. These deals combine KFC's food items with Pepsi drinks to create an attractive package that customers can enjoy. It also ensures the promotion of both Pepsi and KFC as a result.

And a final example would be the companies offering frequent flyer miles (such as KLM) partnerships with hotels, car rental agencies, and restaurants.

Job Titles are associated with Cooperative Marketing

1) Marketing Manager

The marketing manager oversees the overall marketing strategy of the business. This includes developing a cooperative marketing plan, as well as creating campaigns to promote both products and services.

2) Brand Manager

The brand manager is responsible for overseeing the branding of a business's products and services. This includes developing advertising and promotional material, as well as ensuring that the product's brand is consistent across all marketing channels.

3) Market Research Analysts

Market research analysts are responsible for gathering and analyzing data about consumer behavior. They use this data to create marketing strategies that can increase the reach of a business's products and services.

4) B2B Sales Managers

Business-to-business (B2B) sales managers are responsible for developing relationships with other businesses to increase sales and profit. This includes negotiating co-op marketing agreements, as well as managing customer relationships.

5) Digital Content Strategists

Digital content strategists' role in co-op marketing programs involves creating content that is both engaging and search engine friendly. This includes developing effective SEO strategies, as well as crafting compelling copy for websites, emails, and social media channels to promote all the partners involved in the co-op marketing partnerships.

COOPERATIVE BENEFITS

A cooperative's benefits to producers are the ability to maintain or increase market access, reduce risk, and generate more sales. Its strategies would allow producers to have access to pricing and marketing opportunities that otherwise may not have been available. Producers may not be aware of various marketing opportunities and, even if they are aware, they may not have been able to access them because of size requirements or high costs associated with these opportunities.

Cooperatives provide an opportunity for effective coordination that improves marketing system performance by unifying and exerting power to raise total returns to agricultural producers. System rewards from improved coordination have been most visible through efforts of farm input cooperatives at the regional and inter-regional levels in the plant food, crop protectant, petroleum, farm credit, and energy sectors.

CATEGORIES OF COOPERATIVES

Many different types of cooperatives exist. Structurally, cooperatives may vary as much as the products or services they provide. Because of the variety of possible structures and functions, classification is not standardized across all cooperative ventures. Below are several short descriptions of selected cooperative structures.

Marketing Cooperatives

Marketing cooperatives handle most types of farm products. These cooperatives enable producers to 1) correct market failure where prices are too low or buyers have left the market, 2) provide a service not available otherwise, 3) gain market power (negotiating power) against much larger buyers, 4) spread risks and costs, and 5) have adequate volume to operate on a large enough level to meet the demands of buyers or a greater level of efficiency. This classification of agricultural cooperatives is the largest segment by sales value.

Niche-Market Cooperatives

As a subset of Marketing Cooperatives, some local cooperatives seek to serve a specialized clientele. These cooperatives do not strive to become large because their smaller customer base wants specialized products and/or services. Others are small by nature of the products they handle and the territory where the items can be produced. While some of these cooperatives may be very successful, the opportunities they represent and their overall impact are both limited.

Marketing Agencies-in-Common (MACs)

MACs are a strategic alliance among marketing cooperatives that join to market under a common agreement. MACs serve as marketing agents for their members to achieve economies of size in marketing their like or complementary products. These cooperatives also share the large costs associated with developing brand names and provide a way to acquire and sell nonmember products when expanding product lines. The agency will usually have exclusive rights to sell members' products in some or all markets.

Supply Cooperatives

Supply Cooperatives, the largest number of agricultural cooperatives by type, derive most of their business volume from the sale of production supplies, machinery and equipment, and building materials. Many also handle farm, ranch, and home items, such as heating oil, lawn and garden supplies and equipment, and food.

Service Cooperatives

The smallest of all agricultural cooperative types by number, Service Cooperatives provide specialized services related to the business operations of farmers, ranchers, or cooperatives, such as trucking, storing, and drying. Cooperatives that provide these services to their members offer a way for producers to become more productive by lowering their costs.

Joint Ventures

Joint Ventures exist across all classification types, and offer another alternative coordination among cooperatives. As shown in a USDA Agricultural Cooperative Service Research Report "A joint venture is a business entity, created and supported by other businesses, that has a limited objective related to solving a problem facing each of its owners." Cooperatives are, in this sense, joint ventures. Formed by members to provide quality goods and services the members need at the lowest possible cost, joint ventures may be organized as Limited Liability Companies (LLC), partnerships, corporations, cooperatives, unincorporated associations, or merely contractual arrangements. A joint venture that does not meet its objectives may be disbanded without becoming a major disruption to the participants. Joint ventures can be either be short-lived or continue for decades.

New Generation Cooperative

A New Generation Cooperative, a complex legal structure rather than a type, is often formed by producers who perceive the best opportunity for continued economic success hinges on their ability to retain more of the value-added dollars generated from their production. This type of cooperative is not legal in all states. Distinguishing features include:

- Limited and defined membership
- Delivery rights and obligations with specified quantity and quality
- Substantial up-front producer equity
- Tradable equity shares that can fluctuate in value
- The right to deliver product to the cooperative is linked to legal responsibility of the producer to provide that product, accomplished through a stock purchase and legally binding marketing agreements.

New Generation Cooperatives are based on significant up-front investment of producer equity as opposed to equity retained over time in traditional cooperatives. Producers provide up-front investment to capitalize the business through the purchase of delivery rights, which would also ensure the cooperative's supply. In return, producers receive compensation based on contracts entered into by the cooperative on their behalf.

VALUE CHAIN

The definition of a value chain is a set of business activities involving the creation, commercialization, and correction of products or services.

A value chain is a model that includes every step a company goes through — from the initial idea through delivery to the customer — to create a good or service. The value chain includes initial design, materials sourcing, manufacturing, marketing, sale, delivery and after-sale service. If that sounds a lot like a supply chain, it should. Value chains encompass more business activities than supply chains, but the main difference is their customer-focused point of view.

By studying the value chain, businesses can go step by step to find places to add values that customers look for when choosing where to spend their money. Not every business has the time or resources to perform a full analysis of its value chain — that would require a deep look at every step of production for every product — but many companies benefit from some value chain analysis on their highest-cost products, specific departments or anywhere they feel that a deeper look is needed before implementing efficiency improvements.

An example of a value chain in manufacturing is the creation of S'well water bottles. First, someone had to come up with the idea for S'well water bottles. Then, they had to design the innovative water bottle using software and other tools. Then, they had to source a manufacturer for developing the product. After outsourcing the manufacturer, they may have to acquire raw materials for the manufacturer to use.

Once the product is created, they have to sell the product — which, in this case, is a combination of wholesale, retail, and direct-to-consumer. Then, they have to service the product which, in this case, is likely handling returns. Regardless of their business model, they must create and deliver the product to the end customer, whether that's an individual or a retail store.

All of these steps create a value chain — literally, a chain where value can be extracted or added in real time at every step of the chain. When executed well, a value chain framework can double as a competitive strategy that offers a differentiation advantage for your products.

The goal of the value chain model is to help a business gain an advantage over its competitors by increasing the value its products offer to customers. Once decision-makers or managers map out the steps in the value chain — either for one product or as a broad look at a company's processes — they can analyze the costs and rewards of each step. That analysis then informs decisions about decreasing costs or increasing the value of a product in the eye of the customer. Lower costs can lead to higher profit margins or lower prices for the good, creating a "cost advantage" over competitors. And when customers view a product as more valuable than a comparable good, they are often willing to purchase it more often or pay higher prices, giving the business a "differentiation advantage".

For example, let's say a company's value chain analysis highlights that its use of high-quality raw materials is driving up the cost of manufacturing. If the company's goal is to gain a cost advantage over competitors, it can consider cost-cutting measures like changing suppliers or outsourcing costly parts of the process. If the business is aiming for a differentiation advantage, it can emphasize its high-quality materials and manufacturing processes in its marketing, positioning the product as a premium item — and charging a premium price. Both approaches to competitive advantage are possible when a business understands its value chain, and both have the same ultimate financial goal — higher profits.

Value Chain Origins

The term "value chain" was first coined in 1985 by Michael E. Porter of the Harvard Business School in his book *Competitive Advantage: Creating and Sustaining Superior Performance*. Its second chapter opens with the following lines, introducing what Porter called the "value chain": "Competitive advantage cannot be understood by looking at a firm as a whole. It stems from the many discrete activities a firm performs in designing, producing, marketing, delivering and supporting its product."

Porter goes on to emphasize customer value over cost as the crucial point of view from which to seek competitive advantage: "Value is the amount buyers are willing to pay for what a firm provides them ... Value, instead of cost, must be used in analyzing competitive position since firms often deliberately raise their cost in order to command a premium price via differentiation".

Porter's work showed businesses that focusing simply on reducing costs is only a fraction of the battle to win customers and stay competitive. By framing the customer's opinions and preferences as a business's primary focus, the value chain helps businesses differentiate from competitors and gain advantages in the market — even if they raise costs in the process. Customers are often willing to pay higher prices for products they perceive as higher value, whether that value comes from perceived higher quality, specific features or through marketing, customer service and sales techniques.

Porter's value chain model is still used today by businesses to create and maintain competitive advantage.

How Do Value Chains Work?

The value chain breaks up a business's processes and expenses into individual steps and weighs each one against the value it adds to the product. To determine how effectively value is added, many companies analyze sales data or employ surveys and market research to hear directly from customers about how they value products and what they think should be improved or added to a particular good or service. By analyzing the value created at each step, businesses can more accurately price their products and keep their demand high — both for their premium products and their lower-value alternatives.

For example, if a business makes and sells musical instruments, its value chain would include the procurement of raw materials — like the wood used for the body of a guitar and the metal in the electronics — the entire manufacturing process, marketing, sales and support. For the guitar manufacturer Fender, higher-quality wood and more skilled craftsmen are employed to create the American-made Stratocaster compared with Stratocasters made in Mexico. By spending more on labor and materials in the United States, Fender increases the value of an American-made guitar and charges almost double the price of a Mexican-made guitar. While they share many components, the steps in the value chain that vary between the two guitars change each product's value, costs and the price customers are willing to pay. By analyzing sales data and surveying musicians, Fender can correlate the prices for both guitars with the value difference that customers "feel" between the two goods, maintaining demand for both options.

The Importance of a Value Chain

Value chain modeling is important for businesses trying to gain advantages over their competition, or maintain advantages they already have, because it helps them precisely identify where in their processes customer value is created. In his book, Porter described the importance of the value chain like this: "A systematic way of examining all the activities a firm performs and how they interact is necessary for analyzing the sources of competitive advantage... A firm gains competitive advantage by performing these strategically important activities more cheaply or better than its competitors".

Industries are constantly evolving through new technologies, processes, suppliers, marketing strategies and, most important, changing customer demands. Businesses seeking to stay ahead of the curve need to evolve alongside customers' ever-changing wants and needs by regularly analyzing and improving the value that their products offer.

They can do this through studying and optimizing steps in the value chain. If a business is the lone supplier or far ahead of the competition, finding advantages based on value differentiation may not be a top priority. In that case, the value chain can be analyzed through the lens of supply chain best practices to find lower costs or higher productivity, which increase margins.

Virtual Value Chain

The internet has shifted many customers and businesses from only physical goods and services to a mix of physical and virtual. That shift has created new types of "virtual value," such as data and user experiences, leading to the virtual value chain concept. The virtual value chain focuses on these steps:

- ***Information gathering***: Businesses first must collect as much information as they can on their customers, industry, the current state of the market and regulations to ensure that they are providing their goods or services effectively and satisfying customers' needs.

- ***Organization of information***: Data collected by companies must be organized so it can be studied and analyzed. Without proper organization, the sheer volume of information captured can render it useless to the business, overwhelming even the savviest managers.
- ***Selecting what will be shared with customers***: During this phase, businesses decide which information they will use to provide their product or service. For example, if a streaming service has collected enough data on the formats its customers prefer, this step will establish how the business's content will be delivered to customers.
- ***Synthesizing information***: The virtual product is finalized and prepared for delivery to the customer. Formatting, virtual "packaging" and user interface are major aspects of synthesis.
- ***Information distribution***: Finally, the product is delivered to the customer/ user. To use the streaming service example, this is when the customer can finally watch a film. In an analogous physical value chain, this is where the delivery of a DVD would occur. Both physical and virtual value chains have the same goal — satisfied customers buying and using the product.

Value Chain vs. Supply Chain

Many individuals get the value chain confused with supply chains.

Supply chains are systems of people, activities, organizations, and resources involved in delivering a product or service to the consumer.

Wait…how is that different from a value chain?

A value chain encompasses much more than the supply chain does. The supply chain is all about the delivery of goods or services—the outputs—while the value chain is "a set of interrelated activities a company uses to create a competitive advantage." A company's value chain, for example, includes the marketing and servicing of a product, while a supply chain only encompasses the creation and distribution of a product.

If you're confused, just remember:

- Supply chain = supplying products
- Value chain = delivering value

Porter's Value Chain Model

Michael Porter's value chain concept model was established in his 1985 book *Competitive Advantage*. Porter's value chain establishes primary and secondary activities every company goes through in the process of creating value for customers. Michael Porter is an American academic who also created Porter's five forces.

These components of a value chain help create the equation that leads to calculating margins. Margins are the revenue generated from the value chain.

Value Created and Captured – Cost of Creating that Value = Margin

Primary Value Chain Activities

The primary activities in a value chain include inbound and outbound logistics, operations, marketing, sales, and services. Primary value chain activities include every step in the physical creation, sale, maintenance, and support of a product. It's the entire production process of creating a new product. These specific activities can be broken down into Porter's model of the value chain.

Inbound logistics

This includes all of the processes of receiving, distributing and storing of products internally. This is the process of going from raw material to an actual product. Inbound logistics is all about sourcing the raw materials required to create a finished product. In the case of S'well water bottles from above, this includes the stainless steel and copper used in their product. Supplier relationships are integral when it comes to inbound logistics.

Outbound logistics

Outbound logistics refers to the delivery of a final product and the services associated with them; the process of delivering final products or services to the end consumer. The steps in this process may be external or internal — i.e. you might not store your items in your own warehouses. For example, S'well water bottles sells directly to consumers, in stores and in bulk. Each type of selling has a different process for outbound logistics. This includes the warehousing of products.

Operations

Operations is the process of transforming inputs into complete, finished products and services. Operations are all of the transformation activities that turn raw materials into finished goods. This includes quality assurance.

Marketing and sales

Marketing and sales are the business processes an organization uses to influence customers to purchase from your organization instead of a competitor. This includes the benefits offered, how well they're communicated, and if they are sources of value to the end customer.

Marketing and sales is pretty clear — it's the marketing and selling of products. Due to the incredibly competitive world we live in where manufacturing products is easier than ever, high-quality, relevant, and timely sales and marketing can be a make or break. Sales and marketing often drive the distribution channels and channel metrics, based on research.

Services

Services are the activities designed to maintain products and enhance consumer experience. Often includes add-on services, warranties, refunds and returns. Services, like sales and marketing, are becoming more and more significant in delivering products. This is due to the rise of Products-as-a-Service like Peloton or smart thermostats. They are a physical product that rely on recurring revenue through services like new classes or access to data to optimize the product in the future.

Secondary Value Chain Activities

On the other hand, secondary or support value chain activities are everything that supports each phase of the value chain. These include procurement, HR management, technology and infrastructure.

Procurement

Procurement refers to the obtainment of resources to produce the end product. Procurement involves finding vendors and securing contracts for goods and services the business needs to create and deliver a final product. Procurement initiatives can include everything from obtaining a lease for an office to securing a partnership to produce a piece of the end product.

HR management

HR management is how well a company recruits, hires, trains and retains their workforce. HR management is all about human resources and managing people. Because of the changing workforce, human resources is becoming even more important. Human resources is responsible for recruiting, training, motivating, and retaining employees across the organization.

Technology

Technology refers to the equipment, hardware, software, procedures and technical knowledge of an organization. Technology development is becoming hypercritical in the fourth industrial revolution. Today, many companies are focused on technology including automation, cloud computing, and the Internet of Things (IoT).

Infrastructure

Infrastructure includes the company's support systems like legal, accounting and administrative functions. A firm's infrastructure is everything else that goes into building a product that's not directly connected to the final product. This is the general management of an organization including accounting, administration, and legal.

Value Chain Analysis

Value chain analysis is a way for businesses to evaluate each of the activities involved in the creation and delivery of a product.

Businesses conduct a value chain analysis when they want to understand how they can decrease costs or increase product differentiation. The final result in a value chain analysis should be recommendations to optimize each phase or step of the value chain to create higher margins. There are only two ways a business can gain a competitive advantage: Cost reduction or product differentiation.

Cost reduction

If a company is deploying a cost leadership strategy, their goal is to become the lowest cost option for the end user. Typically, companies who succeed in a cost leadership strategy use low-cost materials, offshore their manufacturing to low-cost manufacturing hubs, and have maximum operational efficiency.

McDonald's and their dollar menu or generic brands in stores are cost reduction examples.

Product differentiation

A product differentiation strategy's competitive advantage is through having a unique offering or a specialized finished product. This enables the company to charge a premium price. Product differentiation is usually the result of research and development. Innovative companies creating innovative products deploy this strategy, enabling them to charge a higher price.

In the fourth industrial revolution, we will see mass personalization become a leader in product differentiation strategies.

Examples of product differentiation include Apple and Louis Vuitton.

Cost reduction vs. product differentiation

When analyzing your value chain, it's important to figure out which competitive advantage is your main focus. This will help shape your efforts while enabling you to evaluate the effectiveness of your value chain analysis.

When conducting a value chain analysis, companies are typically either focused on product differentiation, which typically means a bigger investment in support activities, or are focused on increasing margins by cutting costs, which is mainly about optimizing primary activities.

Value Chain Analysis Steps

1. Understand each of the primary and secondary activities in the business

From procuring raw materials and shipping them to factories to delivering a final product to the end consumer, there are dozens of steps in the value chain process. This is the hardest step as it requires a deep investigatory look at each of the primary and secondary activities.

For example, when analyzing the human resource management process, you have to look at everything from where you post job opportunities to how long it takes to onboard a new hire and every step in between. The deeper you go in your value chain analysis, the more results you'll be able to yield.

2. Analyze the cost and value of each activity

When creating your value chain analysis, you must look at the cost drivers of each step. Do you have steps in the process of building your finished product that are low value, high cost?

If we are to keep with the human resources example, how much does it cost to post on job boards? How much time is involved in interviewing candidates on average? What is the average cost of that time? Or, if you want to take the example to manufacturing explicitly, how much does a certain material cost? Are you focused on sourcing the most sustainable materials or the cheapest?

Then, those conducting the value chain analysis should analyze the value that each step brings. Do a majority of top candidates come from one channel? Does checking references really make a difference in the job interview process?

In manufacturing specifically, does sourcing sustainably add value to the organization? Does it bring about product differentiation?

By analyzing both the cost advantages and profit margins of each activity and the value it provides to the organization, you can holistically understand how to optimize each activity.

3. Identify competitive advantage opportunities

Now that you've broken down each process - from procuring raw materials to hiring employees or acquiring new technology - it's time to optimize your value chain. This is why having a focus on either product differentiation or cost advantages is critical.

Whoever is developing the value chain analysis should make recommendations based on how the company wants to improve margins. Companies should first focus on optimizing high cost, low value processes regardless of their focus on differentiation or cost reduction.

The overall goal of any value chain analysis is to increase profit margins while providing utmost customer satisfaction with a final product that meets their expectations.

Value Chain Analysis Example

To understand value chain analysis, let's look at the example of Apple. Apple is a brand focused on product differentiation. Their technology, on average, eclipses their competition by hundreds of dollars, and they're often the first to produce a technology or they dramatically improve upon existing technology.

Let's break down a value chain analysis of Apple into primary and support activities.

Primary activities

Primary activities in the value chain include inbound and outbound logistics, operations, marketing and sales, and services.

Let's start with inbound logistics.

Inbound logistics

Inbound logistics is how a company sources materials from suppliers.

When it comes to Apple, their inbound logistics include sourcing and shipping different types of materials to build their technology. In analyzing this process, the company would look at if their supply is sourced sustainably and if they have the highest quality materials.

Operations

Operations references the process of actually building a finished product. This includes the people and machines involved in the process.

For Apple, this is the method of producing computers, phones, headphones, watches, and more. Apple's product design focuses on high product quality with unique capabilities.

Outbound logistics

Outbound logistics is the warehousing and delivery of finished goods.

Apple sells their products online and in their stores. They must ship products from where they are produced to warehouses and their stores around the world.

Marketing and sales

Marketing and sales is...well, marketing and sales. It's how a brand gets the word out about their product and convinces someone to purchase. This can include social media, online advertising, print advertising, commercials, video content, and more. Apple is known for their "shot on iPhone" commercials and photography, for example. They focus a lot on brand building.

Services

More and more, companies are having to focus on how they service their products after a purchase. Companies are shifting to Product-as-a-Service that utilize subscriptions as a new business model.

Apple focuses quite heavily on customer service. They're also building in subscription models within their App Store and with Apple Music.

Support activities

Secondary or support activities include all of the operational activities that don't directly involve producing a product including firm infrastructure, human resources, technology, and procurement.

Firm infrastructure

Infrastructure encompasses the business management, financial, and legal systems, and quality control within an organization. These are general management roles that must be filled to uphold the business.

Apple has their main headquarters in Cupertino, California but they also have satellite offices around the world to help maintain their research, manufacturing, and distribution.

Human resources

Human resources is pretty self explanatory - it's the management of human capital.

Apple employs over 137,000 individuals around the world. They have to have robust human resource management practices in place to keep the ball rolling.

Technology

Technology not only includes the technology a business uses to operate and produce products, but also the technology development process of producing new, innovative products and processes.

Apple is a technology company. They use technology to lower costs and to differentiate their products while also creating new products.

Procurement

Procurement is the sourcing of raw materials from suppliers. Apple has suppliers around the world for different pieces of technology and parts that go into each of their products.

VALUE CHAIN APPROACH

The value chain approach has distinctive features in terms of both i) the scope used in analyzing an industry and ii) the tangible and non-tangible considerations used in designing and implementing interventions. The features discussed here are not necessarily unique to the value chain approach; but few, if any, other economic development approaches simultaneously emphasize all of these features:

- A market system perspective
- A focus on end markets
- Understanding the role of value chain governance
- Recognition of the importance of relationships

- Facilitating changes in firm behavior
- Transforming relationships
- Targeting leverage points
- Empowering the private sector

Value chains are situated within broader economic systems.

The value chain approach is one of several market systems approaches to development. In recent years this type of methodology has seen a surge in popularity among a variety of donors in a diversity of contexts. While they differ in their terminology, frameworks, principles and even definitions of a system, what these types of approaches have in common is the foundational belief that the poor and their economic opportunities are profoundly influenced by the dynamic systems in which they participate. By influencing how those systems perform, we can improve opportunities and outcomes for the poor. The value chain approach seeks to understand the firms that operate within an industry—from input suppliers to end market buyers; the support markets that provide technical, business and financial services to the industry; and the business environment in which the industry operates. Such a broad scope for industry analysis is needed because the principal constraints to competitiveness may lie within any part of this market system or the environment in which it operates. While it may be beyond the capacity or mandate of a donor or implementing agency to address certain constraints, the failure to recognize and incorporate the implications of the full range of constraints will generally lead to limited, short-term impact or even counter-productive results.

The end markets into which a product or service is sold—whether local, regional or international—provide the opportunities and set the parameters for economic growth. Generally there are multiple actual and potential end markets, each with different demand characteristics and returns. It is therefore important to segment the market: outline each of the potential end markets, what is required to compete in them, and what benefits and risks can be expected by selling into them. Since end markets are dynamic, the identification of trends should complement information about the current situation.

Understanding the role of value chain governance is fundamental to the value chain approach. Governance describes which firms within a value chain set and enforce the parameters under which others in the chain operate. Embedded in governance are inter-firm relationships, power dynamics—both symmetrical and asymmetrical—and the distribution of benefits. While the form of value chain governance is influenced by the characteristics of the product and the degree of specification in the end market, governance patterns evolve over time with changes in markets, products and inter-firm relationships.

The quality of relationships between different stakeholders is a key factor affecting the functioning of a value chain. Strong, mutually beneficial relationships between firms facilitate the transfer of information, skills and services—all of which are essential to upgrading. Value chain opportunities and constraints generally require a coordinated response by multiple firms in the chain—which necessitates trust and a willingness to collaborate. The value chain approach therefore emphasizes a dynamic that has long been recognized: Social capital (networks of relationships and social institutions) are critical to business and competitiveness. In contrast to much enterprise development work in the past, the value chain approach seeks to do more than solve specific identified production and marketing problems. Directly solving problems may create some initial momentum, but building internal capacity to address value chain constraints will empower stakeholders, reduce dependency and ensure sustainability of investment impacts. The focus of the value chain approach is therefore on transforming relationships—particularly between firms linked vertically in the value chain to: i)facilitate upgrading to become more competitive, and ii)adapt to changes in end markets, in the enabling environment or within the chain to remain competitive. Value chain actors make upgrading decisions based on a variety of financial and non-financial incentives. In order to be able to influence the uptake of new market behaviors, the value chain approach seeks to understand the business and cultural norms, risk tolerance levels, environmental factors and other such non-financial determinants.

Why Use the Value Chain Approach?

Globalization of markets ties the sustainability of firms to the competitiveness of the industries in which they participate. Firms within an industry in a country or region must increasingly compete—even in local markets—with firms and industries from across the globe. To succeed in global markets, entire industries (or value chains) must be able to deliver a product to the consumer more efficiently, with a higher quality and/or in a more unique form than the value chains in competing countries.

In this way, competitiveness at the firm and industry levels are interdependent. Increasing the competitiveness of the firm is only effective at sustainably creating wealth and alleviating poverty when the competitiveness of the industry is similarly raised by interventions at all levels of the value chain.

How is the Value Chain Approach Implemented?

In addition to the features of the approach described above, the following implementation principles can be used to design and implement successful value chain development programs:

- ***Facilitating changes in firm behavior.***The value chain approach seeks to facilitate changes in firm behavior that increase the competitiveness of the chain and generate wealth for all participating firms, thereby contributing to inclusive economic growth. Changing firm behavior requires an understanding of the financial and non-financial incentives of the various stakeholders—why they behave in the way they do, and what is needed to motivate them to change their behavior. Implementers of the value chain approach identify firms within the industry with the incentives, ability and willingness to address constraints and facilitate upgrading throughout the chain.
- ***Transforming relationships.*** By making the benefits of win-win relationships explicit to stakeholders, some firms can be encouraged to change the way they relate to others. However, sometimes conflicting incentives and high levels of mistrust diminish the effectiveness of such simple appeals to self-interest.

- ***Targeting leverage points.*** Value chain project implementers target points of leverage that have a multiplier effect on interventions in order to maximize impact and outreach. Points of leverage include economic and social structures, commercial incentives and social norms and incentives.
- ***Empowering the private sector.*** The goal of the value chain approach is to enable private-sector stakeholders to act on their own behalf: to upgrade their firms and collectively create a competitive value chain that contributes to economic growth with poverty reduction. The value chain analysis and strategy development process is therefore participatory to the extent possible. The role of the donor and implementing partner is to facilitate and support implementation of the competitiveness strategy by the private sector in such a way that ensures that development objectives—economic growth, poverty reduction and other concerns such as sustainable natural resource management—are also met.
- ***Learning and Adaptive Management*** . Inherent in this approach is the challenge of working in markets that are dynamic and trying influence behavior that is unpredictable. Achieving successful outcomes in such a context requires continual learning and adaptation to know what is working and under what conditions.

Features of the Value Chain Approach

A Market System Perspective

Taking a value chain approach necessitates understanding a market system in its totality: the firms that operate within an industry—from input suppliers to end market buyers; the support markets that provide technical, business and financial services to the industry; and the business environment in which the industry operates. Such a broad scope for industry analysis is needed because the principal constraints to competitiveness can lie within any part of this market system or the environment in which it operates. While it may be beyond the capacity or mandate of a donor or implementing agency to address certain constraints, the failure to recognize and incorporate the implications of the full range of constraints will generally lead to limited, short-term impact or even counter-productive results.

The decision of where to intervene in a value chain should be primarily driven by the end goal of sustainable economic growth with poverty reduction. Interventions that target a particular part of a value chain (e.g., processing) or group of beneficiaries (e.g., small-scale producers) must therefore be designed and implemented:

- within the context, and with an understanding, of the value chain as a whole; and
- with an explicit focus on benefits to MSEs and the poor.

A Focus on End Markets

The end markets into which a product or service is sold—whether local, regional or international—provide the opportunities and set the parameters for economic growth. Generally there are multiple actual and potential end markets, each with different demand characteristics and returns. It is therefore important to segment the market: outline each of the potential end markets, what is required to compete in them, and what benefits and risks can be expected by selling into them. Since end markets are dynamic, the identification of trends should complement information about the current situation.

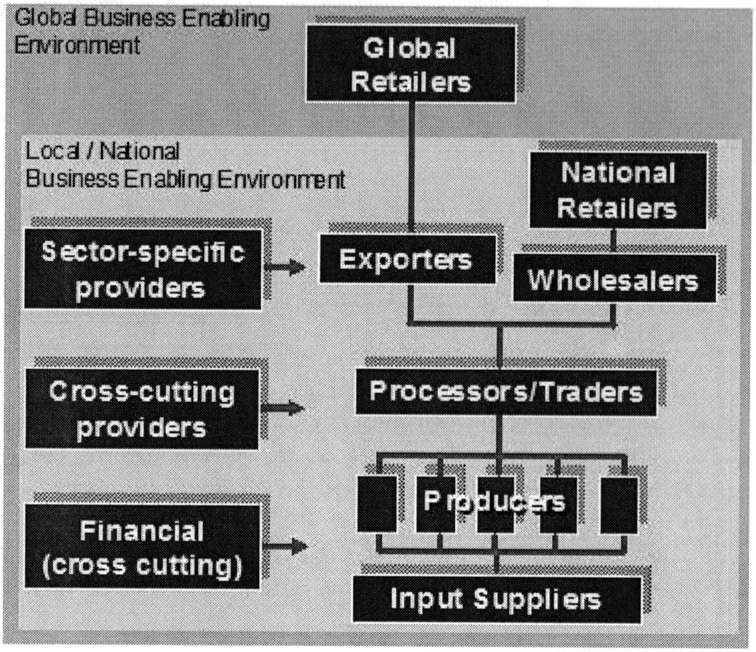

Figure 1. A Market System Perspective.

Source: https://www.marketlinks.org/sites/default/files/styles/medium_no_crop/public/book/images/Value_Chain_Framework_Figure_0.jpg

By benchmarking key attributes (e.g., quality, price, reliability of supply, flexibility, time from order to delivery) against competitors, industry stakeholders can see where they have a competitive advantage and where they need to upgrade in order to compete. The information needed for benchmarking can often be obtained through simple interviews with end-market buyers; secondary information alone is generally insufficient.

Buyers can often also provide information on market trends. Using market-trend information, together with information about the capacity and constraints within the value chain and its environment, industry stakeholders can develop a strategy to position themselves in the market: competing through a combination of price, quality and innovation. To sustain end-market competitiveness, this strategy will have to be continually revised in response to changes in the end markets, in the enabling environment or within the chain itself. Additionally, inter-firm relationships need to be such that firms are able and willing to act cooperatively in response to new threats and opportunities in the end market over time.

Understanding the Role of Value Chain Governance

Value chain governance is a concept that is fundamental to the value chain approach. Governance describes which firms within a value chain set and enforce the parameters under which others in the chain operate. Embedded in governance are inter-firm relationships, power dynamics—both symmetrical and asymmetrical—and the distribution of benefits. While the form of value chain governance is influenced by the characteristics of the product and the degree of specification in the end-market, governance patterns evolve over time with changes in markets, products and inter-firm relationships.

Increasing the competitiveness of a value chain typically requires an emphasis on consistent product quality, traceability and on-time delivery. These changes, in turn, often require a different relationship between buyers and sellers to exert the control needed to meet the demands of higher value markets. Importantly, governance pat-terns also affect the ability of in-country supply chains to integrate into global markets. Where there are no systems for introducing global standards, national value chains are excluded from global opportunities. Without knowledgeable and resourced lead firms providing information on end market demand and services to facilitate upgrading, in some cases, it is impossible for a value chain to become or remain competitive. Thus, value chain governance is a level of organization that facilitates or hinders upgrading and the ability to respond to market changes, especially in global markets.

Recognition of the Importance of Relationships

The quality of relationships between different stakeholders is a key factor affecting the functioning of a value chain. Strong, mutually beneficial relationships between firms facilitate the transfer of information, skills and services—all of which are essential to upgrading. Value chain opportunities and constraints generally require a coordinated response by multiple firms in the chain—which necessitates trust and a willingness to collaborate. The value chain approach therefore emphasizes a dynamic that has long been recognized: Social capital (networks of relationships and social institutions) are critical to business and competitiveness.

In contrast to much enterprise development work in the past, the value chain approach seeks to do more than solve specific identified production and marketing problems. Directly solving problems may create some initial momentum, but building internal capacity to address value chain constraints will empower stakeholders, reduce dependency and ensure sustainability of investment impacts. The focus of the value chain approach is there-fore on transforming relationships—particularly between firms linked vertically in the value chain—to:

- facilitate upgrading to become competitive, and
- adapt to changes in end markets, in the enabling environment or within the chain to remain competitive.

Factors Influencing Relationships

The nature of relationships is defined by a number of factors, including:

- supply and demand market dynamics
- the degree of control needed during production and processing to meet market requirements
- the capacity of producers
- the need for support services and the capacity of service providers
- socio-economic and cultural factors

Ongoing Analysis and Learning

Most value chain development projects operate in highly dynamic markets. In these markets, prices fluctuate, standards change, new competitors arise, and policies shift. No matter how well it is conducted, a project's initial value chain analysis is likely to be out-of-date to a greater or lesser degree during the later years of the project. The analysis must therefore be updated periodically.

Furthermore, value chain development projects try to influence behavior. They encourage firms and individuals to take on new practices, adopt new technologies, sell into new markets, and create new kinds of market relationships. But market actors each respond differently to different incentives, depending on their risk tolerance, skills, capacities and experience. It is therefore not possible to predict with certainty how individuals, firms or industries will respond to project initiatives. Achieving successful outcomes in such a context requires continual learning to identify what is working and under what conditions, a periodic reassessment of project assumptions, and ongoing adaptation of interventions in response to project learning and changes in the operating context.

VALUE CHAIN DEVELOPMENT

Micro and Small enterprises in developing countries often emerge when entrepreneurship is the only viable employment option; most of these enterprises are very small in size, fragmented and with limited access to markets. Their financial and productive capacity gives them very limited bargaining power and their voice is often not heard when it comes to designing policies. They operate in the informal economy, often with poor working conditions and without access to social protection. Some of these challenges can be addressed by collective action organizations like cooperatives or business associations.

While collective action organizations can be present at all levels of value chains, the focus of this briefing paper is mainly on the part of chains where micro and small enterprises operate. It looks at how organizations, like cooperatives or business associations, can help producers and small enterprises in addressing constraints within a value chain. It puts forward recommendations about the role of these organizations in the value chain development process.

Smaller actors in a value chain face problems often more forcefully than bigger enterprises. Limited resources and capacity make it difficult for small enterprises to become suppliers to larger firms, compete in value chains and enter highervalue markets. While large firms can often use their bargaining power in their supply chain, small enterprises need to follow the decisions taken by others. Often they have no other choice than to accept prices or product requirements that are given by a buyer.

The figure on the right shows the image of a generic value chain with several trade linkages between processors/traders and producers. Intermediary traders play a crucial role in the value chain and often have better market information and more financial resources than small producers. The trader relates to each of the small producers individually and can potentially use his bargaining position to exercise pressure on small producers (for lower prices etc.). This asymmetric bargaining power in a chain can lessen small producer revenues and, thus, limits their opportunities for improved livelihoods. Producers often do not have proper information on market conditions and processes and therefore run the risk of being treated unfairly.

But the fragmentation of small producers is not always in the interest of the intermediary buyer. Having fragmented suppliers is costly due to the arising transaction costs. Buyers often want to buy large quantities with good and stable quality, in other words, find reliable business partners. So buyers would also have an interest in dealing with a single trading partner. Constraints that affect small producers and farmers in the end can have an impact on the overall performance and competitiveness of the chain and as such will also affect large buyers. So potentially both traders and small producers need effective mechanisms by which the issues of fragmentation can be addressed. Producer associations or cooperatives provide a possible way of dealing with these concerns.

Collective Action Organizations

Collective action organizations come in many "shapes and sizes" depending on the purpose and activities of the organization. In this brief cooperatives and business association are presented as examples of a collective action organization.

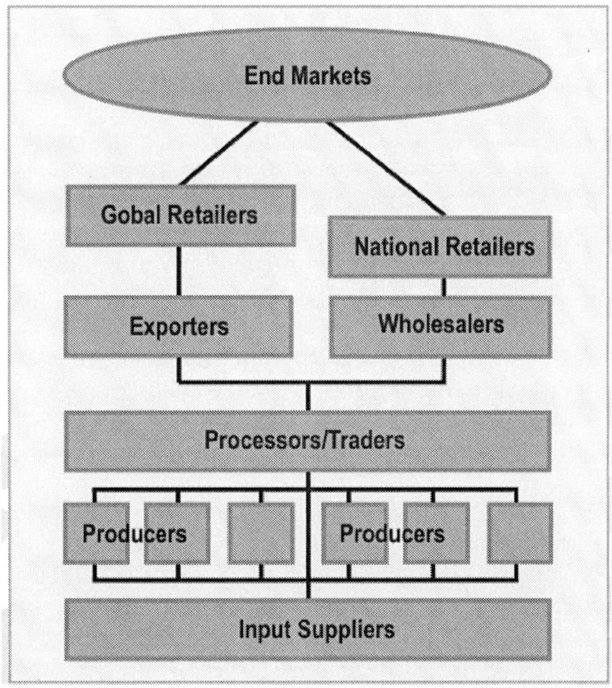

Figure 2. Collective action organizations.

Source: https://www.ilo.org/wcmsp5/groups/public/---ed_emp/---emp_ent/---ifp_seed/documents/publication/wcms_182602.pdf

Collective action organizations can play a key role in helping enterprises and producers to address value chain requirements irrespective of their exact legal form. They can facilitate and leverage market linkages for small scale entrepreneurs and producers, improve their bargaining power and access to market information.

For instance, joint purchasing, financial and other activities enable organizations to achieve economies of scale that cannot be achieved by single firms. Members of collective action organizations can potentially benefit from networking, collaboration and joint initiatives. Collective action organizations are often members of and thus linked to a bigger structure such as a cooperative union, a federation or a chamber of commerce.

Engaging with Collective Action Organizations in Value Chain Development

The role of the collective action organization in a value chain depends on the activities it conducts. The organization can be linked to a value chain both vertically (buyer-seller relationships) and horizontally (inter-firm coordination, linkages to services providers and to policy makers). In the past organizations, especially cooperatives, used to have a more defensive role and focus on horizontal coordination (e.g. collectively selling the members' produce). However, the role of the organizations has changed. Nowadays organizations are taking on more proactive roles, higher-up or further-down the chain and engaging in value chain integration.

They must consider vertical linkages in the chain as well and combine horizontal and vertical coordination. This often goes hand in hand with a diversification of services these organizations provide to their members.

Vertical Activities

Cooperatives and business associations can have an important role in providing information about market requirements and supporting their members in complying with them. The organizations can help for example by providing training and improving skills in modern production and management techniques. For instance, the Supirisara Rural Economic Development Entrepreneurship Association in Kurunegala, Sri Lanka, was established to improve dairy farmers' access to business development services and increase their bargaining power, organize trade fairs, link members to new buyers and suppliers, undertake marketing and common purchasing as well as providing members with information on market trends and opportunities.

Horizontal Activities

Horizontal activities have a strong potential to reduce transaction costs and create economies of scale. Horizontal activities include grouping together to increase small producers′ bargaining power and therefore, strengthening their position in the value chain. This is often a key role of collective action organizations. Joining forces can result both in a more stable and profitable relationship with intermediary buyers as well as help producers getting access to cheaper inputs when by pooling their purchasing power and buying in bulk.

Collective action organizations can also be active players in trying to influence the business environment under which they have to operate. The organization can not only represent its members vis-a-vis buyers but also towards local and national government and play an advocacy role, exercising influence on rules and regulations that might affect the operations. The organization can give enterprises a chance to participate in decision-making processes and also help with new regulations. Many organizations, especially cooperatives, do also provide finance and business services to their members. Alternatively they can help in linking up to existing financial institutions and business service providers to collectively get a better deal for services provided to members.

Risks of Collective Action Organizations

The most important actors of the collective action organization are its members. Their engagement and sense of ownership is key. Collective action organizations set up by outsiders or for the wrong reasons are in a great risk of failure. If an outside agent (such as a NGO or government) sets up a collective action organizations in combination with financial help, there is a risk of the organization becoming dependent on the financial aid and it thus might not respond to the incentives set by its market context. Such a set-up has a high probability of failure as in the long-term the organization needs to be able to operate in the market.

Collective action organizations like any other (commercial) organization are also at risk of being mismanaged. Leading the organization requires entrepreneurial and managerial skills, which members of the organization might not always have. Especially small organizations might not be able to afford to hire professional managers owning the needed skills. Furthermore, managers may take an advantage of the information they have and pursue their own interests instead of interests of the organization.

There are also risks associated to other types of opportunistic behaviour at the expense of others, like free-riding. A free-rider can be a non-member who receives benefits of the collective action organization without contributing respectively or a member receiving (and paying for) inputs of her cooperative whilst side selling her produce. In both cases the free-riders are undermining the business activity of the organization.

How Can Value Chain Development Help?

Value Chain Development enables policy makers and value chain stakeholders to get a better understanding of their role and potential in a specific Value Chain. A Value Chain Development approach can help in providing crucial information about end-markets and about key underlying constraints that hinder further development. This in turn can inform and enhance the work of business associations and cooperatives or help small entrepreneurs in the decision of why and how to form a collective action organization. Collective action organizations give a voice and representation to producers and small enterprises enabling a more informed and empowered dialogue with other value chain stakeholders. However, it is important to remember that the success of the organization largely depends on the local situation, engagement of people and whether members have a sense of ownership or not.

MARKETS LINKAGES

Markets Linkages connect the organisations involved in producing the products and delivering the services for any and every market. As such when linkages are absent or weak, markets become inefficient. Businesses and donor programmes operating in developing countries with poor linkages are often forced to source goods and services from outside the local economy. The benefits of investing in linkage development are significant. Whilst linkage creation does take time and effort, linkages enable long term market development and deepening, drive cost and efficiency savings and support inclusion of the poor in the market economy. Thus, through supporting the development of market linkages, businesses and programmes alike can ensure that their short term investment has a long term impact that will ultimately lead to improved local capacity, create jobs and accelerate growth.

Whilst many large firms have long recognised the need to build linkages along their supply and distribution chains, the aid sector as a whole has been slow both to recognise the importance of this and to make progress. Building linkages improves the efficiency of programme implementation and, by not seeking ways in which to build the capacity of local organisations so that they can undertake to provide donors (or large firms) with goods and services, all stakeholders are missing an important opportunity.

In developing countries, complex environments, market failures, information asymmetries and low business capacity represent significant challenges that require time and commitment to overcome. In light of this, creating linkages as an integral part of the implementation of projects has more often than not been perceived by practitioners to be at odds with the donor focus on results and VfM. Those implementing projects have also cited the increased risk of using untested SME suppliers as a reason for not contracting them to deliver goods and services to donor programmes. The literature, however, highlights the fact that, if implemented correctly, there is no increased risk associated with engaging local SMEs. Furthermore, as donors increasingly recognise the commercial and developmental benefits of creating linkages, there is increasing expectation that all project managers and practitioners have a strategy in place to support linkage development.

Large firms, with their commercial focus, face many of the same challenges. In the past, the benefits of building the capacity of local suppliers and distributors was seen to be outweighed by the time and effort it takes to promote local market development. Given the overriding objectives of a corporate entity are increasing output and profit, exchanging trusted, reliable international suppliers for potentially poor local suppliers was viewed with some suspicion. However, increasingly the cost savings, improved efficiency and flexibility achieved through working with local suppliers, combined with the importance of obtaining a 'license to operate' and a commitment to corporate social responsibility has resulted in many larger firms undertaking local linkage schemes as part of their overall business strategy.

There is extensive literature that demonstrates the positive impact linkages can have on the local community, on SMEs, for those larger firms that successfully implement such schemes, and the wider economy.

The social license to operate generated through such market and business linkage schemes is also a key consideration for both donor and private sector led interventions.

From the perspective of businesses, creating local links can help to overcome the negative social and political attitudes that are often harboured towards the private sector. In the past, the need for donors to have a license to operate has largely been ignored as donors assumed the license came from the fact that they were funding programmes with grants. This is no longer a safe assumption and increasingly donors must address their own 'license to operate' issues to avoid the accusation that aid spend is a mechanism to employ international consultants and provide business to their own goods and service providers.

Through reviewing the literature on what has already been done in this area and by undertaking interviews with those practitioners that have experience in implementing successful business linkage strategies, either through specific linkage programmes (both business and donor led) or as a part of donor programmes, this topic guide aims to consolidate and select those interventions that are most effective. Specifically, the paper will address the following:

- The conceptual basis for market linkage development.
- The challenges hampering the formation of market linkages.
- Approaches used in relation to 1) supplier and distributor development; 2) enabling linkages through establishing/improving information and communication services; and 3) strengthening linkages through policy and business environment initiatives.
- What this mean for practitioners.

Market Linkage Interventions

First, the facilitators of market linkage interventions are described, defining what the key drivers of each are. This is followed by a detailed analysis of the particular interventions that can be implemented in order to address the challenges set out above. Although there is inevitably some cross over as to what activities can be utilised to tackle specific challenges, we have broadly categorised the interventions under the following headings as a guide to which activities are most suited to addressing the problems: 1) supplier and distributor development; 2) information and communication services; and 3) the strengthening of linkages through policy and business environment interventions. Each section sets out the benefits, theory of change, interventions and lessons learnt related to each of these areas.

In order to offer practical examples of each of the interventions, selected programmes that have undertaken market linkage activities have been presented alongside the interventions. It should be noted that most of these are drawn from specific market linkage programmes (private sector, donor and Government) rather than programmes that have developed market linkages to support the delivery of their objectives. This is because there are very few examples of the latter other than market development programmes (e.g. M4P initiatives) which by definition work to use linkages to develop markets.

Linkage Facilitators

We have divided the facilitators into three groups, donors, B2B, and the public sector. Whilst there are obviously some common drivers for creating linkages for all of them, such as cost savings and more efficient delivery of services and goods, the underlying agenda of each participant is driven by different objectives. Understanding these is important when deciding which interventions are best suited to achieving those goals.

Donors

There are a number of donor funded programmes that specifically aim to support the development of market linkages as a programme output, recognising that without support the development of linkages will be too slow, especially where the domestic private sector is very weak, such as in post conflict and fragile state situations. In addition, there is currently a largely untapped opportunity to increase the efficient delivery of donor programmes through integrating the development of local market linkages into their own programme delivery, whatever market they are operating within.

Through developing local supply and distribution channels, donors themselves benefit through cost savings and the efficiency gains made through a more reliable, better functioning local supply networks. Furthermore, the absence of a social license to operate can be detrimental to the implementation of projects. Engaging local SMEs involved in such chains can therefore provide donors with a means to obtain a license to operate and develop a rapport with the local business and policy environment.

Although developing such linkages requires some upfront costs, the longer term impacts will result in better overall value for money (VfM); as well as cost savings gained for future programmes able to contract locally. Building linkages ensures that the programme continues delivering benefits beyond the lifetime of the project. Furthermore, as a result of supporting linkages, overall programme impact and spill-over effects can be increased significantly.

Business-To-Business

Numerous businesses, especially larger companies, have implemented their own market linkage programmes. There are several drivers underpinning such strategies:

- Lower procurement, production and distribution costs
- Improved productivity
- Opportunities for CSR combined with profitability
- Enhanced reputation and license to operate
- Integration into new markets
- Ability to reach new customers at BoP
- Reduction in foreign exchange needs through import substitution
- Flexibility in design and production changes due to proximity of local suppliers
- Compliance with local content rules

As corporate entities, a key consideration for businesses is the cost savings that can be made through developing reliable local suppliers and distribution systems. Improved linkages also lead to the development of local markets and ensure inclusive business. The ultimate development impact of such a scheme is increased jobs and incomes for those who, as a result of linkage initiatives, are included in large firm supplier and distributor chains.

Public sector

The public sector drivers underpinning market linkage support include overall improved private sector functioning. Developing linkages and supporting local SMEs enables the development of existing and new markets, both domestic and foreign, and enhances the efficiency of markets. Furthermore, by streamlining business related procedures, the public sector can take an active role in promoting inward foreign investment.

Ultimately, market development leads to increased local economic participation and growth, a key driver for governments. This helps generate jobs, higher incomes and therefore economic growth.

Better linkages also increase the cost effectiveness and efficiency of government procurement systems through improving local suppliers' ability to participate in the procurement process.

The full list of drivers associated with public sector linkage creation and development of local supply and distribution chains are presented:

- Improved economic activity and local economic development
- New markets (domestic and foreign)
- Increased employment and productivity
- Long term increase in local and regional competitiveness
- FDI attracted
- Diversified economy
- Added purchasing power
- Improved products and services
- Participation of large companies in local business
- Balance of payments benefits when products are exported and substituted for imports
- Development of local services providers catering to SMEs

Supplier & Distribution Development

In many developing countries where businesses and donor programmes work, the key issues constraining market linkages are poor local supplier and distributor capacity. As such, many business, donor and government initiatives have focused on the development of local SMEs in order to overcome this challenge.

Interventions

Figure 3 presents the theory of change for the most useful interventions for local supplier and distributor development.

In practice, even simple strategies can promote market growth inclusive of local SME businesses. Various interventions have already been tried and tested and should be used as a clear roadmap for future practices:

Training

Many local suppliers and distributors lack the technical capacity to undertake the provision of services and products to larger firms or programmes. Lack of experience and understanding of buyer procurement protocols also hampers their participation in global supply/distribution chains. Targeted training sessions can help local enterprises bridge these skills and management gaps to help them meet global standards.

Evidence shows that providing tailored training courses to local companies covering the topics listed below will build local business capacity and help firms deliver global standard goods and services to larger firms.

- Procurement processes/tendering and bidding for contracts
- Improve supplier knowledge of business standards
- Basic business management
- Business accounting
- Sales and marketing support

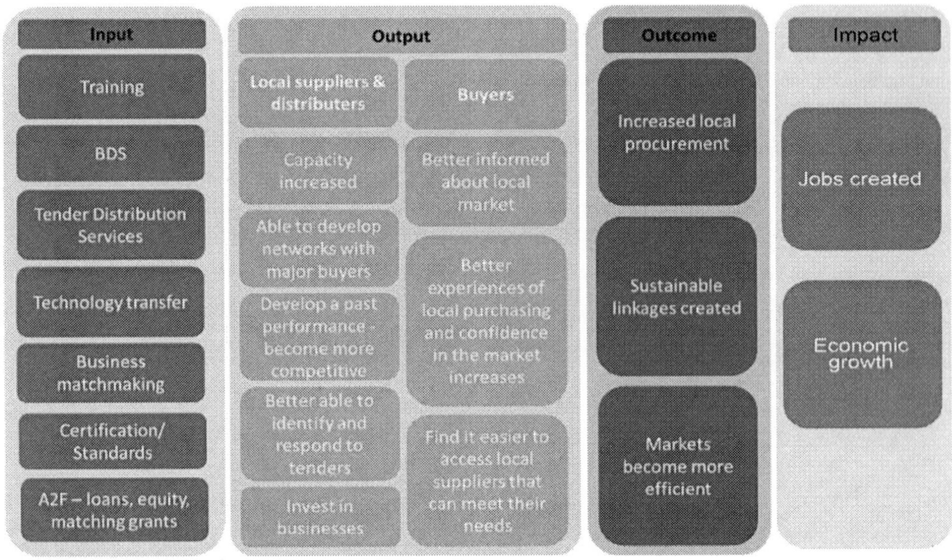

Figure 3. Theory of change for supplier & distributor development interventions.

Source: https://encrypted-tbn2.gstatic.com/images?q=tbn:ANd9GcQBVpURLQaaw-fvS0qltVYJ20OyJXrjJHJwGU_k3SiBGQOqIScсc

While technical skills courses will vary depending on the target sector/ industry, improving general business practices will ensure that basic systems are in place to meet the demands of suppliers.

Business development services (including embedded)

BDS are defined in the broad category of all non-financial capacity building services provided to local entrepreneurs and businesses. In the case of Business-to-Business linkages, evidence suggests that BDS is most effective when it is embedded as one company can share and develop best practices (through training, consultancy and business plan development) or even provide operational support such as transport, advertising and accounting.

Technology transfer

There is strong evidence that the availability and use of technology can increase the impact of linkage interventions. Positive spill-overs into host countries through buyer/supplier linkages are more likely to occur when the technological gap between foreign and local firms is relatively small.

The technological capabilities of local firms are key determinants of their ability to qualify as suppliers to firms operating in increasingly competitive markets. A number of initiatives have adopted measures to encourage technology transfer from buyer firms to supplier firms and to strengthen technological cooperation between the two. A number of governments have set out technology transfer requirements to induce the transfer of technologies from TNCs to local firms that are subcontractors of foreign affiliates. Other initiatives have involved buyers affiliating themselves as partners in technology upgrading programmes, offering them access to technological and managerial know-how.

Finance

Financing is one of the most common tools to develop supplier and distributor capacity. While there are several other interventions required to develop linkages, it remains an important part of improving the health of the local private sector. Capital inputs can be a necessary catalyst to advance key industries and allow them to be self-sustaining enough to not require similar levels of financing in the future. Financing schemes can come in the form of loans, equity investments, or matching grants/cost sharing. Within B2B initiatives finance may come from the purchasing company itself or through their support in obtaining external finance. Facilitators are also not always the direct sources of finance, but may also help enterprises secure support from banks or other sources of finance.

Certification & Standards

To reduce both the time and costs associated with carrying out appropriate due diligence procedures, businesses can be supported to gain certification to meet an approved set of standards to work with either SMEs or large foreign businesses. In contrast to business verification, certification is a longer-term system of approval that is recognisable amongst buyers. Rigorous individual evaluation of local businesses is costly and inefficient As such, credible certifications can give future buyers confidence in the ability of a wide range of SMEs. This will lower due diligence costs and encourage firms to work with a greater number of local suppliers.

There is substantial literature on the implementation of supplier and distributor development interventions. Many buyers have implemented some form of M&E strategy whilst executing linkage interventions and have subsequently identified a number of key considerations that make it more likely a linkages programme will have the right impact. The specific lessons that are most frequently cited in the literature include the following:

- ***Multiple interventions:*** Successful initiatives/programmes implement several interventions in conjunction, to varying degrees, catered to the desired market outcome. The Anglo Group's example of financing mining operations while contracting SMEs to meet service demands is one such example of a selective approach.
- ***Start early:*** Building the capacity of local businesses takes time – the earlier the program starts, the greater the opportunities.
- ***Anchor company participation:*** Experience has shown that anchor companies are reluctant to participate in linkage programmes unless they have some control over the selection of local supplier and distributors. This is to ensure that they have confidence in the partnerships. Therefore, ensuring that large firms are involved in the selection process is critical to making linkage initiatives sustainable.

- ***Commitment and culture of long term thinking:*** Linkages take time to evolve and require patience. They require 5,10,15 years of effort and as such linkage practitioners need explicit support from senior levels and procurement managers.
- ***Performance measures and incentives:*** Suppliers and distributors should be aiming at achieving targets with an incentive structure in place (e.g. increasing contract size as performance improves). This is particularly relevant to those large companies implementing linkage schemes.
- ***Measuring returns:*** It is important to develop tools that help companies and practitioners measure the impact and/or financial return of their linkage activities, specifically the extent to which they create or protect value helps engender commitment. E.g. Planning and Financial Evaluation Tool (FV Tool) designed by Deloitte, Rio Tinto and IFC.
- ***Active participation of SMEs:*** Participating SMEs must have a sense of ownership, play an active role in their development process, and demonstrate a willingness to change their business practices.
- ***Defining criteria:*** The selection of SMEs who can participate in the interventions should be focused, with only those that meet the criteria selected to participate in linkage intervention. This will ensure that SMEs without potential are filtered out. An ineffective selection wastes valuable resources and can jeopardize the sustainability of programme outcomes.
- ***Sector selection:*** Some sectors will deliver higher returns than others. The Building Markets initiative found that the top three sectors for employment generation were construction, healthcare, and transport/ logistics. In Haiti, construction accounted for 51% of all jobs created, the vast majority of which were more sustainable over the long-term (higher than the average lifetime of 6 years).
- ***Best practice guidelines:*** In conjunction with large companies/ programmes, it is important to develop best practice guidelines that are specific to industries and business activities. E.g. Unilever's sustainable tea initiative provides guidelines to tea farmers.
- ***Enterprise centres:*** Should initiatives have access to adequate funds then setting up a one-stop-shop for SMEs, where they can access contract opportunities, eprocurement systems, ICT, BDS, training courses, can aid the linkage development process.
- ***Encourage diversification***: SMEs should be encouraged to diversify their client base to ensure they do not become totally dependent on one buyer and to safeguard their sustainability.

Enabling market linkages through information and communication services

Information systems are fundamental to the creation of sustainable linkages. Procurement related interventions such as tender distribution services, supplier databases and matchmaking activities help both buyers and suppliers expand their networks. Whilst SMEs are better able to find opportunities, buyers benefit from receiving more bids. With better access to such platforms, practitioners are also able to source local partners more easily. In fragile and conflict affected states or in countries with a poor private sector, services which undertake due diligence of local businesses and which take a more hands on approach to matchmaking firms are particularly important as it helps increase trust in the reliability of SMEs. As a result, businesses that may not have felt confident enough to invest and start operation in that country are enabled somewhat to do so. Besides improving the quality of business services, information platforms can also act as a key tool for SMEs to research and find out about good practice and innovation; disseminating knowledge (e.g. farming techniques) and market information (e.g. commodity prices).

Information and communication failures impact negatively on market linkages in a number of ways. In environments where local businesses have typically relied on informal networks to conduct business transactions, SMEs are often excluded from linking with viable business partners outside their networks (both regional and international) as they are unaware of many of the tender opportunities offered by larger firms.

Similarly, without databases, matchmaking and tender distribution services, large international entities struggle to tap into the local supplier and distributor networks. From a practitioner's viewpoint, where implementers of donor programmes are often setting up projects in countries where they have not necessarily worked before, it is apparent how difficult it can be to tap into local networks. When identifying partners to supply goods and services, there is a heavy dependence on collaborating with other firms who have experience in those countries. Without formal information platforms, firms must rely on informal networks and feedback from competitors and partners to identify local suppliers.

In order to overcome these challenges, many linkage initiatives have focused on interventions that aim to establish platforms and systems that collect, distil and disseminate information for both buyers and suppliers.

Interventions

The theory of change underpinning the information services interventions is presented in:

- *Business supplier databases and inventories:* Supplier databases keep a record of different SMEs and TNCs for businesses, donors and governments alike to access when designing programmes or business ventures. Buyers can use this type of database to find suppliers who meet their specific demands, and a regulated set of standards. Information on main business activities, past collaborations, financial data and other topics can help form effective linkages. It can also provide up to date information about innovative programmes and policies.
- *Business verification:* In order to give international buyers confidence in the local suppliers' ability to provide goods and services, intermediary actors can help identify and verify potential firms. Verification services help streamline the contracting process in an environment unfamiliar to new buyers. Intervention from an authorised body, be it from the private or public sector, can help enforce minimum criterion to ensure firms hold to set standards and promote the longevity of local businesses. This process may be accompanied with other BDS services to help ensure that quality controls are in place.

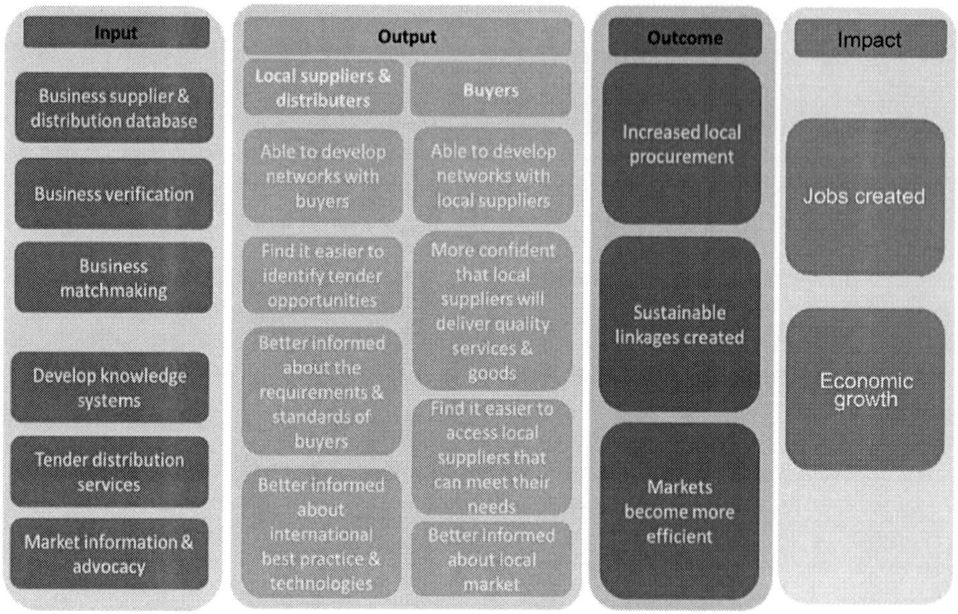

Figure 4: Information services theory of change.

Source: https://encrypted-tbn2.gstatic.com/images?q=tbn:ANd9GcQBVpURLQaaw-fvS0qltVYJ20OyJXrjJHJwGU_k3SiBGQOqISccc

- *Business matchmaking:* For local businesses, connecting with one business (particularly a TNC) can open up the way to future opportunities and help the local market integrate into a global supply chain. Business matchmaking can help facilitate and speed up this process.

Business matchmaking services help connect national and international buyers looking for goods and services with verified local businesses. Business matchmaking is a more active approach of establishing contracts between international buyers and local suppliers, particularly when there are technological constraints. Both parties are able to identify the needs of the buyer and the capacities of the supplier. Interventions include site visits, vendor promotion events, product sample collecting, and networking events between buyers and suppliers (exhibitions and trade fairs).

- *Tender distribution services and tender simplification:* The purpose of tender distribution services is to expose as many suppliers as possible to relevant tendering opportunities. It must help mitigate problems of access and awareness. A successful system collects tender announcements and business opportunities for distribution to local companies. Announcements can be distributed via the internet, local news outlets or radio. Through amalgamating tenders to make them available through one platform, local suppliers can easily find relevant opportunities, saving them both time and resources.

Tender distribution systems must be as inclusive as possible. Publishing tenders in local dialects can help rural communities access opportunities.

Technological gaps can be overcome by traditional modes of communication, such as presentations to rural farm or microfinance collectives. TDS benefits both suppliers and buyers as it provides a simple and more open market to work in.

Simplifying the procurement process also encourages local suppliers to bid for contracts. Reducing the size of contracts, simplifying procurement documentation and forms, ensuring procurement notices are written in local language are all means by which to ensure local SMEs are more likely to tender for work.

- *Market information & knowledge management systems:* Information asymmetries to do with basic market information also exist. This is particularly important to suppliers whose only entry into supply chains is through unreliable middle-men. For instance, rural market participants can lack vital information on local market prices, demand for niche products (such as cash crops) and minimum bulking demands. Most existing systems focus on farmers, but small retailers would also benefit from knowing wholesale and competing retail prices.

Additionally, in many developing countries, the absence of efficient knowledge systems means that it is hard for local suppliers to find information on global best practice. Centralised systems are critical for local supplier capacity development as they can be accessed by multiple actors to capture knowledge and disseminate useful information. They function as a collection point for action research, guidelines on best practice, evaluations and reviews to help improve the technical ability of SMEs, as well as the inform the implementation of future programmes.

- *Advocacy:* Advocacy targeted at buyers must not only stress the social benefits of sourcing locally (such as job creation), but also include detailed market research and financial analysis to speak to the lowered costs associated with buying from local firms. These measures can encourage businesses to source locally.

Furthermore, advocacy initiatives should aim to set up lines of communication between the buyers/suppliers and government in order to generate political momentum to influence policy. From a business perspective, policy and regulatory advocacy can be undertaken to promote and facilitate the formation of business linkages through strengthening enabling environment and engaging in public policy processes. SMEs in developing countries often lack a voice at the national/government level. Large firms, however, have a platform and can use their influence to pressure governments into making reforms.

REFERENCES

1. Birchall, Johnston. "Co-operative Principles Then and Now." Co-operatives UK, 2011.
2. Cook, Michael L., and M. Ryan Haley. "Cooperative Value Chain Management." Journal of Business & Industrial Marketing, vol. 20, no. 7, 2005, pp. 376-384.
3. Fabiani, Jean-Louis, et al. "Co-operative Marketing of Agricultural Products in Europe: Research, Practice and Policy." European Commission, 2013.
4. Franks, Jeremy R. "Co-operative Enterprise: Facing the Challenge of Globalization." Routledge, 2016.
5. Morrison, Alastair. "The Co-operative Movement in Scotland: Industry and Society, 1880-1970." John Donald, 2008.

6. North, David. "Co-operative Values in a Changing World." Co-operatives UK, 2007.
7. Patel, Rajeev, and Vijay S. Vyas. "Cooperative Marketing: A Case Study of Dairy Cooperatives in Gujarat, India." Journal of Rural Cooperation, vol. 36, no. 2, 2008, pp. 227-248.
8. Singh, Shikha, et al. "Performance and Impact Assessment of Farmer Producer Organizations (FPOs) in India." International Food Policy Research Institute (IFPRI), 2018.
9. Srivastava, R.K. "Co-operative Marketing of Agricultural Produce in India." Deep & Deep Publications, 2006.
10. United Nations Food and Agriculture Organization (FAO). "Cooperative Value Chain Approaches: Agribusiness Cases from Asia." FAO, 2015.

7 GENDER EQUALITY AND THE COMMUNITY OF PRACTICE APPROACH

INTRODUCTION

A Community of Practice (CoP) is a group of people who share a common interest or passion for something they do and interact regularly to learn from each other and improve. The concept, coined by cognitive anthropologists Jean Lave and Etienne Wenger in 1991, revolves around three dimensions: the domain (shared interest), the community (group of people), and the practice (the shared repertoire of resources, experiences, and knowledge). A CoP is not merely a community of interest or a professional network. It involves members who actively engage in joint activities, discussions, and exchanges to learn from each other. It's more about the social learning process that occurs when people with a common interest collaborate over an extended period to share ideas, find solutions, and build innovations. CoPs can be informal or formal, online or in person, within an organisation or spanning multiple organisations. They can serve various purposes such as knowledge sharing, best practice transfer, professional development, innovation, and problem-solving. By participating in a CoP, individuals can develop their abilities and build social relationships that contribute to their personal and professional growth.

Gender equality refers to the state in which access to rights or opportunities is not affected by gender. It is a basic human right and a fundamental principle of social justice that advocates that all human beings, regardless of their gender, should be free to develop their personal abilities and make choices without the limitations set by stereotypes, rigid gender roles, or prejudices. In the context of social norms, gender equality means the equivalence in life outcomes for women and men, recognising their different needs and interests, and requiring a redistribution of power and resources. It is not about affirming that women and men are the same, but rather about acknowledging their differences and ensuring that these differences don't confer rights, privileges, or opportunities to one group over the other. Gender equality involves promoting the full participation of women and men in society. This includes equal participation in decision making, economic opportunities, access to education and healthcare, and freedom from violence and harassment. It also includes shared responsibility for household and childcare tasks.

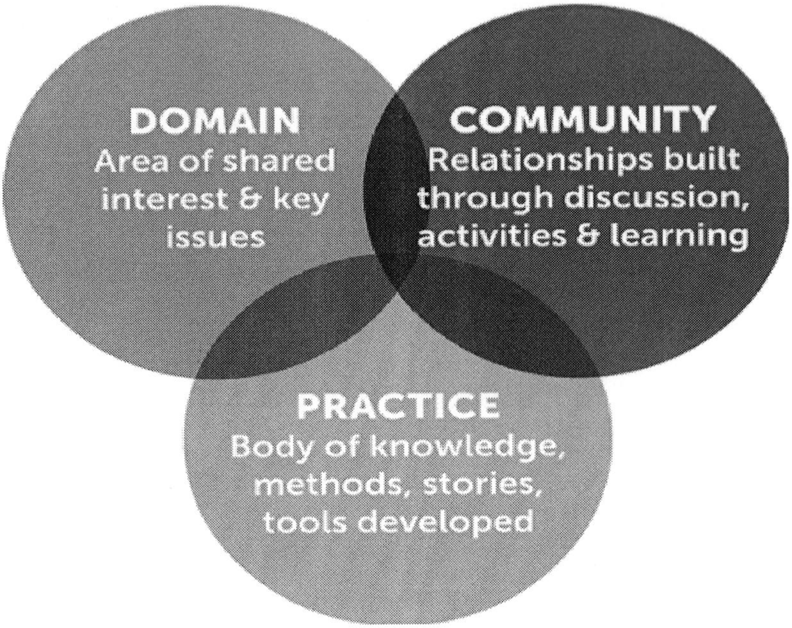

Figure 1. Illustration of community of practice (CoP) components.

Source: https://miro.medium.com/v2/resize:fit:828/format:webp/0*c3OIxTRNRFdM_7KI

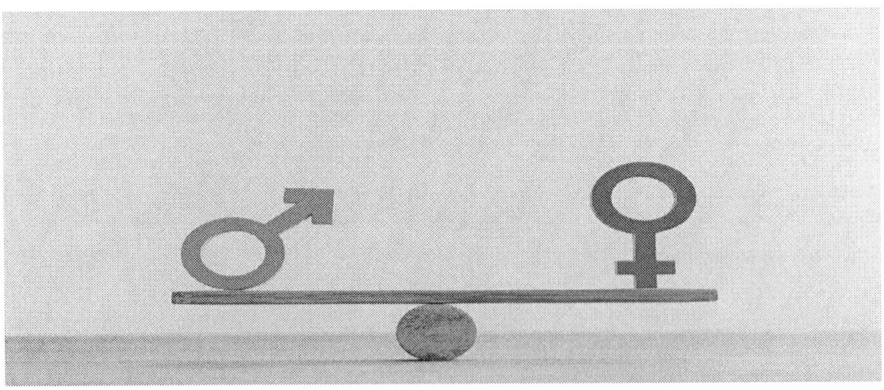

Figure 2. Image of gender equality.

Source: https://abmagazine.accaglobal.com/content/abmagazine/global/articles/2024/jan/business/pay-inequality-crackdown/_jcr_content/middle-content/container/image.desktop.jpeg/1704883459151/08january-cpd-bus-pay-transparency-ie-article.jpeg

In recent years, significant progress has been made towards achieving gender equality globally, although much remains to be done. Persistent gender disparities exist in various forms, including the gender wage gap, the under-representation of women in leadership roles, the lack of access to education for girls in some regions, and gender-based violence (GBV). A CoP facilitates collective learning and sharing of experiences among its members who are bound by a shared interest or domain. The concept could be instrumental in promoting gender equality, by creating a space for dialogue, sharing of knowledge and best practices, and initiating collective action to challenge gender norms and stereotypes, and advocate for equal rights and opportunities for all, regardless of gender.

HISTORICAL OVERVIEW OF GENDER EQUALITY

Historically, gender equality has been a struggle worldwide, with women often positioned in subordinate roles to men. In many cultures, women were viewed primarily as homemakers and their participation in the public sphere was restricted. Many societies have upheld patriarchal norms that disproportionately affected women's political, economic, and personal freedoms.

However, the fight for gender equality has a long and rich history. The late 18th and early 19th centuries marked the first wave of feminism, with a focus primarily on legal issues, primarily women's suffrage. In the United States, for example, the Seneca Falls Convention in 1848 was a significant event that galvanized women's rights activism. Despite significant resistance, the movement eventually resulted in women gaining the right to vote. The second wave of feminism in the mid-20th century broadened the debate to a wider range of issues: sexuality, family, the workplace, reproductive rights, de facto inequalities, and official legal inequalities. This wave also drew attention to domestic violence and marital rape issues, the establishment of the rape crisis and battered women's shelters, and changes in custody and divorce law. The women's liberation movement of the 1960s and 1970s, for example, advocated for equal pay, equal rights, reproductive rights, and the elimination of societal sexism. The third wave of feminism, beginning in the 1990s and continuing into the early 21st century, has sought to challenge and expand common definitions of gender and sexuality. This wave, with its roots in the academic study of intersectionality, centres on the understanding that women's experiences are shaped not only by gender, but also by other factors such as race, socioeconomic status, and sexuality.

THE CURRENT STATE OF GENDER EQUALITY GLOBALLY

As of my knowledge cut-off in 2021, progress has been made globally in the struggle for gender equality, but disparities still persist. Significant achievements have been seen in the fields of education and health. For example, gender parity in primary education has been reached in most regions, and improvements in women's health, particularly maternal health, have been substantial. However, challenges remain, particularly in political representation, economic participation, and the fight against GBV. Globally, only a quarter of all parliamentary seats are held by women, and women's representation in senior management roles and entrepreneurial work remains low. The gender wage gap is a persistent problem worldwide.

The COVID-19 pandemic also had a disproportionate impact on women, from health to the economy, security to social protection, exacerbating already existing gender inequalities. Women were more likely to be front-line workers or to lose their jobs and took on the majority of the increased housework and childcare. In terms of GBV, it's a global issue that persists in every society, with harmful practices like child marriage and Female Genital Mutilation (FGM) still widespread in certain regions.

In conclusion, although progress has been made towards gender equality, it is evident that much work remains to be done. The Sustainable Development Goals set by the United Nations highlight gender equality as not only a fundamental human right, but a necessary foundation for a peaceful, prosperous and sustainable world. It is clear that to achieve this goal, gender equality must remain at the forefront of global efforts.

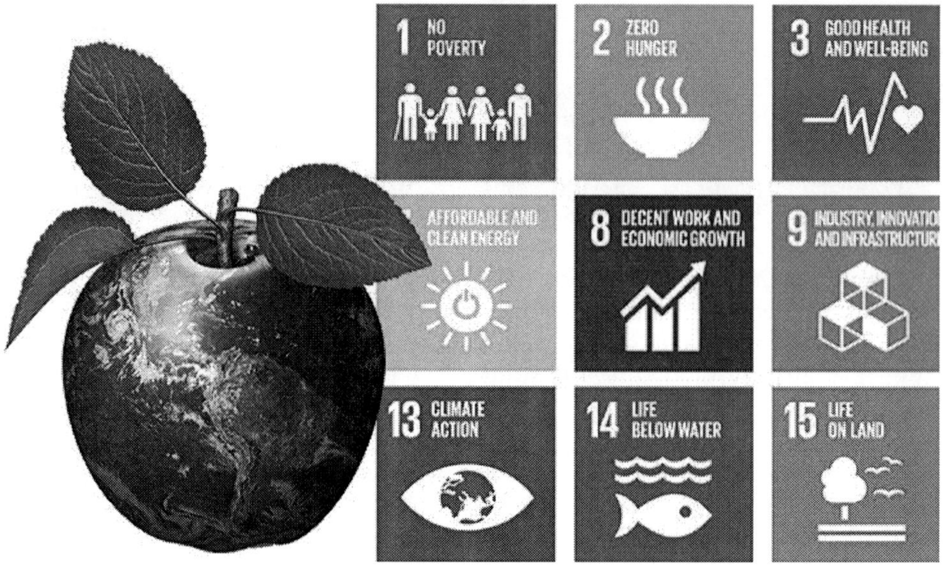

Figure 3. Image of sustainable development goals.

Source: https://miro.medium.com/v2/resize:fit:1100/format:webp/1*tvlsCy6RNAX7RN0X-JnYJig.jpeg

THE IMPORTANCE OF GENDER EQUALITY

Gender equality is paramount for various reasons. It is a fundamental human right and a cornerstone of a fair and prosperous society. Achieving gender equality is critical for economic growth; it leads to a more diversified workforce, driving productivity and economic prosperity. It also results in healthier and more educated families, thus contributing to alleviating poverty. From a social perspective, gender equality helps eliminate biases, stereotypes, and violence. It ensures that every individual, regardless of their gender, has the same freedoms, opportunities, and rights, allowing them to contribute and benefit from economic, social, cultural, and political developments in society. Thus, gender equality not only empowers individuals, but also fosters societal progress and development.

Economic Benefits

Gender equality brings with it a multitude of economic benefits, acting as a driver for sustainable development and economic growth. These benefits are multifaceted and include workforce diversification, increased productivity, poverty reduction, and improved national prosperity.

- ***Workforce Diversification***: When men and women have equal opportunities on the job market, the workforce becomes more diverse. This diversity encourages a wide range of skills, perspectives, and ideas, fostering creativity and innovation. Research suggests that companies with gender diversity are more likely to outperform their less diverse counterparts, highlighting the economic advantages of an inclusive work environment.
- ***Increased Productivity***: Gender equality on the job contributes to increased productivity. Equal pay and opportunities for training and professional development, regardless of gender, can boost employee morale and motivation. Additionally, organisations that provide supportive and flexible working conditions for both men and women witness higher levels of staff retention and productivity.
- ***Poverty Reduction***: Gender equality plays a crucial role in the reduction of poverty. Women constitute a significant proportion of the world's poor due to discriminatory laws or societal norms that limit their access to resources, education, and opportunities. By promoting gender equality and empowerment of women, we can help lift both women and their families out of poverty. Studies have shown that women are more likely to invest a larger portion of their income back into their families, leading to improved child health and education, which in turn can break the cycle of poverty.

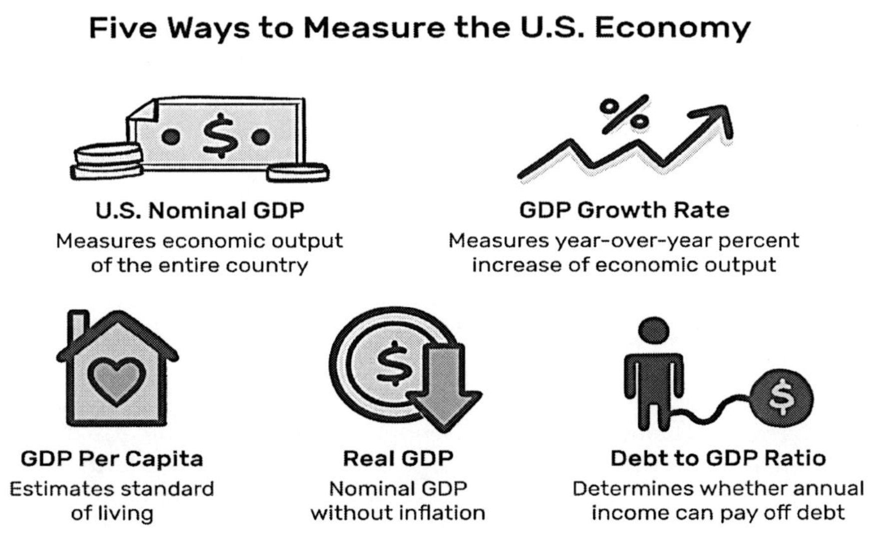

Figure 4. Illustration of five ways to measure GDP.

Source: https://www.thebalancemoney.com/thmb/aEdWOno0kVsokv368Xh2_P8EY-58=/750x0/filters:no_upscale():max_bytes(150000):strip_icc():format(webp)/u-s-gdp-5-latest-statistics-and-how-to-use-them-3306041-Final-3eaf7113efd34bdcbca4688d05d59ce3.png

- ***Economic Growth*:** Gender equality boosts economic growth. The World Bank has found that if women had the same lifetime earnings as men, global wealth could increase by $160 trillion, an increase of 14%. Furthermore, according to the McKinsey Global Institute, achieving gender equality could add $12 trillion to global GDP by 2025.
- ***Resilient Economies*:** Economies that harness the full potential of women and men are more resilient. They can recover more quickly from economic downturns because they can draw on the full talents of their populations. Gender equality can also lead to better financial management at both the household and national levels. Women tend to be more risk averse in their financial decision-making, which can contribute to economic stability.

In conclusion, gender equality offers numerous economic benefits, making it an essential aspect of a thriving economy. Recognizing and promoting gender equality is not just a moral and social imperative, but an economic one as well. Countries and companies that prioritize gender equality stand to reap substantial economic gains, contributing to sustainable and inclusive growth. On the contrary, those that do not prioritize gender equality miss out on the valuable contributions women could make to economic progress, hampering their own growth and development.

Social Benefits

The realization of gender equality has numerous social benefits that contribute to the development of a more just, equitable, and prosperous society. These benefits extend beyond individual women and men to families, communities, and societies as a whole.

1. ***Improved Education*:** Gender equality in education leads to more educated societies. When girls are given the same educational opportunities as boys, they gain the skills and knowledge to function effectively in society. Educated women are more likely to participate in decision-making processes, which can lead to the development of policies and programs that benefit a broader segment of society. Furthermore, girls' education has been associated with delayed marriage and childbirth, lower fertility rates, and better health and survival rates for children.
2. ***Enhanced Health*:** Gender equality is closely related to improvements in health. Women with more control over their lives and resources are better equipped to seek and access health care services for themselves and their families. In addition, gender equality can help mitigate harmful practices such as genital mutilation or cutting (FGM/C) and child marriage, which have significant health implications.
3. ***Decreased Domestic Violence*:** Gender equality contributes to a decrease in domestic violence. By challenging traditional gender norms that condone violence against women, societies can reduce the prevalence of domestic violence. Empowered women are also less likely to tolerate abuse and more likely to seek help.
4. ***Stronger Communities*:** Gender equality fosters stronger communities. Women often play a crucial role in community building activities, from education and health to conflict resolution. When women have equal voice

in community decisions, these decisions are more likely to consider the needs of all community members, leading to more inclusive and effective community initiatives.

5. ***Promotion of Human Rights***: Gender equality advances the realization of human rights for all. The equality between men and women is a fundamental human right, as recognized by international treaties and agreements such as the Universal Declaration of Human Rights of the United Nations. Gender equality ensures that all individuals can enjoy their rights, regardless of their gender.
6. ***Social Justice***: Gender equality fosters social justice. A society cannot truly be fair and just if half its population is subject to discrimination or exclusion. Gender equality promotes the values of fairness and justice and challenges the structures and stereotypes that perpetuate inequality.

The social benefits of gender equality are extensive and transformative. They ripple out from individual women and men to the broader society, fostering healthier, better educated, more just, and more inclusive communities. Gender equality is not just a women's issue, it is a societal issue that requires the commitment and action of all members of society. The realization of gender equality promises a better future for all.

Psychological Benefits

The achievement of gender equality brings about significant psychological benefits, positively influencing the mental and emotional well-being of individuals and societies as a whole. These benefits manifest themselves through improved self-esteem, reduced mental health issues, healthier relationships, and improved social attitudes and norms.

1. ***Enhanced Self-esteem***: When gender equality is promoted, both men and women experience an improved sense of self-worth. They feel recognized and valued for their abilities and contributions, rather than being confined or judged by their gender. This recognition not only boosts individual self-esteem, but also motivates individuals to fully participate in social, economic, and political life.
2. ***Reduced Mental Health Issues***: Gender equality can contribute to reduced levels of anxiety, depression, and other mental health issues. Discrimination and GBV, which women experience disproportionately, are significant risk factors for a variety of mental health problems. By promoting equality and tackling these harmful practices, we can create a safer, less stressful environment that fosters mental well-being.
3. ***Healthier Relationships***: Gender equality facilitates healthier interpersonal relationships. In a context of equality, relationships (be it romantic, familial, or professional) are more likely to be based on mutual respect, shared responsibilities, and equitable power dynamics. This fosters communication, understanding, and respect, contributing to improved relationship satisfaction and psychological well-being.
4. ***Positive Role Modeling***: Gender equality provides positive role models for younger generations. When children see that women and men share

responsibilities and opportunities equally, they are more likely to develop a sense of fairness and justice and carry these values into adulthood. This not only benefits their psychological development, but also contributes to a future generation that values and promotes equality.

5. ***Shifting Societal Attitudes*:** Achieving gender equality contributes to changing societal attitudes and breaking down stereotypes. Stereotypes can limit individuals' aspirations and potential, causing stress and dissatisfaction. By promoting gender equality, societies can challenge these stereotypes and broaden the range of acceptable behaviors and roles for both women and men. This frees individuals to pursue their interests and ambitions, leading to increased satisfaction and mental well-being.
6. ***Increased Empathy and Cooperation*:** Gender equality fosters an environment of empathy and cooperation. When the focus shifts from differences and hierarchy to equality and mutual respect, people are more likely to develop empathic understanding and cooperate with one another. This empathy and cooperation contribute to a sense of community and connection, improving psychological well-being.

Gender equality has profound implications for psychological health. It not only fosters individual self-esteem, well-being, and satisfaction, but also promotes healthier relationships and societies. The psychological benefits of gender equality are an essential aspect of human development and societal progress, further highlighting the need for continued efforts toward achieving gender equality. Gender equality is not just about economic empowerment or social justice, it is also about mental health and happiness, making it a crucial aspect of human well-being and social health.

CHALLENGES TO ACHIEVING GENDER EQUALITY

The achievement of gender equality presents numerous challenges, many rooted in long-standing cultural norms and systemic biases. Discriminatory laws and social norms continue to perpetuate gender inequality worldwide, preventing women from accessing education, jobs, and political representation equally. Gender stereotypes often limit women's roles and reinforce harmful practices. Economic inequalities persist, as seen in the gender wage gap and the lack of women in leadership roles. In addition, violence against women, including domestic violence and sexual harassment, remains a major global issue. The intersectionality of gender with other factors such as race, religion, and socioeconomic status often compounds these challenges. Furthermore, the COVID-19 pandemic has exacerbated many gender inequalities, posing new hurdles to gender equality. It's clear that overcoming these challenges requires systemic change, dedicated resources, and a commitment to gender equality at all societal levels.

Sociocultural Barriers

Sociocultural barriers play an important role in perpetuating gender inequality. These barriers are embedded in the societal and cultural norms, practices, and beliefs that define gender roles and expectations. Overcoming these barriers is a complex task that requires a deep understanding of the underlying social structures and cultural contexts.

1. ***Stereotyping and Social Norms***: Stereotyping is one of the most pervasive sociocultural barriers to gender equality. Stereotypes can limit the roles and behaviors considered appropriate for men and women, confining them to traditional gender roles. For example, women are often expected to assume the primary responsibility for domestic work and childcare, limiting their opportunities for education and career advancement. Men, on the other hand, are often expected to be the primary breadwinners and may face social stigma for taking on "feminine" roles or occupations.
2. ***Patriarchal Structures***: Many societies operate under patriarchal structures, where power and authority are held predominantly by men. These structures are reinforced through social, religious, and cultural practices that privilege male leadership and marginalize women's voices. This not only limits women's participation in decision-making processes but also perpetuates norms that normalize gender inequality.
3. ***Gender-Based Violence***: Gender-based violence is a brutal manifestation of gender inequality, deeply rooted in power imbalances between men and women. Societies that tolerate or normalize such violence create an environment of fear and insecurity for women, hindering their full and equal participation in all aspects of life.
4. ***Educational Inequalities***: In many cultures, girls' education is undervalued, resulting in fewer educational opportunities for girls compared to boys. This gender disparity in education perpetuates women's socioeconomic disadvantage, reducing their access to well-paying jobs and positions of influence.
5. ***Economic Dependence***: In some societies, women are economically dependent on men, often due to a lack of access to income-generating opportunities or restrictive norms around women's work. This economic dependence can limit women's autonomy and decision-making power, maintaining gender inequalities.
6. ***Religious and Cultural Beliefs***: Certain religious interpretations and cultural beliefs can be used to justify and maintain gender inequalities. Practices like child marriage, female genital mutilation, and preference for male children are examples of how cultural and religious beliefs can serve as barriers to gender equality.
7. ***Intersectionality***: The intersection of gender with other forms of social identity, such as race, class, ethnicity, and sexuality, can compound gender inequality. Women belonging to marginalized communities often face multiple layers of discrimination and exclusion, making the pursuit of gender equality even more complex.

Addressing these sociocultural barriers is vital to achieving gender equality. It requires the transformation of deeply established attitudes and norms, which is no small task. However, through comprehensive education, policy reform, and social dialogue, these barriers can be removed. Achieving gender equality not only involves changing laws and policies, but also involves transforming the cultural and social norms that define and limit the roles, opportunities, and potential of women and men.

Institutional Barriers

Institutional barriers to gender equality are systemic practices, laws, and regulations that hinder the achievement of equality between women and men. These barriers often manifest themselves in educational systems, workplaces, governments, and other social structures. Addressing them requires comprehensive institutional reforms and a commitment to achieving gender equality at all levels of society.

1. ***Discriminatory Laws and Policies***: Despite significant progress, many countries still have laws that directly discriminate against women, limiting their rights and opportunities. These may include laws related to property rights, inheritance, marriage, divorce, and citizenship. Such laws perpetuate gender inequality and hinder women's empowerment.
2. ***Gender Wage Gap***: The gender wage gap is a clear manifestation of institutional gender inequality. On average, women earn less than men for the same work. This gap is driven by various factors, including occupational segregation, discrimination, and undervaluing the work traditionally performed by women.
3. ***Underrepresentation in Leadership***: Women are often under-represented in positions of power and decision-making. Whether in politics, business, academia, or other sectors, men often outnumber women in leadership roles. This under-representation can perpetuate gender biases and hinder the development of policies and practices that promote gender equality.
4. ***Inadequate Legal Protection***: Although many countries have laws against GBV and discrimination, enforcement is often inadequate. Furthermore, many women do not have access to legal recourse due to factors such as lack of information, financial resources, and social support.
5. ***Lack of Access to Education and Training***: Institutional barriers often limit women's access to education and vocational training. These barriers can include gender-biased curricula, lack of safe and accessible facilities, early marriage and pregnancy, and cultural norms that prioritize boys' education.
6. ***Workplace Discrimination***: Women often face discrimination on the job, including biased hiring practices, unfair treatment, sexual harassment, and limited opportunities for advancement. These practices not only violate women's rights but also limit their economic potential and contributions.
7. ***Healthcare Inequality***: Women's health needs are often inadequately addressed within health systems. This can include a lack of focus on women's reproductive health, inadequate healthcare provision during and after pregnancy, and a lack of gender-sensitive approaches to healthcare.
8. ***Barriers to Political Participation***: Women's political participation is often limited by institutional barriers such as discriminatory laws and regulations, biased party practices, violence against women in politics, and the double burden of work and family responsibilities.

These institutional barriers are deeply rooted in societal structures and require comprehensive efforts to remove them. Addressing them involves not only revising discriminatory laws and policies but also challenging the gender biases that underpin these institutional practices. This requires the commitment of all levels of society, from governments to organizations, communities, and individuals. With concerted effort, these institutional barriers can be overcome, paving the way for a world where gender equality is a lived reality for all.

Individual Barriers

Individual barriers to gender equality are personal beliefs, attitudes, and behaviors that reinforce gender inequality. These barriers are often internalized from social norms and can be unconsciously perpetuated by individuals, regardless of their gender. Addressing these barriers requires self-awareness, education, and a commitment to change.

1. ***Gender Stereotypes and Biases***: At an individual level, gender stereotypes and biases can significantly influence perceptions and behaviors. These biases can lead to discriminatory behaviors, such as favoring men over women for leadership roles or perpetuating the notion that certain tasks or professions are "male" or "female."
2. ***Lack of Awareness or Denial***: Many individuals do not know about gender inequalities or may deny their existence. This lack of awareness can prevent people from recognizing and addressing their own biases or challenging discriminatory practices.
3. ***Fear of Change or Backlash***: Some people resist gender equality because they fear change or anticipate negative consequences. For example, men may fear losing their traditional privileges, while women may fear backlash or ostracism for challenging social norms.
4. ***Internalized Sexism***: Women and men can internalize sexist beliefs and attitudes. This internalized sexism can lead women to undervalue their abilities, limit their ambitions, or tolerate discrimination and violence.
5. ***Victim-Blaming Attitudes***: Victim-blaming attitudes, where victims of GBV are blamed for the harm they suffer, are another individual barrier to gender equality. These attitudes can deter victims from seeking help and perpetuate a culture of impunity for perpetrators.
6. ***Passive Acceptance of Inequality***: Some people passively accept gender inequality as a natural or inevitable part of life. This passive acceptance can hinder individual and collective efforts to promote gender equality.
7. ***Privilege Blindness***: Privilege blindness refers to the inability of individuals to recognize the privileges they enjoy due to their gender, often resulting from societal norms that favor their gender. This blindness can prevent individuals, particularly men, from acknowledging gender inequality and their role in perpetuating it.
8. ***Lack of Male Allies***: Gender equality is not just a 'women' issue - it requires the active participation of men as allies. However, some men do not participate in gender equality efforts due to lack of understanding, fear of emasculation, or the misconception that gender equality does not benefit them.

Overcoming individual barriers to gender equality requires self-reflection, education, and a commitment to change. Individuals must challenge their biases, educate themselves about gender equality, and take action to promote it in their daily lives. It's important to remember that everyone has a role to play in promoting gender equality. By addressing these individual barriers, each person can contribute to a more equal and just society.

THE COMMUNITY OF PRACTICE APPROACH

The CoP approach is a social learning theory and practice that fosters knowledge sharing and learning in a community setting. It revolves around the concept that learning is a social process that happens most effectively in a collaborative environment where individuals with common interests or professions share knowledge, experiences, and insights. CoPs can be found in various contexts, from businesses and educational institutions to online platforms. They are characterized by a shared domain of interest, a vibrant community that interacts and learns together, and a practice defined by resources, experiences, and methods. In the context of gender equality, the CoP approach can be highly instrumental, fostering collective learning, spreading best practices, and promoting effective strategies for overcoming gender-based barriers.

Definition and Explanation

The concept of the CoP was developed by theorists Etienne Wenger and Jean Lave as a framework to describe the process of social learning. This approach emphasizes the idea that learning is not just an individual or isolated activity, but a dynamic and social process that takes place within a community of individuals who share a common interest or profession.

A CoP is defined by three crucial elements: the domain, the community, and the practice.

1. ***Domain***: Domain refers to a shared area of interest or field of knowledge that brings people together. Creates common ground, gives members a sense of shared identity, and guides their learning. The domain can be broad, such as 'education', or specific, such as 'gender equality in rural education'.
2. ***Community***: The community is the group of individuals who engage in collective learning in a shared domain. They interact, participate in discussions, share information, and help each other. The relationships built among community members foster mutual respect and trust, creating a safe space for learning and knowledge exchange.
3. ***Practice***: Practice refers to the body of knowledge, methods, tools, stories, cases, documents that community members share. It's through the process of sharing and debating these practices that members learn from each other and develop personally and professionally.

These elements interact dynamically in a CoP, leading to continuous learning, innovation, and evolution. The CoP approach is widely applicable, being used in companies to improve performance, in education to improve learning and teaching strategies, and in social sectors to address complex issues, including gender equality.

In the context of gender equality, the CoP approach can be an empowering tool. CoPs focused on gender equality would bring together individuals and organizations dedicated to this cause, creating a platform where members can share experiences, learn from successful initiatives, and collaboratively find solutions to common challenges. By fostering continuous dialogue and collaboration, CoPs can accelerate the spread of best practices and innovative solutions, empowering members with the knowledge and skills needed to promote gender equality in various contexts. It offers a space for challenging stereotypes and biases, sharing strategies to overcome institutional and individual barriers, and promoting the social, economic, and psychological benefits of gender equality. It also provides a supportive network for people engaged in the challenging work of advancing gender equality. CoPs also encourage members to reflect on their practices, learn from their successes and failures, and continually improve their strategies. This reflective practice is vital in a field as complex and context-dependent as gender equality. It enables practitioners to adapt and evolve their practices in response to changing conditions and learnings.

In conclusion, the CoP approach is a powerful strategy for fostering social learning and promoting gender equality. By bringing people together around shared interests and goals, CoPs provide an environment where knowledge can be created, shared, and applied, leading to innovative solutions and practices. In the pursuit of gender equality, this approach offers a promising avenue for collaborative learning and collective action.

Historical Development of the Community of Practice Approach

The CoP approach has its roots in the field of social learning theory and has evolved over time through the work of several influential scholars. The historical development of the CoP approach can be traced back to the late 1980s and early 1990s.

1. ***Jean Lave and Etienne Wenger***: In their groundbreaking book, 'Situated Learning: Legitimate Peripheral Participation," published in 1991, Jean Lave and Etienne Wenger introduced the concept of communities of practice. They argued that learning is a social process that occurs through participation in authentic activities within a community. They emphasized the importance of social interactions, shared practices, and the development of a sense of identity and belonging within the community.
2. ***Wenger's Expansion of the CoP Concept***: On the basis of the work of Lave, Wenger further developed the concept of CoPs in subsequent publications. In his book "Communities of Practice: Learning, Meaning, and Identity," published in 1998, Wenger elaborated on the three key dimensions of CoPs: domain, community, and practice. He emphasized the role of social learning and the creation of knowledge through participation in communities.
3. ***Application in Organizations***: The CoP approach gained traction in the business and organizational context, thanks to the work of Wenger and his collaborators. They applied the CoP framework to various organizational settings, demonstrating how CoPs can foster knowledge sharing, innovation, and organizational learning. This application

highlighted the potential of CoPs to address complex challenges and promote collaboration within and across organizations.

4. ***Broader Application in Education***: The CoP approach found further application in the field of education. Educators recognized the importance of social learning and collaboration among students and teachers. CoPs were seen as a way to create supportive learning communities and enhance professional development among educators. Wenger's work on communities of practice in educational settings helped shape the discourse on educational reform and teacher professional learning.
5. ***Evolution and Diversification***: Over time, the concept of CoPs has evolved and diversified. Scholars and practitioners have adapted and applied the approach to various fields and contexts, including healthcare, sustainability, technology, and social change. The understanding of CoPs has expanded to include both face-to-face and online communities, recognizing the role of digital platforms in facilitating virtual communities of practice.
6. ***Integration with Technology***: With the advancement of technology, digital platforms have become essential for supporting and improving CoPs. Online communities of practice have emerged, providing platforms for knowledge sharing, collaboration, and networking across geographic boundaries. These digital CoPs have allowed global connections and facilitated the rapid dissemination of information and resources.
7. ***Continued Research and Application***: The CoP approach continues to be an active area of research, with scholars exploring its theoretical foundations, dynamics, and practical implications. It remains a valuable framework to understand social learning and to foster collaboration and knowledge exchange in various fields.

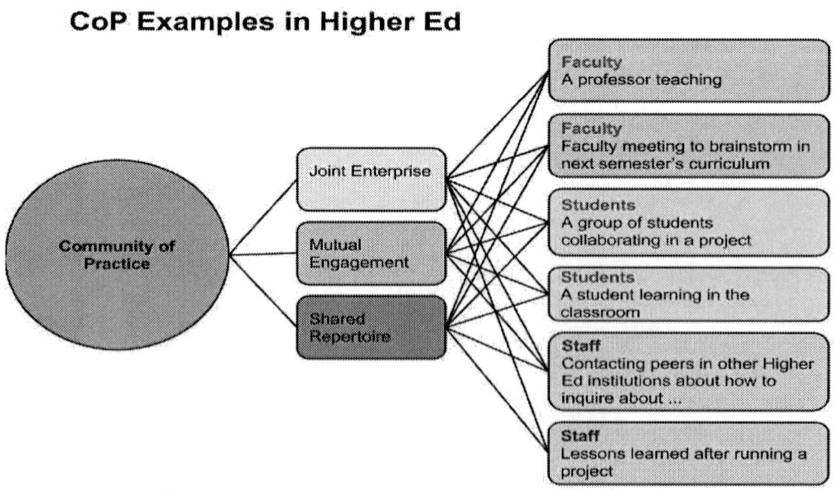

Figure 5. Reflections on Wenger's community of practice.

Source: https://bpb-us-e1.wpmucdn.com/you.stonybrook.edu/dist/a/37/files/2015/02/CoP-29dz9rs-300x225.jpg

In summary, the CoP approach has evolved from its inception as a social learning theory in the early 1990s to a widely applied framework to foster collaboration, knowledge sharing and learning in various domains. Its historical development has seen its application expand from organizational contexts to education and beyond. The integration of technology has further expanded the possibilities and reach of CoPs, making them more accessible and inclusive. As research and practice continue, the CoP approach is likely to further evolve, adapting to the changing needs and contexts of communities and organizations.

Current State of the Community of Practice Approach

The CoP approach continues to be a relevant and influential framework for fostering collaboration, knowledge sharing, and learning in various fields and contexts. Its current state reflects both its enduring impact and its adaptation to the evolving landscape of social learning and technology.

1. ***Diverse Application***: The CoP approach has found widespread application in different sectors and disciplines. It is utilized in organizations to improve knowledge management, innovation, and employee development. In education, CoPs are used to support professional learning communities among teachers and promote student engagement. The approach is also applied in fields such as healthcare, sustainability, social change, and technology, where communities of practitioners come together to address complex challenges and share best practices.
2. ***Online Communities of Practice***: With the increasing prominence of digital platforms and on-line connectivity, the CoP approach has extended its reach through virtual communities of practice. Online CoPs provide opportunities for knowledge sharing, networking, and collaboration across geographical boundaries. Social media platforms, discussion forums, and online learning communities have become spaces where individuals with shared interests and professional goals come together to learn, exchange ideas, and collaborate.
3. ***Global Connections***: The CoP approach has facilitated global connections and collaborations between individuals and organizations. Digital platforms enable practitioners from different countries and cultures to engage in cross-cultural dialogue, exchange diverse perspectives, and collectively address global challenges. This globalized approach expands the pool of knowledge and experiences available within CoPs, enhancing innovation and problem-solving.
4. ***Technology Integration***: The integration of technology has transformed the way CoPs function and interact. Online collaboration tools, video conferences, and knowledge management systems have simplified communication and facilitated the sharing of resources, documents, and experiences. The use of technology also allows for the capture and dissemination of tacit knowledge, ensuring that valuable insights are not lost as individuals join or leave a community.
5. ***Emphasis on Diversity and Inclusion***: The current state of CoPs places an increasing emphasis on diversity and inclusion. Recognizing the value of

multiple perspectives and experiences, efforts are being made to create inclusive spaces that welcome individuals from diverse backgrounds and identities. CoPs are evolving to ensure that marginalized voices are heard and power imbalances are addressed, promoting equity within the community.

6. ***Research and Learning*:** The CoP approach remains an active area of research, with scholars continuously exploring its theoretical foundations, dynamics, and impacts. Research focuses on understanding the conditions that facilitate effective CoPs, examining the role of leadership, exploring strategies to sustain and scale communities, and evaluating the outcomes and impact of CoP initiatives. This ongoing research contributes to the refinement and development of the CoP approach.
7. ***Challenges and Opportunities*:** Despite its many benefits, CoPs also face challenges. Sustaining active participation, ensuring a balance between online and offline interactions, and addressing motivation and commitment issues are among the challenges faced by CoPs. However, these challenges also present opportunities for innovation and improvement, prompting practitioners and researchers to develop strategies to improve engagement, foster meaningful connections, and measure the impact of CoP initiatives.

The CoP approach is alive and thriving in the landscape of social learning and technology today. Its diverse applications, integration of digital platforms, emphasis on diversity and inclusion, and ongoing research efforts demonstrate its relevance and adaptability. As organizations and communities recognize the value of collective learning, collaboration, and knowledge sharing, the CoP approach will continue to evolve and play a vital role in fostering innovation, professional development, and positive social change.

APPLICATION OF THE COMMUNITY OF PRACTICE APPROACH TO GENDER EQUALITY

The CoP approach has great potential for the application of gender equality initiatives. By bringing together individuals and organizations with a shared interest in promoting gender equality, CoPs provide a platform for knowledge sharing, collaboration, and collective learning. CoPs focused on gender equality can serve as spaces where members exchange best practices, discuss strategies for overcoming barriers, and share resources and experiences. They create opportunities for cross-sectoral collaboration, enabling diverse stakeholders to work together towards common goals. Through the CoP approach, people engaged in gender equality work can gain support, build networks, and develop innovative solutions to address the complex challenges and systemic barriers that hinder progress toward achieving gender equality.

The Potential of Community of Practice in Promoting Gender Equality

The CoP approach has immense potential to promote gender equality by fostering collaboration, knowledge sharing, and collective action. CoPs provide a platform for individuals and organizations to come together, exchange ideas, learn from each other, and work towards common goals. Here, we explore the potential of the CoP approach to advance gender equality and create meaningful change.

1. ***Knowledge Sharing and Learning***: CoPs offer a space for sharing experiences, best practices, and lessons learned in the field of gender equality. Members can exchange information on effective strategies, innovative approaches, and successful initiatives. This knowledge sharing helps to disseminate valuable information and expertise across diverse contexts and organizations. It allows individuals and organizations to learn from each other's successes and failures, contributing to continuous improvement in the promotion of gender equality.
2. ***Building Networks and Collaboration***: CoPs bring together diverse stakeholders, including policymakers, activists, researchers, practitioners, and community members, fostering collaboration and the development of networks. By facilitating connections among these stakeholders, CoPs enable the sharing of resources, expertise, and opportunities. These networks can lead to powerful collaborations that amplify efforts, leverage resources, and drive systemic change for gender equality.
3. ***Addressing Complex Challenges***: Gender equality is a multifaceted issue that requires a comprehensive and interdisciplinary approach. CoPs provide a platform for collective problem solving and the exploration of innovative solutions. By engaging stakeholders from various sectors and backgrounds, CoPs facilitate a holistic understanding of the challenges and opportunities to advance gender equality. This collective approach allows the identification of systemic barriers, the development of strategies to overcome them, and the implementation of context-specific interventions.
4. ***Empowering Individuals and Organizations***: CoPs empower individuals and organizations engaged in gender equality work by providing a supportive and collaborative environment. Through participation in CoPs, individuals gain access to a diverse range of perspectives, expertise, and resources. This exposure improves your understanding of gender issues, builds your capacity to address challenges, and strengthens your confidence as agents of change. Additionally, CoPs offer opportunities for professional development, mentoring, and peer support, fostering the growth and empowerment of individuals committed to gender equality.
5. ***Advocacy and Policy Influence***: CoPs can play a crucial role in advocating for gender equality at various levels, including influencing policy and decision-making processes. By collectively amplifying voices, sharing evidence-based practices, and presenting a unified front, CoPs can influence policies, legislation, and institutional practices. They provide a platform for knowledge translation, where research findings and insights are shared in accessible ways to inform policy discussions and shape gender-responsive approaches.
6. ***Community Engagement and Social Norms***: CoPs engage with communities at the grassroots level, promoting dialogue and raising awareness about gender equality issues. They create opportunities for community members to share their experiences, challenges, and aspirations. CoPs can facilitate

community-led initiatives, empowering individuals to challenge harmful gender norms, stereotypes, and discriminatory practices. By involving communities, PPPs ensure that gender equality efforts are contextually relevant, inclusive, and sustainable.

7. ***Monitoring and Evaluation*:** CoPs can contribute to the monitoring and evaluation of gender equality initiatives by developing shared indicators, evaluation frameworks, and data collection methods. Through collaborative monitoring and evaluation, CoPs can assess the impact of interventions, identify areas for improvement, and refine strategies. This evidence-based approach strengthens accountability, enhances learning, and allows adaptive programming in the pursuit of gender equality.
8. ***Scaling Up and Replication*:** Successful gender equality initiatives developed within CoPs can be scaled up and replicated in different contexts. CoPs serve as incubators for innovative practices that have demonstrated positive outcomes. Through collaboration and shared learning, CoPs can support the dissemination of successful interventions, ensuring that effective strategies are adapted and applied to address gender inequalities on a broader scale.

In conclusion, the CoP approach has significant potential to promote gender equality. By facilitating knowledge sharing, collaboration, and collective action, CoPs empower individuals and organizations to address complex challenges, build networks, influence policies, engage communities, and contribute to monitoring and evaluation efforts. The CoP approach offers a dynamic and inclusive platform to foster collaboration and drive meaningful change toward achieving gender equality. By harnessing the power of collective learning and collaboration, CoPs can play a vital role in advancing gender equality across sectors and communities.

CHALLENGES AND OPPORTUNITIES IN APPLYING THE COMMUNITY OF PRACTICE APPROACH

The application of the CoP approach in promoting gender equality is not without challenges and opportunities. One challenge is to ensure active and sustained participation of diverse stakeholders in the CoP. Balancing the interests, priorities, and availability of members can be complex. Additionally, establishing effective communication channels and platforms for knowledge sharing can be a challenge, particularly in contexts with limited access to technology or low digital literacy. However, these challenges also present opportunities. They can stimulate creativity and innovation by finding inclusive and accessible ways to engage stakeholders. Furthermore, overcoming these challenges can strengthen the resilience and effectiveness of the CoP, fostering a sense of ownership and commitment among members. By addressing these challenges and leveraging the opportunities, the CoP approach can be a powerful tool in driving gender equality by promoting collaboration, knowledge sharing, and collective action.

Identifying and Overcoming Challenges

Identifying and overcoming challenges is crucial for the successful application of the CoP approach to promote gender equality. By recognizing and addressing these challenges, CoPs can effectively harness the power of collective action, knowledge sharing, and collaboration. Here are some common challenges in applying the CoP approach and strategies for overcoming them:

1. ***Engagement and Participation*:** One of the primary challenges is ensuring active and sustained engagement of various stakeholders in the CoP. To address this, it is essential to clearly communicate the purpose, benefits, and value proposition of the CoP to potential members. Engaging key influencers and opinion leaders within the community can help promote participation. Regular and meaningful interaction, such as sharing relevant resources, organizing events, and facilitating discussions, can foster a sense of belonging and encourage active participation.
2. ***Communication and Knowledge Sharing*:** Effective communication and knowledge sharing are fundamental to the success of CoPs. However, limited access to technology, language barriers, and varying levels of digital literacy can pose challenges. Overcoming these challenges requires employing a variety of communication channels that accommodate diverse needs and preferences. This could include using multiple platforms, such as online forums, social media groups, virtual meetings, and offline gatherings. It is also essential to ensure that knowledge sharing is inclusive and accessible by translating materials into local languages, using plain language, and employing visual and audio formats.
3. ***Sustainability and Continuity*:** CoPs must maintain their momentum and relevance over time. This requires strategies to maintain engagement and continuity, as members may face competing priorities or turnover. Creating a governance structure that allows shared leadership, roles, and responsibilities can help distribute the workload and prevent overreliance on a few individuals. Documenting and organizing knowledge and resources in a central repository ensures continuity and facilitates onboarding of new members. Periodic evaluation and reflection can help identify areas for improvement and keep the CoP dynamic and responsive to changing needs.
4. ***Power Dynamics and Inclusivity*:** Power dynamics and hierarchies can impact the effectiveness of CoPs in promoting gender equality. It is essential to create a safe and inclusive space that encourages diverse perspectives, active participation, and shared decision-making. Addressing power imbalances may involve establishing guidelines for respectful communication, facilitating inclusive discussions, and actively seeking input from marginalized voices. CoPs should also actively strive for gender balance in membership and leadership positions to ensure equitable representation.
5. ***Resource Constraints*:** Limited financial and human resources can pose challenges in the application of the CoP approach. Collaborating with strategic partners, leveraging existing networks, and accessing funding opportunities can help overcome resource constraints. Identifying and mobilizing local resources, such as community spaces, volunteer expertise, or inkind contributions, can also be valuable. Furthermore, focusing on leveraging the strengths and expertise within the CoP itself can help maximize available resources.

6. ***Monitoring and Evaluation***: Monitoring and evaluating the impact of CoP initiatives can be challenging. Defining appropriate indicators, establishing data collection mechanisms, and ensuring the availability of reliable data can be complex. Engaging CoP members in the evaluation process can improve their ownership and commitment. Using participatory evaluation methods, such as collaborative data collection and reflective practices, can capture qualitative insights and assess the effectiveness of CoP interventions. Regular evaluation allows for adaptive management and evidence-based decision-making.
7. ***Scaling Up and Replication***: Scaling up successful CoP initiatives to wider contexts can be challenging due to variations in resources, cultural norms, and institutional structures. To overcome this, it is crucial to document and disseminate best practices, case studies, and lessons learned. Providing guidance on adapting interventions to different contexts can enable replication. Engaging policymakers, influencers and stakeholders at higher levels can facilitate the scaling of CoP initiatives and the integration of gender equality considerations into broader policies and programs.

Identifying and overcoming challenges in applying the CoP approach is essential to promote gender equality. Strategies such as effective engagement, inclusive communication, sustainability measures, addressing power dynamics, resource mobilization, monitoring and evaluation, and scaling up can help navigate these challenges. By recognizing and actively addressing these obstacles, CoPs can maximize their potential to drive positive change, foster collaboration, and contribute to the advancement of gender equality.

Leveraging Opportunities for Maximum Impact

The use of opportunities is crucial to maximize the impact of the CoP approach in promoting gender equality. By capitalizing on favorable conditions and strategic advantages, CoPs can effectively drive change, foster collaboration, and create lasting impact. Here are some key opportunities that can be leveraged for maximum impact.

1. ***Networks and Partnerships***: CoPs provide a platform for building networks and partnerships across sectors, organizations, and communities. Leveraging these connections can enhance the reach, influence, and effectiveness of CoP. By collaborating with like-minded organizations, academic institutions, government agencies, and grassroots movements, CoPs can tap into diverse expertise, resources, and networks. This enables the sharing of best practices, collective advocacy, and joint initiatives that amplify the impact of gender equality efforts.
2. ***Technology and Digital Platforms***: The advent of digital platforms and technology has created unprecedented opportunities for knowledge sharing, collaboration, and mobilization. CoPs can take advantage of these tools to overcome geographical barriers, facilitate virtual interactions, and engage a wider audience. Online platforms, social media groups, webinars, and virtual conferences offer cost-effective means of communication and

dissemination of knowledge. Harnessing the power of technology can enhance the accessibility and scalability of CoP initiatives, allowing global reach and greater impact.

3. ***Policy and Advocacy*:** CoPs can play a vital role in influencing policies and advocating for gender equality at various levels. By leveraging the collective expertise, evidence, and experiences of its members, a CoP can inform policy debates, contribute to the development of gender-responsive policies, and advocate for their implementation. Engaging policymakers, government officials, and key stakeholders through policy dialogues, consultations, and evidence-based advocacy can ensure that gender equality concerns are effectively integrated into policies, strategies, and programs.
4. ***Knowledge Generation and Dissemination*:** CoPs are excellent platforms for generating and disseminating knowledge that informs gender equality interventions. By fostering a culture of learning, research, and innovation, CoPs can contribute to evidence-based practices, generate new knowledge, and disseminate research findings. Through collaborative research projects, case studies, and publications, CoPs can enhance the understanding of gender issues, identify effective strategies, and inform decision making. This knowledge can be widely shared through publications, on-line platforms, webinars, and conferences, creating a ripple effect that extends beyond the CoP itself.
5. ***Capacity Building and Empowerment*:** CoPs provide opportunities for the development of capacity and the empowerment of individuals and organizations. By facilitating peer learning, mentorship, and skill development, CoPs improve the expertise and capabilities of their members. Capacity building activities, such as training programs, workshops, and webinars, can empower people with the knowledge and skills to drive gender equality initiatives. Empowered individuals can then act as change agents within their organizations and communities, multiplying the impact of the CoP.
6. ***Community Engagement and Ownership*:** CoPs thrive on active community involvement and ownership. By involving local communities, grassroots organizations, and beneficiaries in CoP initiatives, the approach can achieve greater relevance, sustainability, and impact. CoPs can actively engage community members through participatory approaches, community-led projects, and inclusive decision-making processes. This participation fosters a sense of ownership, builds trust, and ensures that interventions are contextually relevant and responsive to the needs and aspirations of the community.
7. ***Learning and Reflection*:** CoPs are learning communities where members continuously reflect on their practices, share experiences, and adapt their approaches. This culture of learning and reflection allows for iterative improvements and innovation. By creating spaces for reflection, evaluation, and feedback, CoPs can improve the effectiveness and impact of their interventions. Regular learning events, knowledge-sharing

sessions, and reflection exercises allow CoP members to critically analyze their work, identify challenges, and develop innovative solutions.

8. ***Cross-Sector Collaboration***: CoPs provide opportunities for cross-sector collaboration, bringing together actors from different sectors, including government, civil society, academia, and the private sector. Leveraging this diversity of perspectives and expertise enables holistic approaches to addressing gender inequality. Collaborative initiatives that involve multiple stakeholders can result in comprehensive interventions that address the complex and interconnected factors that contribute to gender inequality. Using the strengths and resources of each sector, CoPs can create synergies and achieve greater impact.
9. ***Advocacy for Social Norm Change***: CoPs can play a pivotal role in challenging and transforming harmful social norms and attitudes that perpetuate gender inequality. By leveraging their collective voice and influence, CoPs can advocate for social norm change at the individual, community, and societal levels. Engaging with the media, organizing awareness campaigns and working with influencers and opinion leaders can help challenge gender stereotypes, promote gender equality messages, and create an enabling environment for change.
10. ***Policy and Program Innovation***: CoPs are fertile grounds for innovation in policies, programs, and interventions aimed at promoting gender equality. By bringing together diverse stakeholders, CoPs foster an environment conducive to creative problem solving and experimentation. This allows the development of innovative approaches that address emerging challenges and gaps in gender equality. CoPs can serve as incubators for the testing and scaling of innovative ideas, contributing to the development of evidence-based and contextually relevant solutions.

Leveraging these opportunities can maximize the impact of the CoP approach in promoting gender equality. By harnessing networks, technology, policy advocacy, knowledge generation, capacity building, community engagement, learning, cross-sector collaboration, norm change advocacy, and program innovation, CoPs can create transformative change. It is through strategic and intentional utilization of these opportunities that CoPs can drive lasting impact, foster gender equality, and contribute to the achievement of a more equitable and just society.

FUTURE DIRECTIONS FOR GENDER EQUALITY AND THE COMMUNITY OF PRACTICE APPROACH

As we look to the future, there are several promising directions for advancing gender equality through the CoP approach. First, there is a need to increase the focus on intersectionality within CoPs, recognizing the interconnected nature of gender with other social identities such as race, ethnicity, sexuality, and disability. This approach acknowledges the unique challenges facing individuals who belong to multiple marginalized groups and promotes more inclusive and comprehensive strategies. Second, the use of technology and digital platforms will continue to be a key future direction, enabling greater access, participation, and collaboration within CoPs. This includes exploring the potential of virtual reality, artificial intelligence, and online learning platforms to improve knowledge sharing and capacity building. Third, strengthening the evidence base for CoP interventions is crucial, with a greater emphasis on rigorous monitoring, evaluation, and research. This will provide empirical insights into the effectiveness of CoPs in promoting gender equality and inform evidence-based practices. Finally, the promotion of greater global collaboration and cross-regional learning between CoPs can lead to the exchange of diverse perspectives, innovative approaches, and shared best practices. By building bridges between CoPs operating in different contexts, we can accelerate progress toward gender equality on a global scale.

Trends and Developments to Watch

As we navigate the path towards gender equality, there are several emerging trends and developments that hold significant potential to shape the future landscape. By staying attuned to these trends and harnessing their potential, we can drive positive change and accelerate progress. Here are some key trends and developments to watch:

1. ***Intersectionality and Inclusivity***: There is a growing recognition of the importance of intersectionality in addressing gender inequality. Intersectionality acknowledges that individuals experience multiple dimensions of identity simultaneously and that these intersections can create unique forms of discrimination and disadvantage. Moving forward, there will be a greater focus on understanding and addressing the complex interplay between gender, race, ethnicity, sexuality, disability, and other social identities within gender equality initiatives. Embracing intersectionality and adopting inclusive approaches will foster more comprehensive and equitable solutions.
2. ***Youth Engagement and Activism***: Young people around the world have been at the forefront of advocating for gender equality and challenging social norms. Youth-led movements, such as #MeToo and Fridays for the Future, have demonstrated the power of youth participation in driving social change. Moving forward, it is crucial to amplify the voices of young activists, engage them in decision-making processes, and provide platforms for their participation in CoPs. Empowering and supporting youth-led initiatives will shape the future of gender equality movements.
3. ***Technology and Digital Transformation***: Technology continues to play a transformative role in advancing gender equality. The increasing accessibility of digital platforms, mobile connectivity, and social networks has enabled rapid dissemination of information, mobilization of communities, and amplification of voices. Harnessing technology for gender equality initiatives will be a key trend to watch. This includes leveraging digital tools for awareness raising, knowledge sharing, virtual collaborations, online training, and advocacy. It also involves addressing the digital gender divide to ensure that technology is inclusive and accessible to all.
4. ***Private Sector Engagement***: The private sector is increasingly recognizing its role and responsibility in promoting gender equality. Businesses

are integrating gender equality principles into their operations, supply chains, and corporate social responsibility initiatives. There is a growing emphasis on diversity and inclusion in the workplace, equal pay, and ethical business practices. Collaboration between CoPs and the private sector can foster innovative solutions, resource mobilization, and scaling up of gender equality interventions.

5. ***Data and Evidence-based Approaches***: The availability of reliable and disaggregated data is crucial for effective gender equality interventions. There is a growing emphasis on data collection, analysis, and utilization to inform evidence-based policies and programs. Moving forward, there will be an increased focus on generating sex-disaggregated data, qualitative research, and participatory approaches to understand the complex dynamics of gender inequality. Strengthening data systems and investing in research will allow better targeting, monitoring, and evaluation of gender equality initiatives.
6. ***Policy and Legal Reforms***: Policy and legal reforms play a vital role in advancing gender equality. Governments are increasingly enacting legislation and policies to address gender disparities and promote gender-responsive governance. Continued efforts are needed to implement and enforce these policies effectively. Additionally, there is a need for policy coherence, where gender equality is integrated across all sectors and policy domains. Monitoring policy developments and advocating for gender-responsive policies will be essential in the future.
7. ***Global Collaboration and Learning Networks***: The power of collaboration and knowledge exchange across borders cannot be underestimated. CoPs are increasingly participating in global collaboration and learning networks to share best practices, lessons learned, and innovative approaches. Building bridges between CoPs operating in different regions and contexts allows cross-cultural learning, exchange of experiences, and joint advocacy efforts. Strengthening these networks will enhance collective impact and foster a global movement for gender equality.
8. ***Climate Change and Gender***: The intersection of climate change and gender equality is gaining recognition as a critical area of focus. Climate change disproportionately affects women and girls, exacerbating existing gender inequalities. It is essential to address the differential impacts of climate change on women and men, promote women's leadership in climate action, and integrate gender perspectives into climate policies and programs. CoPs can play a crucial role in bringing together stakeholders from the gender equality and environmental sectors to foster collaboration, develop gender-responsive climate strategies, and advocate for gender-just climate policies.
9. ***Health and Well-being***: The COVID-19 pandemic has highlighted the intersection of gender equality with health and well-being. Women have been disproportionately affected by the pandemic, both in terms of health impacts and socioeconomic consequences. Moving forward, there will be a need to prioritize women's health, ensure access to healthcare services,

address GBV and promote mental well-being. CoPs can contribute by sharing best practices, developing gender-responsive healthcare policies, and strengthening the capacity of healthcare systems to address gender-specific needs.

10. ***Education and Empowerment***: Education is a powerful tool for empowering people and promoting gender equality. Investing in girls' education, promoting gender-responsive pedagogy and challenging gender stereotypes within educational systems are crucial to achieve long-term change. CoPs can collaborate with educational institutions, teachers, and community organizations to develop innovative approaches that address barriers to girls' education and foster gender-equitable learning environments.

Staying attuned to these trends and developments will be key to shaping the future of gender equality initiatives and the role of CoPs. Embracing intersectionality, leveraging technology, engaging the private sector, promoting data-driven approaches, advocating for policy reforms, fostering global collaboration, addressing climate change and health, and prioritizing education and empowerment will contribute to the advancement of gender equality. By proactively responding to these trends, CoPs can effectively drive change, inspire collective action, and create a more equitable and inclusive future for all.

Potential Innovations and Their Impact

As we strive for gender equality, there are several potential innovations that have the potential to significantly impact and accelerate progress in this area. These innovations take advantage of advances in technology, research, and social practices to address persistent challenges and create new opportunities for gender equality. Here are some key innovations and their potential impact:

1. ***Technology for Gender Empowerment***: Technology has the potential to empower individuals and communities by providing access to information, resources, and opportunities. Mobile applications, online platforms, and digital tools can be used to provide gender-responsive services, such as healthcare, education, finance, and entrepreneurship support. These innovations can bridge geographical and social barriers, particularly in marginalized communities, and provide women and girls with new avenues for empowerment and economic independence.

2. ***Artificial Intelligence and Data Analytics***: Artificial Intelligence (AI) and data analytics have significant potential to advance gender equality. These technologies can help identify patterns, trends, and biases in gender-related data, enabling evidence-based decision making and policy formulation. AI-powered chatbots and virtual assistants can provide personalized information and support for gender-related issues. Furthermore, AI can be used to address gender biases in algorithms and ensure fairness and inclusion in automated decision-making processes.

3. ***Feminist and Gender-Sensitive Design***: Incorporating feminist and gender-sensitive design principles into the development of products, services, and infrastructure can create more inclusive and equitable solutions. Designing

with a gender lens takes into account the diverse needs, experiences, and perspectives of different genders, ensuring that the design is accessible, safe, and inclusive for all. This approach can lead to innovations such as gender-responsive urban planning, inclusive healthcare facilities, and technology products that address specific gender-related challenges.

4. ***Gender-Equal Leadership and Representation***: Achieving gender equality requires the promotion of women's leadership and representation in all areas of society. Innovative strategies and initiatives can be developed to increase women's participation in decision making processes, including quotas, mentoring programs, and leadership development initiatives. Creating an enabling environment for women's leadership can drive systemic change and challenge gender norms and stereotypes.
5. ***Social Norm Change Campaigns***: Addressing harmful social norms and attitudes is critical to achieving gender equality. Innovative social norm change campaigns can challenge deeply entrenched beliefs and behaviors that perpetuate gender inequality. These campaigns can use various media, including social media, art, and storytelling, to promote positive gender norms, challenge stereotypes, and encourage inclusive and respectful behaviors. By engaging individuals and communities, these campaigns can foster collective action and create social transformation.
6. ***Intersectional Approaches***: Intersectionality recognizes the interconnected nature of social identities and the need to address overlapping forms of discrimination and disadvantage. Innovations that embrace intersectionality can promote more inclusive and comprehensive approaches to gender equality. This includes considering the specific needs and experiences of individuals at the intersections of gender, race, ethnicity, sexuality, disability, and other social identities. Intersectional innovations can lead to more targeted and effective interventions, ensuring that no one is left behind.
7. ***Virtual and Augmented Reality for Empathy-building***: Virtual and augmented reality technologies have the potential to foster empathy and understanding by allowing individuals to experience different perspectives. These technologies can be used to raise awareness about gender inequality, simulate challenging situations faced by marginalized groups, and encourage empathy-building exercises. By immersing individuals in virtual experiences, these innovations can facilitate attitude and behavior change, promoting empathy, and support for gender equality.
8. ***Partnerships for Innovation***: Collaborations and partnerships between various stakeholders, including governments, civil society organizations, academia, and the private sector, can drive innovation and amplify the impact of gender equality initiatives. Public-private partnerships can leverage resources, expertise, and networks to develop and scale innovative solutions. Cross-sector collaborations can also facilitate knowledge exchange, research, and collective advocacy, fostering a collaborative ecosystem that nurtures innovation and accelerates progress toward gender equality.

9. ***Gender-Responsive Education and Training***: Transforming education and training systems to be more gender-responsive is crucial for promoting gender equality. Innovative approaches can include integrating gender equality into curriculum and pedagogy, promoting girls' access to STEM education and careers, and providing gender-sensitive training for teachers and educators. By equipping individuals with knowledge, skills, and attitudes that challenge gender stereotypes and promote equality, these innovations can foster long-term social change.
10. ***Financial Inclusion and Economic Empowerment***: Access to financial services and economic opportunities is a vital aspect of gender equality. Innovations in financial technology, such as mobile banking and digital payment systems, can expand financial inclusion for women, particularly in underserved communities. Microfinance initiatives and entrepreneurship support programs tailored to women's needs can improve economic empowerment and promote women's economic participation. These innovations can create pathways for women to generate income, build assets, and have greater control over their financial lives.
11. ***Men and Boys as Allies***: Engaging men and boys as allies in the pursuit of gender equality is an important innovation. Initiatives that promote positive masculinity, challenge harmful stereotypes, and foster respectful and equal relationships can contribute to the decomposition of patriarchal norms and behaviors. These innovations can address the root causes of gender inequality and create a more inclusive society where men and boys actively support and advocate for gender equality.
12. ***Gamification for Behavior Change***: Gamification, the application of game-design elements in non-game contexts, can be harnessed to promote behavior change towards gender equality. Gamified platforms, apps, and initiatives can incentivize and reward people who engage in gender-equitable actions, fostering positive behavior change. By making efforts to achieve gender equality interactive, enjoyable, and engaging, gamification innovations have the potential to create a lasting impact and sustain individual commitment to equality.

These potential innovations hold significant promise for advancing gender equality. Using technology, embracing intersectionality, challenging social norms, fostering partnerships, and promoting inclusive design, we can harness the power of innovation to create a more equitable and just society. These innovations have the potential to address systemic barriers, change attitudes and behaviors, and empower individuals and communities. By continuously exploring and implementing these innovations, we can pave the way for a future where gender equality is truly realized.

UNDERSTANDING GENDER EQUALITY COMMUNITIES OF PRACTICE

CoPs are social constructs that facilitate the convergence of individuals who have a common interest or specialized knowledge to foster collaboration, exchange knowledge and participate in collective learning. CoPs exhibit distinct attributes:

voluntary participation, collective objective, and reciprocal involvement among their constituents. Gender Equality CoPs function as forums where individuals with expertise in gender equality, including professionals, researchers, practitioners, and activists, come together to share their experiences, knowledge, and effective strategies on gender-related topics. These communities offer a platform for people to engage in interactions, acquire knowledge from each other, and collaboratively strive for the promotion of gender equality. Gender equality refers to equal treatment and opportunities for individuals of all genders without discrimination or bias. CoPs facilitate collaboration and knowledge acquisition to promote gender equality. The individuals involved establish a conducive atmosphere that fosters active participation, exchange of knowledge, and collaborative development of solutions. Several important rationales underscore the importance of CoPs in promoting and advancing gender equality.

1. CoPs foster communication and cooperation among various stakeholders. CoPs facilitate interdisciplinary discourse and the sharing of varied viewpoints by fostering collaboration among professionals, policymakers, academics, and activists in different sectors. Establishing partnerships, connected initiatives, and collective efforts to achieve gender equality objectives can be facilitated through collaboration within a CoP.
2. CoPs facilitate the exchange of information, experiences, and best practices, thereby serving as a platform for knowledge exchange. The sharing of insights, lessons obtained, and evidence-based approaches among members facilitates the dissemination of useful data. Knowledge exchange plays an important role in improving collective understanding of gender-related topics, providing valuable information for decision-making processes, and improving the overall quality and efficacy of initiatives that promote gender equality.
3. CoPs provide avenues for ongoing learning and the enhancement of professional growth. By actively participating in discussions, taking workshops, and participating in knowledge exchange activities, members of a CoP can improve their skills, broaden their knowledge, and stay informed about emerging trends and practices. Continuous learning is a vital component that facilitates personal and professional development of individuals, thus improving their effectiveness in the realm of gender equality.
4. The concepts of innovation and creativity are integral to the discussion at hand. CoPs create a conducive atmosphere that promotes the cultivation of innovative ideas and the expression of creativity. The collaborative knowledge and varied viewpoints within a CoP facilitate the examination of novel concepts, the joint construction of knowledge, and the advancement of inventive resolutions. This phenomenon can lead to innovative methodologies and tactics to mitigate gender disparities.

Key Principles and Values of Effective COPs

To guarantee the efficacy and durability of gender equality CoPs, it is imperative to adhere to the fundamental principles and values that govern their operation. Several fundamental principles and values can be identified as critical.

1. Trust and respect serve as foundational principles within CoPs, fostering a sense of cohesion and collaboration among its members. Establishing a secure and all-encompassing environment where individuals experience a sense of worth and respect facilitates the transparent and sincere exchange of ideas, stimulates engaged involvement, and cultivates a feeling of affiliation.
2. Shared Purpose and Goals: CoPs should have a distinct and mutually agreed purpose and goals that are directly aligned with the pursuit of gender equality. A shared vision aligns efforts, fosters cooperation, and maintains a concentrated focus on promoting gender equality.
3. Active engagement and involvement of members are essential components for the success of CoPs. All individuals within a group must have equal opportunities to actively participate, contribute their specialized knowledge, and exchange knowledge with their peers. Active participation of individuals within a CoP cultivates a feeling of personal investment and dedication.
4. CoPs must possess a robust learning orientation. This encompasses a cultural environment characterized by a disposition toward curiosity, the pursuit of knowledge, and a willingness to embrace novel concepts. It is imperative to foster an environment where members are motivated to examine their experiences, critically analyze underlying assumptions, and actively participate in ongoing learning and enhancement endeavors.
5. Being adaptable and flexible is crucial for CoPs to respond effectively to evolving needs and contextual changes. This involves demonstrating responsiveness to new problems, accommodating various perspectives, and adapting activities and approaches by feedback and developing knowledge.
6. Knowledge Management: CoPs have mechanisms that facilitate knowledge acquisition, structure, and distribution. This may involve the establishment of repositories, the construction of knowledge-sharing platforms, and the utilization of communication channels that facilitate convenient access to information and resources.

Examples of Successful COPs Related to Gender Equality

Several Gender Equality CoPs have successfully promoted gender equality. These CoPs have made substantial contributions towards advancing the cause of gender equality. Several notable examples can be mentioned.

1. The Gender and Evaluation Community of Practice (CoP) is dedicated to enhancing the quality of evaluation practices by incorporating a gender-responsive approach. This platform facilitates the collaboration of judges, scientists, and practitioners to exchange knowledge, tools, and approaches that foster the advancement of gender equality within evaluation practices.
2. The Women's Economic Empowerment CoP aims to advance women's economic empowerment on a global scale. This platform facilitates the

exchange of knowledge, fosters discussions on innovative approaches, and identifies strategies to advance women's economic empowerment by bringing together practitioners, policymakers, and researchers.

3. The Women, Peace, and Security Network is a CoP that serves as a platform for the collaboration of activists, scholars, and policymakers in addressing matters about women, peace, and security. The platform functions as a medium for exchanging experiences, advancing policy reform, and facilitating women's substantial involvement in peacebuilding endeavors.
4. The Gender-Based Violence Prevention Network is a CoP that centers its efforts on preventing gender-based violence (GBV). The platform facilitates knowledge exchange and collaboration among practitioners, researchers, and policymakers to disseminate effective strategies, tools, and resources for preventing and mitigating gender-based violence.

The examples above illustrate the importance and potential of Gender Equality CoPs in fostering collaboration, facilitating knowledge exchange, and encouraging collective efforts to achieve gender equality. Community-driven initiatives are emphasized for their ability to effectively tackle complex gender issues and catalyze transformative action across multiple spheres.

In summary, gender equality co-programs function as forums for collaborative efforts, sharing knowledge, and collective acquisition of knowledge. They play a crucial role in facilitating collaboration among various stakeholders, facilitating the exchange of best practices, advocating for ongoing learning, and catalyzing innovation within gender equality. The effectiveness and sustainability of a given entity can be ensured by adhering to fundamental principles and values. Through a comprehensive understanding and effective use of gender equality CoPs, individuals and organizations can make substantial contributions to the advancement of gender equality and the establishment of more inclusive societies.

PLANNING AND DESIGNING A GENDER EQUALITY COP

Before establishing a Gender Equality CoP, it is imperative to ascertain its objective and scope. This necessitates elucidating the precise areas of concentration, thematic emphases, or objectives that the CoP endeavors to tackle within the wider framework of gender equality. When determining the purpose and scope, several factors should be considered.

1. One of the primary objectives of this study is to identify and analyze the key challenges that are currently being faced. The CoP aims to tackle the significant challenges and gaps that exist in the domain of gender equality. Potential focus areas may include distinct concerns such as gender-based violence, promoting women's economic empowerment, or engaging in policy advocacy efforts.
2. Establishing and Delimiting Areas of Emphasis: Identify distinct areas of concentration within the selected field, considering factors such as pertinence, influence, and practicability. Narrowing the scope of a CoP contributes to its effectiveness and influence.
3. Evaluating Niche Expertise: Evaluate the current level of expertise and knowledge possessed by the potential members and stakeholders of the

CoP. Identifying areas of expertise is crucial in selecting focus areas and ensuring a comprehensive range of expertise and abilities within the CoP.

Defining the Target Audience and Stakeholders

To optimize the efficacy and pertinence of the Gender Equality Community of Practice (CoP), it is imperative to delineate the intended recipients and interested parties involved clearly. This entails identifying the various people, groups, and communities that will benefit from, contribute to, and actively participate in the CoP. Several factors need to be considered when establishing the target audience and stakeholders.

1. Professional Experiences: The objective is to ascertain the professional backgrounds of the target audience, which may include individuals in positions of influence such as policymakers, researchers, practitioners, activists, or representatives from specific sectors such as health, education, or finance.
2. Geographical Scope: Determine the geographic extent of the CoP, encompassing the national, local, regional, or international levels. The prospective reach and variety of the CoP's members are determined by this factor.
3. Stakeholder mapping involves identifying key stakeholders, encompassing government departments, nonprofit groups, educational institutions, and international organizations. These stakeholders possess the potential to contribute to and derive benefits from the activities of the CoP.

Setting Goals and Objectives for the CoP

Establishing explicit objectives and goals for the Gender Equality Community of Practice (CoP) is of utmost importance in providing direction for its endeavors and assessing its effectiveness. Several factors to consider when establishing goals and objectives are:

1. The SMART approach emphasizes the importance of setting goals and objectives that are specific, quantifiable, doable, pertinent, and time-bound. This practice aids in enhancing clarity and concentration, thereby facilitating the evaluation of progress and achievement.
2. Multiple Hierarchical Levels: It is important to take into account the goals and objectives that exist at various levels, including the individual, corporate, and systemic levels. This approach facilitates a comprehensive examination of gender equality, encompassing immediate necessities and long-term consequences.
3. Ensuring Alignment with Broader Goals: It is imperative to ensure that the goals and objectives of the CoP are in line with larger gender equality goals, policies, and international agreements, such as the Sustainable Development Goals, or SDGs, or national gender equality strategies.

Developing a Governance Structure and Roles

Establishing a system of governance and delineating the roles and duties are imperative for ensuring the efficient operation of the Gender Equality Community of Practice (CoP). This encompasses the following:

1. Establishment of a Coordinating Body: It is recommended to establish a coordinating body or core team that will assume the responsibility of overseeing the activities of the CoP. This body will facilitate coordination among members and ensure a strict commitment to the CoP's vision and values.
2. The roles and responsibilities of individuals within a given context or organization are crucial elements that contribute to the overall functioning and success of the entity. These roles and responsibilities outline the specific roles and responsibilities of the coordinating body, encompassing various positions, namely chairpersons, instructors, knowledge supervisors, and communication coordinators. Establishing a clear and distinct demarcation of their responsibilities and anticipated performance is essential.
3. The guidelines for membership. This proposal aims to establish comprehensive membership guidelines encompassing various aspects such as membership criteria, admission procedures, and expectations about active involvement and engagement.

Establishing Guidelines and Protocols for Participation

To foster a cooperative and all-encompassing atmosphere, it is imperative to establish explicit guidelines and protocols about engagement within the Gender Equality Community of Practice (CoP). When establishing guidelines and protocols, it is important to consider various factors.

1. Development of a Code of Conduct: It is recommended to establish a comprehensive code of conduct that delineates anticipated conduct, emphasizes the importance of valuing diversity, and upholds principles of inclusivity, thereby fostering an environment that is secure and nurturing for all participants.
2. The establishment of guidelines about the maintenance of confidentiality and privacy is crucial, particularly in instances where the sharing of private data or personal experiences occurs within the CoP.
3. Decision-Making Processes: The decision-making procedures, such as reaching an agreement or voting mechanisms, are defined to ensure transparent and equitable decision-making within the CoP.
4. Conflict Resolution: Establishing protocols for effectively managing disagreements or disputes that may emerge within the CoP, focusing on fostering transparent communication, maintaining a respectful discourse, and employing mediation techniques when required.

Determining Communication and Knowledge Sharing Mechanisms

Facilitating cooperation and education within the Gender Equality Community of Practice (CoP) is contingent upon effective interaction and exchange of information mechanisms. When evaluating communication and knowledge-sharing mechanisms, several factors need to be taken into consideration.

1. Implementing online platforms, such as websites, discussion forums, or social media groups, can effectively enhance communication, facilitate

information sharing, and promote networking among members of the CoP.

2. Regular webinars, seminars, or virtual meetings are recommended to facilitate knowledge sharing, enhance skill development, and foster interactive discourse within the CoP.
3. Promoting peer education and mentoring is advocated within the CoP, fostering an environment where members can exchange specialized knowledge, offer guidance, and facilitate one another's growth in their professional pursuits.
4. Establishment of a Resource Repository: Construct a comprehensive resource archive or knowledge base that centralizes pertinent publications, research papers, toolkits, and exemplary methodologies, facilitating convenient access to valuable resources for members of the CoP.

Securing Resources and Sustainability for the CoP

Acquiring resources and establishing long-term sustainability for the Gender Equality Community of Practice (CoP) is imperative to maintain its ongoing influence. Several factors should be considered when contemplating the security of resources and the promotion of sustainability.

1. Funding Opportunities: Investigate potential sources of funding from governmental entities, philanthropic foundations, or international institutions that are in alignment with the goals and aims of the CoP. The individual should engage in the process of crafting grant proposals or actively pursue collaborative partnerships to obtain the necessary financial resources.
2. Identification of Potential In-Kind Contributions: The objective is to identify interested in-kind contributions that members and stakeholders can provide to support the activities of the CoP. These contributions may include meeting areas, technical support, or expertise.
3. Partnership Development: Cultivate alliances with pertinent organizations, institutions, or networks that pursue gender equality to optimize resource utilization, exchange knowledge, and augment the CoP's scope and influence.

Establishing evaluation and monitoring systems is crucial to assess the progress, outcomes, and impact of the CoP. This aids in illustrating the significance and efficacy of the CoP to individuals or groups with a vested interest, such as stakeholders and prospective funders.

Through meticulous strategic planning and deliberate design, organizations, and individuals can establish a Gender Equality CoP that encompasses crucial elements. Considering these fundamental aspects, a dynamic and influential collaborative platform can be created to advance gender equality, facilitate knowledge exchange, and cultivate collective efforts.

ESTABLISHING AND LAUNCHING A GENDER EQUALITY COMMUNITY OF PRACTICE (COP)

The recruitment and participation of individuals are crucial stages in establishing a Gender Equality CoP. This fosters a heterogeneous, engaged community that contributes to shared goals and objectives. When examining the process of recruitment and engagement, it is important to take into account the following factors:

1. Targeted Outreach: Employ strategies to identify prospective members of the CoP by leveraging networks, professional organizations, and pre-existing initiatives focused on promoting gender equality. Implement a focused approach to engage and extend invitations to individuals possessing pertinent knowledge, expertise, and a mutual commitment to promoting the advancement of gender equality.
2. The value proposition is clearly defined. Effectively convey the significance and advantages of becoming a member of the CoP, including providing a supportive network, opportunities for learning, and the potential to contribute to collective endeavors to promote gender equality.
3. Member Profiling: Construct a member profile or registration form to collect data about members' proficiency, areas of interest, and aspirations regarding gender equality. This facilitates comprehension of the varied skills and knowledge within the CoP.
4. Strategies for Active Member Engagement: Employ tactics to foster active member participation. This may encompass consistent communication, soliciting their input on CoP endeavors, and offering avenues for members to share their specialized knowledge via workshops, conferences, or working groups.

Creating an Inclusive and Safe Space for Participation

Establishing an inclusive and secure environment is of utmost importance to cultivate substantial engagement within the Gender Equality CoP. This fosters an environment of trust, mutual respect, and effective communication among the individuals involved. When establishing an environment that is inclusive and promotes safety, several factors should be taken into consideration.

1. Development of a Code of Conduct: Formulate a comprehensive code of conduct that delineates anticipated behaviors and guarantees the establishment of a respectful and inclusive milieu. It is imperative to underscore the zero-tolerance policy towards instances of harassment, discrimination, and any manifestation of disrespect.
2. Promoting diversity and inclusion is imperative within the CoP. This can be achieved by proactively engaging individuals from various backgrounds, encompassing diverse genders, ethnicities, age categories, and geographic regions. It is imperative to achieve an equilibrium between various perspectives and experiences.
3. Facilitated Discourse: Employ facilitation techniques to foster discussions and activities that promote equal participation and guarantee the inclusion of all perspectives. Facilitate avenues for people who may experience marginalization or possess limited opportunities for expression to contribute their unique perspectives actively.
4. Confidentiality: Develop protocols for upholding confidentiality during

discussions about sensitive subjects or disclosing personal anecdotes. Assure individuals that their input will be handled in a manner that upholds respect and ensures confidentiality.

Organizing Launch Events to Generate Enthusiasm

Establishing the Gender Equality CoP with enthusiasm and dedication is crucial for laying a solid groundwork and fostering active participation among its members. There are several factors to consider when contemplating the organization of launch events or activities.

1. The vision, goals, and purposes of the CoP should be clearly articulated during the launch event. Emphasize the prospective influence and communal advantages of engaging in the CoP.
2. Including esteemed and influential guest speakers from the domain of gender equality is recommended to impart their valuable insights and experiences. The presence of individuals within a CoP can elicit enthusiasm and foster a sense of dedication among its members.
3. Interactive Sessions: Develop interactive sessions that foster active engagement, such as discussion boards, workshops, or collaborative group activities. These sessions can enhance networking, foster the exchange of knowledge, and enable the identification of shared challenges and opportunities.
4. Membership Pledges: Foster a culture of active participation and support among members by encouraging them to publicly commit to and pledge their dedication towards the objectives of the CoP. This practice cultivates a collective sense of personal ownership and shared duty among the individuals involved.

Facilitating Initial Knowledge Exchange

Engaging in the transfer of knowledge and networking initiatives during the initial phase of a CoP fosters connections and establishes a foundation for subsequent collaborative endeavors. Several factors should be considered when facilitating the initial knowledge exchange and networking.

1. Introduction Sessions: Facilitate initial sessions wherein participants can exchange their respective backgrounds, areas of expertise, and anticipated outcomes. This facilitates the establishment of connections, the identification of areas of shared interest, and the promotion of potential collaborations.
2. Implementing online discussion forums or platforms provides a means for members to actively participate in continuous dialogues, exchange valuable resources, and solicit guidance or constructive criticism from their peers. Promote and foster active engagement among participants while prioritizing inclusivity and respect within discussions.
3. It is recommended to organize webinars or workshops centered on pertinent subjects within the domain of gender equality. Extending invitations to guest speakers or subject matter experts is recommended to impart their expertise and foster engaging dialogues among the participants.

4. One strategy to enhance knowledge exchange and collaboration within the CoP is the implementation of peer learning circles or small working groups. These circles or groups aim to facilitate targeted discussions, foster collaborative learning, and encourage the exchange of experiences and best practices among members.

Addressing Potential Challenges

Identifying and resolving potential challenges and conflicts is imperative to facilitate a seamless development phase for the Gender Equality CoP. When contemplating the resolution of challenges and conflicts, several factors should be taken into account:

4. Facilitated discussions: Offer avenues for inclusive and productive discourse among participants to address potential concerns or conflicts effectively. Promote the practice of active listening, foster an atmosphere of respect for a range of perspectives, and facilitate the identification of shared interests and goals.
5. Conflict Resolution Mechanisms: It is imperative to implement well-defined conflict resolution processes, such as negotiation or facilitated discussions, to effectively tackle conflicts in an equitable manner characterized by mutual respect. It is imperative to establish an environment where members experience a sense of support and have confidence that their concerns are given due consideration.

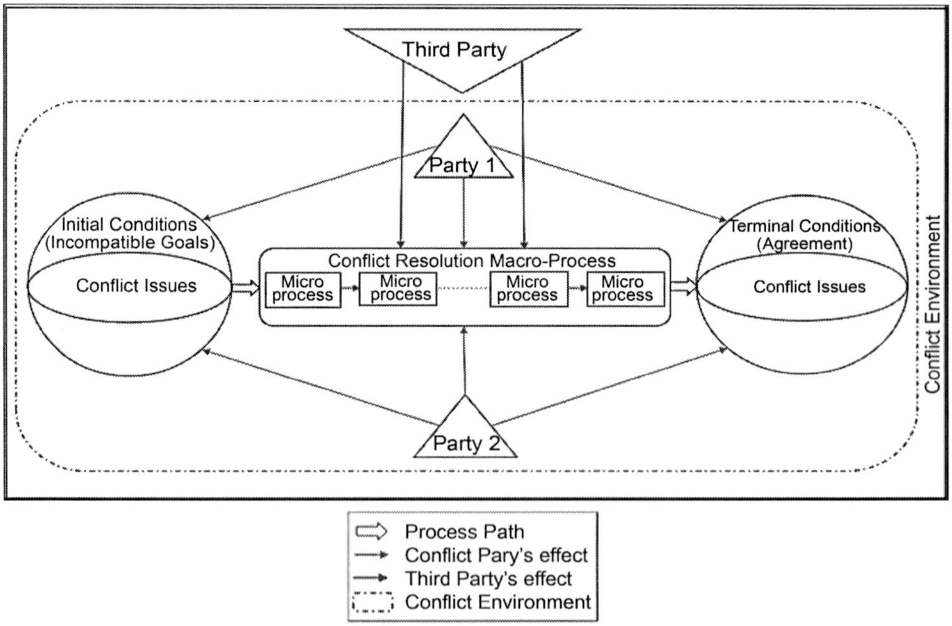

Figure 6. Illustration of Conflict Resolution Mechanisms structure.

Source: https://www.researchgate.net/publication/334103814_Transboundary_Water_Conflict_Resolution_Mechanisms_Substitutes_or_Complements

6. One important aspect to consider in organizational decision-making is transparency. Transparency refers to the openness and clarity with which decisions are made and communicated. To ensure fairness and inclusivity, it is imperative to uphold transparency in the decision-making procedures within the CoP, thereby mitigating any potential notions of bias or marginalization. It is imperative to ensure that decisions are made collectively and effectively communicated to all members involved.
7. Sustained Communication: Cultivate enduring communication channels to effectively address obstacles, collect input, and ensure CoP members are well-informed of the CoP's advancements. It is advisable to consistently solicit member feedback to enhance the CoP's operational efficiency and effectively tackle any arising concerns.

Through prioritizing recruitment and engagement, establishing an inclusive and safe environment, coordinating impactful launch events, facilitating the exchange of knowledge, and proactively addressing potential challenges, the initial stage of establishing the Gender Equality CoP can establish a strong basis for continued collaboration, learning, and collective efforts.

ENGAGING STAKEHOLDERS AND CREATING PARTNERSHIPS

The active involvement of stakeholders and the establishment of partnerships are essential elements for the achievement and long-term viability of a Gender Equality CoP. The amplification of the CoP's impact and the facilitation of resource mobilization is achieved through collaboration with external stakeholders, other CoPs, and existing initiatives and platforms. There are several factors to consider when involving stakeholders and establishing partnerships.

1. It is recommended to involve pertinent government agencies promoting gender equality to establish unity with prevailing national strategies and policies. Encourage active engagement in CoP initiatives, such as contributing specialized knowledge, offering valuable resources, or fostering meaningful policy discussions.
2. Non-Governmental Organizations (NGOs): Engage in collaborative partnerships with NGOs possessing specialized knowledge and extensive experience in gender equality programming. These organizations have the potential to provide significant contributions in terms of valuable insights, the sharing of best practices, and the facilitation of community involvement or advocacy initiatives.
3. Academia: Foster collaborations with educational institutions that engage in research and offer specialized knowledge in gender equality. Engage in collaborative research endeavors, facilitate educational workshops or seminars, and access scholarly resources to support the implementation of evidence-based practices.

It is recommended to involve civil society organizations that specifically prioritize gender equality and the advancement of women's rights. These organizations can offer perspectives from the grassroots level, mobilize communities, and engage in advocacy efforts aimed at policy change or social transformation.

Engaging in collaborative efforts with other CoPs and networks to enhance the overall influence and effectiveness.

1. CoP Networks: Facilitate the identification and establishment of collaborative partnerships with other CoPs that address similar or complementary subject matters. CoP networks offer valuable prospects for exchanging knowledge, collaborative endeavors, and the pooling of resources. By harnessing the advantages of multiple CoPs, the influence of individual endeavors can be magnified.
2. Engage in collaborative efforts with interdisciplinary networks that intersect with gender equality, including but not limited to networks focused on human rights, social justice, and sustainable development. These networks offer prospects for interdisciplinary knowledge exchange, advocacy for policy changes, and collaborative efforts in addressing gender-related matters.
3. It is recommended to actively participate in international platforms or initiatives prioritizing gender equality, such as United Nations agencies, regional organizations, or global campaigns dedicated to promoting gender equality. Engage in pertinent conferences, discussions, or working groups to actively contribute to global dialogues and harness international knowledge and resources.

Utilizing strategic collaborations to enhance resource acquisition and facilitate collaborative endeavors:

1. It is advisable to pursue funding collaborations with donors, philanthropic groups, or social responsibility programs that share a common goal of promoting gender equality. Collaborative funding requests or joint initiatives have the potential to attract a greater amount of resources and provide sustained support for the long term.
2. Shared Resource Pooling: Engage in collaborative efforts with partners to establish shared resource pools, encompassing various assets such as knowledge repositories, training materials, or databases for research purposes. The act of pooling resources within a CoP has the potential to enhance operational efficiency, mitigate redundancy, and amplify the overall effectiveness of the CoP's endeavors.
3. Joint Collaborations: Recognize potential avenues for collaboration with partners, such as coordinating meetings, seminars, or policy dialogues. Collaborative endeavors augment prominence, fortify endeavors supporting a cause, and engender novel knowledge and perspectives.

Establishing collaborative partnerships with current gender equality initiatives and platforms to foster synergistic outcomes.

1. Establish connections with extant gender equality networks or platforms operating at regional, national, or local scales. Engage in their endeavors, exchange insights, and recognize prospects for cooperation to optimize effectiveness and prevent redundant endeavors.
2. Gender Equality Initiatives: Foster synergy and bolster existing gender equality initiatives, promotions, or programs through alignment

and support. This encompasses the promotion of their activities, the mobilization of support, and the integration of their resources and expertise into the work of the CoP.

3. Policy platforms refer to the set of principles and objectives that guide the actions and decisions of a political party or candidate. These platforms outline the specific Participate in policy platforms or forums that promote gender equality and advocacy. Engage in policy discourse, offer recommendations grounded in empirical evidence, and foster cooperation in the formulation or execution of policies.

Through active stakeholder engagement, collaboration with other CoPs and networks, utilization of partnerships, and the establishment of synergies with current gender equality initiatives and platforms, the Gender Equality CoP has the potential to effectively harness collective endeavors, resources, and expertise, resulting in heightened influence and long-term viability. These collaborative efforts and partnerships facilitate the exchange of knowledge, mobilization of resources, implementation of joint initiatives, and advocacy for policy changes, ultimately driving forward the objectives of promoting gender equality.

EVALUATION AND CONTINUOUS IMPROVEMENT

The evaluation and continuous improvement processes are crucial in guaranteeing the efficacy, pertinence, and influence of a Gender Equality CoP. By monitoring activities, collecting feedback, and implementing necessary adjustments, the CoP can effectively respond to evolving requirements and optimize its capabilities. Several factors to take into account when assessing and enhancing performance are:

Monitoring and evaluating the effectiveness of the CoP is a crucial aspect to consider.

1. The process of defining and setting Key Performance Indicators (KPIs) The task at hand involves the establishment of KPIs that are in congruence with the goals and objectives of the CoP. These indicators encompass various measures, including but not limited to the number of individuals actively engaged, activities related to knowledge sharing, collaborative initiatives undertaken, the impact of policies, and outcomes related to capacity development.

2. Implementing mechanisms to systematically collect pertinent data on CoP activities, participant engagement, and outcomes is crucial. Various methods can be employed to gather data, such as polls, interviews, involvement logs, or website analytics. The consistent gathering of data offers valuable insights into the functioning of the CoP and its advancement in attaining its objectives.

3. Impact Assessment: Regularly perform impact assessments to ascertain the influence of the CoP on people, organizations, regulations, or broader outcomes related to gender equality. This may encompass the utilization of empirical research, interviews of qualitative nature, or quantitative analysis to examine indicators such as behavioral modifications, enhanced practices, or the impact on policies.

Gathering input from constituents and stakeholders to enhance performance:

1. Implementing member surveys is recommended to collect valuable feedback about their experiences, levels of satisfaction, and suggestions for potential enhancements. Please inquire about the individuals' perspectives regarding the perceived value, relevance, and efficacy of the CoP in facilitating their efforts toward promoting gender equality.
2. Stakeholder Engagements: Conduct consultations with key stakeholders, such as government agencies, NGOs, and academia, to actively involve them in understanding their viewpoints on the impact of the CoP and identifying potential areas for enhancement. This can encompass various methods, such as conducting interviews, organizing focus group discussions, or facilitating stakeholder workshops.
3. Peer Learning and Reflection: Foster peer learning sessions or reflection exercises within the CoP to promote the exchange of observations, lessons learned, and recommendations to improve the CoP's effectiveness. Promote an inclusive and productive discourse among participants.

Implementing essential modifications to guarantee the CoP pertinence and influence.

1. Analyzing feedback entails examining the feedback obtained from members and stakeholders to identify prevalent themes, areas of strength, areas requiring improvement, or emerging needs. It is imperative to give careful consideration to recommendations that have the potential to augment the CoP's pertinence, involvement, and efficacy.
2. Continuous Learning and Adaptation: Utilize the feedback and insights acquired to implement essential modifications to the CoP's activities, methods of communication, or engagement mechanisms. Promote adopting a culture prioritizing ongoing learning, experimentation, and adaptation in response to changing requirements and member feedback.
3. The involvement of CoP members in the decision-making process and the collaborative development of improvement strategies is essential. Encourage active participation in dialogues regarding strategies to tackle obstacles, capitalize on favorable circumstances, and enhance the CoP's initiatives to foster a sense of ownership and shared accountability.
4. Exploring possibilities for cooperation with external partners, stakeholders, or groups should be undertaken to address feedback and identify gaps. Collaborative efforts have the potential to augment the capacity of a CoP, expand its scope, and introduce fresh viewpoints and resources.

Implementing evaluation and ongoing enhancement processes enables the CoP to adapt, acquire knowledge, and maintain relevance within the ever-changing context of gender equality.

Through the systematic monitoring of its effectiveness, collecting feedback from members and stakeholders, and implementing necessary adjustments, the CoP can enhance its impact, cultivate a culture of learning, and facilitate constructive transformation in the promotion of gender equality.

REFERENCES

1. Aikman, S., & Unterhalter, E. (2005). Beyond Access: Transforming Policy and Practice for Gender Equality in Education: Oxfam.
2. Ali, F., & Syed, J. (2017). From rhetoric to reality: A multilevel analysis of gender equality in Pakistani organizations. Gender, Work & Organization, 24(5), 472–486.
3. Allee, V. (2000). Knowledge networks and communities of practice. OD practitioner, 32(4), 4–13.
4. Barreto, M. E., Ryan, M. K., & Schmitt, M. T. (2009). The Glass Ceiling in the 21st century: Understanding Barriers to Gender Equality: American Psychological Association.
5. Bryant, L. D., Burkinshaw, P., House, A. O., West, R. M., & Ward, V. (2017). Good practice or positive action? Using Q methodology to identify competing views on improving gender equality in academic medicine. BMJ Open, 7(8), e015973.
6. Chen, D. H. (2004a). Gender equality and economic development. World Bank Policy Research Working Paper, 3285.
7. Chen, D. H. (2004b). Gender equality and economic development: The role for information and communication technologies. Available at SSRN 610329.
8. Coe, I. R., Wiley, R., & Bekker, L.-G. (2019). Organizational best practices towards gender equality in science and medicine. The Lancet, 393(10171), 587–593.
9. Costanza-Chock, S. (2020). Design Justice: Community-Led Practices to Build the Worlds We Need: The MIT Press.
10. Cruess, R. L., Cruess, S. R., & Steinert, Y. (2018). Medicine as a Community of Practice: implications for medical education. Academic Medicine, 93(2), 185–191.
11. Cuddy, C. (2002). Cultivating communities of practice: A guide to managing knowledge. The Bottom Line, 15(2).
12. de Carvalho Leal, L. Y., de Souza, E. R., Júnior, J. A. S., & Dos Santos, M. A. (2020). Comparison of soil and hydroponic cultivation systems for spinach irrigated with brackish water. Scientia Horticulturae, 274, 109616.
13. De Soysa, L., & Zipp, S. (2019). Gender equality, sport and the United Nation's system. A historical overview of the slow pace of progress. Sport in Society, 22(11), 1783–1800.
14. Demaidi, M. N., & Al-Sahili, K. (2021). Integrating SDGs in higher education—Case of climate change awareness and gender equality in a developing country according to RMEI-TARGET strategy. Sustainability, 13(6), 3101.

INDEX